RED-BUTTON MEN

RED-BUTTON MEN

Red-Button Years, Volume 3

KEN FULLER

By Ken Fuller

Non-Fiction:

Radical Aristocrats: London Busworkers from the 1880s to the 1980s (1985)
Forcing the Pace: The Partido Komunista ng Pilipinas, From Foundation to Armed Struggle (2007)
A Movement Divided: Philippine Communism, 1957-1986 (2011)
The Lost Vision: The Philippine Left, 1986-2010 (2015)
The Long Crisis: Gloria Macapagal Arroyo and Philippine Underdevelopment (2013, 2019)
Hardboiled Activist: The Work and Politics of Dashiell Hammett (2017)
Raymond Chandler: The Man behind the Mask (2020)

Journalism:

A Mad Desire to Read: Books and their Authors (2020)

Fiction:

Foreigners: A Philippine Satire (2019)
Love and Labour (2019)
Romance and Revolution (2020)
Red-Button Men (2021)

ISBN: 979-7602-7656-8

CONTENTS

PART ONE

1919

1

When Mickey Rice had been elected to the red-button union's executive council, he was replaced as union rep at Middle Row bus garage by Dick Mortlake, who had been secretary of the branch since its formation in 1913. Although a former classical flautist from a moderately well-off family, Dick had long been accepted by his more proletarian workmates as one of their own. His presence on the buses was, in fact, not particularly remarkable for, as Mickey had often noted, working for the London General Omnibus Company was a bit like being in the French Foreign Legion: you met all sorts. Anyway, the members at Middle Row trusted Dick to do both jobs and, as the garage was one of the smallest in the fleet, he found that he was able to represent the members at local level and conduct the secretarial work with ease. With the forthcoming formation of the United Vehicle Workers, however, with seats for just two London busworkers on its executive council, at the request of the old red-button left Mickey had stood aside so as not to split the votes for Barney Macauley and Ernie Fairbrother, who were duly elected and would take office on 1 January; by agreement with Dick Mortlake, Mickey then decided to stand for his old position of garage rep.

This would bring him into closer contact with the new garage superintendent Victor Wiggins, who had been appointed following the promotion of his predecessor, the gentlemanly West Country man James Shilling, to divisional level. Wiggins was a different kettle of fish: still in his mid-thirties, tall and with a somewhat forbidding demeanour, he had worked his way up from driver, first to point inspector, then to allocation official in a number of garages in North London.

Shortly after his arrival at Middle Row in early December, Wiggins made a point of making Mickey's acquaintance, having one of the garage officials stamp "See GS" on the sign-on sheet next to his scheduled duty. Seeing this, Mickey had looked up and smiled at the official on duty at the window, a decent enough chap called Sid Phillips.

"Any idea what he wants, Sid?"

"Oh, just to say hello, I think, Mickey."

"On whose time?"

Sid laughed, remembering when, almost seven years earlier, on his first day on the job Mickey had been instructed to see the garage superintendent because he was wearing the red union button on his uniform jacket; the matter had ended badly for Mr Butcher, the official who had issued the instruction, and Mickey had been paid thirty minutes' overtime for the interview. "Yeah, come to think of it, Mickey," Sid chuckled now, "this could be a re-run of 1913."

"Maybe, Sid." Mickey shrugged. "Although I doubt it."

But, in a sense, it was.

Mickey knocked and put his head around the door. "You want to see me, Mr Wiggins? Mickey Rice."

Victor Wiggins, who was interviewing a point inspector seated before him, inclined his head to get a clear view of Mickey. It was, Mickey saw for the first time, quite a head: Wiggins' light bushy hair was already receding and so, perhaps to compensate for this, he had allowed it to grow so that it resembled a sizeable cloud sitting just beyond the cliff-face of his brow.

"Give me ten minutes, Mr Rice."

"Or shall I come back another time?"

"No, no, just give me ten minutes."

"So I'll get a tea on the van, then."

"Entirely up to you, Mr Rice." A trace of impatience there. "Mr Turpin will let you know when I'm free." He returned to the matter in hand, writing on the pad before him.

Well, Mr Wiggins, thought Mickey, I hope you know what you're doing. He climbed aboard the refreshment vehicle—Middle Row was not large enough to have its own canteen—and ordered a tea. In due course, Inspector Turpin—real name Jack but inevitably referred to as Ben, after the cross-eyed star of the silver screen—rapped the window to let Mickey know that the garage superintendent was now available. Turpin usually stood at Paddington Station, and Mickey assumed that his meeting with Wiggins concerned a driver he had placed on report. Mickey gave him a thumbs-up and, with a grimace, swallowed the rest of his tea.

"Ah, Mr Rice! Come in."

Wiggins rose from his seat and offered Mickey his hand. "Good morning, Mr Rice." He sank back into his chair and barely managed to banish a flicker of annoyance when Mickey sat opposite him without first being invited to do so; he spent a moment regarding the man: thirty-one years of age, broad-shouldered, clear-eyed with even features. It had to be admitted that he had a certain presence. Worse, he was said to be intelligent.

Mickey raised his hands. "Well, Mr Wiggins, what can I do for you?"

"Oh, just an introductory chat, Mr Rice. I thought that we should make each other's acquaintance sooner rather than later, as you are a member of your union's executive council." It was clear from his stiff attitude that this was something he felt he *should* do rather than something he *wanted* to do.

"Not for much longer, Mr Wiggins."

"Oh really?" Wiggins, obviously not a keen observer of trade union amalgamations, seemed genuinely puzzled. "And why is that, might I ask?"

"Come 1 January, we'll be the United Vehicle Workers, and there will be only two seats on its executive for London busworkers." He shrugged. "Simple as that."

Puzzlement gave way to concern. "And so you will have no union position?"

Mickey smiled. "That depends on the Middle Row membership, Mr Wiggins."

"Ah, you will be going for a local position."

The bugger probably thinks I see myself as branch chairman, thought Mickey. "Yes, I'll run for rep."

"Oh." Concern had now escalated to something approaching dismay, and the garage superintendent had paled. "But Mr Mortlake..."

"Has volunteered to step aside. He will remain as branch secretary—if elected, of course."

"Oh, I see. Well, this does put a different complexion on the matter, Mr Rice."

"On which matter, Mr Wiggins?"

"Well...the matter of our future relationship, I suppose." Rather than having a somewhat distant relationship with a member of the red-button executive council, Wiggins was now faced with the prospect of finding Mickey, who had a reputation as someone who could not be tricked, bought or brow-beaten, on the other side of his desk every time there was a problem.

Mickey nodded. "Oh, yes, it certainly does, Mr Wiggins."

The garage superintendent spent a moment in thought, a frown upon his brow as he considered his hands upon the desk. He looked up, brightening somewhat. "I see, incidentally, that both you and Mr Mortlake have applied for three days' annual leave at the end of this week."

"That is correct, Mr Wiggins." He was buggered if he would explain without a direct question.

Wiggins inclined his head, raising an eyebrow. "Union activity, Mr

Rice? Or is it something political?"

"Neither, Mr Wiggins." Mickey maintained his straight face. Interesting, though, that Wiggins seemed to be completely in the dark, which could only mean that garage gossip stopped at his door, which in turn implied that his attempts to build relationships with his officials and the crews was about as successful as this current effort.

"Well, I daresay that it's none of my business…"

"Correct again, Mr Wiggins."

The way Wiggins blinked and sat back in his chair, you would have thought that Mickey had slapped his face. It was obvious that since embarking on the road to officialdom he never been spoken to in this manner, and he was momentarily as a loss for words.

Mickey let him stew for a moment and then, feeling somewhat sorry for him, softened and allowed himself to smile. He sighed. "If you must know, Mr Wiggins," he said, regretting the precise formulation as it left his mouth, "we're getting married."

Wiggins now saw—mistakenly as it turned out—his way back, throwing up his head and laughing. "Well, Mr Rice, I assumed that you and Mr Mortlake were fairly close, but…"

"Yes, yes, Mr Wiggins, very droll." Mickey's poker face was back. "Perhaps I should have said that we're having a joint wedding."

It took Wiggins some seconds to bring his laughter under control. "Ah! Forgive me, Mr Rice, but the way you said that…" Seeing that Mickey was not at all amused—or, perhaps more accurately, that he had no intention of sharing Wiggins's merriment—and realising that life in the months ahead was probably not going to be easy, he regarded him soberly for a few moments. "I *do* hope we'll get on, Mr Rice."

It was Mickey's turn to frown thoughtfully as he tried to make out this strange newcomer. He shrugged. "What do you want me to say, Mr Wiggins?"

Wiggins placed his elbows on the desk and crossed his hands before him, looking earnest now. "I'd like you to say, Mr Rice, that you'll help me see that this garage is run efficiently, with a minimum of lost mileage and good staff attendance figures."

Mickey felt like laughing. What came out was more of a snort than a laugh. "That's not my job, Mr Wiggins."

"So you have no interest in maintaining mileage and improving the attendance figures?"

"I can see the importance of maintaining mileage from the point of view of the company and the travelling public. But you're right: I have no interest in helping you achieve better results—at least directly."

"And indirectly?"

"My interest is in seeing that staff are treated fairly and that their working conditions are as humane as possible. If I'm successful in that, I think you'll find that the figures for mileage and attendance will improve."

Wiggins' face was impassive, but as Mickey held his gaze his right eye began to flicker. "You seem to overlook another way in which you can contribute to those results, Mr Rice."

"Oh, really?"

"Of course: avoid unnecessary strikes."

Mickey got to his feet. "Well, if that will be all, Mr Wiggins..."

"No it will *not* be all, Mr Rice. You'll leave when I tell you to leave, so sit down!"

Mickey sat, a broad smile on his face.

"What is it that you find funny, Mr Rice?"

"You'll see soon enough, Mr Wiggins."

Wiggins regarded him in silence for several seconds as he brought his anger under control. Eventually, he took a deep breath and expelled it. "Now, let's see if we can continue this discussion sensibly. As I was saying, the mileage figures would be improved if you were to avoid unnecessary strikes."

Before long, thought Mickey, he'll be offering to take me off the road a couple of days a week in return for my "co-operation." He said nothing.

"Do you not agree, Mr Rice?"

"I can neither agree nor disagree, Mr Wiggins, because I've no idea what you mean by *unnecessary strikes*."

Wiggins threw back his head, glancing at the ceiling in recollection. "Well, Mr Shilling tells me that on one occasion, during the war, you threatened a strike if the women washers were not paid the men's rate."

"And what was the result?"

"Well..." Wiggins, distinctly uncomfortable, cleared his throat. "It is true that it was agreed that the women would be paid the same as the men, but this could have been achieved by going through the procedure."

"I very much doubt that, Mr Wiggins. In fact, it was the company which failed to use the machinery, by employing women washers at lower rates without even discussing the matter with the union. And, of course, in the event there *was* no strike."

"But by preventing crews from signing on at this garage, Mr Rice, you caused considerable lost mileage."

"If I had not taken the action I did, Mr Wiggins, there would have been the possibility of a *fleet-wide* strike, so I think you could say that I saved mileage rather than lost it."

Wiggins conceded defeat by raising his hands and letting them fall to the desk. "Perhaps I could have chosen a better example, Mr Rice."

"To be honest, I'm surprised at your choice of subject, Mr Wiggins."

A frown. "And why is that, Mr Rice?"

"Because mileage is being lost right now, Mr Wiggins."

Confusion. "I'm not at all sure that I follow…"

Mickey whipped out his pocket watch. "We were due out of the garage thirty-seven minutes ago, Mr Wiggins."

Reality dawned and Wiggins exploded. "You mean to tell me that you've been sitting here when you should have been on the road!"

Mickey sighed and crossed his arms. "Mr Wiggins, on the sign-on sheet next to my duty number there is a message: 'See GS'—See Garage Superintendent. I assume that it was stamped on your instruction. When was I likely to see that message?" He unfolded his arms and spread his hands. "Why, when I was signing on, of course. I came to your office immediately but saw that you were with Inspector Turpin, so I asked whether you would prefer to see me some other time. Did you ask whether I was due to take a bus out? You did not. Instead, you told me to give you ten minutes. During the course of our discussion, I got up and was about to leave, but you told me—instructed me—to sit down. 'You'll leave when I tell you to leave,' you said. So, yes, I've been sitting here when I should have been on the road, but the fault is yours, Mr Wiggins, not mine."

Back in the output, Mickey nodded to Billy Franklin, his conductor. "Give us your log card, Billy."

"How'd it go, Mickey?" murmured Sid Phillips from the other side of the allocation window.

"Oh, not so bad, Sid. He just wanted a chat about the mileage figures and how they might be improved." He pushed the log card through the window.

"What's this for, Mick?"

"So you can turn us at Russell Square, Sid."

"Did Mr Wiggins agree to this?"

"Yes, he did—eventually." Mickey winked at the official and gave him a thumbs-up.

Sid Phillips stifled a laugh.

2

At Paddington Green, just before the Harrow Road met the Edgware Road, sat Paddington Town Hall, a red-brick, two-story building in the classical style, white cornerstones lending it a Continental flavour. At eleven o'clock on that Saturday morning, Mickey Rice and Annette Fré, and Dick Mortlake and Gladys Rogers, presented themselves at the Register Office for the purpose of marriage. The witnesses were Mickey's brother Eric and his wife Elsie, union organizer George Sanders, and Gladys's mother Mary. They were accompanied by Jacko, the almost nine-year old son of Eric and Elsie, and six-year old Jimmy, Gladys's son by her late husband. Heavy overcoats were not required, as that December was a mild month. By bus they arrived and, not long after 11.30, with the exception of George Sanders who rode his Triumph Trusty motorcycle, by bus they departed, taking a number 6 down to Marble Arch, where they changed to a number 7.

"Our weddings," Annette murmured to Mickey in her Belgian accent as they changed buses, "are I think very proletarian."

At the insistence of the children, they sat on the open top deck of the number 7—Mickey's own route, Dick having recently transferred to route 31 after more than six years travelling between Wormwood Scrubs and Liverpool Street—and as they progressed down Oxford Street Mickey was reminded of that day in June 1913 when, having just arrived in London, he had travelled westward on this route with his brother Eric, exulting at being in London. Now, the pavements teemed with Saturday-afternoon shoppers, their numbers swollen by the introduction of the 48-hour week in so many trades, their pockets heavier than they had been for several years due to the post-war boom; and down the street, buses in the London General livery picking up and dropping off, picking up and dropping off; and, as the buses bunched, they slowly crossed Oxford Circus, with the children kneeling on their seats and straining for a glance down Regent Street. The conductor, a short Cockney called Alfie Wright, came up and, beaming, offered a congratulatory hand to Mickey, Dick and their new wives, refusing to take the fares of those who, unlike the two grooms, had no travel passes.

Minutes later, to protests from the children, they made their way down the outside staircase and alighted. Crossing the road, they sauntered down Dean Street, a fifteen-minute walk taking them to Gerrard Street, where they passed the headquarters of the London and Provincial Union of Licensed Vehicle Workers, widely known as the red-button union. Here was where Annette worked in the ledger department, Eric Rice was stationed as a full-time officer and Mickey attended meetings of the executive council.

"Come this way in a few weeks' time and you'll see the removal lorries outside,"
Eric remarked. The United Vehicle Workers would begin life on 1 January, and before then every stick of red-button furniture and office equipment would have to be transported to 45, Emperor's Gate, Kensington, the headquarters of the new union.

"I think I will miss it," said Annette.

"Miss it?" queried Eric in a tone which, although intentionally good-natured, was, as were many of his pronouncements, open to misinterpretation. "You haven't been there more than five minutes, girl!"

This was not much of an exaggeration, for Annette had begun working for the union just nineteen months earlier, and even this short period had been interrupted by an absence of some weeks in Belgium, following a misunderstanding with Mickey.

"Oh," Annette responded in spirited fashion, "my brother-in-law is *tres amusant*, but this is where I met my husband."

"Ha ha, you tell 'im, girl," said Gladys in support.

"That is true, sis, that is true," said Eric, turning to Annette and inclining his head. "No offence intended."

Annette gave him her twinkling smile.

"Ah, this is the place I'm going to miss," sighed Mickey as they approached the venue of the joint wedding reception.

"Oh, Guido's café is okay," said Eric, "but it's not *that* good, is it?"

"It's where I fell in love with my wife, bruv," explained Mickey, immediately regretting that Eric had now been slapped down twice.

The Italian café operated by Guido Russo and his wife Emilia had been decorated with a message on each of the two front windows:

Congratulations	Congratulations
Mickey and Annette!	Dick and Gladys!

As the party approached, Guido, who had obviously been watching the street, stepped through the door and stood, a sommelier towel over his right wrist, as he greeted the guests of honour. *"Buon giorno, signore et signori."* A balding man of around sixty, he smiled pleasantly and touched one of the boys on the shoulder. *"E anche i bambini: buon giorno."* When the last person had filed through the door, Guido scowled at George Sanders' motorbike, which was parked on the pavement, next to the wall of the café; he snapped his wine towel in disapproval and entered his domain.

*

Those inside the café rose to applaud the wedding party, which was led by Mickey Rice in a light grey, single-breasted suit, a white carnation on his lapel, and matching tie. Annette followed, wearing a figure-hugging white ankle-length dress which shimmered like silk but was more probably, given the price of silk, viscose; she wore no makeup apart from the lightest of lipsticks and the subtlest shadow for her eyes with their almost Oriental cast; short a year ago, her dazzling blond hair now touched her shoulders. As rumour had it that Dick Mortlake came from a family that had at one time been well-off, it might have been expected that he would have looked particularly splendid on his wedding day. But no, that was not Dick's style. There was nothing wrong with his suit: a dark grey, it was newish, clean, and recently pressed, but it did not look right on him; perhaps nothing would look right on him. It was, maybe, his shape that was to blame, for he was tall and thin with little in the way of a chest. But it was attitude as well, for he had already loosened his tie. Gladys, with whom Dick had lived for three years, was, on the other hand, somewhat more than splendid. She was a large woman without being fat—large and powerful enough, in fact, to have, during the "women's strike" of 1918, broken the nose of a strike-breaker who was later promoted to inspector—and today her body inhabited a silky material printed with a huge floral design in gold, green and scarlet which was wrapped about her tightly enough to give a suggestion of hips and bust while leaving her actual body a mystery; the colour scheme was echoed by scarlet lipstick and gold earrings with green stones. As Gladys entered the café, the applause swelled and Mickey thought that she must surely be pleased by that. He noticed, however, that as Dick turned to her, probably to congratulate her, she frowned and pointed to his tie, seemingly scolding him.

Guido had pulled the tables together to form a large square, and as Mickey's gaze travelled over it he saw not just George Sanders but chairman of the union's executive council Dennis Davies and his comrade from the cab section Morris Frankenberg, EC member Barney Macauley, organising secretary Ben Smith, organiser Archie Henderson, long-term British Socialist Party activist—and unrecognized Soviet Ambassador—Theo Rothstein, Annette's immediate boss Dougal McGregor from the finance department, Meg Arnold, a former Middle Row conductor and friend of Gladys, and the Middle Row branch chairman Malcolm Lewis.

As Guido showed the wedding couples to their seats at the top of the square, he pointed to two piles of gift-wrapped packages in a corner. "The wedding gifts, Mickey." Although he smiled gratefully, Mickey found himself wondering how they would manage to carry them back to Alexander Street.

Earlier in the week, Annette had used her lunch break to discuss the menu for her wedding reception with Guido.

"Italian, Mickey thinks," she had ventured.

"All of it?" This had been almost whispered by a frowning Guido. "But they are all English, Annette."

"Apart from me and Comrade Rothstein, yes. Oh, and Brother McGregor is Scottish. And so is Archie. And Brother Lewis, of course, is Welsh. Then, you and Emilia. Ah, I almost forgot: you are to be guests."

"But why, Annette?" Guido's shoulders were raised, his palms outstretched. "And how? Emilia and I must serve you."

"Why?" Annette smiled. "Because you are our friends. How? Is it possible that you could employ two waitresses for the afternoon?"

Guido's head oscillated from side to side, his eyes narrowing. It was, thought Annette, the gesture of a man who is considering a proposal to which he already knows he will agree. "Yes, it is possible. And thank you for your invitation. It will be our great pleasure to attend as guests...But the food, Annette. Are you sure it should all be Italian? You know most of these English are not familiar with the foods of other countries."

"With the two wedding couples, you will have no problem—although I am not too sure of Gladys," Annette explained patiently. "Comrade Rothstein is a man of the world. The others...well, it will be a nice surprise for them, I think."

"Will there be children?"

"Ah, yes: two boys. Maybe, to be safe, you should have available servings of—what are they called?—*les pommes frites*."

"Chips."

"Yes, chips, and maybe some sausages, so when it comes to the main course the children can choose."

"And so, for the main menu...?"

She smiled. "Mickey says I should ask you for an Italian menu, but if possible to do it on the cheap, as he puts it."

Guido laughed. "Ah, Mickey! Do not worry; I will not overcharge him." An afterthought brought about a raising of the eyebrows in what could have been alarm. "So Mickey will be paying the bill alone?"

"No, no, no: Dick, Bridegroom Number 2, will also contribute."

"Ah, good." He inhaled before getting down to business. "Alright. I would suggest six courses instead of the usual seven. Normally, the meal would start with the *aperitivo*—welcome drinks and small bite-sized snacks—but I think we should leave out this course. This will help to keep costs down and will remove the danger of the English drinking too much before they begin to eat."

Annette laughed. "That is very good thinking, Guido. But you raise the question of drink. What wines should we have? Champagne?"

Guido smiled and raised a hand. "On this question, the two bridegrooms can relax. I have already had a visit from George Sanders, who told me that the officers had made a collection for this purpose. It is all paid for, Annette. He also suggested champagne, but I advised him that because of the cost involved we should have *Prosecco*, which we call Italian champagne. And, of course, for the red we will have your favourite: *Montepulciano*."

Annette brought her palms together. "Oh, that's wonderful, Guido!" She had been introduced to this red wine with the almost spicy taste by her father, in an Italian restaurant they had sometimes visited in Liege before the war, and she in turn had introduced Mickey to it.

"And for the men, if they require it, we also have bottled beer."

It had taken just a matter of minutes to decide on the rest of the menu.

And here they were, tucking into the *antipasti*: thinly-sliced ham, olives, sliced aubergine, modest amounts of lettuce and tomato, accompanied by glasses of *Prosecco*, lemonade for the boys. It was all very informal.

"The bubbles keep going up my nose," giggled Gladys.

"Er, pardon me, Guido, but what is this?" The question came from Eric Rice, who was pointing his fork at a slice of aubergine.

"That, my friend, is what we call *melanzana*. In England it is known as aubergine, but the Americans call it eggplant."

"We also call it aubergine," said Annette. She smiled across at Eric." It is very nice."

"'Ere, dad, watch this." This from Jacko who, once he had his father's attention, closed his eyes and dropped a slice of aubergine into his mouth. "Mmm...yummy!"

Eric followed his son's example, nodding as he chewed. "Yes, very nice."

"How are you doing, Jimmy?" Dick enquired of his stepson.

Jimmy, in reply, tilted his plate to show that its contents had already disappeared inside him. "Why can't we have this at home, Mum?"

Annette glanced across at Guido, murmuring, "We may not need the sausages."

The *primo piatto* consisted of *ravioli*, pasta envelopes with a meat and cheese filling served with a tomato-based sauce. This caused no problems, although Gladys and Elsie, fearing later sickness caused by the overeating of rich food, made sure that the boys received only small portions.

"That's a fine bit of cloth you're wearing, Mickey," George Sanders called across as they rested between courses. George, of course, had a Gold Flake between his fingers.

Mickey fingered his lapel. "Yeah, not bad, George."

"Must have cost you a pretty penny."

"Six bob, mate."

"*What?*"

"Mind you, I have to get it back to the shop by five o'clock, so I'm hoping we'll soon be finished here."

Annette slapped her husband's hand. Theo Rothstein, who was familiar with and enjoyed London banter of this nature, was the first to laugh.

Guido, seated next to Theo, turned to him. "So you understand this kind of humour, Comrade?" At the time of the armistice celebrations thirteen months earlier, Guido had revealed himself to be a member of the *Partito Socialista.*

"I do, Guido. I have, after all, been in this country for almost thirty years. I'm particularly fond of the kind of joke that Mickey has just made because it could only come from a worker. Can you imagine a bourgeois joking about returning a hired suit?"

There was a little confusion when the sorbet arrived, as Malcolm Lewis whispered to Meg Arnold, "Is this the pudding?"

"Damned if I know," Meg muttered in reply. "No, it can't be, because there's still all this cutlery on the table."

"The *sorbetto*," announced Guido to the company at large, having noticed a number of mystified expressions, "is to clear the palate in preparation for the main course."

Jacko's spoon was already in his mouth, eyebrows raised as he nodded his approval to Jimmy.

There were sighs and gasps of pleasure when Guido's two hired waitresses—both women in their thirties—served the main course: braised chicken thighs in a tomato and basil sauce with rice. Archie Henderson, an organiser who had defected from the conservative blue-button union during the 1915 tram strike, grasped his stomach, wailing "How will I ever...?" Ben Smith, a pioneer of the old London Cabdrivers' Union, raised his eyes from his plate and growled, "You'll find a way, Archie."

For most of the party, the dessert, *tiramisu*, was a novelty, and not one they would soon forget.

"What is this dish made of, Guido?" asked Theo Rothstein after two mouthfuls.

"Basically, Theo, it is lady fingers..."

"Lady fingers?"

"Yes, you know—sponge fingers..."

"Ah, as in diplomat pudding?"

"Yes, that is right. Do you like diplomat pudding, Theo?"

Theo shrugged, chuckling, "I don't know; the only time I tried to order it the Lyons Corner House had run out."

"Tell them the story, Theo," Mickey encouraged him.

Theo, debonair in his three-piece suit and his smartly trimmed beard, looked around the room, eyes twinkling behind his glasses. "Would you like to hear a story of my diplomatic exploits, comrades?"

"Theo, I could listen to you for hours, regardless of the subject," said George Sanders, "so yes, I'm sure we would like to hear your story."

"Seconded," said Malcolm Lewis, who had heard Theo address meetings of busworkers on a couple of occasions.

Theo tugged on his waistcoat and raised his chin. "Very well, comrades. In January 1918, along with Maxim Litvinov, who was then our Soviet Ambassador—although just as unrecognised by the British government as I am today—I attended a meeting with a man called Bruce Lockhart and a representative of the Foreign Office. Lloyd George had acknowledged the need for a semi-official form of contact between our two countries, and so Lockhart was to be his man in Russia and Max—although still unrecognised as ambassador—would be our man in London. The purpose of our meeting, therefore, was to finalise this unofficial arrangement.

"We were meeting in the Lyons Corner House on the Strand—on the second floor to be precise. I hear you ask, why a Lyons Corner House?" He spread his hands. "Why not? In fact, it had been my practice to meet in these restaurants because, as one of my London comrades had argued, we were unlikely to see in such places anyone we knew." He paused and looked along the table at George Sanders, who winked.

"So, there we were, in the Lyons restaurant on the Strand. We discussed the unofficial arrangements over lunch, following which Max wrote a letter to Trotsky, who was then People's Commissar for Foreign Affairs, introducing Lockhart to him. At the conclusion of this, it was suggested that we celebrate the success of our negotiations by ordering dessert. Ah! I had just the idea, for after I had noticed diplomat pudding on the Lyons' menu some weeks earlier, the London comrade I mentioned just now explained to me what this dish was. Ah, yes, said Comrade Litvinov, very appropriate, so how about it, Mr Lockhart? So we called a waitress— I expect you know that they call them *nippies*, presumably because they are expected to nip here and nip there, wasting not a second in the pursuit of profit for their employer—and ordered four portions of diplomat pudding. Alas, the young lady soon nipped back to our table to apologise for the fact that every single portion of diplomat pudding had already been consumed." He shrugged. "Possibly the staff of the French Embassy had beaten us to it. Anyway, upon hearing this news, Max Litvinov threw up his arms and cried, 'You see, not even Lyons will recognise me!'"

The laughter and applause came, but Theo had by now turned to Guido.

"Guido, a thousand apologies for interrupting you! *Tiramisu!* We had got as far as lady fingers…"

Guido touched the corner of his eye with the back of his hand. "Ah yes! Lady fingers soaked in coffee, with cream cheese and whipping cream, Comrade."

Theo raised a finger. "Mind you, comrades, it is perhaps just as well that we did not celebrate our success, because the results of our negotiations turned out to be rather *less* than successful: within weeks, Lockhart was found to be providing financial and other support to the Whites, and so he was arrested and deported. The British government then retaliated by treating poor Max in like fashion." The finger came up again as another thought struck him. "Which is how, in case you were wondering, this humble Russian— actually Lithuanian— journalist came to be appointed to the lofty rank of Soviet Ambassador." The finger now went to his chin as he frowned in thought. "Maybe, the next time I am in a Lyons Corner House, I should put it to the test and attempt once more to order diplomat pudding." A shrug. "If Lyons recognises me, how long can Downing Street delay the inevitable?"

As the laughter subsided, it dawned on everyone that the consumption of solids was at an end and the time had arrived for coffee, more wine, and speeches.

Dick turned to Mickey, murmuring, "It seems we need a chairman."

"Want me to do it?"

"Why, when we have an experienced chairman in the form of Dennis?"

"Fair enough. Your man, by the way, is about to crash by the look of him." He nodded at Jimmy who sat, his eyelids drifting southwards, at Gladys's side.

"Don't you worry about him, Mickey," assured Gladys as she began to create a space on the table in front of her son. "A pity that he'll miss the speeches, though."

"Now there's a sensible lad," Dennis Davies pointed at Jimmy, whose head was now on the table, as the chairman rose to assume his duties.

"Drunk as a lord!" cried Dick, attracting affectionate laughter from most and a scowl from his bride.

"Comrades," Dennis commenced, "I think I speak for all of us when I say that it is a great, great pleasure to be a part of this wonderful occasion, and so thank you Mickey and Annette, Dick and Gladys, for inviting us to share it with you. And thank you, Guido and Emilia for providing such a wonderful meal. In one sense, this is a sad occasion, because for those of us who work at the offices of the red-button union, and those of us who meet there occasionally, this café became the place where we not only enjoyed each other's company but where we experienced the warmth and hospitality of Guido and Emilia, and for some of us this may be the last time we will be here, as in just a couple of weeks' time we will have a new union and new premises. So, comrades, let's hear your appreciation for Guido and Emilia."

As the applause filled the room, Guido held back a tear, nodding in gratitude, while a more composed Emilia announced, "Comrades, this does not have to be your last time here: your office may close, but we will still be open!"

This brought forth laughter and a renewed burst of applause, through which Barney Macauley made himself heard. "Dennis, we should also thank the two waitresses who have served us so efficiently this afternoon. Would it not be appropriate to ask them to join us for coffee and a glass of wine at this stage of the proceedings? We're all comrades after all!"

As Dennis sought the approval of the two wedding couples for this suggestion—which came swiftly enough, Mickey nodding and indicating two spaces at the opposite side of the square from where he sat—Barney leaned forward to peer past Theo Rothstein, attracting the attention of Guido. "Guido, the tall one is a fine-looking woman, is she not?"

Guido smiled, nodding. "She is, Comrade, she is."

"Would she be married at all, Guido?"

"A widow, Barney, unfortunately."

"Oh," said Barney with less than total sincerity, "I'm sorry to hear that."

Guido winked at him.

"Now, Comrades," resumed Dennis, "before I call on the witnesses to give their estimates of the newlyweds, Theo here has a brief message."

Theo stood and took a single sheet of paper from his inside pocket. He smiled. "Don't worry, comrades, this is not a speech but a letter. You know, there are two people who would have loved to be here today but were unable to make the trip. I refer, of course, to Annette's parents, Emil and Jeanne Fré. Emile is a printer, an active member of his union and, I am happy to say, a thorn in the side of the leaders of his political party, the Belgian Workers' Party. Comrades, they are unable to be here for the simple reason that they are rebuilding their lives back in Liege, having spent several years during the war here in London, where Emile worked for the Twentieth Century Press." He waved the letter. "This is their message to Mickey and Annette."

Dearest Daughter and Son-in-law,

It pains us to be absent on what will hopefully be one of the happiest days of your lives, but we are content in the knowledge that our daughter is now married to a fine young comrade and that you are both gainfully employed. We treasure the memory of those few times when we were together as a family in London and hope that in the near future you will be able to visit us here in Liege—and possibly present us with a grandchild.

You may be interested to know that our party, although so lacking in militancy and internationalist spirit, gained 30 seats in the elections of 16 November, while the Catholic Party lost 29 seats. Now, we both have 70 seats, and so, as there are 186 seats in the Chamber, a coalition has been formed. As a condition of our participation, we have demanded a number of progressive reforms: the legalisation of picketing, old-age pensions, the eight-hour working day, etc. In this, we should be successful, but of course it will not be socialism. For that, we workers will need to build a more committed and determined party.

Well, sweet ones, we send our deepest love to you and wish you happy and productive lives. Please pass on our fraternal regards to all the comrades with whom you will be working to bring about a fairer society and a better world.

Until we meet again!

Emile and Jeanne Fré.

It was now Mickey who struggled to hold back the tears as he placed his arm around Annette and drew her to him, kissing her brow while Guido led the applause.

"Well, I'll tell you what," said Dennis Davies as he regained his feet. "I wish I'd had a mum and dad like that! Now to the final business of the afternoon, when Eric Rice and George Sanders—and anyone else who feels like it—will say a few words about the newlyweds. For my own part, let me just say that Mickey and Dick, although they're busmen, have made their own distinctive contributions to the cab section of our union. I well remember the meeting of the Vigilance Committee where Dick made as sharp an analysis of the cab trade as I've ever heard, dividing us into semi-proletarian journeymen and petty-bourgeois owner-drivers. And who could forget when, at that meeting at The Ring in 1917, Mickey stood up before twelve hundred journeymen—they'd kicked me out of the chair because I was an owner-driver—and pretty much convinced them that they'd be daft to strike against a fare-increase. But that's enough from me. Here's someone who's known Mickey a lot longer than me: his brother, Eric!"

For a moment, Eric stood there, tall and thin with his gingerish moustache, looking down at the table in front of him. At length he shrugged, growling, "Well, what can I say? He's been almost a brother to me."

That got laughter with a nervous edge to it—nervous because people were not *quite* sure that it was intended as humour; that "almost" was a bit of a worry. Mickey made himself smile but he wondered whether Eric was making a not-too-subtle reference to the biological fact that they were only half-brothers and the political fact that on some matters they were no longer of the same mind.

"I come up to London some years before Mickey, did the Knowledge, got my cab licence and became active in the old London Cabdrivers' Union. Mickey followed me to London in 1913, having done a few years on the Reading trams. I remember that day. George had said I should discuss the possibilities open to 'im—not just for work but for union activity. After I'd told him all the things that were wrong with the bus conductor's job, he said, 'Okay, I'll take a crack at it.' Just like that."

When he turned to look at Mickey it was if he had trouble identifying the person before him as the young man who had first set foot in London six years earlier. There now seemed no danger that Eric would suddenly lurch into animosity, for he appeared to have realised that what he had been feeling for his brother in recent times was not envy but admiration.

"And by Christ, didn't he take a crack at it! First day on the job, he took on the surliest, most anti-union official in the garage and come out on top. *And* he screwed half an hour's overtime payment out of the old man for the privilege of interviewing him over his wearing of the red button." Eric had suddenly fallen back into the accent of his home town, pronouncing *out* as *eht*; perhaps he imagined himself back in Reading, explaining Mickey's progress to their mutual acquaintances. "And it was later that same year that we got recognition by the London General and Tilling's, due in no small part to the efforts of men like Mickey. God, he put himself abeht, organising the men in Middle Row garage—along with Dick, Malcolm and others, it's true—and when it came to the recognition strike that garage was one of the first to come eht. And soon as the recognition agreement was signed, Mickey became the local rep."

He paused, smoothing down his moustache. "Then, of course, he became a driver. It didn't take long for him to make a name for hisself in the union—by Christ, George, do you remember that speech he made when the EC come back from the first wage negotiations without a reduction in hours? He certainly give 'em some stick! Didn't he just! Then in 1917 he was elected to the EC. Seeing the way he conducted hisself, I had to admit that he was leaving me behind. The arguments he come up with, an' the way he put 'em forward, you woulda thought that he'd been sittin' on that council for *years*." He sighed. "In 1913 when he first come up here, comrades, I was 'is big brother." A chuckle as he looked across at Mickey. "The way things stand now, though, I reckon he's *my* big brother."

Affectionate murmurs about the room, Elsie and Gladys's mum dabbing their eyes.

Eric took a sip from his water glass. "Mehth's a bit dry. Anyway, here we are at the start of another chapter in the Mickey Rice story, and it seems like he's hit the jackpot. Not only is Annette beautiful, but she's a fine socialist, and I just want to wish you both the happiest possible future, and to let you know that if either of you is ever in trouble you can rely on me. My love to both of you." He blew them a kiss and sat down.

Mickey surprised himself by leaving his seat and walking around to Eric. His brother stood and for a moment their eyes locked. Then they threw their arms around each other.

"Thank you, brother," said Mickey. "I love you, Eric."

"You know, air Mickey, this sort of thing ent done in Reading," Eric responded. "I love you too, bruv."

Jacko was tugging at Elsie's dress. "Mum, Mum, why are you and Dad crying?"

"It's what people do when they're happy, son."

Jacko frowned. That was news to him.

"In that case," said Barney Macauley, who had moved a few tables down to join the tall waitress, "I should be bawling my head off."

Dennis Davies stood up for what he hoped would be the last time. "Well, comrades," he said with a smile on his face, "I've chaired a few events in my time, but never one like this." He turned to Sanders, "George, you're on."

Having stubbed out his cigarette, Sanders rose to his feet. At almost fifty, George Sanders was still a handsome man. Hair and moustache were tinged with grey but his figure was still lean and his broad forehead and erect stance suggested power and rectitude.

"Comrades, Brother and Sister Mortlake have each made valuable contributions to our union and the class to which they belong. And I do mean the *working* class, comrades, although of course Dick traces his origins to the petty bourgeoisie. There is absolutely nothing wrong with that; the petty bourgeoisie, after all, gave us Marx and Lenin. The important thing is not which class a person is born into but which class he or she identifies with and struggles alongside and on behalf of. But Dick has done more than that: he has *become a member* of our class, and I and a few more people in this room remember the precise *day* that transformation took place.

"It was the day of our Annual Delegate Meeting in 1914, comrades, and Dick was the delegate from his branch. Now, it was obvious that he had never spoken at an event of this size before, and you could see that he was nervous. And it wasn't just the size of the event that was causing him concern: he came from a different background from these rough proletarians, and while he didn't necessarily look any different from them, he knew that when he began to speak, they would be able to tell that he wasn't really one of them. Now, it wasn't so much, I suppose, that the other delegates would have been bothered by any of this; no, it was more a case of Dick *thinking* that he didn't fit in. Anyway, he had prepared a three-page speech on the evil of long hours at the wheel and what we needed to do about it, and as he placed it on the lectern there were distinct signs of a tremor."

He paused there for a moment and looked across at Dick who was, a grin on his face, impressed by the fact that George had not only such a clear memory of the event but that the older man had known precisely what he had been feeling as he stood on the rostrum.

"But then someone did him a favour. Somehow, news had got out that Dick Mortlake had previously been a classical flautist, and a lad from the cab section shouted out, 'Come on, give us a tune on yer flute!' For a few seconds, Dick just stood there, looking around the conference hall, and at first I thought he'd completely dried up. But no: calm as you please, he picked up his speech from the lectern—no evidence of the shakes now—and put it back in his pocket. Then he tells 'em he'd *love* to give 'em a tune on his flute, but it was impossible. Why? Because he was completely knackered after the hours he'd worked the day before, getting home at one o'clock in the morning. When was the last time you had the opportunity to listen to some proper music, he asked them, or even to go to a picture palace? He said he's been to a picture palace a few weeks earlier, and all around him men were snoring and talking in their sleep. When some members of the audience told them to shut it or get out, Dick came to their defence, shouting, 'Leave them alone! They must be vehicle workers, and they need their rest!' Earlier, the chairman had said that if any delegates had too much to drink during the dinner-break he'd send 'em home to the wife and kiddies. 'You'll be doing them a favour,' said Dick. 'How else would they get a chance to spend time with the wife and kiddies?'

"Oh, comrades, he had us rolling in the aisles! By the end of his speech, he was fully accepted as one of us—a busman and a member of the working class. *That* was the day when Dick Mortlake became a member of our class!"

George allowed the applause to subside and then smiled across at Gladys. "And today Dick has tied the knot with Gladys, formerly the conductor on Mickey Rice's bus. Let me start by saying that if anyone doubts that a woman can do what is sometimes referred to as a man's work, Gladys is here to show the fallacy of that belief. According to Mickey, in fact, she was the best conductor he ever had. Gladys proved herself as a worker; but she also proved herself as a trade unionist." He nodded, eyes narrowed in discernment. "By Christ she did! When, last year, the Committee on Production made the mistake of awarding a five-bob war bonus to the men and telling the women they'd get nothing, Gladys showed her leadership qualities. She attended as an observer when the EC discussed the matter and told the members of that august body—Mickey included—that if they failed to resolve the matter expeditiously, the women would solve it themselves and that, pretty much, is what happened. It's true that it took longer than it should have done, because we wanted to ensure that this would be a national dispute, and the employers were dragging their heels, giving excuse after excuse. So one morning Gladys decided that enough was enough, and she led the women of Middle Row onto the stones and began contacting the other garages in the division, and pretty soon the whole of the London fleet was out and members in the provinces were also taking a stand. And it seems that there was a woman—or women—very much like Gladys on the trams at London United, because they struck at pretty much the same time as Middle Row, and so we now had a bus *and* tram strike. And, as we all know, that strike was successful, and the women were paid the war bonus. So Gladys"—he raised his glass in her direction—"I salute you."

He splashed some more *Montepulciano* into his glass and raised it once more. "And now, comrades, let's drink to Dick and Gladys— a new proletarian family!"

*

Now the party began to wind down. Gladys's mother Mary felt called upon to say a few words, as did organizing secretary Ben Smith, but it was Morris Frankenberg's very practical contribution which signaled the end of the proceedings. "Comrades," he said, "I believe I saw a puzzled expression on Mickey's face when he saw the wedding gifts piled against the wall, and he was obviously wondering how he and Dick were going to get them home. Well, let me advise the newlyweds that there are two taxis parked just down the street, and Dennis and I will be delighted to convey them and their gifts to Bayswater."

When, after the fond farewells, Mickey made his way to the door, a stack of gifts in his arms, he noticed that Barney Macauley was still seated at the table with the tall waitress.

"You not making a move, Barney?" he called over the top of the gifts.

Barney turned a mischievous grin on him. "Not just yet, Mickey; I've offered to give a hand with the washing up."

3

Riding home in Morris Frankenberg's taxi with Annette beside him, Mickey was reminded of the first time they had travelled to his flat together. That had been on a number 7 bus, after the armistice celebrations at the red-button office. He had been happy just to have her beside him; happier still when the bus lurched or braked a little sharply, causing his body to press into hers. She had agreed to spend an hour alone with him in the Alexander Street flat. He had surprised her that night by making no attempt to make love with her. They had talked, they had kissed, but it had gone no further. It was not until much later that Mickey had explained that he had been restraining himself not due to any prissy sense of propriety but because he had first to disentangle himself from a sexual relationship with another woman. Once he had told her that he had done that, she had come to the flat one sunny summer Sunday morning and the inevitable, the wonderful, had finally occurred and as he had entered her he had seen that golden aura about her blond head which told him that this was more than sex.

They had used the weeks after Annette had moved into the flat in November to become accustomed to each other's bodies and to the circumstance of living together. It is possible that, given their political views, they would not have bothered with formal marriage, but they had needed to ensure that Annette's residence in the country was secure.

Now, it might have been assumed that, having lived in what was sometimes called sin for several weeks, they would not be particularly eager to get home from their wedding celebration and litter the bedroom floor with their clothes prior to effecting a congress in these new circumstances. But this was not the case. In the taxi, Mickey was almost unbearably aware of the warmth of Annette's thigh against his and she, as she often did when becoming aroused, was twisting on the seat. As they were dropped off at the door, Mickey had to take Annette's hand to restrain her from dashing to the flat while he thanked Morris for his kindness. But when the taxi pulled away it was a dash for both of them, Annette's early lead reduced to naught by the necessity of waiting while Mickey placed the wedding presents on the ground and took the key from his pocket to open the front door, a frustration she was forced to endure a second time at the door to the flat, by which time she had two items of clothing in her hands. Even so, aided by the intricacies involved in the removal of female clothing, Mickey was first on the bed, stark naked, on his back. He could not help noticing, as he awaited the unclipping of the garter belt and the unrolling of stockings, that the slight paunch he had developed in recent years as a result of sitting behind a wheel all day had, despite his efforts to get rid of it by frequent visits to the swimming pool at the Wedlake Street Baths just along the Harrow Road, still clung to him.

"I must do something about this," he said, slapping his stomach.

She laughed. "And I must do something about *this*," she said, giving his penis a light slap, encouraging it to life.

She crawled towards him now, her breasts brushing his chest, her face, flushed somewhat by the afternoon's wine, bearing an openly predatory expression. She let her body fall onto his and they kissed, open-mouthed, hungrily. As they came up for air, Mickey stretched luxuriously, feeling her warmth against him. "Oh, this is sooo nice," he murmured.

But, of course, Annette had fallen asleep; and so, within a minute, did he.

*

"Well," Dick drawled in his best upper-class accent, "he *has* been known to have that effect on people."

This was when, upon returning home after the Sunday evening recital at the Wigmore Hall, Dick told him that a few members of the audience had walked out during the performance of one of the Satie pieces.

"Why don't we go to a concert during our two-and-a-half-day honeymoon?" Mickey had suggested in the week before their wedding.

"Oh, how wonderful!" Annette had responded. "Yes, I would like that."

"The question, then: *which* concert?" He walked across to the coffee table where he had deposited that day's edition of *The Times* and turned to the Entertainments Index. "Have you ever heard the *Organ Symphony* by Saint-Saëns, or Tchaikovsky's *Violin Concerto*, my sweetheart? Oh, I'm sure you would love them. Trouble is, there's no sign of them in the listings."

Annette extended her hand. "May I, my love?" As she scanned the column, she began to issue sounds, at first dismissive and then more enthusiastic. "Ah, this looks interesting, my love."

"What's that, sweetheart?"

"It is not a concert, though: a piano recital."

"Just the piano?"

"*Oui*, by someone called Francis Poulenc."

"Belgian?"

"I do not know, but probably French, as the music is French."

"And what is the music, sweetheart?"

She bit her bottom lip. "Oh, I do not know whether you will like it. It is...modern, I suppose."

"Jazz? If there's such a thing as French jazz."

"No, no, no. It is..." She searched for the words but could not find them.

"Do *you* like it?"

"Why, yes, I like some of it, but..."

"That's good enough for me, then."

"No, my love, our musical tastes might be quite different." She brightened. "Ah, Dick will know how to explain it! We will ask Dick!"

"Ah, Debussy and Erik Satie," said Dick when they tracked him down. "Their kind of music is sometimes called *avant-garde*. You know, new, experimental."

"So it's the kind you can't whistle," pronounced Mickey, looking a little glum.

Dick laughed. "Yes, you *would* have a bit of a job whistling some of it."

"But some of it is very pretty," protested Annette. "*Clair de Lune,* for example."

"That's very true, Annette. I was actually thinking more of Satie when I said that. But listen, Mickey, did I hear you once say that you liked the paintings of the Impressionists?"

"You may well have, because I do."

"Well, the music of these composers has been called the musical equivalent of Impressionist painting. It creates a *mood,* if you know what I mean."

"Oh, that doesn't sound so bad." Mickey seemed relieved.

"And where is the recital?"

"The Wigmore Hall."

"That place has a *very* interesting history."

"Go on."

"Used to be called the Bechstein Hall. It was built by the German piano company, next-door to its showroom in Wigmore Street. Then came the war, and the company fell afoul of the Trading with the Enemy Act and its property was seized. They were forced to stop trading, and the hall was sold at auction for about half of what it was worth. A couple of years ago, it reopened as the Wigmore Hall."

And so, the day after their wedding, they found themselves seated in the Wigmore Hall, a venue of modest size. Mickey sat hand in hand with Annette, holding in his free hand a programme which resembled a small menu card. The titles of the pieces were all, of course, in French.

"What's a *gnossienne* when it's at home, sweetheart?" Mickey whispered, trying not to chuckle.

Annette blushed, afraid that he might have been overheard. "It's a word invented by Satie. It means, I think, a dance-like piece." She smiled. "*Excellent* pronunciation, Mickey."

"And *gymnopedies*?"

"No idea, my sweet."

The audience contained a mixture of types: those who frequented concert halls and dressed accordingly, although not overdoing it for this small hall, and a fairly large minority wearing clothes that were studiedly casual, many of the men with open-necked shirts although sometimes with a woollen scarf around their necks; with this latter group, corduroy appeared to be quite popular. Mickey had seen these types on several occasions previously, usually at the Hands off Russia movement rallies, and he recalled Harry Pollitt's dismissal of them at the launch meeting.

"Sweetheart," he whispered, leaning close to Annette, "would you say that this kind of music is popular with the bohemian set?"

"Oh, yes, very much so, Mickey."

That set him back on his heels, for it seemed that his wife bore these middle-class posers little—or no—ill-will. Well, perhaps he would learn something this evening—about the music, about bohemians, and about Annette.

The pianist appeared onstage and bowed to the audience before taking his stool. He did not flick back his tails before seating himself because he had no tails to flick; instead, he was dressed almost as casually as some of the bohemians in the audience, in a suit with a faint check pattern. He was a kid, surely not much more than twenty.

According to the menu card, M. Poulenc was to commence with a few of his own compositions and, apparently, he did. They were like nothing Mickey had heard before. The first was almost tuneless and devoid of emotion, and sounded as if it might be modeled on a nursery rhyme; the second resembled a hymn, but dribbled away into nothing. These were—thankfully!—very short pieces, but the surprisingly enjoyable third piece was rattled off by Poulenc in less than twenty seconds, at the end of which Mickey felt cheated, tricked.

Feeling his attention drift, he scanned the audience in an attempt to read the various reactions. Most of the regular concert-goers looked either bored or mystified, but that was to be expected. The bohemians were rather more interesting: true, the more honest among them looked somewhat puzzled, as if this was not quite what they had expected, but others at least affected enjoyment and some may *actually* have been enjoying the music. Mickey's attention was particularly drawn to one young man who listened to each piece with closed eyes, nodding in an apparent attempt to penetrate its logic; with most pieces, short as they were, this was as far as he got, but by the fourth one he knew what to expect, and was ready to greet its conclusion with a silent exclamation, eyes springing wide open, as if to announce to all about him that he had fully understood it. Mickey was reminded of his single visit to the National Gallery but was put in mind not of the Impressionists but of the young groom in Hogarth's "The Wedding Settlement." At the time, he had been filled with an almost overwhelming desire to bring his palm into stinging contact with the young man's ear, and his feeling towards the contriving bohemian was remarkably similar.

Annette, who had noticed his scowl, patted his arm. "I am so sorry, my love." A shake of her blond head. "It is truly awful."

Mickey almost laughed. "Patience, my sweet, patience. It may improve when he gets to the Satie pieces," giving no thought to the fact that Annette was almost certainly more aware of this than he.

And so it did.

Poulenc led off with Satie's *Gnossienne* No. 1, and Mickey was immediately captivated by its dreamlike simplicity. When Annette squeezed his hand, he squeezed back. "Told you," he whispered.

This was followed by the first of the *Gymnopedies*, and Mickey could now understand Dick's meaning when he had likened *avant-garde* music to the paintings of the Impressionists. Yes, he was back in the National Gallery, but this time he stood before Renoir.

And then disaster struck. For reasons best known to himself, Poulenc chose to follow these two charming pieces with the prelude to the first act of a play called *Les Fils des Étoiles*, which Annette thoughtfully translated as *The Sons of the Stars*. In the first few minutes, hardly anything happened, and this would continue for almost eighteen minutes, making it the longest piece of the recital. Once again, Mickey's attention drifted to the audience. After about six minutes, it was clear that some of the regular concert-goers were appalled, and at ten minutes a few made for the exit. None of the bohemians appeared puzzled now because, of course, the music was so simple, but some were clearly bored by its sheer uneventfulness; the poser whom Mickey had compared to Hogarth's young bridegroom attempted to continue his act, but even he was unable to keep it up for eighteen minutes.

"Don't think I'll try whistling that one," said Mickey, this time making no attempt to lower his voice, causing several people in the nearby seats to chuckle. Annette slapped his hand.

Poulenc then resurrected his recital, restoring the audience to consciousness by performing Debussy's demanding *L'Isle Joyeuse* followed by the sublime *Clair de Lune*.

And that was it.

"Bit of a mixed bag," Mickey commented as he and Annette got to their feet.

"Sorry, sorry, sorry," Annette whispered sibilantly.

"No, no, some of it was very nice. Besides, I've learned something this evening."

Annette looked sceptical. "What have you learned, Mickey?"

"That you can feed anything to a certain class of people, even though it's pretty meaningless, and as long as you tell them that it's modern, up-to-date and intellectually challenging they'll not only accept it but see things in it which are simply not there."

PART TWO

1920

4

At Middle Row garage, disciplinary hearings were reserved for Thursday mornings, unless of course the alleged offence was more serious and had to be dealt with immediately. On Tuesday, 30 December, Mickey had entered the office of Victor Wiggins in order to clarify the arrangements.

"Yes, Mr Rice, what can I do for you?"

Mickey planted himself on the chair opposite Wiggins. "As you know, Mr Wiggins, I take over as rep in two days' time, and I thought it might be good sense if we had a little chat about certain arrangements."

Wiggins whipped out a watch from the pocket of his waistcoat. "What time do you start work, Mr Rice?"

Mickey chuckled. "Oh, you're alright, Mr Wiggins; there's plenty of time before I sign on."

Wiggins forced a smile. "Glad to hear it. Now: arrangements."

"Yes, I'm thinking in particular of disciplinary day."

"Ah, yes, Thursday."

"That's right, but this particular Thursday happens to be New Year's Day, so I thought it might be sensible to postpone it for a week, or at least shift it to another day."

"Did you, indeed?" Wiggins crossed his arms and regarded Mickey through narrowed eyes. "Thinking of pushing the boat out on Wednesday evening, Mr Rice?"

"Not at all, Mr Wiggins, but some people might be thinking of it: possibly some of the witnesses, perhaps even you." He shrugged. "I was hoping that you would agree that a clear head is needed for a disciplinary hearing."

"It's also necessary for driving or conducting a bus, Mr Rice, and so whether or not someone is attending a disciplinary should make no difference. In this industry, staff presenting themselves for duty should be sober. Full stop."

An exasperated sigh escaped Mickey's lips. Clearly, this fool thought that any suggestion coming from him must have an ulterior motive and therefore should be resisted. It was inexperience writ large. "But some of the witnesses neither drive nor conduct a bus. I'm thinking of point inspectors, garage officials...and the like."

"Well, I'm sure that's very considerate of you, Mr Rice, but I think that on this occasion we will manage without your advice. The disciplinary hearings will go ahead on Thursday—*this* Thursday." He lifted his chin, seemingly proud that he had not only survived this confrontation with the dangerous extremist Mickey Rice, but had prevailed. "Now, is that all?"

"Not quite."

Wiggins consulted his pocket watch once more. "Well?"

"Arrangements for the day—*my* arrangements for the day."

"You will be stood down for the day, Mr Rice, don't worry about that."

Wiggins was being deliberately provocative and Mickey was provoked. He placed his elbows on the garage superintendent's desk and leaned forward. "Mr Wiggins, if you took the trouble to discuss the working of this garage with Mr Shilling before he left, you will know that I have never been one of those reps who constantly seek to be stood down on the slightest pretext. I am interested only in providing a service to my members, and I would ask you to remember that." His expression hardened. "And I find any suggestion to the contrary to be insulting. Now let's move on: arrangements."

"I will expect you to arrive in the garage at 0830 hours, Mr Rice." If Wiggins seemed relieved that Mickey gave no indication that he expected a response to his claim of altruism, it was probably because he did not have one. Now he was simply asserting his authority.

"What time is the first hearing?"

"0900."

"Then I'll be here at 0800."

He could hardly argue with that, could he? No, but he could argue with the assumption upon which it rested.

"That's entirely up to you, Mr Rice, but between hearings you will be allowed thirty minutes to consult with your members."

"That's fine if thirty minutes is sufficient; if not, I'll take as long as necessary."

"This is not negotiable, Mr Rice."

"That's right: it's not." Mickey withdrew his watch from his pocket and stood up. "I sign on in two minutes, so I'll bid you good morning, Mr Wiggins."

Mickey walked to the door without looking back, followed by the eyes of Victor Wiggins, who still had no idea how he was going to deal with this rep.

*

Jack Doyle was an Irishman in his fifties and a bus conductor of long standing. He was of medium height, still slender, and most women would have considered him handsome, with his dark hair brushed straight back and his thin moustache always neatly trimmed, although his flushed appearance bore witness to the fact that he was a man who liked a drink. Nevertheless, such minor physical shortcomings were more than compensated for by the style he brought to everything he did.

Prior to making up his waybill at the conclusion of a duty, Jack Doyle would be seen in the output office, removing a pencil from the breast pocket of his uniform jacket with a flourish, and giving a quick glance at the ceiling while he brought the tip to his lips to moisten it; there would be a further flourish as he brought the pencil down to the waybill and he was off, rapidly calculating the columns before him and entering the totals. He was never known to make a mistake. Once he had paid in, he would reach into his side pocket as he turned away from the counter and draw out a packet of Players Navy Cut from which he removed a cigarette and, with a flourish similar in form to the one he bestowed upon his pencil, bring it to his mouth; next came the box of Swan Vestas, the match ignited on his thumbnail. Once the cigarette was alight and drawing well, he would douse the flame with a single shake of the wrist and insert the spent match into the bottom of the box rather than simply discarding it on the floor. Jack Doyle was a tidy man.

Sometimes, Mickey would see Jack in the bar of The Eagle after a branch meeting. He stood with his left elbow on the bar next to his cigarettes and matches, and when he picked up his pint with his right hand the little finger was extended. Style. He resembled, Mickey thought, an aging gunslinger. Once, Mickey saw him take out a cigarette and flick it in the air, where it spiraled three or four times before landing in Jack's mouth—and the lighted match was there to greet it. Jack shook the life from the match before dropping it in the nearest ashtray and looking across at Mickey to give him a wink. Mickey had grinned and mimed applause. And he saw from this performance that Jack's style was not natural, but practiced.

And now Mickey was about to learn that thiss style extended to waking up in the morning. Jack was up on a disciplinary. The charge: a single instance of poor timekeeping.

"So you were an hour late on Tuesday morning, Jack." They were sitting in the refreshment vehicle which, by arrangement, always arrived early on discipline day.

A flourish as a cigarette came to Jack's mouth. "I was, Mickey."

"Did they lose mileage because of it?"

"Did they buggery! No, they put a poor sod on the spare list into my harness as soon as the minute-hand clicked past my sign-on time."

"And what happened when you turned up, Jack? Did they find work for you?"

Jack picked a flake of tobacco from his tongue and flicked it into the ashtray. Even in this, there was style. "They did. I ended up standing by for an hour and then doing a full duty on the 31s after Jimmy Abbott failed to show."

"Then they don't have much to complain about, do they?"

"They do not, but I *was* late, after all."

"Even so, I can't see you getting more than advice, Jack." Advice; caution; final caution; dismissal: that was how the disciplinary procedure went, unless it was a charge of gross misconduct, in which case, regardless of the previous record, it would, if proven, merit instant dismissal.

"Do you have any previous, Jack?"

"Not a thing, Mickey, apart from a similar occurrence five years ago."

"And what did you get for that?"

"Advice."

"There you go, then, Jack. You're home and dry."

"Ah, but that was with Mr Shilling. The fockin' eedjit we're seeing this morning is, so I'm told, a different species of being. And see the head on him! You'd think the cunt combs his hair with a firework,"

"Well, he does have an obsession with lost mileage. The fact that no mileage was lost due to your late arrival of Tuesday will go down well with him."

"Well. I should certainly hope so." Jack regarded the tip of his cigarette and blew gently on it until it glowed red. "But are you not going to ask me why I was late, Mickey?"

"Is it relevant, Jack?"

"Fockin' right it's relevant."

"Well, I was assuming you were out for a drink the night before."

"I'm out for a drink every fockin' night, but that wasn't why I was late!"

"Okay, Jack, calm down; I'm on your side." Mickey squinted across at the man he was about to represent. Knowing that he had enough information to get the man off with advice, he hesitated to ask the question, even though he knew the answer would be a corker; the danger was that it could complicate an otherwise straightforward case. "So why were you late, Jack?"

"I forgot to switch on the gas."

Mickey succeeded in preventing outright laughter, but he did snigger. "You might want to explain that, Jack."

"I will, but you'll need to stop that sniggering." This was what Jack had come for. He dogged his cigarette, leaned back and took a deep breath, running his palms over the table-top as though smoothing down the pages of his defence brief. "I have a very large kettle, Mickey, one of those with a whistle on the spout. Every evening before I go to the pub, I throw some tea in the teapot and fill that kettle to the very brim. And out I go. When I get back home after closing time, I light the gas under the kettle—very low, mind you, *very* low—before laying down for my beauty sleep. When it's time to rise and shine, that kettle will be whistling like an express train, so I'm out the bed, pour some water into the teapot, go and brush me teeth while the tea's drawing, then pour the tea. After I drink the tea, I'm out the door and on me way to the garage. That's what *usually* happens, except that on Monday night I forgot to light the fockin' gas!"

"Is this the same thing that happened five years ago?"

"Exactly the same."

"And you told this story to Mr Shilling?"

"I did, Mickey, and he loved it."

"And your penalty was advice."

"Correct."

"And what was the advice, Jack? Don't be late again?"

"No, don't forget to light the fockin' gas."

*

"Happy New Year, Mr Wiggins!"

This was Jack Doyle as he entered the garage superintendent's office behind Mickey Rice. The greeting was loud enough to make Mickey jump, but the effect it had on Victor Wiggins was rather more dramatic. Brow clenched, Wiggins brought his palms to his temples, which appeared to be the location of the damage.

"Yes, yes, Mr..."—a glance at the charge sheet—"Doyle." His face was a ghastly white and his eyes looked as if they had been bathed in the juice from a can of raspberries. "Sit down, Mr Doyle—and you, Mr Rice." When he picked up the charge sheet, there was a tremor to his hand. Victor Wiggins was very obviously drunk or, at least, suffering from a severe hangover.

"Good morning, Mr Wiggins," said Mickey, smiling to let him know that he was perfectly aware of the condition he was in.

"Is it? Well yes, good morning Mr Rice."

Jack Doyle, grinning broadly, looked at Mickey with raised eyebrows, silently mouthing, "D'ye smell the drink on 'im?"

"Time-keeping, Mr Doyle." Wiggins, eyes closed, placed his right hand on the edge of his desk, his index and middle fingers tapping softly. "Bad time-keeping so often leads to lost mileage."

"Often, Mr Wiggins," Jack conceded, "although not on this occasion."

"A set of lucky coincidences, Mr Doyle: there happened to be a spare conductor standing by, and later in the morning another conductor failed to report, and you were available to work his duty. But the important thing, Mr Doyle, is the *principle*." It must have taken considerable effort for him to get this out. He opened one eye, with which he regarded Jack Doyle. "I've been looking at your record, Mr Doyle..."

"So you'll have seen that it's good one."

Wiggins began to nod until the sudden pain told him that this was a bad idea. "It is a good one, yes. Usually, you appear to have no problem in reporting for duty on time. In fact, your time-keeping is far better than average. Tell me, did you train yourself in any particular way?"

"Well, I suppose it began when I was in the Army, Mr Wiggins. You don't have the opportunity to oversleep there."

Mickey had not known that Jack had been in the British Army, but he was not surprised, being well aware that employment opportunities were never all that plentiful in Ireland, and that, despite the growth of nationalist feeling, many men had joined up— or, of course, simply crossed the Irish Sea in search of a job.

"Oh, you served during the war?"

"Which war would that be, Mr Wiggins."

"Why, the last one of course."

"No, I gave that one a miss."

A suggestion of disapproval touched the damaged and suffering visage of Victor Wiggins. "Any particular reason, Mr Doyle?"

Jack cocked an eye at his representative. "Will I answer that one, Mickey?"

Mickey shrugged. "It has no connection with the charge, Jack, so it's entirely up to you. You're under no obligation to."

Wiggins tried, despite his evident distress, to adopt a determined and forceful expression. "When I ask a question, Mr Rice, I expect it to be answered."

"Then ask a question about Mr Doyle's time-keeping, Mr Wiggins."

"Now, now, lads," said Jack, ostensibly to calm matters, "I don't mind answering the question, even though I'm not obliged to. Do you still want an answer, Mr Wiggins?"

"Of course."

"You're sure now?"

A sigh as the eyelids fluttered closed. "Quite sure."

"There were a couple of reasons. For one thing, I was already well into my forties when war was declared and I didn't fancy getting my arse shot off as I tried to run as fast as a twenty-year-old. Secondly, I had no grudge against German workers, Austrian workers, Turkish workers or Hungarian workers, so I had no good reason to try to kill any of 'em."

"Are you saying you had no good reason to fight for the preservation of the British Empire?"

Wiggins was losing—had lost—control of the hearing, but Mickey, having no interest in helping him get back on track, had allowed him to stumble on.

"I haven't said that," Jack replied, "but I'll certainly say it if that's what you want. In fact, I'll shout it: I HAD NO REASON TO FIGHT TO PRESERVE THE BRITISH EMPIRE!"

Victor Wiggins' palms were over his ears, his eyes screwed shut. He was making a sound which could only be described as a whimper. He waited for several seconds and then, satisfied that silence now reigned, he gradually brought his hands down onto the desk. Having brought the whimper under control, he looked across the desk at Jack Doyle. "Now I'll tell you what I'm going to do, Mr Doyle. I had it in mind, given your good record, to give you advice regarding your time-keeping. In view of your behaviour here this morning, however"—a self-important sniff, a squaring of the shoulders—"I intend to administer a final caution."

"You what!" Jack exploded. "You haven't even discussed my lateness! You've not even asked me if there was a *reason* for it." Jack was obviously dying to tell his kettle story.

Mickey held up a hand. "Alright, Jack, that's enough. Leave it to me now."

Mouth downturned, Wiggins leaned back into his chair, as if expecting a blow from Mickey.

Still seated, Mickey leaned over the garage superintendent's desk and addressed him in hushed tones, having no wish to be overheard by the officials in the allocation office next door.

"Mr Wiggins, two days ago, I suggested that as today is New Year's

Day the weekly disciplinary hearings be postponed. Why? Because people—witnesses, such as point inspectors, garage officials, etc.—may well have been celebrating the night before and clear heads were essential for disciplinary hearings. But you refused." He paused, giving Wiggins a glare which could only mean that a raised voice was not far behind. "TODAY, you arrive pissed out of your mind, in no fit state to hold a pen, let alone a disciplinary hearing. And NOW you say that Mr Doyle, for being late once in five years is to receive a final warning. And he's quite right: you have asked for no explanation for his lateness. Oh, but you say his behaviour today has contributed to your decision to award a final caution. Well, Mr Wiggins, that is not how the disciplinary procedure works. Any penalty arises ONLY from the charge which appears on the charge sheet. You might, however, find it appropriate to charge Mr Doyle regarding his behaviour today." He shook his head. "But that would be very unwise, Mr Wiggins, very unwise indeed, because your own behaviour, to say nothing of your demeanour, would come under scrutiny at the subsequent disciplinary hearing—which, of course, would have to be chaired by another manager."

Mickey took a breather, sitting back. Thinking—or hoping—that he had finished, Wiggins opened his mouth.

"Wait! You'll know when I'm finished, Mr Wiggins." Mickey sighed. "The question is, what do we do now; or more specifically, what do *I* do now? I think I have two choices, Mr Wiggins. First, I could call the buses in." He watched as Wiggins flinched. "That would be a piece of cake: Jack Doyle, a well-liked man in his fifties, is given a final caution—one step away from dismissal—for being late once in five years. Believe me, Mr Wiggins, I'd have no trouble rallying them to Jack. The trouble is, everyone would be saying *Ohh, Mickey Rice is only on his first day back as rep and by ten o'clock he's pulling the buses off the road.* That's what people would say, not realising that this was due not to the mindless militancy of Mickey Rice but to the outrageous behaviour of Victor Wiggins.

"The second alternative would be to call the full-time officer and have him tell your divisional office to send a manager down to Middle Row, where Victor Wiggins is attempting to conduct disciplinary hearings while pissed out of his mind. That, Mr Wiggins, would be the end of your own managerial career, at least for a lengthy spell. But people would be saying, *Ohh, that Mickey Rice was only on his first day back as rep and by mid-morning the garage super was out the door.* " Mickey pondered for a few seconds and then shrugged. "In fact, I don't have much of a problem with that option, and I suppose it's the one you would prefer, because there would be no lost mileage. What do you say?"

Victor Wiggins was—almost—a broken man. "L-l-l-look, Mr Rice, I m-m-m-may have made a mistake here. B-b-b-but there must surely be a l-l-l-less extreme option."

"Oh, there is, Mr Wiggins, there is. All I've done is outline the options open to *me*. The less extreme ones are those open to *you*."

Eyes narrowed, Wiggins inclined his head as he attempted to divine what these options might be.

Deciding to help him out, Mickey leaned forward again, prodding the top of the desk with his index finger. "*First*, you bid Mr Doyle good morning and send him out of here with a record as clean as it was when he walked in." He looked at Wiggins full in the face. "You with me so far?"

It took a few seconds, but Wiggins eventually nodded—bugger the pain. "Y-e-e-e-s."

"And secondly, you postpone the rest of today's disciplinaries until next week." That look again. "Yes?"

A sigh, but also a look of relief. "Yes, I'll do it."

Mickey got to his feet. "Jack, we're finished. Fancy a cup of tea?" He turned to Wiggins who, while still wan and hollow-eyed, appeared to have recovered somewhat. "So shall I tell the members waiting to see you that they have another week to wait, Mr Wiggins?"

Wiggins nodded. "If you would, Mr Rice, if you would."

Stepping into the garage, having led the way out of the office, Mickey heard Victor Wiggins calling. "Oh, but the way, Mr Doyle, what *was* the explanation for your lateness?"

Jack, in the doorway with this hand on the knob, looked back over his shoulder. "Forgot to light the fockin' gas, didn't I?"

5

The third week of February was dry and mild in London, and the red-button men found it pleasant to walk through Kensington on their determined way to their new headquarters building.

Were there still red-button men in 1920?

True, there was no longer a red-button union, its merger with the blue-button Amalgamated Association of Tramway and Vehicle Workers having been registered on 20 December 1919 as the United Vehicle Workers, the numbers of which were further increased by the adhesion of such as the Amalgamated Carters, Lurrymen and

Motormen and the Halifax and District Carters, Draymen and Horsemen's Association, names sounding so foreign to southern ears. Even more foreign, though, were the practices of those who now led the new union, particularly those of the new general secretary, Stanley Hirst, and the men closest to him, like John Cliff, who had chaired the executive committee of the blue-button union in the last six years of its existence and was now joint secretary of the Joint Industrial Council for tramworkers. Those men used to the freedom and democracy of the red-button union, the London and Provincial Union of Licensed Vehicle Workers, not only longed for the red-button days but insisted, when they could, on red-button ways. So yes, there were still red-button men.

For Stanley Hirst, this was a cause for complaint. "Occasionally, I have found to my regret," he had said, "that although we are now one union there is still a tendency to discuss certain matters in terms of 'reds' and 'blues.'"

Bus driver Mickey Rice, formerly a red-button executive member, had found himself astonished at the figure cut by this new general secretary. Stanley Hirst was short—extremely so—and although still in his early forties with fairly even features, to Mickey he resembled Mr Punch, or the sort of wrinkled, hook-nosed old man you might see depicted in a book of children's fairy tales. This was not reassuring.

"Aye, he's but a wee man is Stan," Archie Henderson had said when Mickey had raised the matter with him.

"Dumpy, I would say," Mickey Rice had responded.

"He's put on some flesh since I last saw him, but that was back in 1915, at the time of the tram strike, when he was the assistant. He's been general secretary of the blue-button for two years and more now, and it's easy to see where he spends the extra salary."

Archie was a former blue-button organizer who had switched buttons—"Off with the blue and on with the red!" had been his cry at the time—when the blue-button union had dragged its feet during the London tram strike of 1915.

"I suppose, though," he continued, "that we should make allowances for the hard life he's had: left school at ten and went into a mill up in Huddersfield before going on the trams."

"Mm, maybe," muttered Mickey Rice, unconvinced.

Archie and Mickey did not meet professionally these days because Archie had been promoted to national organiser for the commercial sector, with responsibility for drivers of lorries and vans; Ben Smith, who had pioneered the organisation of the London cab section and been elected as organising secretary of the red-button union, was national organising secretary for the same sector. George Sanders, champion of London's busworkers, had been kicked upstairs to occupy the post of national organising secretary for buses and cabs. Mickey was convinced that this pattern was deliberate: Hirst had moved the old red-button officials away from their bases of support, giving them less opportunity to mobilise the membership against unpopular decisions. It could be said that Sanders had been hit twice, because while red-button assistant organising secretary he had also edited the union's journal, his status as an elected official giving him a certain amount of freedom to chastise the leadership in its pages; given his current national responsibilities, it was unlikely that he would have been able to shoulder responsibility for the journal, but just in case the new rule book made it clear that the editor could be suspended by the executive council, subject to appeal. Former general secretary Alfred "Tich" Smith, meanwhile, had been appointed as parliamentary secretary of the new union, but this was possibly a case of personal ambition, Tich having stood for the East Dorset seat in 1918, coming from nowhere to gain 4,000 votes.

There were just six red-button men who turned into Emperor's Gate this morning: Mickey Rice, 30, soon to complete his seventh year on the buses; Lenny Hawkins, 34, who worked with Mickey at Middle Row garage; Malcolm Lewis, 32, chairman of the Middle Row branch of the union; Reuben Topping, 35, of Willesden garage, who had spent several of the war years in prison as a conscientious objector; Harry Beard, 42, from the old steam garage called Nunhead; and Ernie Sharp, 39, from the New Cross tramshed.

Their mission was to claim one of the red-button rights as yet untested since the amalgamation: the right of lay members to attend meetings of the executive council as observers.

"You think they'll sling us out?" asked tall and skinny Lenny Hawkins.

"Oh, I think so, Len," replied Mickey Rice, well-built and thought to be handsome.

"Well, they'd better not try any rough stuff," warned Harry Beard, a large, red-faced man.

"Been meaning to ask you, Harry: how are things at Nunhead since the London General took you over?" asked Mickey.

Nunhead had been operated by the National Steam Car Company, which had run its buses on steam generated by paraffin. In May the previous year, shortly after the red-button's final negotiations with the London bus companies, the company had checked its books and decided that the costs of labour and paraffin ruled out any prospect of it continuing to operate in the capital, and it had therefore withdrawn some of its buses in May and the remainder in November; the mighty London General Omnibus Company had stepped in, purchasing the garages at Nunhead and Putney, accepting the 1,300 displaced staff into employment and running its own vehicles on the routes.

"I'd have to say," replied Beard, "that we're now feeling a bit more secure in the job and confident that the wages will be paid on time."

Mickey laughed. "You know, even before we submitted last year's claim Ben Smith predicted that the Steam Car Company wouldn't last."

"Some of us were saying that years ago," Beard chuckled.

*

And here they were: Transport House, 45 Emperor's Gate, tucked into a corner of this sedate residential area. The six men paused and looked up at the imposing structure, Mickey Rice, arms crossed, narrowing his eyes.

"Looks almost respectable," murmured Ernie Sharp.

"That's what I'm afraid of," said Mickey Rice, causing the others to laugh.

"Ahh," remarked Rueben Topping, "but it's *ours*."

"Well," said Mickey, "let's put that to the test. Come on, lads."

Mickey led them up the steps, through the double doors and into the lobby, where the receptionist—a new man, medically retired from the trams—raised his eyebrows in enquiry.

"EC meeting," snapped Mickey and, as the man lifted a finger, led his party swiftly to the stairs.

As they passed, Harry Beard glanced from his pocket watch to shake his head in disbelief at the receptionist, who grinned and grunted "Cuttin' it fine, mate."

Out of curiosity, Mickey called a halt on the first-floor landing, motioning the others to wait for him while he entered the door and stepped stealthily down the corridor to the ledger room, where he peered through the glass panel. Yes, there she was, on the nearside of the room, her blond head bent diligently over a ledger, her brow clenched in concentration as she ran her finger down a column of figures: Annette, his wife of two months. Wife: the concept was still a novelty to him, and often, as now, he found it impossible, knowing that she was in the vicinity, not to move closer to her, if only to lay his eyes upon her. Part of him wanted her to look up and see him, because he knew that then she would, after overcoming her surprise, give him that twinkling smile; but it would be a mistake to give anyone the impression that she was party to this morning's little adventure, and so he walked briskly back to the landing where, having given his companions a thumbs-up sign, he led them up the next flight.

The executive chamber, occupying almost half of the second floor, was not quite as large as the old meeting room in Gerrard Street, headquarters of the red-button union, although it was sufficiently spacious for its intended purpose, for the "gallery"—the rows of chairs at the rear of the latter, democratically provided for those lay members who wished to witness the executive proceedings—was here absent. As Mickey and his companions entered the chamber, the executive meeting had not commenced and, with EC members and officers standing about the room, casually chatting, they were not immediately noticed. The long table, transported from Gerrard Street, occupied the centre of the chamber, and this, as Mickey well knew, would just accommodate the EC members and a handful of officers. There were, on each side of the room, a number of chairs placed against the wall, and while these might have been intended for those national officers who could not be accommodated at the table, there were, Mickey calculated, sufficient of them to seat his party of intending observers.

Being recently elected from various parts of the country, some of the EC members, being not yet well-known to each other, possibly thought that the six late arrivals were of their number; others may have assumed that Mickey and company were members of a delegation, the presence of which they would be informed once the meeting got underway. No one, anyway, thought to challenge them. There were, of course, men in the room who recognised an interloper when they saw one: busman Barney Macauley had winked across the table at Mickey, and Archie Henderson had brought a hand to his mouth, feigning shock at the sight of him.

George Sanders, nearing fifty and showing more forehead than ever, drew heavily on his cigarette as he sidled up to Mickey and shook his head ruefully. "You're going to get yourself into trouble, Mickey. What are you up to?"

Mickey shrugged as if the answer might be obvious. "We've come to witness the executive meeting, George—a fine old red-button tradition."

Sanders smiled, possibly relieved that the purpose of the visit of Mickey and his comrades was not more serious. "Oh, I see." He held Mickey's gaze. "You realize he'll have you thrown out?"

"I'll be surprised if he doesn't, George."

Sanders nodded. "But you'll have made your point."

"Exactly."

A sigh. "Okay. Well, he'll be here any minute now, so sit yourselves down against the wall here and try not to be noticed."

In they came: John Cliff, thirty-seven, short, bespectacled, in a three-piece suit, and Stanley Hirst, grim-faced, drably dressed and even shorter; they had, Mickey realised, been in Hirst's office, preparing for the meeting, discussing tactics and deciding what they might concede if demands were to be made upon the union. Well, he thought, they won't have been able to prepare for the demand we've got for them. He watched as they strode—short men do sometimes stride, as if hoping that by stretching their legs to their furthest extent they might grow an inch or two—to the head of the table, thankfully taking the route on the opposite side of the room. The EC members and officers now took their seats and silence descended.

Cliff spent a few moments glancing about the room, as if to remind himself of the identities of those gathered there. Then he cleared his throat, shuffled the papers in front of him and, looking now at the six strangers seated along the wall to his right, said, "We appear to have visitors, General Secretary."

"Visitors?" The nose of Mr Punch came up and he blinked as, stretching, he attempted to peer over the heads of the EC members seated to his right.

They should provide him with a cushion, thought Mickey.

"Yes, General Secretary, there appear to be six gentlemen seated along the side there who are unknown to us." He grimaced. "And when I say unknown to *us*, General Secretary, I mean to you and I." He glanced over to where George Sanders and Archie Henderson were seated. "I daresay they are known to some in the room."

Mr Punch got to his feet and leaned forward with his fists on the table. "Then I suggest, Chairman, that our visitors announce themselves and state their business."

Mickey Rice stood, recalling the day in 1914 when, at the EC meeting called to consider the package of wages and conditions put forward by the London General Omnibus Company, he had stood in the gallery and savaged the proposals on hours; but this was not an occasion of that nature at all; today he must exude calmness and sobriety.

"My name is Mickey Rice, Brother Hirst..."

"Ah, yes, former EC member!" recalled Hirst now. "And your business here?"

"I and my comrades really have no business as such, Brother Hirst. We're simply here to observe the EC meeting, as lay members of the LPULVW did since its formation in 1913." He paused, noticing several faces being covered by hands on the other side of the table. "So please don't let us interrupt your meeting." Now Barney Macauley's shoulders began to heave.

"Well, that may have been the case, Brother Rice," said Hirst, grimacing at the very notion, "but we are now the United Vehicle Workers, and that is not the way things are done any longer."

"What have you got to hide?" piped up Lenny Hawkins.

"*Hide?* That's got nothing to do with it!" thundered Hirst. "This EC is the highest committee in our union and it has the right to meet and debate without interruption or disruption! I must, therefore, ask that you leave immediately."

"Can I ask, Brother Rice," said John Cliff with a canny grin, "whether the London membership feels that it should be accorded privileges over and above those enjoyed by the general membership? Do you imagine that there is something special about a London vehicle worker?"

Mickey, seeing immediately that Cliff was a cleverer man than Hirst, paused thoughtfully before answering. "Yes," he said firmly, "there *is* something special about the London vehicle workers: more than any other group, it was the London vehicle membership which fought to make the red-button union democratic; it was the London vehicle membership that opposed the war-mongers; and it was the London vehicle membership which, by their militancy and discipline, achieved wages and conditions that are without equal in the passenger industry." He paused. "But no, we seek no special privileges, Brother Cliff. We are simply asserting a right enjoyed by London busworkers—*and* tramworkers and cabdrivers—in the seven years of the red-button union."

"But we are now the United Vehicle Workers!" insisted Hirst.

"But was our right to attend EC meetings as observers rescinded during the amalgamation negotiations?" Mickey came back at him. "No, it was not!"

Mickey could see now that the former red-button men on the EC were nodding, and George Sanders and Archie Henderson wore broad smiles; but as yet no voice was raised.

But John Cliff thought he had a trump card up his sleeve. "You say, Brother Rice, that you seek no special privileges, but that is not right, is it? You claim the right to attend EC meetings, and for you that might be physically possible. But what about our members in Leeds, Glasgow, Manchester, Liverpool?" He shook his head with that canny smile. "Are they second-class members, Brother Rice?"

Although Mickey was ready for him, he hesitated, nodding as if to acknowledge Cliff's argument, which surely must have validity. But no. "Brother Hirst has said that this highest committee of our union must be allowed to conduct its business without the possibility of disruption or interruption. But what is the highest *policy-making* body of our union? Isn't it the Annual Delegate Meeting?" He nodded. "Of course it is. And isn't it a fact that lay members are free to attend the ADMs as observers?"

The old red-button men seated around the table were now laughing, and one or two brought their hands together; even some of the blue-button men were smiling. But still no voice was raised.

Stanley Hirst was clearly unnerved, having sensed the previously unthinkable possibility that he might lose control of his executive. He now stood again, looking across the room at Mickey Rice. "Alright, that's enough discussion! I ask you again, Brother Rice, to leave this chamber. If you refuse, you will leave me no alternative but to have the police called, and they will eject you."

The wave of dismay which now swept over the members of the executive was, thought Mickey, almost visible. And they were affected not just by Hirst's threat to call the police against his own members, but by the words proceeding that threat: "That's enough discussion." Having lost the argument, Mr Punch curtails the discussion. The old blue-button members were probably used to this undemocratic behaviour, but the red-button boys and the other newcomers must be finally realising where this long-sought amalgamation had landed them. If the fool had any sense, he would have simply put the matter to the vote, as he would almost certainly have been able to swing his inbuilt majority behind his expulsion order.

Now, finally, a voice was raised: Barney Macauley's, of course. Macauley, in his fifties, burly and bald, thumped the table. "Wait a minute, Chairman! Are we going to have the police decide the business of this EC? Put it to the vote! I move that the six guests be allowed to remain in the chamber! Put it to the vote!" Behind Macauley, seated against the wall, pioneer of the old Cabdrivers' Union Ben Smith was scratching a substantial sideboard and silently nodding.

"Seconded!" cried Ernie Fairbrother, another former red-button member.

"The meeting has not been formally opened, and so there *can* be no vote!" argued John Cliff, voice raised against the hubbub of muttering which had erupted from the table. "The police have been called!"

And, in due course, they arrived, a sergeant and a constable visited by considerable confusion as they entered the executive chamber to find it filled with men and tobacco smoke.

"Excuse me, gentlemen!" called the sergeant, wafting away the smoke with his right hand. "Who's in charge here?"

Somewhat surprisingly, it was Cliff who stepped forward, hand extended. "John Cliff, sergeant. Thank you for arriving so swiftly."

Taking his hand, the sergeant frowned down at him. "There's seems to have been some mistake, Mr Cliff. We was told there had been a break-in."

Cliff grinned sheepishly. "Well, not a break-in as *such*, no. We were about to begin our meeting when we discovered half a dozen men who had no right to be here." He pointed in the direction of Mickey Rice and his companions, who were now standing, although it was not clear whether they were preparing to resist or comply with the instructions of the police. "They have refused to leave and so we called you."

"I see, sir." The sergeant had taken a notebook from his pocket and now wetted his pencil on his tongue. "And you are the owner of the building, sir?"

"In a sense, yes."

Macauley, who had joined the huddle, now intervened. "*We*," he said, sweeping an arm to take in those seated around the table, "are the owners of the building: the executive council of the United Vehicle Workers."

"And we," said tramworker Ernie Sharp who, along with Mickey and the rest of his group, had edged nearer the door, "are also the owners: *members* of the United Vehicle Workers, so how can you kick us out of our own building?"

The constable, who was playing no part in this confusing affair, cast his eyes about the room and suddenly stiffened. Out went his finger. "Excuse me, sir, but is that George Sanders?"

"Do you have a warrant for his arrest?" joked Macauley.

The sergeant's eyebrows went up. "You know him, Albert?"

"Well, I've met him. Friend of a friend, you might say. Helped us out in the first strike in 1918."

The sergeant turned to Cliff. "Please ask Mr Sanders to join us, sir, if you would be so kind."

"George!"

Sanders ambled over, cigarette between the first two fingers of his right hand, looking first to the sergeant, then to the constable, whereupon his frown was transformed into a smile and he transferred the cigarette to the corner of his mouth and extended his hand. "Albert Bell!" he exclaimed. "Last seen on the picket line at Nunhead!"

"Good memory, Mr Sanders," replied the constable. "That must have been four years ago."

"Five," Sanders corrected him, "and if you look around you'll probably see someone else who was there."

Harry Beard took a step forward. "That would be me, constable. Nice to see you again." The Nunhead men had been on strike at the time and Albert Bell had been assigned to keep order on the picket line.

"Yes, yes, yes, I remember," said Albert Bell. He frowned. "But don't tell me you're picketing your own union now!"

The Nunhead man laughed. "Well, in a sense I suppose we are, yeah."

Albert Bell turned back to Sanders. "I suppose you know that poor Bernard Sharkey was sacked after the second strike last August?" After a successful strike in 1918, under a new commissioner the Metropolitan Police had improved the pay and conditions of the force; a second strike in 1919, called to achieve recognition of the police union, had attracted only sparse support, as a result of which the union was crushed and the strikers dismissed.

Sanders nodded. "Of course, but he landed on his feet: he's on the buses now, driving out of Willesden."

"You don't say! Well, I'm glad to hear that..."

John Cliff coughed demonstratively. "This reunion is all very heart-warming, but I would be grateful if we could return to the business at hand so that I can open our EC meeting."

"Yes, Mr Sanders," said the sergeant, "there seems to be a lot of confusion as to who actually owns the building, and I was hoping that you might help us out."

"Well, *technically*..." Sanders began.

"It's alright, George," said Mickey Rice. "We'll be going now."

The sergeant looked at Cliff. "Satisfied, Mr Cliff?"

Cliff nodded. "Thank you, sergeant." He turned to Sanders. "See them off the premises, George."

"The police or the members?"

For response, Cliff turned and walked to rejoin Hirst at the head of the table.

*

"It seems that you and Cliff don't exactly hit it off, George," observed Mickey Rice as they stood outside the building.

"Does that surprise you, Mickey?"

Mickey grinned. "Hardly, George."

"Anyway, lads," asked Sanders, "what do you think you accomplished this morning?"

"We've shown that blue-button bunch that we're prepared to fight for our rights," said Malcolm Lewis. Malcolm had been back in the uniform of the London General Omnibus Company for barely a year, having in January 1919 led the soldiers of his unit of the Army Service Corps in a strike to secure their demobilization—and to let the authorities know that they had no intention of being sent to Russia to fight the Bolsheviks.

"We let them know that this is *our* union," said the tramworker Ernie Sharp, who had deployed the same argument in the days when a previous EC of the red-button union had disregarded the wishes of the membership.

Lenny Hawkins, Harry Beard and Reuben Topping nodded their assent.

But Sanders was looking for more than this. "Mickey?"

Mickey Rice sighed. "You remember when we attended that joint meeting with the executive of the National Union of Railwaymen last year, George? Well, for weeks afterwards I was haunted by a picture of that NUR executive. There they were, seated either side of Jimmy Thomas and Charlie Cramp, not one of 'em with a smile on his face or a glint in his eye. Before meeting us, Thomas and Cramp had given them the line and they were expected to stick to it." He glanced around at his five companions. "As far as we were concerned, the purpose of that meeting was to urge the NUR to call upon the other members of the Transport Workers' Federation to bring their members out in support of the railwaymen. But J.H. Thomas, M.P. was obviously opposed to causing further disruption in the country, as this would upset his parliamentary colleagues. So he sat there, telling us that the time was not ripe, that we should give it another day or two. And his executive members also sat there, saying not a word, showing no emotion. As I told a meeting of my branch at the time, they reminded me of clockwork soldiers who had been wound up—or not wound up—by their owner.

"And I began worrying about our amalgamation with the blue-button union. I couldn't help wondering, George, if the general secretary of the new union—and it was bound to be Hirst—would expect our executive to behave like the NUR men.' He shrugged. "Well, from what we've seen today, I think we have to accept that Stanley Hirst and his sidekick John Cliff are cut from the same cloth as Jimmy Thomas.

"So our intention today, George, was to show the members of the UVW executive that Stanley Hirst and John Cliff are not men to be afraid of, that it's possible for lay members to stand up to them and beat them in argument. And, I suppose, I hoped to give a bit of encouragement to the executive members to do exactly that." He shrugged. "Okay, in the event it was only Barney who spoke up, but you could see that others were losing their nervousness."

By the time Mickey had finished, there was a broad smile on the face of George Sanders. He nodded. "Well done, Mickey. It's a start."

*

"Well, what did you make of this morning's little drama?" asked John Cliff as he and Stanley Hirst sat in the general secretary's office after the conclusion of the EC meeting.

Hirst folded his hands on the desk and grimaced. "I wouldn't be surprised if Sanders was behind it, Johnny."

"That's possible, Stan, but this Rice character has a head on his shoulders by all accounts. He probably wouldn't *need* to be put up to it."

"They both need watching, then." Hirst sniffed. "Eh, listen to this. During the dinner-break one of our lads told me a nice little story. I think you'll appreciate it Johnny."

"Come on, then, let's hear it."

"A man claims that he's never had a serious quarrel with his wife. Whenever anything crops up upon which they don't agree, they compromise. For example, he says, when it came to choosing the wallpaper for their drawing-room he chose red and his wife plumped for blue, but after a short argument they compromised. 'Oh,' says his friend, 'and what colour did you compromise on?' Says the husband: 'Blue.'"

6

"And why was it necessary for you to be involved, Mickey?" asked Annette that evening.

He had arrived home two hours after her and now, after they had eaten the meal which she had prepared, he had explained the events of that morning.

"Apart from the fact that it was my idea, you mean?" He was

genuinely puzzled. Why was she questioning his involvement? And why did she appear so aloof—almost as if she were offended.

"But why did you have to be involved? That surely was not necessary."

"Well, I suppose not. But I *wanted* to be involved, sweetheart."

"The others could have made their position clear, surely?"

"Well, on second thoughts maybe it *was* necessary that I be there."

"But was it necessary that you stand outside the ledger department, staring at me?"

Ah, it was beginning to make sense now: he had embarrassed her.

But there was more. "Everyone in the building was talking about the incident at break-time—and they know that you are my husband."

He frowned. This was becoming serious. If Annette persisted in criticising his involvement in the executive chamber incident, they were headed for a collision. He recalled now how perilously close to disaster a few of his arguments with Dorothy had drifted. Luckily, he also remembered how he had—on one or two occasions, anyway—navigated those rapids, and Annette now handed him the opportunity to employ similar skills.

"Why did you stand there looking at me, Mickey?"

"But you didn't see me."

"Of course I saw you!"

"Do you really want to know, sweetheart?"

Her attitude softened. "Yes, please tell me," she said in a softer tone.

He took her hand in his and looked into her eyes. "Because I love to look at you, *ma chérie*. And so every chance that I get, I...look at you. And besides..."

The danger was past and she was ready to fall into his arms. "Yes, Mickey?"

"When I see you at work, it reminds me of when we first met at the Gerrard Street office—you, frowning down at a ledger, ink on your fingers..."

Involuntarily, she raised her right hand to inspect her fingers and then, realising the foolishness of the gesture, let out an exclamation—"Poof!"—and allowed the hand to fall.

"In a strange way, my love," he said, "I just find that...exciting."

Ah, now she smiled that twinkly smile, her slightly slanted eyes glowing. "I think I know what you mean, but..."

Oh, all buts must be intercepted! "You mean like when you told me, when we were together in Guido's café early in our relationship, that you were becoming excited when I told you that I would like to make love to you?"

She closed her eyes and nodded. "Oh, you remember! Yes, like that."

He smiled at her. "You were moving in your seat"—he moved his buttocks to and fro—"like this, sweetheart." He inclined his head slightly. "Why were you doing that, *ma chérie*?" He cupped her face with the palm of his left hand.

"You must know, my darling." Her right hand moved to the buckle of his belt.

"Because you were becoming wet?" he murmured.

She swallowed, then, lengthening the sibilant esses, whispered, "Yes. Of course."

By stages, they moved to the floor, the sofa, the bedroom.

When it was over, and they lay naked upon the bed, she asked drowsily, "My darling, please promise me that you will not again do anything like the protest today while I am working there."

He realised now that there would possibly come a time when love-making would not heal the breach between them.

"No, I can't promise that, sweetheart."

Silently, Annette turned her back to him and slept.

7

"And what do you consider the chances to be of direct action to compel the withdrawal of British troops, George? How is it looking?"

The question came from Theodore Rothstein, the unrecognised Russian Ambassador. He sat with George Sanders on the second floor of the Lyons Corner House at the junction of Rupert Street and Coventry Street, a favourite meeting-place for them. Waitresses—"nippies"—hurried from table to table in their black and white costumes.

The question, Sanders realized, concerned not his own union in particular but the whole British trade union movement. He sighed and lifted his eyes from the tabletop. "It's not looking very likely at the moment, I'm afraid, Theo. In fact, it's looking doubtful whether the movement is willing to strike for its *own* political demands."

Rothstein, short and smartly dressed, shrugged his eyebrows. "You mean nationalization of the coal mines, George?"

"Exactly. Although it was recommended by the Sankey

Commission, Lloyd George told the miners quite bluntly that there would be no nationalization. So, knowing that public opinion would probably not support them if they struck for it, what were the miners to do?"

"They started a public propaganda campaign."

"They did." Sanders prodded the table-top with his forefinger. "And in doing that, Theo, I think they handed the TUC the excuse to move away from any form of direct action."

Impressed with Sanders' reasoning, Rothstein nodded.

"Mind you, they wasted no time: not more than a fortnight after the Lloyd George meeting in October, they were addressing a meeting of four thousand people at Manchester Free Trade Hall, and the following day they were placing their case before the Liverpool Chamber of Commerce.

"Then on 9 December came the TUC Special Congress, which was to have discussed the government's Russia policy as well as coal nationalisation. As we might have expected, the railwaymen's so-called leader Jimmy Thomas got up and told the delegates how he favoured political activity over industrial action. Then the miners' general secretary Frank Hodges told them that the TUC's Parliamentary Committee, the miners' executive, the Labour Party and the Co-op Party had *already* agreed a plan for an intensified propaganda campaign over the next few months. Well, after that it was obvious that direct action was out of the question, and when Will Thorne—another leader who, like Thomas, can't make up his mind whether he's a trade unionist or a politician—moved that consideration of direct action be deferred until an adjourned Congress after Parliament reassembled in February, it was passed unanimously."

Sanders spread his hands. "If there was to be no direct action for coal nationalisation, it was obvious that there would be none in support of our Russian comrades, Theo. But the Congress heavily criticised the government's position on Russia and called on it to immediately consider the Soviet peace proposals. Despite Churchill's promises, British troops were still in Russia; they should be withdrawn, the blockade should be lifted and trade relations should be opened. The Congress demanded an independent and impartial inquiry into the political, industrial and economic conditions in Russia and instructed the Parliamentary Committee to appoint a delegation to visit the country to see for itself. A further report would be made when the Special Congress reconvened. All this was unanimously agreed, Theo, although I don't think we should take too much comfort from that."

Theo Rothstein, frowning slightly, inclined his head quizzically. "What do you mean by that, George?"

"I think a good part of the delegates were simply relieved that there was no question of industrial action."

"Ah, yes, maybe so, maybe so." He sniffed, reached for the coffee pot and topped up his cup.

Sanders took his packet of Gold Flake from his side pocket, selected a cigarette and lighted it. "What are the chances of our Cabinet recognising the Soviet government in the near future, Theo?"

Rothstein sighed. "Things are moving, but very slowly, George. On the day Parliament was opened, Lloyd George urged trade with us. But, as you will have seen, the Tory press is still very hostile, and the *Morning Post* has gone so far as to suggest that Poland should be armed. A few days later Minister of War Churchill maintained the anti-Soviet line regardless of what his Prime Minister might have said."

"And then there was that extraordinary letter from Gough and other officers in *The Times*..."

Rothstein grinned. "General Sir Hubert Gough, the man who led the Curragh Mutiny, when officers announced that they would not allow themselves to be used against Unionists opposed to Irish Home Rule. One would have thought from this that he was a died-in-the-wool reactionary, and yet here he was, with others it is true, calling for peace and trade relations with Russia."

"And he had been chief of the British Military Mission in Russia..."

"In Northwest Russia—the Baltic," Rothstein corrected him. "And it may well be that this latest outburst was born of his sore feelings over his sacking last year. Or, of course, he may simply be a realist: now that the Whites have been defeated everywhere except the Crimea and the Caucasus, peace is surely inevitable." He took out a handkerchief and began polishing his glasses.

"It was interesting to see that a day or two after that letter appeared the Supreme Allied Council announced that it would discourage neighbouring countries from waging war against Russia."

Rothstein waved a hand dismissively. "Hypocrisy, George, pure hypocrisy."

"You think so?"

"Yes, because they also said that they would offer every assistance if such neighbouring countries were attacked—by us, George— within their borders. It doesn't take much imagination to see how this might work in practice: one of these countries—Poland, most probably—disregards this advice and attacks us, and the Allies simply sit and watch; but the Red Army pushes back the attack and then, the moment we cross the border of the aggressor nation, what happens? Up goes the French and British cry for intervention once more!"

Sanders, eyes narrowed, drew on his cigarette and nodded. "Yes, I can see how that might happen."

"And that is what we must be prepared for, George." He leaned forward and lowered his voice. "Look, George, as direct action by the trade union movement seems to be out of the question at the moment, I believe that action at local level should be given precedence. For example, Sylvia Pankhurst and that young Harry Pollitt and others are very busy in the East End, particularly in the area of the docks, leafleting dockers and seamen in support of Russia."

"Yes, I sit with Harry on the committee of the Hands Off Russia movement, so I'm aware of his activity."

"Ah, of course."

"But, Theo..." Sanders waved a distracted hand. "Help me out here: our government has agreed to trade with Russia, so how at the same time can it still be thinking of intervention."

Rothstein gave him a patient smile. "The government," he said slowly, "has agreed to trade with Russian *cooperatives*, without recognising the Soviet government, which is not quite the same thing at all. Anyway, the All-Russian Central Union of Consumers' Cooperatives has appointed its delegation."

"Anyone I know?"

A grin. "Max has been appointed as chair of the delegation."

"Litvinov? But they'll surely never let him back into the country."

Rothstein shrugged. "Maybe not, but the comrades probably think it's worth a try: if the government allows Max in, despite the fact that he was arrested and deported last year, it will indicate a sharp change of posture."

Sanders shook his head. "Don't hold your breath, Theo."

"I hear what you say, George."

*

Sanders tipped a small amount of milk into his cup and poured the remaining contents of the teapot on top of it. "Where are we on communist unity, Theo?"

Rothstein sighed. "We're getting there, George, we're getting there, although Sylvia Pankhurst is proving somewhat difficult."

"Her position on parliamentary activity?"

"That and her opposition to the proposal that the new party should seek affiliation to the Labour Party. Did you see Tom Quelch's critique of her position in the 19 February issue of *The Call*?"

Sanders nodded. "I did. More like an attack than a critique, though, Theo."

A shrug from Rothstein. "Well, maybe so. But if you saw her article in her own paper two days later, you would better understand how she provokes such reactions."

"What did she say?"

"Oh, that the Comintern had already dismissed the Labour Party as a potential affiliate, and so why should British communists insist on affiliation to a rejected party? That throughout Europe communists were breaking with social democracy, and so why was the British Socialist Party line so different from this trend? That kind of thing."

"Actually, Theo, that's an interesting argument."

Rothstein almost spluttered. "Ah, I see that in repeating Comrade Pankhurst's comments I am in danger of convincing you with them, George, so I must stop."

They both laughed.

"But Sylvia is surely serious about communist unity, Theo. Although her Workers' Socialist Federation converted itself into a communist party at its conference last June, it decided to retain the old name while awaiting the outcome of the unity process."

"Some might interpret that as Sylvia, having laid the groundwork, simply awaiting the opportunity to break with the rest of us and announce the formation of her own communist party."

Sanders grimaced as he sipped his cold tea. "Well, we'll know soon enough, I suppose."

Theo fell silent, a worried frown creasing his brow.

"Are you going to tell me, Theo?"

Rothstein looked up, blinking. "Tell you what, George?"

"Whatever it is that's causing you to look so worried."

"Yes, I think I will," he said following a thoughtful pause. He sighed. "It is connected with the preparations for the formation of the party. Some months ago, a very good comrade presented me with a cheque for a considerable amount, £500 made out to cash, to assist with the various expenses involved."

"Made out to cash? The comrade must trust you."

"Yes, yes, but I also promised to provide him with an itemised list of outgoings." He sighed again. "I very much regret that I was unable to honour that pledge for some time."

Sanders leaned forward, a look of concern on his face. "Go on, Theo."

"The cheque was stolen from my briefcase, George."

A look of relief came over Sanders' face. "Oh, is *that* all! You had me thinking it was more serious for a moment, Theo."

"But George, I can't help thinking that it is *not* all, and that it is in some way connected with a further attempt to have me deported."

"Whatever makes you think that, Theo?"

"Because no attempt was made to cash the cheque. I reported its loss to the comrade, and when he checked his account he found that there had been no withdrawals. So he put a stop on the cheque and issued me another, which I promptly cashed." He shrugged, "So no problem there."

"And you have no idea when the cheque was stolen, or where you were at the time?"

"Foolishly, I allowed that cheque to remain in a little pocket in my briefcase for a few weeks before I decided to cash it. And, of course, when I went to the pocket it was empty. It could have happened at any number of places: in the various newspaper offices that I visit, for work or otherwise, at public meetings I have attended, at one of the private meetings of the Hands Off Russia committee to which I have been invited..."

Sanders, who sat on that committee, made a joke of it. "You mean Billy Watson?"

W.F. "Billy" Watson, a member of the Hands Off Russia committee and a leading light in the London Workers' Committee, had been charged with sedition after a speech he made at a Hands Off Russia rally in February 1919. While he was in prison, it was revealed in the House of Commons that he had been a Special Branch informer since mid-1918, receiving three pounds a week.

"Watson would have been an ideal candidate, but he was not released from prison until December last year, following which he was persona non grata as far as the socialist movement was concerned." Theo shrugged. "He would not have had the opportunity."

Sanders brightened. "But listen, I don't see why you're so worried: the cheque wasn't cashed, and so no harm was done."

Theo almost scowled with impatience. "But George, it is the very *fact* that it was not cashed that is so worrying. It is as if to the person who stole it, or to the people he works for, possession of the cheque itself was far more important than possession of the money it represented. Sooner or later, I think, it will in some way be used against me."

"How *can* it be, Theo? Your name was not on it."

"But the name of the person who wrote it *was*, George."

8

January and February had been fairly quiet on the industrial action front for the United Vehicle Workers. In late January, the Transport Workers' Federation had submitted a claim for a ten-shilling wage increase for lorry drivers, and the UVW had, ahead of the other unions in the sector, authorised the Fed to file for strike action on its behalf, although it was realised that it would be some weeks—possibly months—before this came to a head.

In February, the London cabdrivers—or, rather, the proprietors and owner-drivers—held a one-day strike in protest at an increase in petrol prices, demanding retention of the sixpence-per-hiring wartime bonus and a fifty-percent fare increase. As was often the case these days, the journeymen drivers, who hired their cabs from the proprietors, took a different view: receiving free petrol from the proprietors, they argued against a fare-increase on the grounds that this would mean fewer hirings and/or reduced tips. Thus the UVW found itself in the position of having to argue on behalf of the Owner-Drivers Branch that the Home Secretary should grant a fare-increase and for the journeymen that he should leave the tariff unchanged. As national organising secretary for cabs and buses, George Sanders would have found this embarrassing, and so he deputed Eric Rice, brother of Mickey and a long-time organiser, to present the journeymen's case. An amused Edward Shortt, the Home Secretary, suggested that the UVW meet the proprietors to discuss the share of any increase which should go to the journeymen.

It was in March that George Sanders was put to the test, and according to some, like Mickey Rice, he failed to pass it. He was made aware of the issue during a visit to his office by Bernard Sharkey, who had known Sanders for several years; Sharkey had been dismissed from the Metropolitan Police force for his participation in the strike of August 1919 and had, at Sanders' suggestion, applied for employment at the London General Omnibus Company.

"The bastards have given me notice!" cried Sharkey as he entered

Sanders' office.

Startled, Sanders sat back in his chair, his first thought being how Sharkey had managed to get past the receptionist and his secretary. A man might be your mate, but there was a procedure to be followed. "Isn't this a matter for your local officer, Bernie?" he asked, attempting to not appear too brusque. "What did they get you for?"

Uninvited, Sharkey, all knees and elbows, pulled out a chair and sat opposite Sanders. "Get me? They didn't get me for anything, George! They say they have to make room for the returning servicemen."

Sanders' eyebrows shot up. "News to me, Bernie. So how many are we talking about?"

"According to our garage superintendent, several hundred."

"Well this is fucking outrageous, Bernie! And not a word to us!"

"You sure about that, George?" He nodded at Sanders' overflowing in-tray.

Sanders grunted and, taking a handful of letters, already opened by his secretary, licked his finger and riffled through them.

"Oh, balls, you're right, Bernie." He pulled out a single sheet and held it up, shaking it so that it resembled a freshly-caught fish on a line. He placed it on his blotter and proceeded to read. "H.E. Blain, Operating Manager. Due to the imminent return of those members of staff who served in the armed forces and regarding whom this company gave assurances concerning their future employment. With great regret. Necessary to shed 500 staff. These men signed to the effect that their employment would be temporary. We therefore intend." He looked up at Sharkey. "When they took you on, did you sign anything about this being a temporary job, Bernie?"

"Did I buggery! No, I thought I was set for life, George."

"Know anyone else who signed anything like that?"

Sharkey shook his head. "No, mate, I think we were all under the impression that we'd be here for good."

Sanders brought his fist down onto the letter. "Fuck it!"

Sharkey wondered whether Sanders' anger was triggered by the letter itself or his own negligence in not having got to it earlier.

He reached for his telephone and dialled the Electric Railway House number.

"Hello. Mr Blain, please."

"Hello, this is Mr Blain's secretary. How may I help you?"

"You can't love. I need to speak to Mr Blain."

"Mr Blain, I am afraid, is in a meeting."

"Then get him out of it. Tell him George Sanders needs to speak to him."

After a pause: *"Mr Sanders, this is most irregular. Now, what can I do for you?"*

"You're telling *me* it's irregular! I've just seen your letter announcing the dismissal of five hundred of our members. Is this how we're going to conduct business, Mr Blain: no prior discussion, no telephone call, just a letter announcing dismissals?"

A clearing of the throat. "In normal circumstances, Mr Sanders, I would of course have discussed the matter with you. In this case, however, as the men have signed to the effect that their employment is temporary, I thought it hardly necessary. You should have received my letter yesterday, by the way."

Sanders looked across the desk at Bernard Sharkey. "Well, it was obviously delayed in the post! And let me tell you, Mr Blain, that those men signed nothing of the kind, and so I suggest that you withdraw those dismissal notices immediately!"

"Oh, I think they most certainly did, Mr Sanders..."

"Then check their files—each and every one of them!"

A sigh, indicative of resentment at the tone adopted by this trade union chap. "I will see that they are checked, Mr Sanders. In the meantime, if you wish to drop by and discuss the matter..."

"Oh, you can rest assured that we will discuss the matter, Mr Blain, but there are one or two things I must attend to first. I'll be in touch. Good day to you!"

Sanders slammed down the phone and, breathing heavily, seemed to glare across the desk at Sharkey.

"What we gonna do, George?"

Sanders sighed heavily and Sharkey was almost surprised when neither smoke nor flame appeared. "I'll have to get Hirst to call an emergency meeting of the executive council. In the meantime, you get back to the shed and tell the boys to get ready for a scrap."

*

"You know," said Mickey Rice as he sat opposite Dick Mortlake in the refreshment vehicle in Middle Row garage, "sometimes, when there's something on at the union office, I still find myself thinking of going to Gerrard Street before realising that the union is no longer there."

"That union is no longer *anywhere*," said Dick.

Mickey sighed. "Yeah, it's taking some getting used to, and I sometimes wonder whether I ever will."

"Well, things have changed and we all need to adjust, Mickey."

Mickey grimaced. "Dick," he said, a determined look in his eye, "I have no intention of adjusting to this union led by Stanley Hirst."

"Do you regret not running for the EC?" With only two slots on the Executive Council for London busmen, a meeting of the Vigilance Committee, the unofficial body which grouped together the progressive activists in the old red-button union, had decided that Barney Macauley and Ernie Fairbrother, who outranked Mickey in seniority, should be given a clear run.

Another sigh. "Yes and no, Dick, yes and no. On the one hand, I miss making a contribution, taking part in the debates, helping to solve the problems. On the other hand, with only two of our men on the UVW EC, I dread to think of how it will look after our interests when it meets the London General."

A puzzled frown creased Dick's brow. "How do you mean, Mickey? It's not as if the others will be voting against us!"

"No," Mickey replied patiently, measuring his words, "but the other fourteen EC members, with the possible exception of the cabdriver, all represent companies and trades that are paid less than us. My fear, then, is that when the employers propose—as they undoubtedly will—taking back some of the advances we've made, these other EC members may be less able to recognise the importance of the various issues to us. For example, if the London General proposed a package which, while it would be a step backward for us, was still better than could be had on the trams, on the provincial buses, or on the lorries, there might be a tendency for the EC members from those sectors to think, 'Oh well, it's not *so* bad.' You see what I mean, Dick?"

"I do, Mickey, and bloody hell, you've got *me* worried now." He paused. "So what do you mean, Mickey, when you say that you have no intention of adjusting to this union?"

Mickey smiled. "You remember that night last year when, as we walked home after the branch meeting, you mentioned the next amalgamation, the one that Ernie Bevin was working for?"

"I do, Mickey."

"Well, that's what I shall be working for, too."

"Do you think that Bevin will be easier to get on with than Hirst? From what I've seen and heard about him, he'd probably be a harder nut to crack, Mickey."

Mickey nodded. "You're probably right, Dick, but if we handle it properly we should be able to get some concessions out of him. If it comes off, this new union will be huge, and Bevin won't want to jeopardise it by upsetting one of its biggest components—us."

"When you say concessions, Mickey..."

"Well, for a start—and most importantly—we'll want our own committee for London busmen, and it'll be *this* committee, not the EC, that negotiates with the employers and decides whether to ballot for strike action, although the EC would presumably have to rubber-stamp a decision like that."

Dick whistled softly. "That'll take some doing, Mickey."

"That's why we have make sure we have a rank-and-file organisation, Dick."

*

When the EC met on 10 March, George Sanders found that the only anger displayed came from the two London busmen, Barney Macauley and Ernie Fairbrother.

"George is right!" exploded Macauley. "Those men were led to believe that they were being employed permanently. I know, because there's half a dozen of 'em in my own garage! We can't let the employers get away with this."

"But I note that you're not moving a resolution for industrial action, Brother Macauley," observed Stanley Hirst, peering down the table.

"I'm sure that a full discussion will reveal the feelings of the EC and the action it's prepared to take," replied Macauley, barely able to conceal his dislike of Hirst. "And if there appears to be an appetite for strike action, I'll be quite prepared to move it."

"I think, brothers, we should proceed calmly and examine this question in all its aspects." This was Bill Peters, a commercial driver but, as he was from the London area, someone who might be sympathetic. "First of all, we have to consider that the servicemen were told that their jobs would still be here when they returned. So that subject is closed: we can't juggle their interests against those of the men who've been given notice. Now comes the question of what we can do to force the London General to withdraw those notices. Yes, our members could strike, but are their sympathies likely to rest with the servicemen rather than the men who've been employed more recently?"

"This is sheer nonsense!" erupted Ernie Fairbrother. "There's no question of the servicemen being denied their jobs: our concern is to keep the five hundred in employment!"

"Let's have no interruptions," called John Cliff. "Proceed, Brother Peters."

"Alright," continued Peters, "but let's take a look at this a bit more closely. How is this situation different from when the women were let go last year?"

"Chairman, I have to intervene here," said Sanders. "The women were taken on with the explicit understanding that they would be employed until the cessation of hostilities. And that understanding was between both *them* and the employer and the *union* and the employer."

"But the operating manager says that these men were also taken on with the understanding that it would be temporary," Peters persisted.

"The operating manger is a liar," Sanders came back. "Either that, or he's been misinformed."

"Alright, let's say you're right," conceded Peters, "and we were to consider industrial action. Brothers, the timing couldn't be worse, could it?" He looked around the room, expecting a response.

Cliff obliged him. "Through the chair, Bill, through the chair. But tell us: what's wrong with the timing?"

"As anyone who attended the mass meeting at The Ring, Blackfriars Road three nights ago knows, the ten-shilling claim for commercial drivers is being coordinated with a similar claim for the buses and trams. That means, brothers, that there is a real chance that the members in all three sectors will be faced with the prospect of strike action in the not-too-distant future. The question we need to ask ourselves, then, is whether the London bus membership will be prepared to risk the prospect of two strikes in quick succession." Peters raised his palms, indicating that he himself was unable to answer this question. He cast a glance at Hirst. "There's also the question of whether the funds could afford such an enormous outlay of strike pay."

The northern delegates, well-used to the ways of Stanley Hirst, sniggered at this.

"Then what's the alternative to strike action?" asked Cliff.

"Just a minute, just a minute, Chairman," protested Macauley. "Nobody's saying that our lads won't be prepared to strike."

"But maybe there's another way to tackle this," said Sanders.

Given Sanders' well-known appetite for strike action, this gained the attention of everyone around the table.

"We're all ears, George," said a grinning John Cliff.

"The company's argument is that once the servicemen return there will be no work for five hundred men. But here's a fairly easy way to show them that they're wrong."

*

"Is George Sanders going soft in the fucking head?" Mickey Rice demanded of no one in particular as, having just signed on the following morning, he stood in the output office, scowling at *The Times*. The days when he had been the object of good-natured banter regarding his readership of the ruling-class newspaper had long gone, Mickey having convinced his workmates that, a), *The Times*, despite its reactionary editorial line, could be relied upon for comprehensive industrial reports and, b) that it was always useful to know what the other side was thinking.

The other occupants of the output, Lenny Hawkins and Charley Adams among them, gave each other the wink and turned to Mickey. This should be good.

"What's up, Mick?" asked Lenny.

"The EC met yesterday to discuss the five hundred men who've been given notice. Here's George, after the meeting: 'The Executive Council has decided that the time has come to take a firm stand.'"

"Here we go again, lads," anticipated Charley Adams, "so stock up your larders!"

Mickey looked up from the broadsheet. "You'd think so, wouldn't you, if we were taking a firm stand? But no..."

"*Eh?*" Lenny Hawkins looked genuinely disappointed.

"George says that the EC is instructing all members on London buses—*and* the trams, mind you—to refrain from carrying excess passengers, thereby demonstrating that there is ample work for the five hundred men who face dismissal." Mickey threw the newspaper onto the counter in disgust. "Oh, *that'll* scare 'em to death, won't it? I can't see the directors of the London General getting much sleep tonight after they read that. Since when has the union had to *instruct* us not to carry excess passengers? I *never* have!"

"So are we gonna have the opportunity to discuss this?" asked Lenny.

"Six mass meetings in three days' time, buses and trams, so I suppose ours will be at the Holloway Empire."

*

The mass meetings duly took place on the evening of Sunday, 14 March. While some members denounced the proposed action as so weak as to invite ridicule, each meeting adopted a resolution endorsing the EC's proposal for action, which would commence on 20 March. Somewhat to the surprise of the sceptics, this was sufficient to gain the EC a meeting at Electric Railway House, headquarters of the LGOC, the day before the action was due.

"Good afternoon, Mr Sanders," said Operating Manager H.E. Blain, a short man with a trim dark beard. "I believe you know everyone on this side of the table,"—he gestured to George Shave who flanked him—"but I'm not sure I can say the same of your side. The last time we met in this room you were, of course, the London and Provincial..."

"And now we're the United Vehicle Workers," Sanders completed the sentence for him. He looked to his left and right. "Lads, perhaps you could each introduce yourselves to Mr Blain."

During the two or three minutes which this took, Sanders studied Blain, who appeared relaxed, confident, not at all tense. This could mean anything, of course, but Sanders sensed that something was afoot. For example, the man seated next to George Shave was Mackinnon, the chief schedules officer. Why was he here?

"Now, Mr Sanders," Blain began once the introductions were completed, "I think I must begin by extending you an apology. In my letter, and indeed when we spoke on the telephone, I stated my belief that the men we are here to discuss had commenced their employment with us in the knowledge that it would be temporary. It now seems, sadly, that I had been misinformed, and I therefore feel bound to apologise for the initial misunderstanding."

See, thought Sanders, I *knew* there was something afoot; this is just the sprat to catch the mackerel. "Well, that's very gracious of you, Mr Blain, and I thank you."

"Now, this realisation—as well as, of course, your union's spirited opposition to our proposal—has caused us to revisit the matter, and we think we can see a way of avoiding the dismissal of most, if not all, of the five hundred men."

Sanders held his gaze for a while before replying. If Blain was looking for a servile outpouring of gratitude, he had picked the wrong man. "Well," he said in a level tone, "that's very encouraging, Mr Blain. But you could have told me this over the telephone."

That caught him. He's all aflutter now, his eyes flitting from the notes before him to Shave at his side and back again.

"Ah, no, Mr Sanders, because if we are to retain the men—or most of them—in employment, certain adjustments must be made."

Bugger, thought Sanders, he's caught us! He's lured us in and we've fallen for it. Just as he had done when he had accompanied the National Union of Police and Prison Officers to their meeting at

10 Downing Street in 1918, he could now see in an instant how the situation had been choreographed: the company wanted to make a start on clawing back the concessions it had made last year, so it had engineered a crisis in which five hundred jobs were claimed to be at risk; it had probably expected the union to go for strike action and yet, even when the UVW response had been much weaker than this, had called this meeting, prepared to immediately agree to retain the men in return for the real prize.

Sanders sighed. "You have us on tenterhooks, Mr Blain. Let's hear it."

*

"At first," said Mickey Rice at an unofficial meeting of rank-and-file activists in the Crown and Anchor, Clerkenwell Green, a few days later, "I thought I'd been wrong, and I went around singing the praises of George Sanders after he'd forced the London General to back down after threatening a 'no overloading' campaign, which many of us thought was as weak as piss. But *then...*" He looked around the room—Barney Macauley on the top table, having reported on the negotiations, Dick Mortlake next him, taking the minutes, a fair assembly of activists in the body of the meeting—and saw that most were nodding, about to agree with his imminent criticism of the deal, knowing roughly what form it would take. "But *then*, comrades, we saw what had been agreed: apparently the company, to use George's words, 'agrees to allow the men'—bloody big of 'em, eh!—'to remain on books' but 'for the time being at a lower guaranteed week's work than that which has been in operation.' And as if that was not enough, 'the union will give some latitude on the question of spreadover time.' "

During the war, it had been quite common for a spreadover—the time from sign-on to sign-off—to extend to a crippling fifteen hours, and at the negotiations last year, with virtually the whole trade union movement fighting for lower hours and higher pay—and winning!— the London bus section had wrestled this down to a ten-hour maximum. And now...?

"I share your reservations, Mickey," said Barney Macauley, "but bear in mind that these adjustments apply only to the five hundred who were to have been dismissed and *only* for a limited time."

"And what comfort can we take from that?" Mickey came back. "We don't even have a date for the expiry of these concessions! You know what that means, comrades? It means that in the meantime—

and for as long as these conditions last—we'll have a two-tier workforce. You can imagine what the next negotiations will be like, can't you? 'Actually, Mr Sanders,' says Operating Manager Blain, 'we'd rather like to retain these concessions for a little longer, extending them to every new man we take on.' George will lose his temper and demand that, if this happens, one man should graduate to the package as negotiated in 1919 as each new man is employed. 'Oh, of course, Mr Sanders, we find that eminently reasonable.' And there you have it: a *permanent* two-tier system. But don't think they'll be satisfied with that. Oh, no, you can bet your bottom dollar that they've just been testing the water this time around, and at the very least they'll be wanting to extend the maximum spreadover-time for all of us." He stood in silence for a moment, speechless, his chest heaving and sweat bathing his forehead. Finally: "Jesus Christ, Barney," he roared, "how could you and George ever agree to this?"

"That's not exactly how it was, Mickey, comrades," Macauley replied. He was struggling to control his temper, unused to being accused of accepting a worsening of conditions. "In fact, George himself was pretty much of the same mind as you, Mickey, suspecting that this was the start of a campaign by the company to take back what we won in 1919. He went further than that, saying that he wouldn't have been surprised to learn that the whole business of the five hundred was just a ruse to draw us into talks. He seemed to think, by the way, that it would have taken a cleverer man than Blain to dream this up..."

"Stanley?" This from Mickey. Sir Albert Stanley, previously managing director, was now, following his few years as president of the Board of Trade, chairman of the Traffic Combine, the empire encompassing London's buses, Underground and some of its trams. Mickey knew him personally, as his late partner Dorothy Bridgeman had once worked in Stanley's office; economic interests apart, they actually got on well.

"Or," said the cabman Dennis Davies from the chair, "Lord Ashfield since last December."

"That's right," said Macauley. "Lloyd George kicked him upstairs as compensation for taking the Board of Trade job from him."

Mickey nodded. "It's possible he was behind it. He's certainly clever enough to have come up with something like this." He shook his head, as if to clear it of this distraction. "But listen, Barney, if George suspected that the question of the five hundred was no more than a ruse, why didn't he call their bluff: 'Sorry, Mr Blain, we can't help you, so you'll just have to let 'em go.' "

"That is *exactly* what Ernie Fairbrother suggested during the first adjournment." He shrugged. "But you can guess what happened."

"Outvoted by the new intake?" suggested Dennis Davies from the chair.

"You've got it. Most of 'em couldn't be convinced that this *was* a ruse, and if it *wasn't* they would have to explain to Stan Hirst that they'd just let five hundred dues-payers walk out the door."

"They surely never said that, did they?" queried a sceptical Malcolm Lewis.

"No one actually *said* it, but you could tell that's what was on their minds, the way they were looking at each other and scribbling notes."

"Well I'll be blowed," commented Dennis Davies, shaking his head. He looked around the room. "Well, comrades, is that it on this particular subject? A sad state of affairs, maybe, but nothing that can't be fixed in the long run."

"Just one point, Chairman," said Mickey Rice. "If this episode demonstrates one thing, it's that the wages and conditions of London busmen *must* be negotiated by London busmen themselves."

"And how do we bring that about, Mickey?" asked Dennis Davies who, as a cabdriver, had obviously not given the matter much thought.

"When the next amalgamation comes along," replied Mickey without pause, "we make it clear to Ernie Bevin that unless we get our own negotiating committee, we'll go our own way."

This brought a roar of assent from the meeting, and for a moment, Dennis Davies looked at Mickey in silence. "Phew!" he said at length. "That's some task you've set yourself there, Mickey." He relaxed, and with a grin on his face asked: "But why do you mention Ernie Bevin? Isn't it possible that Stan Hirst will be general secretary of the new amalgamation?"

The wave of laughter which greeted this suggestion gave him his answer.

"Chairman," said Barney Macauley, "Mickey may be in for a pleasant surprise in the near future. None of us are satisfied with the current arrangements, and so George is going to suggest to Stan Hirst that we have an Omnibus Wages Board."

That put a smile on Mickey's face.

*

"Anything else, Barney?" asked Dennis Davies as he checked his pocket watch.

"Just one thing, Dennis. On 11 March, the day after our EC first discussed the question of the five hundred, we had the reconvened special congress of the TUC. That was to consider one matter only: the action that the movement was prepared to take in support of nationalisation of the coal industry. By now, you'll all know the outcome: over three to one against strike action and a similar majority in favour of a propaganda campaign in preparation for a General Election.

"Probably the only thing worth mentioning, comrades, is the very different approaches of the right and the left. On the left, Frank Hodges, general secretary of the miners—Bob Smillie is off sick with a complete collapse of his health, they're saying, and there's some doubt as to whether he'll be back. Frank Hodges told the congress that the miners had placed their faith in the parliamentary machinery, and that faith had been shattered. Those were his words: 'our faith has been shattered.' What he was referring to, of course, was the miners' decision to go along with the Sankey Commission. When the majority report of the Commission came out in favour of nationalisation, however, Lloyd George decided to ignore it.

"For the right, the railwaymen's leader Jimmy Thomas was in his element. He really repeated the speech he made when the special congress opened in December—despite the fact, as he himself admitted, as president of the congress he was supposed to be impartial. This time though, he was acting as though he was the protector of the British constitution—the 'most democratic in the world,' as he called it. We denounced defiance of the constitution over the question of Ireland, he said, so if it were wrong for others, who represented another class, it cannot be right now for us to do the same thing."

"Chairman!" came the voice of Lenny Hawkins. "Barney's lost me. Could we have a bit of explanation? What's the constitution got to do with it?"

Barney Macauley grinned. "Nationalisation of the coal industry, Lenny, would require legislation, and that's the job of a Parliament elected by the people. If this Parliament is against nationalisation, it's up to the people to elect one with a different view, rather than the trade union movement using its clout in an attempt to *force* the current mob to legislate. That's the position of the constitutionalists like Jimmy Thomas."

"So it would also be unconstitutional for us to strike for the nationalisation of the passenger transport industry," suggested Dick Mortlake.

"Or if the whole movement came out against another war," said Reuben Topping.

"Yes, according to the Thomases and the Thornes both of those would be unconstitutional," replied Macauley.

"Despite the fact that the whole of the trade union movement and our families constitute the majority of the population!"

Macauley raised a finger. "Good point, Mickey, but, yes, despite that fact. Now, Thomas argued that political action had in fact never been tried, by which he meant that there had never been a Labour government. Why inflict a great industrial upheaval upon the country, he said, which would inevitably involve violence, when a simpler, constitutional means is at hand, and there's an early possibility of a Labour government?"

"When the ministers will be people like Jimmy Thomas and Will Thorne!" called Mickey Rice. "So we just have to wait for that Labour government, when Jimmy and Will can be relied upon to take the coal industry away from its current owners and place it in the hands of the people—is that right? Fat chance, comrades, fat chance!"

While this earned Mickey a round of applause and some irreverent laughter, he realised that it would be a mistake to assume that everyone in the room shared his scepticism, for he knew there were those, doubtless honest and sincere, who would find his remarks bruising and somewhat uncouth; such men looked upon the Labour Party as their own, a body created by the working class, and, perhaps only semi-consciously they feared that to relinquish belief in the party would be to open the door to a nightmarish alternative: the continuation of the rule of the masters long into the future unless it were curtailed by some form of Bolshevik intervention which, according to the newspapers anyway, would probably be worse. And Mickey knew that unless such men—a good proportion of them, at least—were won over, there could be no such revolution.

For himself, however, this meeting had strengthened rather than weakened his own view. Yes, it was entirely possible that the UVW's acceptance of a worsening of the London's busmen's working conditions, and the special congress's rejection of industrial action for essentially political ends, meant that the pendulum was beginning to swing in the wrong direction again. There had been an outburst of industrial militancy in the years 1910-14, then imperialist war had placed restraints on both trade union action and the thinking of many workers. In the latter stages of the war, particularly after the Russian Revolution, militancy had revived, extending into the post-war period. Now, an economic depression was underway, coupled with the return of the servicemen, and the employer-class was beginning to regain its confidence. If the capitalist class remained in power this would, Mickey thought, be unchanged in 100 years' time, with the pendulum swinging now to the left, now to the right, and the fortunes of the working class rising and falling according to the economic and political climate. This would only change, he knew, if the wealth of the country—its factories, plant, raw materials, transport systems and financial institutions—were taken from the current owners, appropriated by those who actually *created* that wealth, and used for the common good. Some people, even some workers, might be—*were*, no doubt about it—revolted by such a prospect, but Mickey Rice claimed that vision because he saw in it his salvation, and the salvation of all who lived lives like his. "And we," he often pointed out in discussion, "are the majority."

9

I t was 7 April before the UVW team, led by George Sanders and Bob Williams, secretary of the Transport Workers' Federation, visited Electric Railway House to press the claim for a ten-shilling weekly increase in wages for London's busmen. Before they called the employers in Bob Williams, a swarthy Welshman with a widow's peak, painted the background for them.

"You know that this claim is coordinated with the claims of the commercial sector and the trams," he said in his deep coal-trimmer's voice. "Well, in a minute I'll tell you what progress we've made with the tramways companies, but first I should say a few words about the miners. They're after an increase of three shillings a shift. They were offered exactly half of what they had demanded, which according to the government would increase their wages by more than the 130-percent rise in the cost of living since 1914. At the reconvened miners' conference the following day, the South Wales boys were calling for a strike but, having been promised a further offer the following Monday, the conference—by a large majority—agreed to continue negotiations. It might be worth noting, brothers, that this conference lasted just forty-five minutes: that might be an indication of the way the wind is blowing.

"Well, Monday came and the government, on behalf of the owners, varied its approach. 'Strip out the war bonuses and the extra granted by the Sankey Commission,' they said, 'and we'll increase the basic by 20 percent, subject to a minimum of an extra two shillings a shift.' The Miners' Federation has decided to ballot its members, giving them the alternatives of acceptance of the offer or strike action. The result will be announced at another London conference on 15 April, a week tomorrow."

"Any predictions, Bob?" asked George Sanders, already into his second cigarette.

"I reckon they'll accept, George. The majority might be on the slim side, but that's how it looks to me."

"Well, they've got two-thirds of what they were asking for," commented a former blue-button man, "so it's not that bad."

Typical, thought Sanders. "And the trams, Bob?"

Williams uttered a deep sigh. "I have more of a feeling for this, George as, on behalf of the Fed, I'm directly involved." A despairing shake of the head. "My Christ, it's rough going, lads. In mid-March, when the negotiations with the National Joint Industrial Council resumed, there was not the faintest glimmer of hope. As I told the press, it was looking very dark indeed. We met again of 23 March— for eight hours!—and still no agreement.

"Then the members started to threaten strike action, and your bus lads said that they'd be out as well over the Easter weekend if there was no settlement. On the bright side, however, the government said that it would introduce a bill to increase tram-fares, following which the employers made an offer of five bob now and another shilling in June, which the staff side of the NJIC deemed acceptable."

"Following which," said Sanders, unable to suppress a grin, "all hell broke loose." A glance down the table in the direction of the old blue-button men. "In the North, anyway."

*

Bob Williams would have been constrained by a sense of inter-union propriety in recounting this development, but Mickey Rice, at a meeting of the Middle Row branch the previous evening, had let rip.

"So the Northern boys were out at the weekend, and some of 'em are *still* out! Manchester, Salford, Oldham, Huddersfield! The heartland of Stanley Hirst's old blue-button union, brothers, and here they were, telling him what to do with his offer, saying they'd be on the stones until he scuttled back and got a better one from the NJIC!"

"So what has he done about it, Mickey?" asked bespectacled

Charlie Adams, who had occupied the chair while Malcolm Lewis had unwillingly served his time in the Army Service Corps during the war.

"Our Stan," replied Mickey, holding up his copy of *The Times*, "has written to the tramway authorities. Just listen to this! Brother Hirst says he finds the strikes in the North most regrettable, but they prove how unsatisfactory the settlement is. He had urged acceptance because he was convinced that the offer was the best that could be achieved without a national strike or arbitration..."

"So he knew it was rubbish," interpreted Malcolm Lewis from the chair, "but accepted it because he didn't want a strike!"

"That's what it sounds like, Malc. Anyway, he winds up by saying, 'In order to prevent the strike fever spreading to other towns, it seems essential that there should be another meeting of the Joint Industrial Council called at once.'" Manchester and Salford say that they can't improve the offer because they're bound by the national agreement, but if there's a return to work they'll recommend an immediate meeting of the NJIC."

*

"So we'll be back at the NJIC in the near future," continued Bob Williams. "In the meantime, however, I think we have to say that this episode has highlighted one of the drawbacks of the NJIC system for us."

"Oh, and what would that be?" asked, somewhat defensively, Fred Jarvis, a representative of Midlands tramworkers.

"If by a national agreement you mean that wages and conditions should be the same, right across the country, regardless of the size and circumstances of the company, you'll find—as the Manchester lads have just discovered—that you'll be held back by the smaller, less profitable concerns."

Jarvis rubbed his chin. "I can see that, yes." He lifted his head. "Is there a way out of it?"

Bob Williams nodded. "There is: the less fortunate undertakings will have to be allowed to go their own way, negotiating locally."

"Then it wouldn't be a national agreement, would it?" Jarvis came back.

"Yes and no. Some local concerns would have terms and conditions that differed from the main NJIC agreement, but each local package would have to be ratified by the NJIC."

Jarvis nodded. "Worth a try, I suppose. Why don't you put it to them?"

"I will, Fred, I will."

Sanders cleared his throat. "So how does all that affect today's negotiations in your view, Bob?"

"The tram saga has a while to run, George, so I suggest we play it long—no rush. Besides, the Traffic Combine is hardly likely to want to settle the London General negotiations before they know how they stand with their own tram operations."

"What they *will* try to do, Bob, is take back some of the improvements we made last year, so you leave that to me when it comes up."

*

Sanders and Williams shared the job of presenting the case, Sanders discussing the contribution made by the company's operating staff both during the war and more recently, while Williams referred to factors such as the cost of living and wage movements in other industries.

"Thank you, gentlemen," responded operating manager H.E. Blain when they had concluded their presentation. Not a man usually given to humour, there was nevertheless the beginnings of a mischievous grin visible behind his dark beard, which he now turned on Sanders. "I recall, Mr Sanders that last year you made reference to our company's general meeting and the dividend paid. I must conclude from the fact that you have on this occasion made no such reference that you either no longer take *The Times* or, which I think is more likely, that you are aware that the report of this year's meeting would do little to aid your case."

George Sanders smiled across the table at him, silent for a few seconds. "Nice try, Mr Blain, nice try. I *did* read the report of this year's general meeting and while I could hardly have missed the somewhat depressing picture painted by Lord Ashfield of the group's finances, I also noted that the company is pressing Parliament for an increase in fares and, indeed, that one of your prominent shareholders reminded Lord Ashfield that for the past ten years he had warned that the practice of charging fares which barely yielded a profit would lead to only one result."

Blain tried to smile, but was not quite able to achieve it. There was a pause while he tried to overcome this unexpected setback. However, as his notes, which he now consulted, made no provision for an interruption which might dictate a shift in the direction of his argument, and being unskilled at what Lord Ashfield had once, encouraging his managers to practice it, referred to as perpendicular cogitation—thinking on one's feet—he saw no alternative to ploughing on as planned. "And you, Mr Williams, last year were able to cite many examples where hours were being reduced and wages increased, but have apparently little to say on that subject today."

Bob Williams grinned and shrugged his shoulders. "We're not looking for a further reduction in hours today, Mr Blain, but wages are still on the move: the miners look as if they'll settle for an extra two shillings per shift, and I'm reliably informed that the railwaymen will shortly make a submission for an extra pound a week."

Blain seemed to have recovered, and his raised eyebrows signified mild interest rather than alarm. "Oh really? Well, let's now turn our attention to your claim for an extra ten shillings a week. As you are familiar with the financial position of the company, Mr Sanders, you will, I hope, realise that such an increase is quite out of the question. Indeed, *any* increase at the moment would place the company in jeopardy." He looked across the table at Sanders. "Unless, of course, we could find some way to make the increase self-financing."

From the union side of the table there came a chorus of low groans, but Sanders sat quite still, seemingly unreacting.

"While I do not expect you to welcome such a prospect, Mr Sanders, might I ask whether you would be willing to explore the possibilities?"

"I'm sorry, Mr Blain, I was expecting you to put forward a proposal."

"The fact of the matter is, Mr Sanders," Blain began, eyes lowered and brushing his fingers over the table as if he had noticed a dusty patch, "the very generous settlement we arrived at last year has left us with insufficient flexibility when it comes to scheduling and so we would propose some relaxation in the eight-hour day."

"Would you, indeed?" If Sanders' tone was anything to go by, this would be a short meeting. "We seem to have been over this ground fairly recently, Mr Blain, when we—against *my* better judgement, I can assure you—*very* generously allowed you to relax the eight-hour day for the five hundred men you claimed were facing dismissal. That concession on our part has been decidedly unpopular with the men—not just the five hundred but the men in general. Some have gone so far as to suggest that it was, from your point of view, merely the sprat to catch the mackerel, and that you would soon be back to seek the extension of that concession." Sanders raised his hands, palms upward, in the direction of the management side of the table as, speaking softly, he observed, "And here you are, not three months later, doing exactly that."

"But, Mr Sanders, I am sure you must realise…"

"Mr Blain," Sanders interrupted him, his voice raised now, "let me leave you under no misapprehension. You may remember that last year, in this room, my colleague Ben Smith told you that when it came to lengthy working hours, regardless of how long we might debate it, *the men simply would not accept it*. Now you suggest the relaxation of the eight-hour working day. No matter how much you may want it, Mr Blain, and no matter what anyone on this side of the table might think of it,"—here, he threw out an arm in the direction of the former blue-button men—"*the men will not have it!*"

10

And the tramworkers of the North would not have it, either.
A few days later, the strikes in Manchester and elsewhere let to a delegate conference at Central Hall, Westminster. Ernie Sharp of New Cross tramshed, thin-chested and middle-aged, was a delegate to the conference. Had he been able to attend the meeting of the workers' side of the National Joint Industrial Council which preceded the conference, he thought he would have enjoyed himself, for as the members exited from the smallish room which had accommodated it, he overheard Bob Williams, present in his capacity as secretary of the Transport Workers' Federation, telling a journalist that there had been a certain amount of "plain speaking." When an ashen-faced John Cliff, secretary of the workers' side, came out a little later, he certainly looked as if he had been given a good talking-to. Chuckling inwardly, Ernie made his way to the hall where the conference was to be held.

Stanley Hirst assumed responsibility for quelling the rebellion. To whom could he have entrusted this task? Cliff? Given that his action had given rise to the strikes in the first place, this would have been impossible.

"Now, lads," Hirst began in as an avuncular manner as he could manage, "we can all agree that it's a pity it's come to this, but I think we'll see you going back home a little happier than when you came. Clearly, you take the view that five shillings now and a further shilling in June is inadequate. Those of you who have taken strike action have certainly impressed that upon the employers, because they have agreed to reopen negotiations."

The hall was filled with cheers, forcing Hirst to pause. He seemed to know that it would be all downhill from this point on, for he displayed no animation.

Ernie Sharp nudged the delegate seated next to him, a Salford man. "Now for the hard part," he said with a wink.

"Aye, back to work with no guarantees, I reckon," the man replied.

"This is dependent, of course," Hirst resumed, "upon a return to work."

The atmosphere soured immediately. "Nay, Mister Chairman," boomed a northern delegate, in his early thirties, beefy with red hair and the early stages of a beard, as he rose to his feet, "our lads'll not go back unless they have a firm undertaking that there'll be a further improvement. Oh, and by the way, as I came out of the Underground station just now I purchased a copy of the early edition of the evening paper." He took the newspaper from his pocket and waved it at the platform. "You might be interested to know that the National Union of Railwaymen has just submitted a claim for an extra pound a week. A *pound*, brothers!"

This information caused a bit of a rumpus, and Hirst had to wait for it to subside before responding. "I can't speak for the NUR," he said eventually. "But with regard to our negotiations, of *course* there'll be a further improvement. They wouldn't have agreed to reopen the negotiations if that wasn't the case, would they?"

"But I know for a fact," persisted the delegate, "that Manchester can afford the full ten shillings. I've had that from councilors!"

"That may well be the case," Hirst explained, "but some of the smaller concerns may *not* be able to afford it. The whole point of the NJIC is that there should be a *national* agreement, with common terms and conditions."

"And so you're telling me," came the Manchester delegate again, "that we'll be forever tied to whatever the smallest town can afford. 'Ave I got that right?"

Bob Williams, on the platform with the tram leaders and Hirst, now got to his feet. "Chairman and Brother Hirst, might I make a suggestion regarding this problem?" He looked along the top table and, receiving no response from Hirst or the chairman, proceeded. "The Manchester brother is right, of course, and this is one of the drawbacks on the NJIC system in its purest form: if the aim is to arrive at terms and conditions which are common throughout the country—and it has to be said that what you've achieved in this regard is a great improvement on the situation a few years ago—that aim will only be achieved as long as the bank balances of *all* the employers are adequate."

He paused for effect. "Is there a way out of this? Is there an alternative?" He looked around the hall before nodding. "There is, brothers, although it probably won't be to everyone's liking. The alternative is to allow the smaller concerns to negotiate locally, on condition that any agreement they arrive at would have to be endorsed by the full NJIC." He turned to the chairman. "It might be worth considering."

A delegate was on his feet. "But that would mean that my members would be worse off!"

"Relatively, maybe," replied Bob Williams, "but you would end up with the same agreement that the NJIC would have come to. It's not that you would be worse off than that, but that the workers on the larger concerns would be *better* off."

"Alright," said Hirst, "we may have to give that some consideration, Bob. Now, chairman"—turning to John Cliff—"I think we should ask the delegates whether they are prepared to vote on a return to work."

"Whoah! Hold your horses, there, Stanley Hirst." It was the Manchester delegate again. "All this conference can do is *recommend* a return to work. Whether or not we *do* return to work will be decided by our members back 'ome. And that brings me to something we've yet to discuss: this last offer was agreed without consulting the members." He looked around the hall, arms outstretched. "Is *that* any way to run a union, brothers?" He turned to the platform, his arms now stretched in parallel before him. "Is *that* what it's come to?"

Pandemonium erupted, and it was clear to Ernie Sharp that the men were as angry at the way the offer had been accepted behind their backs as at the nature of the offer itself. This being a subject on which he was qualified to speak, he grinned and raised his hand. Perhaps thinking that this mature, modest-looking man might say something to calm things down, the chairman called him.

"Brothers," he began, his deep voice commanding immediate attention, "my name's Ernie Sharp from New Cross, here in London, a former red-button man. You've probably heard of the London tram strike of 1915. Well, that started at New Cross." He paused to allow the applause and cries of acclamation to die. "Now, since this amalgamation this year, we Londoners have been told on several occasions by Brother Hirst that we should forget the old red-button ways. There's no more red and blue, he says: we're all one union." He looked around the conference. "Are we? *Are* we, brothers? It seems to me that some of the practices of the leadership are a bit too blue for our good, and we've just heard about one of 'em from the brother from Manchester." That got a cheer.

"Let me tell you something about the old red-button union. That union of ours was probably the most democratic in the country..."

"Keep to the point, brother, keep to the point," came the chairman's intervention.

Ernie Sharp drew back his head and peered at Cliff through narrowed eyes, and when he spoke his voice was still deep, but soft and low, soft and low, and all the more effective for that. "Oh, what I've got to say is very much to the point, chairman, and if I were you I'd pay close attention to it, because there's a lesson in it for you and everyone else on that platform, with the possible exception of Bob Williams.

"Now, as I was saying, the red-button was probably the most democratic union in this country, but don't make the mistake of thinking that it was always like that. No, brothers, we *made* it democratic, and when I say *we* I mean the ordinary members, like you"—an arm swept over the conference—"and me." He cleared his throat and threw back his head. "For example, in 1914, the negotiations for our Bus Section were somewhat protracted, and it took three ballot before they had an offer they could accept. Now, our executive council was not too happy with this way—the *democratic* way—"of doing things, and so in 1916 they concluded an agreement without balloting the members. The following year, we convened a Special Delegate Meeting and forced the resignation of that executive council, brothers." He looked up at the platform, a smile on his face. "So you see, Chairman, I've kept to the point. And beware, because what we've done before, we can do again."

There followed a prolonged round of applause, some of the delegates standing, and the Salford man seated next to Ernie clapping him on the back, crying "My god, you told 'em brother, you told 'em!" He appeared thoughtful for a moment and then brightened. "Come to think of it, *I'll* tell 'em now," he said, and up went his arm.

"Yes, brother," the chairman called him.

"I move, Chairman, that this delegate conference of tramway members instructs the executive council in future to ballot the membership before accepting any proposal on wages and conditions from the employers!"

More cheers, and over a dozen cries of "Seconded!"

Hirst turned to the chairman. "Just put it to the vote. We don't want any more debate on this."

"All those in favour!"

Unanimous.

"And now," resumed the chairman, choosing his words carefully, "does conference agree to recommend a return to work pending further negotiations on this year's wage claim?"

Not unanimous, but carried by a sizeable majority.

"Well, conference," said Hirst, getting to his feet, "thank you for your attendance and…"

"No, no, no!" cried the Manchester delegate. "We're still not done yet, Stanley Hirst. When I recommend that my members return to work, I want to be able to tell them that they'll be receiving strike pay for the time they've been out."

Hirst sighed. "On behalf of the Executive Council: agreed!"

Hirst had been right about one thing: as the delegates dispersed, they were happier than when they had arrived.

11

Back in the red-button days, the progressive officers and lay members had been able to discuss matters of common interest in the small kitchen at the Soho headquarters of the union. This being no longer possible or politic at Transport House in Emperor's Gate, the group around George Sanders often made their way to the Earl's Court Tavern, at the top end of Earl's Court Road. This early evening in April found Sanders, Eric Rice, Barney Macauley and Mickey gathered around a table in the saloon bar, discussing Russia.

Sanders, a committee member of the Hands Off Russia movement, led off.

"At the end of February, we had a good meeting in the Albert Hall, chaired by Tom Mann. The call was for recognition of the Soviet government and an end to intervention—direct and indirect. Three weeks later, we were back at the Albert Hall as George Lansbury reported on his visit to Russia. A packed meeting." He snapped the fingers of his right hand, as if remembering something. "And, of course, we can look forward to another report-back meeting in a couple of months' time." He looked at each of the other three in turn. "You remember that fact-finding delegation to Russia that was agreed at the special TUC congress in December? Well, Bob Williams is on it! Leaves towards the end of this month."

"Cor, the lucky bugger!" exclaimed Eric Rice.

Sanders nodded. "Yeah, I wouldn't have minded that job meself."

"And the Russian trade delegation?" asked an under-impressed Barney Macauley.

"Although Lloyd George told the House that the delegation was expected soon, a few days later the Overseas Trade Department announced that Litvinov, who was to have led the delegation, would not be welcome here, due to his previous activity, so it wasn't until earlier this month that the delegation arrived in Copenhagen, where they've been negotiating with the Allies."

"So who's leading them now?" asked Eric Rice.

"A comrade called Krassin—Leonid Borisovich, if I remember correctly."

"So when will there arrive here?" This was Mickey.

"Next month at the earliest; that's Theo Rothstein's guess, anyway."

"Will it still go ahead after the Polish invasion?" Mickey again, pushing the discussion in the direction of solidarity action.

Sanders shook out a Gold Flake and placed it between his lips. "Apparently so, Mickey." He applied a match to his cigarette. "And, you know, Theo as much as predicted this attack by Poland."

"This government surely won't negotiate a trade deal while Russia's at war with Poland, will it?" speculated Barney.

Sanders shook his head. "Not a chance."

"And I haven't heard our government calling for a ceasefire," said Eric Rice.

"And you won't, either, unless the comrades push the Poles back to the border—and if they cross it, the Allies have already said they'll come to the aid of any country that Russian troops enter. This is *exactly*"—he slapped the tabletop with the fingers of his left hand—"what Theo said would happen!"

"So we'd better get our skates on, hadn't we!" Mickey exclaimed. "Now's the time to mobilise solidarity action, surely."

Sanders nodded. "That's true, Mickey. I had a pint with Harry Pollitt the other night—you remember Harry, Mickey: he was at the Hands Off Russia foundation meeting. Anyway, Harry's keeping himself busy in the East End, dishing out lit outside the docks every Friday and Saturday night and sticking up placards and posters—on the ships as well as the docks. Sylvia Pankhurst has printed up a huge supply of Lenin's 'Appeal to the Toiling Masses,' and they're being dished out as well.

"Harry was saying that a little while ago a rumour went around that arms would be shipped to Poland, and it was thought that a couple of Belgian barges were being used for the purpose. Guess who's told to work on 'em! You've got it: Harry. Well, acting as if he's a bit nervous about the spread of Bolshevism, he asks whether the barges will be used to help Poland against Russia. Yes, they tell him, these barges will be going to Poland. In that case, says Harry, I ain't working on 'em. Does everyone follow Harry's example? They do not. Harry is sacked, and try as he might he can't get the men to strike. Work was supposed to be finished on the barges on a Sunday, but when it starts snowing the men are sent home—still on double pay; and that double pay might have had something to do with the men's reluctance to strike.

"Anyway, that night Harry holds a meeting in the Old Ford Road—a pretty depressing affair by his account. But he's chatting to a former workmate after the meeting, and this fellow says, with a bit of a twinkle in his eye, 'You worry too much, Harry. Take my word for it, it'll be alright in the end.' And you know what? It was: crossing the North Sea a few days later, the cable towing the barges snapped and the munitions ended up on the sea bed!"

Barney Macauley and Eric Rice burst into laughter, Barney bringing his hands together, Mickey merely smiled and nodded.

"What's up, bruv?" asked Eric.

Mickey sighed. "Look, it's good that the Poles didn't get the arms, but we're gonna need more than sabotage to be of real help to the Russian comrades. How many men were involved in making sure that cable wasn't up to the job? Two or three, I'd guess. But the men as a whole refused to strike. To stop this thing in its tracks, we'll need thousands of workers taking action, making sure our government knows that no munitions will be leaving this country for Poland. And at the end of the day, the official movement will have to be involved." Another sigh. "We've got a hell of a job in front of us, lads!"

Sanders crushed his cigarette-end in the ashtray before looking up and pausing thoughtfully. A sigh. "You're right, Mickey," he said.

12

On 14 April, the Manchester tramworkers voted to return to work. It was in these circumstances that, five days later, a further meeting was held at the headquarters of the London General Omnibus Company regarding the London busworkers' claim.

"Having given the matter considerable thought," said Mr H.E. Blain, operating manager, "we feel we can offer five shillings now and a further shilling in June."

"And you managed to say that with a straight face, Mr Blain," remarked George Sanders, aware of the angry stirring to either side of him.

Blain blinked. "I'm not sure I follow you, Mr Sanders."

"As you must be aware, Mr Blain, the offer you have just proposed is precisely the same as the one put forward by the National Joint Industrial Council for our tram members, and which has led to strike action across the North of England, following which the employers have agreed to reopen negotiations; the NJIC meets tomorrow, in fact."

Blain took this remarkably calmly. "That is so, Mr Sanders, but we both know that you are not comparing like with like: the London busman already earns considerably more than his counterpart on the trams."

"Yes, Mr Blain, and his job is considerably harder. But this bickering will get us nowhere." Sanders gave him a hard look. "This offer will not be acceptable to our members, and well you know it."

"Well, it is the best we can do at this moment in time, Mr Sanders—and even then we have to make it conditional upon your members accepting a maximum spreadover of twelve hours for 25 percent of all duties."

Sanders fell silent. While he had no doubt that the employers genuinely wanted—perhaps, due to the intricacies of effective scheduling, even needed—such a relaxation of the spreadover limit, he could not believe that they expected to get this through in the current round of negotiations. No, this was another game they were playing, hoping that he would explode at this point and force them to withdraw the proposal, in which case the cash already on the table would be accepted out of sheer relief. He shuffled his papers, placed them in his document case and got to his feet. "In which case, gentlemen, we bid you good afternoon. Perhaps you will be good enough to notify us when you have a more reasonable offer to put on the table."

Sanders led his team from the room.

*

"How do you think we should play this one, George?" asked Barney Macauley as they stood outside Electric Railway House.

Sanders considered the tip of his cigarette. "Did you see the result of the miners' ballot the other day, Barney?"

"Yeah, of course. They voted to accept—well, 54 percent of 'em did." He frowned. "Why do you raise that, George?"

"Because when the strongest section of the movement votes to accept an offer it doesn't want, it's a sign that confidence is on the wane."

"So what are you saying?"

"I think it's best that we play this one long, Barney, and save our strength for when we might really need it. We'll ballot on this so-called offer, but no rush. Not much doubt that they'll reject it, of course, but I don't think we have to rush into a strike." He took a final draw on his cigarette before letting it fall at his feet. "No, we'll let the tram lads make the running and just fall in behind them."

13

The day after the busmen's meeting at Electric Railway House, the NJIC for the tramways industry agreed to an immediate increase of six shillings. Realising that this would not be enough to put the matter to bed, Hull Corporation immediately broke ranks and agreed a further four shillings, thus conceding the full demand. Three days later, the employers' side of the NJIC conceded an extra penny per hour which, with the six shillings already granted, would amount to the ten shillings originally demanded. Meanwhile, Bob Williams' suggestion regarding local negotiations for the poorer tramway systems having been adopted, several district councils had failed to arrive at a recommended settlement; the NJIC gave them a further month in which to do so, failing which the matter would be sent to arbitration.

It was not until May that the result of the London busworkers' ballot was announced: 2,882 for acceptance against 8,109 for rejection.

Negotiations were resumed and in the first week of June the LGOC put forward an offer which London's busworkers found acceptable: an increase of nine shillings a week, with no lengthening of the maximum spreadover.

"Here's to success," toasted Barney Macauley, lifting his pint of bitter.

They—Macauley, Sanders, Ernie Fairbrother, Morris Frankenberg, all former red-button men—were in the Adam & Eve on the corner of Palmer Street and Petty France, the meeting at Electric Railway House having wound up in time for a lunchtime drink.

"Past, present or future?" asked Sanders.

"All three. I reckon, George. Last year gave us our biggest success yet, and this year was, at the end of the day, pretty painless. All we had to do was wait until the trams settled."

"Although they tried to frighten us into settling for a few bob less with their threat of twelve-hour spreadovers," said Ernie Fairbrother.

Being a cabbie, Morris Frankenberg's attention was elsewhere. "This wood's been here a good while, by the look of it," he observed, tapping his foot on the floor.

"Eighteenth century," said Sanders.

"Geddon!" said Ernie. "You sure about that, George?"

"That's what the landlord said, the last time I was in here." Sanders looked around at the other three. "Well, are we gonna drink this toast or what?"

"To success," repeated Macauley, and they all drank.

"Mind you," said Sanders, lowering his glass, "I would hesitate before putting money on our chances next year."

"You got a crystal ball, George?" asked Fairbrother.

"No, Ernie, but I'm pretty sure that next year they'll be back for their twelve-hour spreadovers, and I've a nasty feeling that the wind is about to change."

That turned out to be remarkably prescient.

14

Although the delegation—now composed of both Labour Party and TUC representatives—left England on 27 April, it was 10 May before it arrived in Petrograd. Its first stop after crossing the frontier from Estonia, though, was Yambourg, where it was greeted by a modest military parade.

"Well," remarked Alf Purcell with a grin as they watched the parade, "it's certainly nice to feel a bit of protection." Alf—real name Albert—was 47, general secretary of the furnishing trades union.

"It's even nicer to feel *welcome*," replied Bob Williams. He took a great lungful of breath and slowly let it out.

Purcell turned to look at him. "What's all that about Bob? Can't be the first time you've felt welcome."

"No, but it's the first time I've breathed the air of freedom. Just imagine, Alf, this whole vast country—almost a continent—is ruled by our class."

"Or it will be once they've defeated the Whites and chased out the interventionists," chimed in bearded Ben Turner, chair of the delegation and leader of the textile workers.

"I'll drink to that!" exclaimed Williams.

"I'm very much afraid," said Charles Roden Buxton, joint secretary of the delegation, "that it will not be possible to drink to anything while we're in Russia, the Soviet government having banned alcohol for the foreseeable future." Buxton had been a Liberal until as recently as 1917, and Williams had his reservations about him, but he had not put a foot out of place so far.

"Oh, good for them!" enthused Ethel Snowden, a peace campaigner and teetotaller. Williams suspected that this might be one of the few positive things that Ethel, an attractive 38-year-old married to Philip Snowden, MP, would say about Soviet Russia during the entire trip.

*

If Bob Williams had a fear regarding this trip to Russia it was that he would be disappointed by what he saw, and that fear came to the fore as, having arrived in Petrograd, they began to look around the old capital. Whether along broad avenues or in small side-streets, so many stores were shuttered. My god, he thought, how must Ethel Snowden be reacting to this? The thing to do, of course, was to seek an explanation.

"Are all these shops closed due to lack of supplies?" he asked their guide, a woman in early middle age called Vikha, who had told the delegation during the introductions that she had in earlier years been an athlete.

"Many of them, yes," she replied, quite comfortable with the question. "But if we reintroduced capitalism tomorrow, you would see that many of them would reopen."

"Wouldn't that be better for the people?" asked Margaret Bondfield, a 47-year-old former shop-worker who sat on the Parliamentary Committee of the TUC.

Vikha smiled patiently. "Not really, Comrade, because most people would not be able to afford to shop in these stores."

"So when will the supplies get moving again, Vikha?" asked Tom Shaw, a miner's son who, at 47, was now the MP for Preston.

"As soon as the Whites are defeated, and the imperialist countries like Britain and France are forced to stop interfering in our country, the situation with supplies will greatly improve," said Vikha.

So that settled that.

"I can't help noticing," said Ben Turner in an avuncular, sympathetic tone, "that many people look hungry and are not well-clothed."

Vikha nodded. "It is true, Comrades. And they look like that for the same reason that so many shops are closed." She looked over her shoulder at a clock on a public building. "But we must hurry to the Winter Palace, comrades, or we will be late."

There was some speculation among the delegates as to whom they might be meeting at the Winter Palace, but it turned out that they were destined for the old Palace Square—now renamed Uritsky Place in honour of Moisei Uritsky, the head of the Petrograd Cheka who had been assassinated by a military cadet in 1918—in front of the white, gold and turquoise palace, where a spectacular military and naval parade was held in which an estimated 50,000 took part. Most of the uniforms appeared to be in good condition and the soldiers looked healthy. And, Williams noticed, they were not all men.

"Do I see women soldiers in those lines, Vikha?"

"Yes, there are women in our Red Army." When she looked at Williams there was a glint of pride in her eyes. "And some of them are officers."

After the infantry, companies of machine-gunners passed by, their weapons mounted on carts drawn by ponies, followed by three batteries of artillery and two squadrons of cavalry composed of Bakshirs, Muslim soldiers from the southern Urals.

"Comrade Vikha," asked Bob Williams, "can you translate the slogans on the banners for us?"

She smiled. "Of course." Pointing to one of the leading banners, she said, "This one will interest you, comrades. It says 'The English Capitalists are our Enemies; the English Workers are our Friends.'"

Williams was astounded. "So this parade is in our honour?"

Another nod, and an impish grin. "In part, yes. Of course. They did not tell you?"

Unable to speak, moved almost to tears, Williams shook his head.

"And the others, Vikha?" asked Ben Turner.

"Ah, this next one says 'In one hand a rifle; in the other a hammer.' That means that we must be ready to defend the Revolution by armed means and by working in industry to build the things we need. And this one says 'Protect the Fruits of the Revolution.'"

"And this last one?" This from Tom Shaw.

"'Our power rests on labour discipline.'"

Shaw laughed. "Well, that's a slogan you won't find in Trafalgar Square, Bob. Do you agree, Ben?"

"No," said Turner, "I don't suppose you would."

"That just goes to show," said Bob Williams, recovered now, "the difference between the two systems. Nowadays, you'd be laughed at if you put up that slogan back home, but when our class comes to power it'll be something we'll need, just as these comrades need it now."

*

The following evening, the delegation attended the Petrograd Opera House for a performance of Gluck's "Orpheus and Eurydice." The attention of Williams was drawn to the audience, for he noticed that row after row of seats was filled with what only could have been working people, some in clothes that were quite shabby, some of the men in need of a shave. He turned to Vikha, who was seated beside him, placing a hand on her bare arm to attract her attention, and was about to speak when she anticipated his remark.

"Yes," she said, smiling warmly, "there are many workers here. Most of the tickets are distributed to the trade unions, who sell them to their members at a very low price." She was blond, in her late thirties, and Williams could see as she smiled at him that one or two of her molars were made of steel. It was a warm evening and she wore a short-sleeved frock with a floral design.

"Why, that's wonderful," he said.

"Yes, I agree."

He became flustered, suddenly conscious of his hand on her arm. "Oh, I'm sorry..."

She placed her hand on his, so that it stayed on her arm. "It's quite alright, Comrade." Her eyes as they looked into his told him that it really was perfectly acceptable.

"You know," he said, anxious to escape this sudden bond of intimacy which, while unusually pleasant, was at the same time so disconcerting, "I have a comrade in London who argues that music and art would never have existed if the working class had not been creating the wealth to allow artists to follow their non-productive pursuits, and so it should really be seen as the property of the workers."

Vikha nodded, smiling. "Exactly. That is the thinking that guides our policy on culture. But tell me, Comrade, are you fond of opera?"

"In fact, Vikha, I would not claim to know very much about opera. But I like singing—all kinds of singing." He grinned. "I'm Welsh, you see." As he uttered this last sentence, he noticed that his voice assumed the Welsh lilt he had thought lost.

"Ah, your people are singers?"

"Many Welsh people are fine singers, yes."

She patted his hand, which still lay on her arm. "You know what I will do? I will see if it is possible for your delegation to go backstage after the performance and meet the cast."

"Oh, that would be splendid!" The lilt was still there. Looking down at her hand, he noticed her wedding ring for the first time. "Tell me, Vikha, what does your husband do? For a living, I mean."

At that moment, the orchestra, which had completed its tuning up some minutes earlier, sounded the opening bars of the overture, and in reply to Williams Vikha held up a hand: Not now.

Williams followed both the opera and the reactions of the workers in the audience. When, in the opening scene, Orpheus mourned the death of his beloved Eurydice, they grieved with him, heads being shaken sadly; as Eros, called Amore here, advised him that he could travel to the Underworld and return with her, on condition that he did not look at her until she was safely back on Earth, they brightened; when the Furies at first refused to admit him to the Underworld, there was anger, and a few fists were shaken at the stage; there was joy at their reunion, but this turned to deep concern when Orpheus, anxious to convince Eurydice that his refusal to look at her did not mean that he no longer loved her, began to turn, and here there were gasps and even one cry of "No! Don't do it!" and Williams was reminded of the audiences at English pantomimes; they grieved as Eurydice died once more and Orpheus contemplated suicide, until Amore, impressed by the depth of Orpheus's love, restored his lover to life; now their faces beamed and when the opera drew to a close after a four-act ballet and song of praise to Amore by the whole chorus, they were on their feet, applauding wildly.

Vikha turned to Williams. "Excuse, me Comrade, I must speak to Comrade Turner." She touched his arm. "And Comrade..."

"Yes, Vikha?"

"I am a widow." And with that she turned and leaned across to tell Ben Turner, as leader of the delegation, of her intention to lead them backstage.

Williams would never be able to recall the names of the conductor and lead tenor, but nevertheless the delegation was introduced to them and they had a polite—if, on the British side, uninformed—discussion, with Vikha translating.

"I noticed," said Bob Williams, "that there were very many workers in the audience. Vikha has explained that most of the tickets go to the trade unions." He tilted his head quizzically. "You must find these audiences very different from the ones you played to before the Revolution."

The tenor nodded, smiling. "Oh, yes, *very* different. But I will say this: the audiences of today are much more appreciative than during the old times."

"My husband also says this," said a short, plumpish woman in her forties; she was wearing street clothes and Williams at first wondered what connection she had with the opera.

"Ah, forgive me," said the conductor. "Please allow me to introduce Madame Chaliapin."

"The wife of Feodor Chaliapin?" asked Williams. He may have known little about opera, but the whole world knew of Chaliapin, the renowned bass singer.

Madame Chaliapin inclined her head modestly. "The same. I have come to compliment the orchestra and the company on their performance this evening."

"In fact, Madame Chaliapin, we saw your husband in concert just a few days ago at the Estonian Concert Theatre in Reval," said Williams. "Does he still perform internationally as much as he did?"

"Oh, yes, it is no problem for him to travel to Paris or London to perform. To be honest, though, he prefers to sing for Russian audiences. Maybe you will see him again in Moscow; he sings regularly at the Hermitage theatre."

Bob Williams' head was spinning: here he was, a coal-trimmer from Swansea, conversing with the wife of one of the most famous singers in the world.

The delegation was quartered in the seventeenth-century neoclassical Naryshkin Palace on the banks of the Fotanka River, once the home of Russian nobles; during the late war, the last private owner had donated it as a military hospital; it had been nationalised in 1918 and since 1919 housed the Museum of Aristocratic Life. After the delegation's initial arrival, Vikha had given a condensed history of the place, in the course of which she had pointed out that the private owner, Yelizaveta Vladimirovna Shuvalova, had been rather less altruistic than previously thought for, after the palace was taken over following the Revolution, a vast hoard of antiquities and art works had been discovered, concealed in various parts of the palace.

"Of course," said Vikha once they had entered the palace upon return from the opera, "the woman you have just met is not really Chaliapin's wife."

As they had entered, Vikha had gripped the cuff of Williams' jacket to indicate that they should allow the others go before them.

They now stood just inside the entrance, well away from the others.

"Oh, no?"

She grinned and shook her head. "No. He has two families. His legal wife, an Italian ballerina called Iola Tornagi, is in Moscow; she has borne him six children, one of whom died young. The woman you met was Marina Petsold, and she stays here in Petrograd. She has two children by her late husband and she has given Chaliapin two daughters."

Williams chuckled. "How do you come by this information, Vikha?"

She shrugged. "It is not a secret: everybody here knows, but I am not suggesting that you should let the rest of your delegation know." She glanced in the direction of the others. "And now I must go to my room." She lowered her voice. "But before I do, I would ask that, if you are interested in me, you do not lock your door tonight." She raised a finger and looked him in the eye. "This *will* be a secret, Comrade."

*

The room Bob Williams had been assigned was fairly basic: a single bed, a dressing table with a straight-backed chair, a small curtained-off area to serve as a wardrobe, and a sink containing a cracked china bowl; he assumed that this had been part of the servants' quarters. He removed his jacket and shoes and reclined on the bed, wondering whether Vikha would come; part of him hoped that she would not and all of him wondered how he would manage if she did; he had not locked the door. He felt his heart flutter and when he brought a hand before his face the fingers were trembling.

When she arrived, he did not have much of an opportunity to think of what he was doing, but that may have been because he was not doing a great deal. She locked the door behind her and then, hands clasped behind her back, walked to the bed, smiling cautiously at him. She was wearing the same floral-print frock she had worn to the opera. As she approached, Williams swung his legs over the side of the bed.

"I thought you would be in bed, Comrade." She stood before him, taking his large hands in hers.

For the first time, Williams realised how short she was. "I was not sure that you would come," he said, directing his attention to her thin lips, avoiding her eyes.

She inclined her head and gave him a sceptical frown. "Really?"

She was unbuttoning his shirt. "I think maybe you did not want me to come."

"It's. It's not that. It's just that I-I..."

"You are nervous," she purred wonderingly. "Why are you nervous, Comrade?"

"Because I-I..."

"Oh, what a hairy chest you have! And such a *big* chest! Yes, I can see that you are a singer." She smiled coquettishly. "Will you sing to me when we make love, Comrade?"

"Ch-chance would be a fine thing."

Her frown deepened. "What is the meaning of...?" She waved a dismissive hand. "Forget it. Forget it and kiss me, Comrade. I want you to kiss me now."

He did his best. As his lips touched hers, her mouth opened, and she placed her right hand on his neck, pulling him closer, while her left investigated his trousers. The kiss did not last long.

"Forgive me, Comrade, but you are not a very good kisser."

"I've been trying to t-tell you: I-I..."

She patted his crotch with her left hand. "And nothing is happening here, Comrade. By the way, how old are you?"

"Thirty-nine."

"Ah, I also am thirty-nine!" She paused, bringing a finger to her lower lip thoughtfully. "So it cannot be that you are too old."

"No, no, no. It's j-just that..."

"Would you care to feel my breasts? Here." She took his right hand and placed it on her left breast.

"Oh, very n-nice. You're not wearing any..."

"Correct! The underwear I leave in my room." She shrugged. "It seems I am an optimist."

For the first time, Williams wondered why she was doing this. "T-tell me, Vikha: there was a report in the B-British press that w-women in Russia have been n-nationalised..."

She laughed. "Don't be foolish, Comrade. You must know that most of the stories about Soviet Russia in the capitalist press are perversions of the facts." As she realised why he had raised this matter, her mouth fell open. "Oh, you are thinking that I have been assigned to provide this service for you!"

"No, no, no."

Playfully, she brought her face close to his. "Yes, yes, yes, you silly comrade. By the way, it would be better if you *squeezed*, Comrade."

He squeezed her breast. "Oh, yes."

She left his hand where it was and looked into his eyes; her own, he saw, were flecked with gold. "You wish to know why I am doing this? Alright. I told you that I am a widow. Being a widow, I sometimes feel the need for intimate relations. When we talked in the theatre, it seemed to me that you are a sensitive man, and I like to have relations with sensitive men." She pouted playfully. "It turns out that you are perhaps a little *too* sensitive, but I think we can cure this."

"I've been trying to tell you, Vikha: I'm out of pr-practice!"

She leaned back and regarded him seriously, perhaps even sceptically. "Out of practice? Well, perhaps. But let me tell you what I propose. Your delegation is in Petrograd for four more nights, yes? Good. Tomorrow night, I will come to your room again and we will have the most wonderful love-making. How will this be accomplished? I ask you one thing: do not *think*!" She prodded his temple with her forefinger in a manner which was quite painful. "You *think*"—prod!—"far too much! Instead of *thinking*"—prod—"you should be *feeling*!"

She spoke softly now, her slightly husky voice caressing him, soothing him. "Now, my darling, please relax. We will not make love tonight, so you have no need to be nervous. Relax, and your silly stutter will disappear." She took his face between her palms and kissed him lightly on the lips. "You are perfectly relaxed? Good. Now I will show you just a little bit of what it will be like tomorrow night. When I kiss you this time, I want you to open your mouth, darling."

She kissed him hard, forcing her tongue into his mouth, gripping his hair in her hands and pulling him to her. She broke away just once. "Squeeze my breast, my darling—hard." As the kiss resumed, it became clear that Williams was at last getting the practice he claimed to be out of and that he was rising to the occasion.

"Vikha, I think I've recovered," Bob Williams announced, as the kiss finally came to an end.

"That makes me very happy," she said, beaming at him. She gave him a peck on the nose. "But this will be for tomorrow night, when we will make a fresh start. And remember:"—she tapped his crotch, provoking a cry of "Oh, I see what you mean!"—"*feel*, do not think!"

She glided to the door, unlocked it, and was gone.

*

The remaining days in Petrograd were busy enough, with visits throughout the day and often a concert in the evening. The delegation did not always travel together; for example when

Williams, Purcell, Shaw and Skinner visited the Putilov ironworks, famous for its contributions to the revolutions of 1905 and February 1917 and now called the Red Putilovite Plant, the rest of the delegation inspected healthcare centres in the city. With no theatre visit that evening, after dinner they compared notes in a spacious lounge at the palace. Vikha, who had accompanied the health-centre tour, was also present.

"My god, that Putilov factory is some size!" said Tom Shaw.

"How many employed there, Tom?" asked Ben Turner.

It was Purcell who answered. "Thousands, but not as many as there should be."

"Oh?"

"Yeah, some are needed in the Red Army, of course, and then some of the more recent employees have gone back to the countryside."

"Why have they done that, Alf?" asked Herbert Skinner.

"Food, Bert," replied Bob Williams. "The peasants are still well-fed; it's the industrial centres that are short of food, and that problem won't be solved until the transport system is restored to health and improved."

"And ironically, the Putilov works is turning out locomotives and rolling stock, so those who return to the villages are hampering production of the very thing that could ease the situation. Another problem, of course, is that due to the blockade and the activity of the Whites raw materials are more difficult to obtain than they should be."

"I'll be buggered," muttered Skinner, shaking his head. "What are working conditions like? Pretty grim, I'd imagine."

"Actually, not so bad," said Williams. "They have an eight-hour day—although at the moment, of course, there's plenty of overtime."

"Paid at overtime rate?" This from Margaret Bondfield.

"Of course. And here's something you'd be interested in, Margaret: women get paid maternity leave—eight weeks before confinement and eight weeks after."

"Oh, that's very good," she replied. "But I suppose that's because the workers are well-organised at the Putilov factory."

Williams chuckled. "It doesn't work like that here, Margaret. This is Soviet Russia: our class is in charge."

"And so?"

"And so those maternity leave provisions are available throughout industry."

"Are the factories still run by committees?" asked Ethel Snowden. "That must be very inefficient."

"After the Revolution," Williams replied, "the comrades had little choice but to employ the former managers and technicians—those who hadn't flown the coop, anyway. There was a fear of sabotage, and so the unions demanded workers' control of the workshops and factories, which were therefore overseen by boards of stewards. Now that this has outlived its usefulness, they're switching to what they call 'one-man control,' although the unions remain in charge overall. And you're right, Ethel: management by committee was a bit inefficient and, given the huge tasks facing them now, efficiency is a major priority."

Williams noticed that Vikha had been paying close attention to his explanation, and at first he thought that she was monitoring his remarks for possible inaccuracies, but she now smiled and remarked, "I enjoy listening to you comrades because I learn so many English phrases and idioms that are `unfamiliar to me." Her smile broadened. "For example, *fly the coop*. What does that mean, comrades?"

They all laughed.

"It means to escape," explained Les Guest. "You know, like a chicken flapping its wings and flying out of its coop."

"I have to say," said Ben Turner, stroking his beard, "that some of the things *we* saw and heard today are cause for real concern."

"In the hospitals?" That was Tom Shaw seeking clarification.

Purcell caught Williams's eye and winked. He held Shaw in low regard: as Turner and his party had been visiting hospitals that day, from where else could his concern have sprung?

"There are horrendous problems, comrades," Turner continued without answering the question. "Typhus is tearing through the country—and the hospitals. There's cholera too, but typhus is the major problem." He passed a hand over his brow as though the very thought of the problem caused him to break into a sweat. "In some hospitals, half the doctors have fallen victim to it, and most hospitals are ill-equipped."

"When you say ill-equipped..." ventured Shaw.

It was almost a wrathful textile workers' leader who turned on him. "Beds!" he thundered. "Sheets, blankets! Essential medicines! But even simple but crucial things like soap and disinfectant!"

"Because of the transport problems?" asked Purcell.

"Because of the bloody Allied blockade! Russia is dependent on imports for soap and disinfectant!"

"Language, Comrade," murmured Ethel Snowden.

"The blockade has to end—and end soon!" Turner insisted.

Vikha chose this moment to try out one of her newly-acquired idioms. "Chance would be a fine thing," she said, causing all heads to turn in her direction.

*

When she came to his room that night, as previously Vikha wore just a frock and shoes, having left her underwear in her own room. She locked the door behind her and stepped to the side of the bed where Williams lay naked, a towel draped across his midriff.

"I hope you are not thinking, Comrade," she breathed huskily.

He managed a grin. "My mind is a complete blank, Vikha."

"And you are relaxed?"

"Maybe too relaxed."

She inserted a hand under the towel and reached for his penis. "Yes, maybe too relaxed, but we will do something about that."

He extended a hand to her breast. "You mean this, Vikha?"

"No, I mean this," she said, brushing his hand away and with one swift movement removing her frock and dropping it onto the bed.

He had expected her body to be as white as his, drained of colour by long Russian winters, but it was a soft, pale gold; her breasts were larger than his previous tactile exploration had led him to anticipate, the areolas a deeper shade of gold and the nipples erect.

"Oh my goodness."

Once more, her hand burrowed under his towel. A smile came to her face, and she announced: "Let the games commence."

15

On the evening of 16 May, the delegation departed for Moscow. Among the officials who saw them off at the station was a woman who was only ever referred to as Madame Ravitch, Petrograd's Commissar of Public Safety—essentially, the police chief. At the farewell dinner given the previous evening, in a speech translated by the US anarchist Emma Goldman, recently deported from the USA, she had spoken of the women workers of Soviet Russia, concluding, "May the English proletarians learn the quality of their heroic Russian sisters." At the station, Vikha gave each of the delegates the traditional kiss on the cheek; she left Williams until last and, confident that no one was watching, pressed her body to his.

The previous night, in bed after the farewell dinner, Williams had asked if they would meet again.

"It is doubtful, Comrade." She had patted his chest. "You, after all, must return to Britain to wage the revolution."

*

There was no palace for them in Moscow, but a hotel over the front of which hung the slogan "We started the Revolution, comrades—we started it alone; let us finish it together." When this was translated for them, Alf Purcell turned to Bob Williams and quipped, "That'll do me, Comrade!"

Of course, not all citizens were keen on joining the Revolution, let alone completing it, and some members of the delegation were, at their own request, allowed to meet members of the Socialist Revolutionaries and the Mensheviks.

"They complain," said Margaret Bondfield after these visits, "that they are not permitted to undertake political activity or publish their newspapers, and that many of them are imprisoned."

Their guide Dmitri was—or at least affected to be—puzzled by such complaints. He shrugged. "But what do they expect? You may have noticed, Comrade Bondfield, that we are fighting for our lives here. No, that is not quite true: we are fighting for the life of the Revolution, which is the same thing. At a time when we are subject to a blockade by the Allied powers—which, whether we like it or not, has an effect on not just the health but the morale of even our supporters—and when the Whites are still causing disruption, and foreign armies, despite what your Mr Churchill may say, are still on Russian soil, do you really expect us to allow opposition groups to stir further unrest?" He shook his head vigorously. "No, it is not possible!"

Margaret Bondfield made the mistake of looking across at Williams and Purcell, as if hoping that they would come to her assistance. Williams shrugged. "Sounds fair enough to me, Margaret."

The eleven days of their first stay in Moscow passed in a blur. There were the inevitable theatre visits, military parades and outings to schools and mansions taken over by the Revolution and converted to homes for orphaned children. At one stage, Bob Williams commented to Dmitri—a man in his thirties who had lost an arm in fighting against the Whites—that the only groups who did not seem so affected by the shortages were children and the Red Army.

Dmitri grinned. "You are very observant, Comrade. And also very correct. Priority is very deliberately given to the Red Army and to children, the soldiers because they are the protectors of the Revolution, and the children because they are our future."

The first military parade in Moscow was held to welcome the delegation, which was provided with its own stand, and took place on 18 May, involving between three and four thousand soldiers, most of whom were training to be officers. Much more impressive was, two days later, a demonstration to celebrate the formation of the Armed Workers' Militia, under the regime of which every industrial worker was obliged to do two hours' military training twice a week. Thirty thousand workers took part in the demonstration, 12,000 of whom were party members. At the climax of the event, aircraft flew overhead, dropping propaganda leaflets.

Later in the visit, the delegation witnessed a parade of trained officers about to leave for the Polish front, who publicly took an oath of allegiance to the Soviet civilian authorities. Dmitri translated as the oath was chanted by 30,000 voices. "I, a son of the working people, take upon myself the name of a warrior of the Labour and Peasant Government...I undertake to carry this name with honour and to follow the military calling with conscience...I undertake to abstain from any act liable to dishonor the name of citizens of the Soviet Republic; moreover to direct all my deeds and thoughts to the great aim of the liberation of all workers...I pledge myself to the defence of the Soviet Republic in any danger or assault on the part of her enemies...and not to spare myself in the struggle for the Russian Soviet Republic, for the aim of Socialism and Brotherhood of Nations...Should this promise be broken, let my fate be the scorn of my fellows. Let my punishment be the stern hand of revolutionary law."

On 26 May, two days before they left for the south, they visited the Army Physical Culture School for one of their displays, featuring weight-lifting, fencing, boxing and gymnastics.

These events, and a visit to the War Office, convinced Les Guest and Williams that there were not only great improvements in the Red Army but also, as they would write in the delegation's report, that Soviet society was witnessing the growth of a new patriotism that was "determined to resist and overcome all forms of external intervention..."

*

And so to the south.

To travel south, they first went 420 kilometres east to Nizhny Novgorod on the Volga, where they boarded the steamship *Bielinski* which first travelled the 400 kilometres to Kazan in the land of the Tatars before following the Volga as it turned southward. On the 700-kilometre journey to Saratov, they paused at several towns and cities—some of which, like Samara, had names which spoke of antiquity and sunlight—to see how the Revolution fared in those places, but there was also ample opportunity for discussion, for they were accompanied by Comrade Veniamin Sverdlov, acting commissar of railways and the brother of the late Yakov Sverdlov, chairman of the party's All-Russian Central Executive Committee who had perished the previous year in the Spanish 'flu' epidemic at the tragically young age of 33; the Sverdlov family hailed from Nizhny Novgorod.

As their ship ploughed south in the June sunshine, the vast swathes of land between major population centres were populated by the peasantry, and Williams, standing with Sverdlov at the rail of the ship and looking out onto the western bank of the Volga, asked him how this class viewed the Revolution.

Comrade Sverdlov drew on his *papirosa*, a cigarette with a disposable cardboard holder. It was early morning, and although the sky was a deep blue vault spanning this vast land, the sun was not yet as fierce as it would become.

"On the whole, Comrade, the peasantry is not opposed to our government, and there are two reasons for this: first, of course, we have given them land, and secondly those who have endured occupation by the likes of Kolchak, Denikin and Yudenich know that our rule is not so severe. The more conscious elements, as you know, actively support the Revolution, and our task is to ensure that such people become the majority. This is important, because of our total population of 125 million, some 90 million are from the peasantry."

"And how is that task progressing, Comrade?"

Sverdlov smiled. "Like the Revolution itself, it is what you would call a work in progress. But it *is* progressing."

"When we visited the countryside outside Petrograd and Moscow, we noticed that while the clothing and footwear of the peasants were not very good, they were not as hungry as the workers in the cities."

Sverdlov nodded. "That is correct, Comrade, and this is good for them in the short term and bad for us. But it will be bad for all of us unless we get our railways running efficiently once more. This problem, Comrade, is a direct result of the blockade by the Allied governments, which makes it impossible for us to transport to the industrial centres either the food or the raw materials which our industries require. It is not simply that our transport system has been directly attacked in many places—and I will show you examples of this—but that we have been prevented from importing coal, fuel-oil and lubricants."

"At the same time, you have the problem of workers returning to the countryside to obtain food."

Sverdlov nodded sharply. "Correct. Tell me, Comrade, have you met Karl Radek during your visit?"

"The secretary of the Comintern? No, Comrade."

"Well, he has written that those who have fled to the countryside—for understandable reasons, he concedes—should return to the cities, because if the machinery needed by agriculture is not manufactured, agriculture will fail and the whole country will starve." He threw his *papirosa* overboard and leaned closer to Williams. "And he puts forward a very convincing argument, Comrade: if our socialist society has the right to send its soldiers to the front at the risk of their lives, he says, surely it has a greater right to direct the labour of its workers." He met Williams's gaze to determine his reaction. "But perhaps in Britain you oppose the direction of labour, Comrade."

Williams chuckled. "Well, yes, we were opposed to the direction of labour during the war…"

"Ah, you see…"

"Wait, wait, wait. We opposed it because it was done to aid an imperialist war. However, to direct labour in order to save a socialist revolution is an entirely different matter, and I'm sure we would support it."

Sverdlov laughed and placed a hand on Williams's arm. "Ah, forgive me, Comrade: sometimes I forget that you are a Marxist!"

*

Later in the morning, despite the sun, Comrade Sverdlov called the delegation on deck. He stood at the rail, a pair of binoculars in hand, and gestured to the west bank of the Volga.

"Comrades, I would direct your attention to the work being undertaken a few hundred metres from the bank. You may be able to see what is happening with the naked eye, but if not, please feel free to use these binoculars."

"Yep, a gang of men working on the railway embankment," said Alf Purcell, who simply shaded his eyes.

"Can you see what they are doing?" asked Sverdlov.

"Well," said Tom Cox, who had the binoculars to his eyes, "there's an engine there, with just one boxcar, so I suppose they're carrying out some sort of repair work."

"That is exactly what they are doing, comrades. They are relaying the rails where the Whites cut the line. Now, Comrade Cox, as you have the glasses, just follow the line down to the south and tell us what you see."

"Well, nothing yet...No, nothing...Oh, my goodness, the railway bridge is completely demolished! Looks as if there's a building team there, trying to rebuild it."

"And look beyond that, Tom, about half a mile down the line," suggested Alf Purcell.

"Oh, Jesus Christ almighty!"

"*Mr Cox!*" This was Ethel Snowden.

"There's an engine been tipped down the embankment, comrades! But no carriages in sight..."

"The Whites uncoupled the carriages before they pushed the locomotive down the embankment," explained Sverdlov. "As you can see the train was travelling northwards. After the area had been cleared, we were able to send a locomotive to retrieve the carriages and take them back to Saratov."

"It must have taken a lot of men to tip that engine off the tracks," commented Williams. "How did they manage it—leverage?"

"Yes, and on this side they had a team of horses. And you're right, there were very many of them." Sverdlov grinned grimly. "They are not so many now, however..."

"And is this a frequent occurrence, Comrade?" asked Ben Turner.

"Far too frequent for our liking, Comrade Turner, in various parts of the country. But the Whites will soon be defeated, thankfully."

"My goodness," said Margaret Bondfield, "the person with the responsibility for putting it all back together again has a *very* hard task before him. Poor man."

"Thank you, Comrade," said Sverdlov. Seeing her frown, he placed a hand on his heart and bowed his head. "I am, I regret to say, that person. And now, comrades," he said brightly, lifting his head, "I would suggest that we all go inside, as another of my responsibilities is to ensure that none of you suffer sunstroke."

Just outside Saratov, they visited a large locomotive refitting and repair shop where Sverdlov, his sense of urgency doubtless reinforced by the damage caused by the recent raid by the Whites, pleaded with the workers to accelerate the work, and Bob Williams, without giving it a thought, joined in, urging them to greater effort. And the workers, to the surprise of some delegates, responded positively.

"I reckon that must be the first time in your life that you've told men they have to work harder," said Alf Purcell later.

"Now you mention it," replied Williams with a grin, "I suppose it is, yes."

"And the men accepted it!"

"Alf," said Williams, "men will make every sacrifice when they know that it is for national and collective well-being, and equally will resist attempts to exploit their generosity for individual gain."

The *Bielinski* resumed its southward journey, stopping next at Tsaritsyn—renamed Stalingrad five years later—where Sverdlov stood at the rail and pointed to the west, announcing to the delegation: "Just over 600 kilometres in that direction lies Donetsk, in the Ukraine. The Whites laid waste the coal mines there, which is why we are forced to import—or try to import—our coal. But have no fear: the mines will be rehabilitated, and we will once again be self-sufficient."

And finally, as the river took a turn to the south-east, they sailed down to Astrakhan, on the shore of the Caspian Sea. Astrakhan: what a name! And what a history: the Golden Horde; Ibn Battuta, the Muslim Marco Polo; a kremlin built by the city's conqueror, Ivan the Terrible. And across the Caspian lay Persia and the Middle East.

*

On the way back to Moscow, some of the delegates visited the Polish front near Smolensk, where the efficiency of the Red Army was remarked upon. When asked whether it was possible for a Napoleon to arise from among the general staff to lead the opposition to socialism, a senior officer assured Williams that as all officers were now recruited from the working class such a thing could not occur. The delegates were intrigued by a shell that distributed not death but leaflets to the Polish troops, arguing that their ruling class had bamboozled them into fighting against their own class interest.

Back at their Moscow hotel, they were reunited with Dmitri, who persuaded them with his one-armed bear-hugs and hearty handshakes that he had really missed them. Once this round of greetings was complete, he took Williams by the arm and inclined his head towards a quiet spot, indicating that he needed to have a private word with him. Williams, whose mind had, during the trip to Astrakhan and back, often turned to thoughts of Vikha, wondered if a complaint had been forwarded from Petrograd.

Dmitri, considerably shorter than Williams, stood close, looked up at him, patted his lapel with a familiarity that Williams found not at all offensive and said, "Comrade Lenin wishes to see you tomorrow, Comrade."

16

When Bob Williams, accompanied on this occasion by a somewhat taciturn guide called Lev, made his way through the Kremlin, his heart was aflutter and he seemed to be short of breath. At certain points stern guards armed with rifles and bayonets checked their papers before waving them on. When going to meet Herbert Asquith and David Lloyd George in days gone by he had been perfectly calm, but he was about to meet Vladimir Ilyich Ulyanov, known to the world as Lenin, leader of the Revolution! How could he possibly be calm?

And yet sitting opposite the man, he found that his equanimity was almost instantly restored. Possibly the friendly twinkle in Lenin's eye had much to do with this, a characteristic he had previously noted in Theo Rothstein; Theo, of course, was both a comrade and friend to Lenin, who when in London had stayed at Theo's house on Clapton Square. Williams would later write that he found Lenin "simple, genial, and entirely without affectation." Sensing a movement to his right, Williams turned and saw a sculptor working on a bust of the great man. He turned back to Lenin and raised his eyebrows. Lenin grinned and gave a little shrug, as if to say that this was one of the minor inconveniences one must learn to endure when one was considered to be a figure on the world stage. He then jerked his thumb over his shoulder and Williams saw a young man seated at a small desk, beginning to sketch on a pad. He could not have been sketching Lenin, for all he could see was his back. Williams pointed at his own chest and gave Lenin a questioning look, receiving an amused nod in reply. It was now Williams's turn to shrug, a gesture which may have mimicked that of Lenin. They both laughed.

Now Lenin got to his feet and extended his hand over his desk. "You will be relieved to know," he said in passable English as Williams also stood and clasped his hand, "that we will not be using sign language for the rest of our discussion. Welcome, Comrade Williams. I hope that you have found your visit to have been of interest so far."

They began by discussing the situation in Russia, and from his comments and replies Williams was able to satisfy Lenin that he and the rest of the delegation had been provided with an accurate picture of the situation by the officials they had met.

Of the Whites, Lenin was scornful. "They are facing defeat now, and on the brink of falling apart. Yudenich, commander of the White forces in Northwest Russia, attempted to take Petrograd last year but was defeated and chased into Estonia. In the north, Admiral Kolchak, who assumed the title of supreme leader of Russia, and was recognised as such by the Entente, was defeated and was executed four months ago—contrary to our orders, by the way. Kolchak had appointed General Denikin as his successor. Denikin's officers are virulently anti-Semitic." He snorted contemptuously. "They think that our Revolution is some sort of Jewish conspiracy and they have been responsible for the murder of thousands of Jews in their pogroms. Until very late last year, Denikin simply looked the other way. Anyway, he was unable to bear the pressures of the job and he resigned in April and is now in exile. He was succeeded by Baron Wrangel, who had gone into exile due to his differences with Denikin. After Denikin's resignation, Wrangel was brought back as commander of the White forces in the Crimea; he has since formed the so-called government of South Russia, but we are closing in on him and he will be defeated this year."

Lenin uttered a long sigh. "Of course, there was not the slightest possibility of these adventures being undertaken were it not for the promised support of the Allied Powers, Comrade. Likewise, everyone in Russia realises that the Polish offensive was engineered by British and French influence, and supported by British and French direction, training and equipment."

At this point, Lenin's gaze became penetrating. "Talking of which, Comrade Williams, I was very interested to follow the events of last year, when your Triple Alliance was calling for direct action to force your government to end its intervention in Russia and lift the blockade."

"Ah, yes." Williams leaned forward in his chair.

Lenin lifted his hands and shrugged in incomprehension. "I was completely unable to understand the acceptance by the Parliamentary Committee of your TUC the assurances by Churchill and Lloyd George that intervention would cease." He thought for an instant and then shook his head. "No, that is not entirely true. I could *just* understand when the Parliamentary Committee accepted their word, but when the Triple Alliance did so also..." Another shrug, more demonstrative this time.

"There are basically two reasons, Comrade Lenin. First of all, the concept of what is being called *direct action*—by which is meant strike action in pursuit of a political objective—is controversial in our movement."

Lenin chuckled. "Well, it is certainly controversial in the columns of *The Times*."

Williams found himself wishing that Lenin were not quite so well-informed. "Yes, yes, and that is true of the rest of the capitalist press, which on matters of this nature acts as the voice of the ruling class. And if that voice is loud enough, and sufficiently sustained, it will have an effect on certain trade union leaders—those who wish to be considered *respectable*. Their argument is that direct action is unconstitutional because the government against which such action would be directed would have been democratically elected and that, therefore, such political objectives should be pursued via the ballot box. This argument has particular resonance with those members of the Parliamentary Committee who, as well as being trade union leaders, also have seats in the House of Commons."

"You mean men like Thorne and Thomas."

"Exactly!"

"You are presumably aware that after our February Revolution the gasworkers' leader Thorne came to Petrograd to try to convince the workers that Russia should remain in the war."

"Of course, Comrade. Now, the second reason is that some of those men are also members of the Triple Alliance—I refer in particular to J.H. Thomas and Havelock Wilson, president of the seamen's union. Thomas's union, the National Union of Railwaymen, is a member of the Triple Alliance, while Wilson's seamen's union is affiliated to my own Transport Workers' Federation. Wilson, in fact, is a Liberal."

Lenin nodded. "I see. Men such as Thomas, of course, will soon be members of a Labour government."

"So you foresee a Labour government?"

A slight shrug. "It is surely inevitable, either alone or in coalition. The Thomases and the Hendersons, and perhaps the MacDonalds and the Snowdens, will have to be given their opportunity just as Kerensky was given his in this country. But a government under the leadership of such men will do little if anything to benefit the working class."

"Of course not, Comrade."

Lenin leaned forward and clasped his hands. "Tell me, Comrade, how well do you know Bevin?"

"Oh, *very* well: we work together in the Transport Workers'

Federation."

"And what is your estimate of him?"

"With regard to British intervention in Russia and the blockade, he can be depended upon, as he is totally opposed to both of these." Williams grinned. "This, however, does not make him a communist. At the moment, he tolerates those of us who are known to be Marxists, but this may not last."

"Why do you say that, Comrade?"

"Because, as you may know, he is intent upon amalgamating a large number of transport unions into a new organization, of which he will undoubtedly be the general secretary. If the communists become a power to be reckoned with in the new union, he will possibly see them as a challenge to his own position."

"I see. And so how would you characterise his politics?"

Bob Williams spread his hands. "As far as I can see, Ernest Bevin has no strong political beliefs, one way or the other. He is a profoundly *industrial* creature who wants to do the best he possibly can for his members. If he has an ambition, it is to ensure that when he and his team attend meetings with employers, they are treated as equals."

"So he has no political ambitions?"

"Not as such. In fact, he has a profound disliking for professional politicians—particularly those in the Labour Party who come from wealthy or educated backgrounds and think that they can speak on behalf of workers. However, I think it possible that once this new union is formed and Bevin comes to be recognised as a power in the whole movement, there will come a point when the trade union movement alone will not be large enough to contain him."

For the first time, Lenin was jotting a few notes on the pad before him. "That's very interesting, Comrade, *very* interesting." He looked up. "But tell me: once this new transport union is formed, will it not make your federation redundant?"

Williams found this subject both difficult and painful. He sighed. "To be honest, I don't know, Comrade. It's possible, although there will still be a number of transport unions outside of the new amalgamation..."

"But there is a possibility that you will be without employment?"

"I suppose that is possible, although this year I have been elected as president of the International Transport Workers' Federation..."

"I'm sorry; I meant *paid* employment, Comrade."

"Ah, well, if the worst comes to the worst, I'm sure something will turn up."

Lenin grinned. "Of course. And if your communist party grows at the same rate as ours, there would obviously be the possibility of becoming a professional revolutionary."

Williams chuckled. "Yes, that is a possibility I had not considered."

"I understand, by the way, that before you return to Britain you will be meeting representatives of the Italian trade unions and our All-Russian Trade Union Executive."

"Yes, that's right. Comrade Purcell will also be attending the meeting. The intention, I believe, is that we address an appeal to the left of the trade unions for the formation of a more progressive international federation." The previous year, the International Federation of Trade Unions, originally founded in 1913 but then falling victim to the war, had been relaunched. After the first president, G.A. Appleton, resigned when his General Federation of Trade Unions was effectively barred, he had been succeeded by none other than J.H. Thomas.

"The IFTU appears to be a purely European organization," commented Lenin.

"Yes, when the organization declared in favour of the socialization of the means of production—purely as a means of stealing the thunder of the communists, of course—Samuel Gompers decided that the American Federation of Labour would not, after all, be an affiliate."

They both laughed.

Williams glanced at the clock on the wall behind Lenin and saw that the meeting had lasted almost ninety minutes. "Comrade Lenin, I am deeply honoured to have met you, but feel that I must leave you to your work. Before I go, however, there is just one question I would like to ask."

Lenin extended his open palm. "By all means: go ahead, Comrade."

"During these past few weeks, the eyes of our delegation have been opened to many things, chief of which is Russia's desperate need for peace and the resumption of international trade. In view of this, should we, upon our return, throw our energies into working for peace and the opening of trade relations, or should we propagate the ideas of the Third International, working for the overthrow of capitalism in Western Europe—even though this might for a time prevent Russia from obtaining the things it requires?"

Lenin greeted this with a characteristic grin. "Comrade, I am not so foolish as to think that this brief visit will have won all the members of your delegation to the concept of the dictatorship of the proletariat..."

This forced Williams to recognize that he had been speaking as if on behalf of the whole delegation. He swallowed.

"And so I would say this: Let those who believe in peace work for peace, and let those who believe in communism and the dictatorship of the proletariat work for the overthrow of capitalism." He held up a finger. "On the question of peace, however, in my view the capitalists of Western Europe and the USA will not and cannot make *real* peace with us for the simple reason that this great experiment we are undertaking will offer such an example to the workers of the whole world that it will be more powerful than anything our propaganda department might devise."

Williams bowed his head. "Thank you, Comrade Lenin. For those wise words." He began to get to his feet.

Lenin held up a restraining hand. "A few more moments if you please, Comrade Williams. There is something that has been puzzling me."

Oh no, he knows about Vikha, Williams thought in a completely irrational moment. "Of course, Comrade. How can I help you?"

"I understand, Comrade, that earlier this year you were elected as a delegate to the conference of the Second International which is to take place in Geneva in July." Lenin held up his hands. "Help me, Comrade, I am confused. You are a man who has used the term *dictatorship of the proletariat* for some years. In fact, according to the report of the Leeds Convention of June 1917 you used it there, even before our October Revolution. Our Third International, the Comintern, was founded in Moscow last year; its second congress will be held later this year. And yet here you are, accepting election to the conference of the social-democratic Second International." He shook his head. "I truly do not understand, comrade. So perhaps you can help me."

Perspiration had broken out on William's forehead. This was a tricky one, for to be honest he himself had no clear idea why he had agreed to be a delegate. Nevertheless, he thought he could provide an explanation. He cleared his throat.

"First of all, Comrade, let me say that I now have no intention of attending the Geneva Conference, as I consider the Second International to be worse than useless!"

Lenin grinned. "So far, so good, but why did you accept election as a delegate?"

"As you will be aware, Comrade, our party, the British Socialist Party, affiliated to the Labour Party in 1916..."

Lenin nodded vigorously. "Yes, Comrade, an absolutely correct decision!"

"And the Labour Party is affiliated to the Second International—or was, before it collapsed with the outbreak of war. It is therefore committed to the relaunch or refounding of a socialist international, and it was in these circumstances that I was elected in January. As we have yet to form a communist party in our country—something which will, we hope, be achieved this year—there is no British organization which meets the qualifications for affiliation to the Comintern..."

"Ah!" Lenin slapped his brow with the palm of his right hand, a gesture which drew an irritated tutting from the sculptor, who was still beavering away on his bust. Lenin turned to frown at him before returning his attention to Williams. "Are you saying, Comrade, that you do not understand the distinction between affiliation to the Comintern and the attendance of delegates to our congress? We are in a transitional phase, Comrade, as many countries have yet to form communist parties, and so in this period we allow delegates from countries where there is the firm intention to form one." He slapped his brow once more. "Why, this year we will have delegates from your own party, the BSP! And also from Britain there will be delegates from the shop stewards' movement and the International Workers of the World!" He subsided into silence and studied Williams with a frown. "But surely you know this, Comrade," he said quietly.

"I know it now, Comrade, but I did not know it when I was elected as a delegate to Geneva."

"I see, Comrade." He raised a finger. "Such misunderstandings will be avoided in future, of course, once your own communist party has been founded."

"And I can assure you, Comrade Lenin, that I will be working to that end as soon as my shoes touch British soil." He stood. "Thank you again for your time."

Lenin nodded and stood, extending his hand. "Goodbye, Comrade. I hope the remainder of your stay will be fruitful."

As Williams—with his guide Lev, who had been called upon to perform little translation during the meeting—made his way to the door, Lenin remained standing, a thoughtful frown on his face as he watched his guest depart. As Williams disappeared from view, he closed his eyes for a second, shook his head, and resumed his seat.

*

When, some days later, having visited twenty towns and cities and their environs, the delegation departed for England, Bob Williams was still asking himself why he had initially agreed to be a delegate to the conference of the Second International, and he hoped that Lenin's mind was not still similarly exercised.

17

Some industrial activists, Mickey Rice had noticed, were quite abstemious, and Harry Pollitt turned out to be one of these. They—Theo Rothstein, Mickey, Annette, Bob Williams and Pollitt having accepted George Sanders' invitation to go for a drink after a meeting of the Hands Off Russia movement—were in the Crown and Anchor on Clerkenwell Green, grouped around two tables which had been pushed together, and while the others had ordered pints—except Annette who, red wine being unavailable, had asked for a lime cordial and soda—Pollitt made do with a half, which he sipped sparingly. Encouraged by Rothstein, he was recalling his recent experiences in the docks.

"To begin with, I thought May was going to be a very disappointing month," he began. "There was a Danish steamer called the *Neptune* that we knew would be bound for Poland, but try as we might, we couldn't persuade the seamen to strike from the East India Docks." He shrugged. "Well, she sailed and I, along with my comrades, went off to Hyde Park for the May Day celebrations, trying to put this failure behind us. Later, though, we learned that just as the *Neptune* reached Gravesend two firemen came up on deck and called a meeting, explaining to the deckies that the ship was carrying munitions to Poland. The captain put in an appearance, fuming with anger, telling them to carry on with their work. And just then— BANG! The *Neptune* was rammed by another ship—a complete accident, I'm sure—and that was the end of that." He brought his hands together exultantly, and the others, even those who had heard the story before, laughed.

"And then," prompted Rothstein, "came the *Jolly George*."

"Yes," responded Pollitt, "just a few days later..." He paused abruptly, looking around the table. "And would you believe it! The cargo was on the dock clearly labelled 'OHMS...'" Seeing Annette frown, he spelled it out. "'On His Majesty's Service. Munitions for Poland.' Quite blatant! Well, regardless of this, the cargo was actually loaded, but then the dockers sent deputations to Fred Thompson, their London secretary, and Ernie Bevin, assistant secretary of the Dockers' Union, who both pledged to stand by them, whatever action they chose to take."

"Bevin said that?" asked Mickey.

Pollitt nodded firmly. "He did!"

Mickey exchanged glances with George Sanders, as if to indicate that life might not be intolerable if, after the next amalgamation, they found that Bevin was their general secretary. Sanders, however, was non-committal.

"I think I might have told you lads before," said a grinning Bob Williams, who sat on the Transport Workers' Federation committee with Bevin, "that Ernie is a complex man."

"The upshot of all this," said Pollitt, continuing his tale, "was that on 10 May the dockers went on strike and the munitions ended up back on the dock."

Theo Rothstein hit the edge of the table with the fingers of his right hand. "And you know the most encouraging aspect of this story from my point of view, comrades? It is the stance adopted by Ernest Bevin. He is rapidly gaining a reputation within the official working-class movement, and if we are to avoid the commitment of British troops to fight against our revolution, using this war with Poland as an excuse, we will need people like him to stop the government in its tracks."

"What do you think, Mickey?" asked George Sanders. Then he frowned. "Are you okay, Mickey?"

From where Mickey sat, with his back to the window, he had a full view of the interior to the bar, and for some minutes his attention had been drawn to two men seated a few tables away. They were young, one around thirty and the other maybe thirty-five, and not particularly well-dressed; they did not seem to have much to say to each other and their drinks were untouched.

"Yes, George," said Mickey, appearing to emerge from a trance, "I think Ernie Bevin will probably be alright on this issue." He leaned forward and lowered his voice. "But I'd ask you to take a look at the two blokes sitting two tables away from us and tell me what you think. Don't make it obvious; continue the discussion as if I've said nothing."

"Well," said Bob Williams, taking up this advice, "the test will come on 13 July, when the TUC holds its Special Congress at Westminster Hall."

Theo held up a finger. "Bob, it would be remiss of me not to mention that the interim report issued by the Labour-TUC delegation to Russia has surely paved the way for a positive outcome at the Congress. And you were a signatory to that report, Bob." He glanced around the table. "Have you had a chance to read it, comrades? Oh, it is very strong; I don't think we could have wished for more. It recommends—and I think I can recite this accurately because I have only recently transmitted it to Moscow—that 'the entire British labour movement should demand the removal of the last vestige of blockade and intervention, and the complete destruction of the barrier which imperialist statesmen have erected between our own people and our brothers and sisters of Russia.'" He spread his hands. "On behalf of the Soviet government, Bob, please convey my deep and sincere gratitude to your fellow-delegates."

Bob Williams mimed applause. "Bravo, Theo: that is some memory you have. And yes, I will pass your message to the rest of the delegation."

"And how was your meeting with Lenin, Comrade?" asked Rothstein.

Mickey gasped. "You met Lenin, Bob?"

Williams nodded, and to Rothstein: "It was very fine, Theo. You've obviously heard from him recently."

Rothstein grinned and shrugged.

"Well, come on, Bob," urged Pollitt. "Don't keep it to yourself! What did you talk about?"

Williams sighed. "We talked of many things, Harry, but this is probably not the occasion for a detailed report-back. It's probably worth mentioning, though, that he reckons we'll have a Labour government before too long—not that it will be of much use for our class.

"I asked Lenin whether we should concentrate on working for peace or the overthrow of capitalism. His reply was quite straightforward: 'Let those who believe in peace work for peace,' he said, 'and let those who believe in communism and the dictatorship of the proletariat work for the overthrow of capitalism.'"

"As you say, Comrade," said Rothstein, "now is probably not the time for a full report-back, but I hope that we will not have to wait too long."

"I can probably do better than that, Theo: I'm writing a series of articles."

"Oh, really? Who for, Bob?" asked Pollitt.

"Believe it or not, the *Daily Mail*."

"Wha-a-a-t?" This was Mickey Rice.

Williams grinned. "Oh, I've told them what to expect, but they've said I should go ahead." He shrugged. "Anyway, if they back out I'll pull the articles together into a pamphlet."

Pollitt chuckled. "Well, best of luck with that, Bob."

Williams cleared his throat. "Listen, comrades, what I *would* like to talk about is the *effect* that my meeting with Lenin—and, in fact the whole visit—has had on my thinking.

"Some of us—certainly Purcell and I—have returned from Russia determined to offer all possible encouragement to attempts to form a communist party based on the conception of proletarian or working-class dictatorship. We have to make it clear to workers— especially manual workers—that they can have no hope of improving their lot until capitalism is smashed—and that the dictatorship of the proletariat can only come by the assumption of control of the mines, factories, workshops, railways and means of production and transport generally."

He looked around at the others and saw that, despite the fact that he was beginning to sound as if he were on a rostrum, he had their attention. "And I reckon, you know, that there is no reason why— within a year!—the membership of this party we're going to form should not be as great as that of the Russian communist party: 650,000 members. But that will require great discipline. During the coming months we must ourselves give and expect from others as much solidarity and loyalty to the decisions and programme of the communist party as we expect trade unionists to give to their fellows in an industrial dispute."

Another pause, followed by a deep breath. Bob Williams gave the impression of a man who had been working on a speech in his mind and was now impatient to deliver it. "Our movement in Britain has been—*and is!*—chaotic! Why? Because of our intense individualism, and because we possess many *forms* of liberty without the *content* of liberty. The imminent breakdown of the capitalist system makes it imperative that we should subordinate our individualisms, our own personal conceptions regarding tactics, and our own futile sectionalisms in order to consolidate all the forces of the left."

There was a silence around the table. Theo Rothstein chewed his bottom lip thoughtfully, peering at Williams over the top of his glasses. Pollitt sat with his eyes downcast, giving his head a barely perceptible shake. Sanders, eyes narrowed, seemed to be giving Williams' outburst serious consideration, frowning here, nodding there, and Mickey Rice knew that this was because he was, just as Bob Williams had now revealed himself to be, a romantic. Finally, it was Theo who spoke.

"Comrade, you surely cannot believe that the new party will have such a huge membership in the space of a single year." He spoke softly, but everybody heard him.

"Only if we all work as hard and as correctly as we should. I've seen the results that hard work and discipline can produce in Russia, comrades, a country where the working class was barely organized before the Revolution. We, on the other hand, are not starting from scratch..."

"With the greatest respect, Bob," said Mickey Rice, "you're full of enthusiasm because of what you've seen in Russia, but you're losing sight of British realities. British workers haven't had the opportunity to see Russia, and while you're right when you say that we're not starting from scratch, the level of organisation in our labour movement might be high, but its consciousness is trade union, not revolutionary consciousness."

As Bob Williams lifted his head to reply, Harry Pollitt came in. "Comrades, I really think that this is neither the time nor the place to have this discussion,"—he shrugged his eyebrows to indicate the two men at the nearby table—"particularly in view of the company we're in."

"Yes," Mickey asked quietly, welcoming this change of subject, "have you had a chance to take a good look at those two fellows, George?"

"I have. Mickey, and apart from the possibility that they're attempting to eavesdrop on us, I can't see anything unusual."

"Then let's see if I can help you out." Mickey looked around at the others, making sure he had their attention, before quietly continuing. "Do you see what they're drinking? Halves of bitter. Except, of course, they're not actually drinking. Why not? Because they're on duty and want to keep clear heads. Why are they not speaking to each other? Because they're trying to listen to us: you're right, George, they're eavesdropping. Do they look at all familiar to you? No? Well, they should do because they were at the meeting. Is it a coincidence that they wind up in the same pub as us? Hardly, because it's not as if we've strolled a few yards from the meeting: we took public transport from Covent Garden because we—some of us—are regulars at the Crown and Anchor. So they followed us here."

"Mickey," said Theo, placing a hand on the bus driver's shoulder, "I remember that occasion when you acted as security when George and I met at the Lyons Corner House on Rupert Street. I said then that you were suited to this kind of activity, and I say it again now. Well done, comrade." He wrinkled his nose. "However, the results of your keen observation tell me that I should now depart. If the Special Branch men attempt to follow me, perhaps you would be so good as to intervene on my behalf." He got to his feet and nodded at those around the two tables. "Comrades and friends, I wish you a very good night."

And he was gone. Mickey tensed, ready to spring to his feet if the two men made to follow, but they remained seated and for a moment he wondered whether his imagination was over-active, but then Bob Williams came in with: "You're right, Mickey. I remember seeing them at the meeting. They sat apart, at the back, trying to make themselves inconspicuous. At the time, I wondered who they were, because despite the fact that they've obviously made an attempt to look the part—jackets and trousers that have seen better days—I don't recall having seen them before."

"An amateurish attempt at disguise, then," said Harry Pollitt. "If they'd studied our movement they would know that working men tend to smarten themselves up when they attend meetings; it's only middle-class types who dress down, so to speak."

"And coppers," said George Sanders.

"Yes," agreed Pollitt with a laugh, "and coppers."

"But why are they so interested in Theo at this time?" asked a frowning Bob Williams.

"There have been a number of attempts to deport him," Mickey explained.

"But surely he's a British citizen."

Mickey shook his head. "No, he made the application some years ago but was turned down. He'd just written his book about the British record in Egypt, and someone sent a copy to Asquith, who was Prime Minister at the time."

Mickey knew more than he was letting on: for some time Lloyd George had found that Theo, although unrecognised as Soviet ambassador, was useful as a channel to Lenin and the Soviet government, but there were those in the Home Office who despite this—or possibly because of it—wanted him deported. An attempt in 1919 had almost succeeded, but Mickey was able, by prior agreement between the parties involved, to have Sir Albert Stanley, until recently president of the Board of Trade, get a message to Lloyd George, who ordered his release from the ship in the Pool of London which was to have been used for his deportation.

"But why now, just when negotiations for a trade treaty are underway?" persisted Bob Williams.

Mickey sighed and, with a glance across the room to check that the Special Branch men were still present, leaned forward and spoke in a hushed tone. "Maybe they've got wind of the fact that Theo has been playing an important part in the preparations for the formation of a united party."

"Mm, maybe," murmured Bob Williams, and then, with a subtle

nod in the direction of the Special Branch team: "So let's change the subject."

"Comrades." It was Annette, making her first contribution to the discussion and gaining immediate attention with her soft voice. "Comrades, how confident are you that the leaders of the official movement will take a progressive stand at the special congress? A week or so ago I saw in the paper that one of the biggest unions..."

"The railwaymen!" exclaimed Pollitt.

"Yes, the NUR. Its executive announced an embargo on the transport of munitions for Poland, and then some days later it lifted the embargo because so few members were observing it." Her frown swept the others, from right to left. "This, I think, is a strange way to conduct international solidarity."

A round of laughter followed.

"Yes, Annette," said Bob Williams, "you're absolutely right. It is indeed strange—but not at all unusual if your name is Jimmy Thomas! In most other unions, with the Polish forces having occupied Kiev as early as 7 May, the leadership would have immediately launched a campaign amongst the membership to ensure that the embargo held. But Jimmy Thomas is a traitor to both his class and his nationality."

"His nationality?" Annette was confused by this apparently inappropriate reference.

"Jimmy Thomas, the NUR general secretary," explained Mickey, "is Welsh, and so is Bob."

"He seems to have his hands full on the wages front at the moment," commented Harry Pollitt.

"Yeah, it looks as if he's come a cropper with the latest demand for an extra pound a week," said Sanders.

Williams nodded. "Looks like it. But at least the rank and file are organising. They've formed vigilance committees in South Wales, Manchester, Carlisle and Liverpool; and here they have what they call a London Council. They've been working to rule in all those places, mainly with the aim of abolishing the sliding scale."

"Sliding scale? What is that?" asked Annette.

"Their wages gain or lose a shilling a week for every five-point change in the cost-of-living index," explained Mickey.

"And do they ever gain a shilling?"

"They actually gained a shilling recently, sweetheart. But that'll be the last time that happens." Mickey grimaced. "Despite working to rule, the rank and file haven't succeeded in getting rid of it."

"True enough," responded Pollitt, "but at least they're on the move."

"Yeah, you'd have to say that's encouraging," said Mickey, "but the companies and the government are sticking to the sliding scale, and the wage-rises they've just won, from what I understand, vary according to location. Is that right, Bob?"

"It is: one increase for London and the industrial areas and a lower one for the rural areas."

"God help us!" exclaimed Harry Pollitt. "That'll drive a coach and horses through their national unity. They'll never accept that, will they?"

"If the members were balloted," said Bob Williams, "no, they probably wouldn't. But this is the NUR, Harry, and Jimmy Thomas has said that the decision will be made at their annual conference in Belfast on 6 July. A pound to a pinch of snuff he'll talk 'em into it."

"Who's next?' asked Mickey. "The miners?"

Williams nodded. "They say they'll set a day aside at their annual conference—that's also in July—for a discussion of their wage claim."

Mickey sniffed. "How much is left in the whip? We got enough for another?" When they had arrived, each had contributed half a crown to the pot—or, rather, to Sanders' bowler hat, which sat on an empty chair, out of harm's way. Sanders reached for it and gave it a shake. "I would say, Mickey, that we have sufficient. Whose turn to order?"

Mickey stood up. "Mine. Same again all round?" He took the bowler from Sanders and made his way to the bar. "Same again, Wally."

To begin with, in the war years, he and the large landlord had not got on particularly well, as Wally had sometimes tried to enforce the government's nonsensical "no treating" rule and had even, on one occasion, made a half-hearted attempt to censor their discussion; but more recently they had grown closer and for some time had been on first-name terms.

"In which case, Mick, that goes for the damage as well."

"Oh, less one pint of bitter, because one of us has left."

Mickey took a handful of coins from the hat and counted out "the damage" on the bar before handing the bowler back to Sanders.

As Wally placed the first two pints on the bar, Mickey leaned close. "See you've got a couple of new customers tonight, mate."

Wally gave him a sly wink before walking back to the pumps to pull the next two pints. As he returned and put the pints down, he whispered. "Rozzers, Mick, rozzers."

"Yeah, that's what we thought, Wally. You seen 'em before?"

"What were the last two, sir?" Wally asked loudly. Then, lowering his voice, "No, mate, this is their first time here."

"Half a bitter, and a lime cordial and soda for the lady," replied Mickey, followed by a whispered "And probably their last."

"Mind you, Mick," Wally whispered as he brought him the last two drinks, "they've taken a bit of care to look the part. You seen what they're reading?"

Mickey glanced briefly to the table in question and saw there, folded in half on the table, a copy of *The Call*, the British Socialist Party newspaper. He looked up at the landlord and, as if thanking him for his service, winked. "Thanks, mate."

Seated once more, Mickey took a long draw from his pint, set it down and looked around at his companions. "Well, comrades, what do you think these two"—he gestured with his chin at the Special Branch men—"are up to."

"Earlier," said Sanders, "I said I thought they were eavesdropping, and maybe they are, but I suspect that they intend to tail one or more of us when we leave."

"And how do you suggest we handle that?" Mickey looked around the tables again. "Anyone?"

"I would suggest," said Bob Williams, "that we leave separately. That way, we'll get an idea of who they're following."

"Bob," said Mickey, "can you see that newspaper on their table?"

Williams gave it a swift glance. "Yep."

"Can you tell what it is?'

The Welshman looked again, eyes narrowed. "No, it's too far away, and it's folded in two."

Mickey was grinning broadly. "Okay. Well, comrades, I think there's a way to ensure that they leave before us." He got to his feet. "Watch this."

"No!" Annette held out a hand, seeking to restrain him.

"Relax, sweetheart, I'm just going to the Gents."

To reach the toilets on the other side of the bar, Mickey had to walk past the Special Branch men, and he did so without sparing them a glance. His companions watched him go, seriously concerned about what he might be planning; when the expected confrontation failed to take place, there were both exhalations of relief and frowns of incomprehension. When they heard the toilet door slam shut, they relaxed for a while. The tension returned a few minutes later when the heel of Mickey's hand hit the door and he reappeared, expressionless, and began the return journey. Then, reaching the Special Branch table, he suddenly halted, apparently spellbound by something he saw there.

"Whoah!" Mickey looked from the newspaper folded on the table to the two men seated at it, one slim with a ragged ginger moustache, the other on the plump side and clean-shaven. "You read *The Call!*"

Ginger Moustache, clearly caught off-guard, attempted to replace the look of alarm on his face with a smile as he nodded; Mr Plump, on the other hand, looked—glared—not at Mickey but at his colleague, and Mickey had a fairly good idea what he was thinking: *Didn't I tell you not to bring that fucking newspaper!*

One finger pointing at the two men, Mickey turned to call across to his companions: "A couple of comrades!" He turned back to the men, beaming goodwill. "Why don't you come across and join us? It's a bit late now, 'cause we're just having one for the road, but at least we can introduce ourselves. What do you say?"

Mr Plump, who was probably the sergeant to the other's constable, fished out his pocket watch and frowned down at it. "Oh that's very kind of you, brother, but we have to dash. Next time, maybe." He turned to Ginger Moustache. "Come on, Jack, drink up or we'll be late." He turned back to Mickey and winked. "Don't do to keep 'em waiting, does it?" The two men drained their half-pint glasses and stood.

"Oh, that's a pity," said Mickey. "So yeah, maybe next time."

Ginger, almost recovered from the shock, brought a finger to his temple. "Right you are then!"

"Here!" Mickey called after them as they made for the door. "You've left your paper."

Ginger, a little flushed, returned to the table and stuffed the newspaper in his jacket pocket.

Mickey stood at the table until the doors swung closed and then turned to the landlord to give him a thumbs-up. The occupants of his own table were laughing and applauding.

"Well done, Mickey!" cried Harry Pollitt, clapping him on the shoulder as he resumed his seat. "That certainly got rid of them!" He looked across at Bob Williams. "I'd say it's safe now to resume that discussion we were having, Bob."

"About the Russian trip?"

"Yes, and the effect it's had on you. You were giving the impression, Bob, that you thought that our own revolution might be just around the corner. You were talking about how we must conduct ourselves in the coming months and the imminent collapse of capitalism." Pollitt cocked his head to one side. "Was that Lenin's prediction?"

"Not in so many words, Harry, but he certainly expects great things of our party."

"When it's formed," said a dubious Mickey.

"Yes, when it's formed, but he knows that will be soon. He's in regular communication with Theo, after all." Williams glanced up at the wall-clock. "Comrades, I'm afraid I have to make a move."

As Williams made his exit, Harry Pollitt and Mickey Rice, equally baffled by his startling view of the future, exchanged glances. George Sanders picked up his bowler, tipped the few remaining coins onto the table and placed it on his head. "Comrades, *adieu*," he said, with a smile to Annette.

18

Annette flipped over the pages of Engels' *Anti-Dühring* and saw that the third chapter, titled "Classification. Apriorism," was only eight or nine pages long. Should she persevere, or lay the book down for another time? Although she found Engels a more comfortable read than Marx, her command of English—she was reading the 1907 English edition—was not yet sufficient to allow her to read him with ease. She glanced at the clock. 7.45. Mickey would be home in forty-five minutes. Comfortably seated on the sofa in the living room of the Alexander Street flat, two cushions at her back, she thought she might try to read that third chapter before she heard Mickey's key in the lock of the front door, followed by his determined tread on the stairs. She looked around the comfortable room, unchanged since Mickey had lived here with Dorothy Bridgeman, the love he had lost to a German air-raid three years ago. Shortly after they had been married, he had asked Annette if there was anything she wanted to change.

"Why? Don't you like it as it is, Mickey?"

"I do, but I thought that you might want to stamp it with your personality, so to speak."

"So that it does not remind you of Dorothy?"

"In fact, the flat looks almost the same as when we moved in six years ago; the only additions we made were the bookcase and the record player—and even the record player was a gift."

"So Dorothy did not...stamp it with her personality?"

"Not really, and neither did I."

"Well, I think it is perfectly lovely, so let it remain as it is. Besides, if we..."

"If we're going to have children we'll need to move anyway."

"Exactly, my love."

It was now 7.53, and so she bent to the task she had set herself. "Philosophy, according to Herr Dühring," she read, "is the development of the highest form of consciousness of the world and of life, and in a wider sense embraces the *principles* of all knowledge and volition."

But it was too much for her—or maybe she was seated too comfortably—and halfway down the second page of the chapter her eyelids fluttered closed.

*

She came awake with a jolt and immediately looked across the room at the clock. 9.27. He must have crept in so as not to awaken her. She closed the book which was still open on her lap, placed it by her side and swung her legs off the sofa. She visited first the bedroom, then the bathroom. No Mickey. Should she worry? Yes, she should, because while it was entirely possible that he had finished late, it was almost unknown for him to be a whole hour late. Was there a meeting he had not told her about? Dick would know, and if he didn't, he had a telephone, another legacy from his prosperous mother.

Dick stood at the door, scratching his scraggly beard. "I was scheduled to finish before him, Annette, so I didn't see him. No, I don't know of any meeting that he might be attending; when we're both free, we usually go together. But come in and I'll telephone the garage."

"Hello, Annette. Mickey gone missing?" Gladys came from the bedroom wearing a dressing gown.

"I hope not missing, Gladys. And please forgive me if I have disturbed you."

"No, you didn't, love. I was just about to lie down when you knocked." She smiled compassionately. "I shouldn't worry if I were you; he's probably gone for a drink with pals."

Dick, about to dial the number of the garage, looked up. "He doesn't usually, though."

Gladys, arms crossed, gave him a withering look. "No, unlike some people I know."

"Hello? Is that Mr Butcher?" Dick had got through to the garage. "Driver Mortlake here, Mr Butcher. Could you tell me if Mickey Rice finished on time? Only he hasn't arrived home and his wife is a little concerned...I see...Yes, alright...Maybe, although that's not like him...Okay. Goodnight."

Dick turned to Annette. "The garage official says his conductor paid in on time, but he didn't see Mickey because he had no reason to go into the output office, so he doesn't know whether he left the garage alone or with friends." He made a face. "That doesn't help us very much, does it?"

Annette was biting her lip, on the verge of tears. "But thank you anyway, Dick. I am sorry to have troubled you."

"Wait, wait, wait. Why not wait for him here, Annette, rather than sitting upstairs alone, worrying yourself to death. We'll sit with you." He took out his pocket watch. "The pubs will be closing in the next few minutes, so we might not have long to wait."

*

"Now, Mr Rice," said Mr Plump, "perhaps you could give us the names of the people you were with in the Crown and Anchor, Clerkenwell Green the other night."

They had nabbed him as he had been walking home. They were clever, waiting until, at the corner of Westbourne Park Road and Great Western Road, there was hardly anyone about, then pulling up next to him. Ginger Moustache had got out of the unmarked car, blocking Mickey's way and pointing to the open car door. Mickey had regarded him for a moment or two, calculating his chances. He could have flattened Ginger and run off, but then what? They obviously knew where he worked and where he lived. So he'd nodded to Ginger, saying "Good evening, Comrade" as he backed onto the rear seat of the car. It had been a short journey: up Great Western Road, a right turn onto Harrow Road, then into the car park at Harrow Road police station. He assumed that Special Branch officers could make use of any police station with a spare cell or interview room.

They were in the interview room now, the two Special Branch men dressed rather more smartly than previously, and Mr Plump was speaking as if he were giving evidence in court; thus, although they all knew the location of the Crown and Anchor pub in question, it had to be "the Crown and Anchor, Clerkenwell Green." He was also playing the usual cop interview game, asking for the identities of all who had been drinking with Mickey although he was really only interested in one of them—and the identity of that person was obviously already known to him.

"Why are you wasting my time?" Mickey asked. "If you're Special Branch, you already know the identity of the people I was with. And if you don't, then Special Branch is not all it's cracked up to be. So out with it: what do you want to know?"

While Mr Plump sat on the other side of the table from Mickey, Ginger Moustache lurked threateningly behind him, leaning against the white brick wall. "Are you offering us information, Mr Rice?" This from Ginger.

"Don't be silly, Comrade."

"Don't call me Comrade."

"If you don't like it, you should stop trying to fool innocent socialists like me into thinking that you *are* a comrade by walking around with a copy of *The Call* in your pocket."

Mr Plump actually laughed. "My thoughts entirely, Mr Rice." But the laughter was short-lived and he suddenly became serious, placing his forearms on the table between them and leaning forward, his eyes hardening. "Alright, let's do it your way: what were you all discussing with Mr Rothstein in the Crown and Anchor?"

Mickey grinned. "You were close enough to overhear, so why don't *you* tell *me*? Or was I right when I suggested that Special Branch is not all it's cracked up to be?"

Mr Plump sighed. "You're obviously aware, Mr Rice, that we are not based at this station. However, I am advised that there is a vacant cell and unless you become a little more cooperative you will find yourself spending some time in it."

"That's entirely up to you," Mickey replied calmly. "But if that turns out to be the case, you should make sure that the car you used tonight will be available to you for the next few days, because you'll be unable to travel anywhere by bus."

Mr Plump frowned. "Not with you, Mr Rice."

"Oh, I think you are. For years, your people avoided banging up George Sanders under the Defence of the Realm Act because you knew that London would be brought to a halt if you did that. Now, I'm not as well-known or popular as George Sanders, but I am *fairly* well-known." He took out his pocket watch and flipped it open. "I was due home thirty or forty minutes ago. By now, my people will be wondering what's happened to me." He shrugged. "They may think I've stopped off for a drink with a friend or two, even though that's something I rarely do. Come ten o'clock, they'll know that there must be another explanation, because the pubs will be closed." He looked at Mr Plump and held his gaze. "Now what conclusion do you think they'll reach? Earlier in the week, I expose two Special Branch men in a pub known to be frequented by trade unionists and socialists, and a few days later I leave the garage at the end of my duty but never reach home." He frowned theatrically. "Anyone who didn't conclude that this was the work of your organisation would surely be lacking in intelligence." He had thought of saying that such people would be as bright as Special Branch was turning out to be, but wisely decided against it.

"In which case," declared Mr Plump, "we had better get a move on, hadn't we?"

Mickey now estimated that they had known all along, for the very reason Mickey had stated, that they could not hold him for long.

"Was the formation of a communist party discussed with Mr Rothstein at the Crown and Anchor?"

"It was not. But you know that."

"Have you ever heard Mr Rothstein discussing the formation of a communist party?"

"Yes."

Mr Plump, eyebrows raised in surprise, directed a glance at Ginger, who presumably shared his astonishment.

"Go on."

"I once heard him explain the circumstances in which the Bolsheviks split from the Mensheviks."

Mickey sensed Ginger Moustache push himself off the wall and lurch towards him, but Plump held up a restraining hand.

"Dammit, Rice, you know what I mean!" Plump shouted. He then took three deep breaths to calm himself, closing his eyes for a couple of seconds. "Are you aware, Mr Rice," he asked eventually, "that Mr Rothstein provides funds for British socialists to assist them in their plans to form a communist party?"

Mickey held his gaze. "I know nothing about that." This was literally true, although Mickey had long assumed that this was the case.

"Are you aware that he receives these funds from Russia?"

"No." Again, this was the literal truth.

"But surely he has made some of these funds available to you, Mr Rice."

Mickey laughed. "And why would he do that?"

"To support your militant trade union activity and your political activity, of course. Or maybe to reward you for it."

Mickey laughed again and looked at him quizzically. "Have you been reading the *Daily Mail*?"

Mr Plump spread his hands, indicating that in his view the case was beyond doubt. "Come, come, Mr Rice. You, a bus driver, live in a luxurious house in Bayswater."

"I live in a *flat* in a house in Bayswater."

"A very luxurious flat, I think, Mr Rice. And this on a bus driver's wage."

Mickey felt his anger building. "I have lived in that flat since 1914. The house belongs to a friend and fellow busman, who inherited it from his mother. Since 1914, he has charged me only a nominal rent. And nowadays a bus driver's wage is quite adequate—thanks to what you call the *militant trade union activity* of people like me. It seems the *Daily Mail* is lacking in its industrial coverage."

Mr Plump leaned back in his chair, his narrowed eyes regarding Mickey in silence for a while. "What would your trade union and socialist friends think if we let it be known that the answers you have given so far were in the positive rather than the negative? What if we let the world know that you had told us that Rothstein, a foreign national, has been fully involved in the preparations for the formation of a communist party here, and that he has been providing Russian money to this end?"

"I would like to think that they would believe me rather than you." So is this their game? Mickey asked himself.

Mr Plump grinned. "But there are two of us"—a stubby finger waved between himself and Ginger—"and only one of you." He shrugged. "Two against one."

"Then their disbelief would be doubled."

There was a thin cardboard folder on the corner of the table nearest Plump, and Mickey had been wondering what it might contain and how it might be used. Plump now drew it to him but did not open it.

Again, there was that calculating look from Plump, indicating that he might now ask the most important question of all. "Would you say that Mr Rothstein is an honest man, Mr Rice?"

"I would, yes."

The eyes hardened once more and Plump leaned forward, forearms on the table. "Then how would you explain the fact that this honest friend of yours is using some of the money he receives from Russia to feather his own nest?"

"Now you're being silly."

Mr Plump smiled. "Oh really? Then how would you explain this, Mr Rice?" He flipped open the cardboard file and pulled out a small document which, rather than pushing it across to Mickey, he held up, gripping each side with a thumb and forefinger.

It was the cheque for £500, made out to cash and signed by M.J. Rice, that he had handed to Theo Rothstein late the previous year. Plump would presumably ask him how such a large sum of money had found its way into his account in the first place, and this was one question he did not want to answer. Lady Ines Bridgeman, the mother of his late lover Dorothy, had told Mickey that the contents of Dorothy's bank account should go to him, because if they had been married—which at some stage they presumably would have been—the money would legally have been his anyway. More lately, Mickey had come to suspect that in reality the money, although it had indeed come from Dorothy's account, was payment for carnal services he had rendered to Ines. But that was beside the point.

"What is this, Mr Rice?" persisted Mr Plump, waving the cheque in the air as if the ink were still wet.

"That," replied Mickey, summoning a stern expression, "is a stolen cheque."

"It's pretty easy to see what happened: Rothstein receives money from Russia and gives you your allowance..."

"Who stole it—you or one of your agents?"

"Then you write him this cheque to disguise the fact that he's skimming off the top."

"Was it Billy Watson, or one of his mates?"

Mr Plump's face suddenly lost its colour, and Mickey knew that he had him.

"Where did it happen? Did someone put their hand into Theo Rothstein's briefcase during a meeting of the Hands Off Russia Committee? Is that how it happened?"

Plump waved the cheque again. "This is proof..."

"It's proof of nothing and you know it!"

"Why did you give this cheque to Rothstein?"

"Who says that I gave it to Rothstein? It's made out to cash, man!"

"You said yourself, Rice, that the cheque was taken from Rothstein's briefcase." Realising what he had just said, Mr Plump thumped the table with his fist and then, red-faced, stood, a hand clasped over his mouth as he turned away.

Mickey laughed. "Not going to look very good in court, is it?"

Mr Plump whirled and faced him again. "Court? What bloody court? We're not doing this to convince a jury, Rice: we're doing it to convince Lloyd Bloody George that your mate Rothstein should be deported!" He sniffed. "Anyway, we need you to change a few of your answers, so I think we'll ask the station to hang onto you for the night and we'll pay you another visit in the morning."

"You can't hold me!" Mickey protested. "I'm not charged with anything!"

"When it comes to a question of national security," said Mr Plump, "we don't need to charge you immediately. However, in order to make sure the buses are running tomorrow..." He nodded to Ginger.

Mickey sensed Ginger's advance and sprang to his feet. As the tall man's arm went around his throat he brought his right elbow into his solar plexus, sending him staggering back against the wall.

"...Assault on a police officer should fit the bill nicely," concluded Mr Plump with a smile. He threw open the door of the interview room and called down the hall. "Sergeant! Your assistance is required immediately. On the double!"

A tall, fair-haired sergeant, in his early thirties, came running, unnecessarily ducking his head as he entered the door. Mickey noted that his good looks were somewhat marred by an unusually large Adam's apple.

Mr Plump gave him a cursory glance and then threw out an arm towards Mickey. "Put this one in a..." He turned his frown back to the sergeant. "Who are you?"

"Sergeant Lawrence. I've just come on duty."

"Oh, of course. Well, Sergeant Lawrence, find a cell for this one: Michael J. Rice; he is to be charged with assaulting a police officer, to wit my constable here, whose distress you will find readily apparent."

Ginger Moustache was still, in fact, in some pain, bent double and gulping to get his breath back. Mickey stood with his arms folded, as if, having thwarted Ginger's attack, he had no further use for them, although he now realised that the purpose of that attack had been solely to provoke his counter-attack, thus giving some credence to the charge he now faced.

"And how long will we hold him?" asked Sergeant Lawrence.

"Overnight," replied Plump. "We'll return in the morning and continue his interview." He turned to Mickey. "In the meantime, Rice, you had better come up with answers more to our liking."

"That's hardly likely," a defiant Mickey Rice threw at him.

"In that case, Rice, you had better give careful thought to the predicament in which you find yourself. That badge you're wearing was issued by the Public Carriage Office of the Metropolitan Police; if you think they'll let you keep that licence after you're convicted of assaulting a police officer, you've got a surprise coming." He snapped his fingers. "And another thing! The female with you the other night in the Crown and Anchor was your wife, and she, Mr Rice, is an alien citizen."

"But we're married. You can't touch her if she's married to a British citizen!" Mickey struggled to conceal the panic he was now beginning to feel.

"Can't touch her? Can't *touch* her? Of course we can bloody well touch her! Would you like me to tell you how many German citizens we deported during the war, despite the fact that some of 'em had lived here for decades and were married to British citizens?"

"But Britain is not at war with Belgium." That sounded a bit lame, but it was the best that Mickey could do.

Mr Plump leaned forward, his face now red, and raised his voice still further. "That's got nothing to do with it, Rice! She was—and has been for some time—consorting with known Bolshevists!" He watched as Mickey visibly paled. "Ahhh,"—this came out as a long sigh—"now you see what a mess you've got yourself into." He nodded grimly and turn to Ginger. "How are you doing, Jack? Think you can make it to the car park, of shall I ask the sergeant to bring a stretcher?"

Ginger grimaced and straightened up. "Yeah, very bloody funny. Come on, let's go."

"Sergeant, take Mr Rice to his cell and see that he's comfortable. Come to think of it, I'd better come with you to make sure he doesn't try anything, although given his circumstances that's probably unlikely."

The cell had a white tile flooring and yellow brick walls. It contained a narrow bunk upon which lay a pillow and a single folded blanket and, in the corner, a seatless toilet. Mickey groaned as he caught sight of the toilet paper.

"What's up, Mr Rice?" asked Plump. "Does the accommodation not come up to Bayswater standards?"

"Bloody Izal toilet paper."

"Oh, yeah, that'll tear your arse to shreds if you're not careful."

Ginger put his head around the cell door. "What's he moaning about?"

"Doesn't like the toilet paper," Plump chuckled.

For the first time in a long while, Ginger grinned. "Come out to our car when you've locked him up, Sergeant Lawrence, and I'll give you something that he'll find smoother."

In the cobbled car park, Ginger Moustache, now fully recovered from the blow he had received from Mickey, stepped smartly to the car, opened the driver's door and took something from the pocket on the door. "Here you are, Sergeant, tell him he can wipe his arse on this."

Sergeant Lawrence unfolded the document and saw that it was a copy of *The Call*, the newspaper of the British Socialist Party.

*

When he heard the key turn in the lock, Mickey untied his shoes, kicked them off and swung his legs onto the bunk. Nothing Mr Plump had said had worried him until he came to the potential loss of his badge and the deportation of Annette. If he lost the badge, he would be out of a job, and it would therefore be impossible to continue his union work. The deportation of Annette would also mean finding a new job—but this time in Belgium; and, of course, he would need to learn French. This latter possibility struck him as not totally unattractive. He would presumably become involved in the trade union movement in Belgium...but then *he* might be the one to be deported. No, he really needed to hang onto his badge and ensure that Annette remained here. It all depended, he supposed, on how serious the Special Branch men were. And what if they were in deadly earnest? He could simply say what they wanted him to say, couldn't he? Well, yes, he could, but then he would have betrayed the cause to which he was committed and his comrade Theo. And he would then be in the clutches of Special Branch for as long as they found him useful. But maybe they were bluffing. If, as Mr Plump had said, their aim was to convince Lloyd George that Theo should be deported, would what they had be up to the job? They had a cheque made out to cash. Lloyd George was hardly likely to be convinced by that. Yes, they would tell him that it had been found in Theo's briefcase, but what did that prove? Nothing, really. The purpose of the cheque, surely, was not really to demonstrate that Theo was defrauding the Soviet government—the British Prime Minister was hardly likely to be upset by that—but that he had received Soviet funds in the first place, and that these funds were being used to support the formation of the new party. Now he had the opportunity to think about it, it was clear that their story was full of holes. They needed a statement from him. But before whom, if not Lloyd George, did they hope to place such a statement? Someone in the movement?

His speculations were interrupted by the sound of the key rattling in the lock. Sergeant Lawrence walked in, waving a newspaper.

"The tall ginger bloke left this for you," he said, dropping a newspaper on the bunk. "You'd probably like to read it rather than using it for what he suggested."

Mickey reached for the newspaper and, having swung his legs off the bunk, opened it and laughed. "*The Call*. Yeah, I can imagine what his suggestion was. Seems he has a sense of humour after all."

Sergeant Lawrence remained just inside the cell, arms folded as he regarded Mickey. "So you're Mickey Rice," he said finally.

Mickey placed the newspaper at his side and looked at the policeman. "That's right," he said with a frown. "Have our paths crossed before?"

The policeman grinned. "Not really. I had occasion to leave a message with your landlord in August last year."

Mickey's frown deepened until, realising the truth, his face lit up. "Are we talking about Theo Rothstein?"

The policeman nodded. "We are."

In August 1919, when Theo had been taken into custody and held on a ship in the Pool to await deportation, Lawrence had been one of the uniformed policemen assigned to guard him until the ship sailed.

"Mind you, he tricked me. Told me that if I spoke to you or left a message for you, you would be able to tell his friends and family what had happened to him." He chuckled. "There was obviously a bit more to it than that, because the next afternoon they let 'im go. Not that I hold it against 'im; imagine, in this country almost thirty years, his son had served in the Army, and they wanted to kick 'im out."

There had indeed been more to it: having received the message from Gladys just as he was about to leave for work, Mickey had gone straight to Electric Railway House. At one of their off-the-record meetings, Theo had told Lloyd George that if he was ever taken into custody by Special Branch, he would get word to him via Sir Albert Stanley, who was then president of the Board of Trade. He made it clear that he had no relationship whatever with Stanley; but Mickey had, and he would ask him to contact Lloyd George; the Prime Minister agreed to advise Stanley that he was comfortable with this arrangement and that he should do as the emissary asked. By the time of Theo's arrest, Stanley had left the government, but he stuck to the letter of the arrangement, and later that day Lloyd George ordered Theo's release.

Mickey stood up and offered the policeman his hand. "Put it there, mate."

The policeman shook his hand. "I'm Oliver Lawrence, by the way—Olly to my friends."

"You obviously didn't join the strike, then, Olly." At the time of Theo's release, the ill-starred police strike of 1919 had just begun.

"No, mate. Thought about it, though." Olly Lawrence made a face. "I don't suppose you think much of me for that."

Mickey grinned and shook his head. "Not at all, Olly. You made the wise choice: that strike was never going to succeed."

"And all those that *did* join it were sacked."

"I take it, by the way," said Mickey, calculating that he could risk this suggestion, "that you don't have much time for your Special

Branch brothers."

There was just the briefest of hesitations. "You take it right, Mickey. The ones I've come across treat those of us in uniform like shit. And look at what they wanted to do to old Theo, him with an English wife and family. And then look how that bastard treated you, threatening to deport your wife." Suddenly, his eyebrows shot up. "'Ere! You'll never guess who they sent to release Theo from that ship!"

Mickey shrugged. "How would I know, Olly?"

"It was the chubby geezer who was grillin' you! He obviously didn't recognise me. We were only together for a few minutes on that ship, and I was still a constable then, so he probably didn't consider me worthy of much attention."

"Well, well. Small world, eh? But you obviously got on with Theo."

"Oh, yeah. What a nice bloke! A true gent. He had a sense of humour, too. You know what he said that last afternoon? I'd asked him if he fancied a game of cards to pass the time, and he said 'No, thanks, Olly, my taxi will be here soon.' And a little bit after that, blow me if the Special Branch blokes didn't show up to release him!" He frowned and raised a finger. "And now I come to think of it, I'm pretty sure that ginger bloke was one of 'em too. Wouldn't swear to it, mind, but it would make sense if they're a regular double act."

"It would, wouldn't it?" But Mickey did not want their discussion to take this diversion. "Mind you, you're right about Theo. I've known him a number of years now, and everything you say about him is true."

"Yeah, if I do say so myself, I'm a pretty good judge of character. You know, we even discussed the strike, and Theo said that if I decided to join it and got the sack, he knew people who could make sure I got a job on the buses." He nodded at Mickey. "I'm thinkin' he probably had you in mind, Mickey."

"Nah, more likely one of our full-timers."

"He even gave me his card and told me to ring him if I wanted to give the buses a try." He laughed. "Mind you, he almost gave himself away there, because I asked him how I was supposed to ring him if he was halfway across the North Sea. 'Oh, yeah,' he said, 'I wasn't thinking.'"

Bingo. "Did you hang onto that card, Olly?"

"Yep. Put it in me wallet and it's still there."

Mickey gave him the lightest touch on the arm with his hand. "In which case, mate, would you fancy doing me a favour?"

19

"Hello?"

It was 6.30 in the morning and Theo Rothstein had run downstairs to answer the telephone. The line was dead. He sighed, replaced the earpiece and stood looking at the instrument, hands in the pockets of his dressing gown; whoever it was would, realising that he had been sleeping when the telephone first rang, presumably call again. Sure enough, it rang.

"Hello?"

"Mr Rothstein?"

"Yes..."

"I'm an old friend, Mr Rothstein. I saved the card you gave me when we met. But I decided not to go on the buses."

"Aha! I have you now. But be careful: this telephone is not safe."

"I realise that, Mr Rothstein; that's why I haven't mentioned my name, and I'm not going to tell you anything that the authorities don't know already."

"Good lad. How can I help you?"

"I thought you would want to know, Mr Rothstein, that your friend Mickey Rice is being held by Special Branch. He's at Harrow Road police station."

Theo sighed heavily. "Ah." He paused. "Well, thank you, my friend. One day we may give you a medal for the service you have performed. Go now."

"Who is it, Theo?" came a female voice from the top of the stairs.

"A friend, Anna, a friend, so do not worry. Go back to bed."

"It's almost seven," said his wife.

"So let's have breakfast together; then I must go out."

"Where to?"

"That is a very good question, Anna."

*

After breakfast, when Theo went back upstairs to wash, shave and dress, he had still not worked out where to go to impart the news of the incarceration of Mickey Rice. He knew he had to impart it to Albert Stanley—since last December ennobled as Lord Ashfield—because he knew that the chairman of all the companies in the Traffic Combine felt respect for Mickey, if only because he was one of the few working men he had ever met with whom he could hold an intelligent conversation; at least that was the way Mickey told it, although it was also true that Ashfield had had a soft spot for Mickey's late lover Dorothy Bridgeman, who had worked in his office between June 1913 and February 1914.

But how to approach Ashfield? He could telephone him from the post office, but was his line secure? He could telegraph him, but how many others would see the message before it reached him? And he could hardly simply turn up at Electric Railway House because he would almost certainly be followed. The danger of arrest and deportation had abated of late, as Moscow had insisted that, for this very reason, his name be added to the Soviet trade delegation. Internationally, things were showing a gradual improvement. Russian troops, having retaken Kiev in the second week of June, were now engaged in a general advance against the Polish invaders. Ten days after the victory at Kiev, a conference of the Allied governments had decided that trade negotiations should be continued, although on the understanding that there was no question of political recognition of the Soviet government; this, he suspected, was France applying its foot to the brakes. Thus, Theo had diplomatic immunity as a member of the trade delegation, but not as ambassador. Regardless of this immunity, he knew that he was still under surveillance, and that there were forces which would use any opportunity to discredit or politically check him.

Buttoning his waistcoat, he gazed out of his bedroom window onto the green of Clapton Square, now living up to its name in the summer months, and wondered how much longer he would be allowed to remain here. But deportation would not be without its compensations, for while the almost three decades he had spent in this country had led to a sense of attachment and belonging, this was also the length of time he had been absent from his homeland, now bursting with new life—new forms of living, in fact. Yes, he would certainly like to take a look at it, but Anna and the children must be considered; if he were suddenly no longer here, his son Andrew would need to be head of the household and continue his political work.

He turned to the mirror on the bedside table. At almost 50 he was, although short, a presentable man, smartly dressed with a neatly trimmed beard and spectacles behind which his eyes so often twinkled with amusement. But not today. He looked out onto the green once more. The first half of June had been wet, but this morning the sun was out and this early there was already someone seated on one of the benches, legs outstretched as he read a newspaper. The man was facing the house and Theo noted that he did not appear to be turning the pages of his newspaper. No, he's probably looking *over* the newspaper at my front door, thought Theo: the man who will tail me. Dark jacket, charcoal trousers, no hat; can't see his face because of the newspaper. He took his watch from his waistcoat pocket and flipped it open. 8.15. Time to make a move, tail or no tail. If the man followed him, he would simply have to take a chance with the telephone at the Dalston Lane Post Office.

*

"Well, now," said Mr Plump, "let's see if we can make a bit better progress this morning, shall we?"

Mickey Rice scowled at him. "You can try."

Mr Plump effected a smile. "That is precisely what I intend to do, Mr Rice. Shall we start with the cheque? When was it, exactly, that Mr Rothstein asked you to write that cheque?"

Mickey glanced across the table, where Ginger Moustache, with a sheaf of forms before him, was seated next to Mr Plump. He turned back to his interrogator. "What's *his* job this morning?"

"The constable will take your statement."

"Ha! What statement would that be?"

"The statement that you will make in order to prevent your wife from being deported, Mr Rice. So let's get down to it: when did he ask you to write that cheque?"

"He never asked me to write a cheque."

"So it was a regular arrangement: he would hand you the Soviet funds every two or three months and you would write him a cheque. That way, he wouldn't need to ask, would he?"

Mickey scratched his head. "Let me get this right: you think that Mr Rothstein handed me money from Russia for the use of the movement..."

"Correct."

"And that I would pay this into my account and then write him a cheque, made out to cash, for his back-hander."

"Now you've got it. Get this down, Constable!"

"No, this is what *you're* saying, not what *I'm* saying, so put down your pencil, Constable." He laughed. "But why would we go to all this trouble? Why wouldn't he just hang onto the cash he wanted for his back pocket?"

"Because, Mr Rice, I assume that you were required to sign for the receipt of these funds, which Rothstein would then submit to his superiors to show that all was above board."

"So why wouldn't I just hand him back some of the cash after I'd signed the receipt?"

This placed Mr Plump in some difficulty. "Because," he spluttered. "Be*cause*..."

Mickey leaned forward and jabbed a finger at the table top. "Be*cause* the only so-called evidence you've got is a cheque signed by me and this is the only way you can find to make use of it!"

*

Lord Ashfield replaced the earpiece and sank back into his chair. Rothstein: it could only have been him. The caller had not left his name, explaining that "for your own protection it is best that I do not openly reveal my identity, but last year you did me a great service."

"I think I understand. How may I help you?"

"This time I am giving the assistance, Lord Ashfield. I thought you would like to know that one of your employees is being held by Special Branch..."

"Oh, really!" And who might that be? Only one person. "And would this be Mr Rice?"

"Yes. Take my word for it that he has done nothing wrong, Lord Ashfield. They are holding him at Harrow Road police station."

"Very well. Thank you for the information. I will do what I can."

"I am sure that he will appreciate it. Goodbye, Lord Ashfield."

Ashfield sighed. All very well saying that he would do what he could, but what *could* he do? Well, he could call that arrogant Superintendent Quinn, of course. Quinn had called him to Special Branch in 1914 to advise him that Dorothy Bridgeman, a member of his secretarial team, had assaulted a police officer in Liverpool during the great strike of 1911, and that she was a member of the British Socialist Party; he had also learned that Mickey Rice was Dorothy's lover. But Ashfield had found the interview distasteful and, having had experience of the Pinkertons in the USA, he feared that Special Branch was developing into a public-sector version of that organisation. Yes, he would call Quinn and act the outraged transport tsar!

*

An exasperated Mr Plump drummed his fingers on the table. "Alright," he said, looking up at Mickey, "let's come at it from another direction. Give us a statement about what was discussed in the Crown and Anchor." He turned to Ginger. "Take this down as it comes—we can always edit it later."

Mickey sat in silence, looking from one to the other.

"Come on, then," urged Mr Plump. He made a slow winding motion with his right hand. "We were at the Crown and Anchor on Clerkenwell Green..." He glanced at Ginger to check that he had begun writing.

"Wait a bit." Ginger held up a restraining hand, frowning in concentration. "Let's get this in context." As he wrote, he slowly recited the words. "We...was...at...the...Crown...and...Anchor..."

*

"Good morning, this is Lord Ashfield. I need to speak to Superintendent Quinn immediately."

A slight hesitation. *"I'm sorry, sir, but Superintendent Quinn is retired."*

Dammit. "I see. And who has replaced him?"

"Superintendent McBrien, sir."

"Then kindly put me through to him."

"I will try, sir, but the Superintendent is a very busy man."

"Tell him that this matter is of the utmost importance."

"I will convey that to him, sir."

During a delay of almost a minute, Ashfield lifted the top few letters in his in-tray and ran an eye over them.

"Good morning. How may I help you?"

Another Irishman, although this was hardly surprising as the organisation which he now headed was originally called the Special Irish Branch. "Good morning, Superintendent McBride..."

"McBrien, sir."

"I beg your pardon. Good morning, Superintendent McBrien. I am reliably informed that your men are holding one of my employees, a Mr Michael Rice, at Harrow Road police station, and I must insist that he be released immediately."

"Must you, sir? Do you know why he is being held?"

"I assume on account of his politics: he is a socialist."

"And are you sympathetic to his political views, sir?"

Ashfield paused. This man was just as impertinent as his predecessor. "I will tell you what I am *not* in sympathy with,

Superintendent," he replied calmly, "and that is the way in which this country appears to be following the United States in its persecution of political dissent."

"I ask again: are you sympathetic to his political views?"

"No, of course not!"

"Then why do you insist on his release, sir?"

"Because there will be dire consequences if he is *not* released, Superintendent."

"Dear me, that sounds like a threat, Mr Ashmead."

"My name is Ash*field*, Superintendent, *Lord* Ashfield." Ashfield now had to struggle to prevent himself chuckling as he realised the other man's error.

"And what are the consequences to which you refer, sir?" McBrien's tone was now cautious, almost respectful.

"As you may be aware, I am chairman of the London General Omnibus Company. Mr Rice, on the other hand, is one of my drivers. More than that, he is an active trade unionist with a considerable following. If he is not released immediately, and word of his incarceration gets out, *there will not be a single bus on the streets of London, or large parts of it!* Given my position, that is obviously something I wish to avoid. *Now* do you understand, Superintendent?"

A clearing of the throat. *"I believe I do, sir, and I will make the appropriate enquiries."*

"And, I trust, you will issue the appropriate instructions."

"Of course, Lord Ashfield."

*

Mickey Rice laughed aloud.

"What's funny, Mr Rice?"

"Your constable obviously doesn't have a clue what the word *context* means."

Ginger looked offended.

"He also thinks that working people should always be made to sound illiterate." When Mr Plump failed to catch his meaning, he slumped his shoulders so that his fingers brushed the floor and adopted a deep frown to give his face a simian cast. "We was at duh Crown an' Anchor…"

"Oh, got you now. Yes, very amusing, Mr Rice." He thumped the table with his fist, causing Ginger to jump and lose his pencil. "But you seem to have forgotten what I said last night about *Mrs* Rice.

137

Don't you think it's about time you started taking this seriously?"

Mickey gave him a level look. "No, because you're trying to build some sort of case against Mr Rothstein out of nothing! You've got nothing, have you? Admit it!"

There came a knock on the door and the uniformed sergeant who had taken over from Olly Lawrence presented his face. "Telephone for you, Sergeant. Sounds as if it might be important."

Left alone with each other, Mickey and Ginger fell into separate silences, Mickey because he was straining to overhear Mr Plump's contribution to the telephone conversation down the hallway, and Ginger because he had nothing to say. All Mickey could hear, however, was the occasional *Yes, sir*. At the second or third of these, Mickey glanced at Ginger, who grimaced. Sounded like bad news.

When Mr Plump returned to the interview room his face was like thunder. "You," he spat at Mickey, jerking his thumb over his shoulder, "'op it." He turned to Ginger. "And not a word from you, Jack."

As Mickey stepped onto Harrow Road, he took out his watch and saw that he had just about enough time to go home, grab something to eat, telephone Annette at work to let her know he was alright, and then get down to Middle Row garage to sign on for his duty. But sooner or later he would need to speak to Theo Rothstein.

*

First, however, came the discussion with Annette.

Finding the living room empty when he arrived home that evening and assuming that Annette was in the bathroom, he slumped down onto the sofa, stretching his legs and sighing deeply. He sat there for a good five minutes, eyes closed, as he reviewed the experiences of the previous twenty-four hours. One thing was certain: Annette must apply for British citizenship as soon as possible. But where was she?

"Sweetheart!" He gave it a few seconds. "Annette, are you here? Sweetheart?"

She came not from the bathroom but from the bedroom. He turned to his right as he heard the bedroom door and saw that she looked as if she had been sleeping, perhaps even crying. When he had telephoned the office that morning, he had merely assured her that he was safe and sound, telling her that he would explain everything when he got home after work.

He struggled to his feet and took her in his arms. "What's wrong *ma chérie*?" He leaned back and lifted her chin. "Have you been crying?"

She nodded, her eyes avoiding his. "A little, yes."

"But why, sweetheart? There's no reason for tears."

Now she flared. "*Why?* You ask me *why?* Because I have been *worried*, Mickey! You do not think I will be worried when you stay out the whole night? You do not call Dick and so I do not know whether you have accident or or or—are maybe with other *womans*!"

Unable to help himself, he laughed as, unusually, her English went to pieces. "Oh," he mimicked, "so you think I was with othair womans?"

Perhaps realising that she could now rule out this possibility, she too almost laughed. But when she looked up at him her eyes were still filled with tears. "Then tell me, Mickey: where were you last night?"

He knew that if he kissed her now her lips would be warm and he would feel her tears upon his face. But this was explanation time. "I was in Harrow Road police station, sweetheart."

A gasp of dismay escaped her. "Oh, Mickey! What have you done?"

He was irritated, almost angered, by this reaction. Was she completely ignorant of the role of the police? He spoke deliberately, emphatically now, all tenderness having fled. "I have not done *any*thing, Annette. Sit down now and I will explain. In fact, I feel so knackered that if I don't sit down, I'll fall down."

"Knackered?"

"Exhausted. *Je suis fatigue.*"

They sat and he patiently explained what had happened. Her response was, as he feared it might be, disappointing, focusing first on the possibility of her deportation.

"But Mickey, they were saying they would *deport* me!"

"Yes, that's what they said, Annette." He was very tired now, and was not inclined to gentleness or tact.

"And you were willing to risk this?"

"They were bluffing, sweetheart."

"But you did not know this, did you?"

"No, I didn't *know* it, but I was fairly..." He brought himself up short, shocked by the implications of her questions. His look was searching, hard. "Do you think I should have told them what they wanted to hear, then?"

She blinked, hardly knowing how to answer this. "No, but..."

"Do you think I should have betrayed Theo to save you from deportation?"

This was easier to deal with. "Of *course* not, Mickey."

"Well, that is what you're implying!"

Annette appeared to be on the verge of tears again. "I'm sorry, Mickey; I had not considered it carefully…"

Mickey softened. He touched her cheek. "Alright, sweetheart. But listen: you must apply for British citizenship as soon as possible."

She nodded. "Of course, my love." She sighed, signifying that this little crisis was over. "It would have been better, Mickey, if you had told me about Special Branch when you telephoned this morning."

"I decided against it, Annette; it was over, and there was nothing anyone had to do. I was afraid that if I told you, Transport House would get to know about it and someone might start thinking of taking action that would have been unnecessary and possibly unhelpful."

"I see," she said. Yes, she appeared to be thinking, so we'll let your wife spend the next twelve hours imagining all sorts of things. But she smiled. "You must be very hungry, my love."

He nodded, making an effort to ensure he did not close his eyes for fear that they might not open again. "Yes, sweetheart, I am— very."

While Annette prepared their meal, Mickey gave some thought to the wife he was only now getting to know. It was quite apparent that her commitment to the movement was not as firm as he had assumed, but should he really be surprised by this? Her politics had been acquired from her parents, but had obviously not been reinforced by experience. She worked, after all, for a trade union: no class contradictions. And what constituted her political experience in this country? They were both members of the Paddington branch of the British Socialist Party and attended branch meetings fairly regularly, but this was not her country and Annette sometimes became lost during the discussions, particularly when they had an historical slant. In a few months' time, they would presumably join the new communist party, which would be more disciplined than the BSP, and for her this could work in one of two ways, either strengthening her commitment or alienating her. He loved Annette and, despite her often irritating demonstrations of individualism or self-interest, he refused to view her as a lost cause in the political sense; indeed, considering her whole person, he regarded her—and *should* regard her, he thought—as the lovely young woman who had given herself to him but who was in danger of becoming separated from him in the dangerous waters in which they found themselves. It being foolish to blame the political waters for this predicament, he must help her to become a stronger swimmer. A lot would depend on him.

She failed him at the first hurdle when she decided to discuss the donation Mickey had made to the new party.

"Why did you write a cheque for such a huge amount, Mickey," she asked as they ate their meal.

"It was money I didn't really want," he replied, hoping that this discussion would not take the direction he feared.

She chuckled—a good sign. "How can that be possible?"

"For two reasons, Annette: first of all, I had not earned it; and secondly, Dorothy had always said that she would use that money for the movement, whenever the need was sufficiently desperate."

He had thought that Annette might react to this mention of Dorothy, but Mickey's wife was not one to exhibit jealousy over a former lover, especially one who had been dead for three years.

"Why do you ask, sweetheart?" It was, he would later realise, a mistake to ask such a question.

"We could have bought a house with that," she said.

If she failed Mickey by such a comment, he then failed her by, instead of soberly discussing the matter and winning her to a more ethical point of view, finishing the rest of the meal in silence and then, when they were in bed, drawing her to him and, *fatigue* or *pas fatigue*, mounting an attack on her breasts and forcing his way between her legs prior to a display of carnality that had them both gasping at the ferociousness of it; and if Annette felt—as was probably his intention—that this was some form of vengeance for her less than enlightened utterances, she showed no sign of it.

20

July began cool, and astute Londoners predicted that the remainder of the summer would be no summer at all. But it was an eventful month. On 2 July, Krassin, leader of the Soviet trade delegation departed for Moscow, carrying with him the Note containing the British peace proposals: a binding armistice; a declaration from each party that they would pay for the goods and services rendered by the nationals of the other, claims for which would be considered at a peace conference while trade negotiations continued; each party should refrain from interfering in the internal affairs of the other; a pledge for absolute freedom of trade and communications. Six days later, these terms were accepted by the Soviet government.

By this time, the Red Army was making significant gains against

Poland, which on 11 July requested aid from the Allied governments. The latter met at Spa in Belgium, and Britain sent a Note to Moscow suggesting a Soviet-Polish armistice and threatening that if Russia "intends to take action hostile to Poland in its own territory, the British Government and its Allies would feel bound to assist the Polish nation to defend its existence with all the means at their disposal."

Theo Rothstein spread his hands. "Just as I predicted, Comrade," he commented to Mickey Rice, who sat opposite him at a table in the Lyons Corner House on the Strand. "So once again the British labour movement faces the prospect of war. We can only hope that it meets this challenge in a more determined manner than six years ago."

Mickey nodded. "I think it will, Theo." He took a sip of his tea.

A smile from Theo. "I think so, too, Mickey." He cast a meditative gaze around the second floor of the restaurant, where black and white-clad "nippies" hurried from table to table. "If that were the only problem facing me, I would be a great deal happier than I am, Comrade."

"Is there a problem with the unity conference, Theo?" asked Mickey, a concerned frown pinching his brow. Mickey was bursting to thank Theo for helping to spring him from the clutches of Special Branch, but more than that to describe the somewhat confused intention of his interrogator, but Theo had ambushed him with a protracted update on the current situation regarding Russia and Mickey had yet to find an opportunity to impart both his gratitude and his news.

"Not really, Mickey. The conference will go ahead at the end of this month." He sighed. "The problem I have is with Sylvia Pankhurst."

"Ah, because she's formed her own party!"

Somewhat surprisingly, Theo grinned. "Even that is not such a problem." His eyes flared. "Did you see what she has called it? The Communist Party, British Section of the Third International! What arrogance! And where did this new spectre that is haunting British socialism hold its founding congress last month? In a private flat! So no, this organization is not much of a problem at all."

"So she won't be at the unity conference."

"No, and for two reasons: she withdrew from the provisional committee after the BSP insisted that a declaration of unity was necessary before the question of Labour Party affiliation could be tackled; and, of course, she will be in Moscow at the time of the unity conference."

"In Moscow."

"Of course—at the Second Congress of the Third International." He smiled. "Interestingly, she will be there as a delegate from her Workers' Socialist Federation, not from her new so-called party. Although she will be merely a consultative delegate: she will be able to speak, but will have no vote."

"So if her new party is not the problem...?"

Theo let his eyebrows rise and fall. "What is rather more of a problem for me is that Comrade Pankhurst has apparently told Lenin that I am using for my own purposes some of the funds that the comrades send me."

Mickey clapped a hand to his brow. "Ah! Now it all makes sense!"

Theo, lifting his coffee cup to his lips, paused and returned it to its saucer. This time, he raised just one eyebrow. "I sense that you have something important to tell me, Mickey."

"I do, Theo, but first things first: thank you for calling Ashfield and rescuing me from Harrow Road police station."

Theo shrugged and smiled kindly. "I was simply returning a favour, Mickey. Think nothing of it. If anyone deserves thanks, it's probably Constable Lawrence: he was the one taking the risk."

"He's now Sergeant Lawrence."

"Oh, in which case the risk was even greater!" A thoughtful pause. "I wonder what caused him to take it."

"Two things, I think: firstly, he thinks you're a proper gent..."

Theo waved an impatient hand. "And secondly?"

"And secondly he doesn't like Special Branch."

"Ah, yes, I can understand that." He cleared his throat. "And now, Mickey..."

"And now for my news." Mickey placed his palms on the table and leaned forward, lowering his voice. "Special Branch tried to get me to make a statement regarding the very allegation that you have just mentioned. The cheque I wrote last year? They have it."

Theo uttered a deep sigh and leaned back in his chair. "As you say, it now makes sense."

"When I suggested that Billy Watson or one of his mates had provided them with the cheque, they didn't know where to put their faces."

"But we know that Watson could not have stolen the cheque from my briefcase, as he was in prison at the time. But we must assume that he was the one who passed it to Special Branch after his release, and then, much more recently, conveyed this allegation to Sylvia."

"Yes, I imagine so..."

"You seem troubled by that suggestion."

"I am, because it's now *known* that Watson was an informer. Why would Sylvia take his word for anything?"

"Maybe you don't know, Mickey, that after his role was revealed, Sylvia actually defended him. Mind you, in doing this she was maybe defending herself, because Watson had a weekly column—'Workers' Notes,' he called it—in her *Workers' Dreadnought*."

"Ah, I see."

"So you just sat there, refusing to cooperate?"

"Pretty much. After they left for the night, I gave it some thought and realized that they really had nothing except a cheque made out to cash with my signature on it."

Theo looked up, eyes wide, as if an aspect of this affair had just occurred to him. "Did they threaten you, Mickey?"

"Oh, yes. They tricked me into defending myself against one of them. Said I'd face a charge of assaulting a police officer, in which case I could wave goodbye to my licence and my job. Then, of course, they threatened to deport Annette."

This brought a sharp intake of breath from Theo. "You must be careful, Mickey."

Mickey's chuckle had little humour in it. "What was I to do—give them the statement they wanted?"

Theo smiled kindly. "No, of course not, Comrade, but Annette should apply for British citizenship as soon as possible."

"I've already told her that, Theo."

Theo was frowning. "But I can't understand how that cheque is meant to prove that I have been feathering my nest."

Mickey laughed. "I know, I know. What they claimed was that you were passing funds to me and I would then put them into my account and write you a cheque for your rake-off. I know it makes no sense, and I told them that. Wouldn't it be more straightforward, I said, to simply hand you back some of the cash? At first, you know, they said that they wanted my statement in order to put it before Lloyd George, so that he would agree to your deportation."

Theo found this amusing. "But would Lloyd George hold it against me if I was cheating my own government?"

"That's precisely what I said to them! It now seems, though, that they had set their sights rather lower."

"To what end, though?"

"To smear your name in the movement—or, as seems to have been the case, with Lenin."

Theo nodded gravely. "Yes, that is it, I suppose." He sighed. "And now I must do something about it."

"Like what, Theo?"

A characteristic shrug. "I probably need to have a chat with Vladimir Ilyich."

"Talking of whom, after the Special Branch men left the pub that night, Harry Pollitt put a couple of questions to Bob Williams. Was it Lenin, he asked, who gave Bob the impression that Britain's revolution might be just around the corner?"

Theo leaned forward. "And what did he say to that?"

"He said that Lenin had not used those words but that he expected great things of our new party; he gave the impression that Lenin did in fact think that our revolution might be close."

Theo laughed. "But previously Williams had told us that Lenin had predicted the formation of a Labour government! Now that is what I would call a glaring inconsistency."

Mickey nodded. "Yes, he did say that, didn't he?" A frown crossed his brow. "So what do you think Bob is up to, Theo?"

A sigh from Theo. "After that evening in the pub, I contacted Vladimir Ilyich and advised him of the somewhat extreme things Comrade Williams had been saying. His reply was of some depth." He grinned. "It is the view of Vladimir Ilyich that Williams is not without positive qualities—he was, he said, very perceptive regarding Bevin—but that he exhibits some of the petty-bourgeois vacillation he has criticized in his pamphlet, *The Proletarian Revolution and the Renegade Kautsky*."

"Petty-bourgeois vacillation? But Bob Williams was a coal trimmer!"

Theo nodded. "*Was*. But for almost a decade he has been a trade union functionary, a position in which he has, possibly, acquired these characteristics. And what are they? Lenin says that wide sections of the petty bourgeoisie vacillate and hesitate, one day marching behind the proletariat and the next day taking fright at the difficulties of the revolution. Sometimes, indeed, they even project themselves as super-revolutionaries, and possibly Comrade Williams is in this phase now. But then they become panic-stricken at the first defeat or semi-defeat of the workers, grow nervous, run about aimlessly, snivel, and rush from one camp into the other—just like our Mensheviks and Socialist-Revolutionaries.

"Incidentally, you can study the phenomenon of the super-revolutionary in Lenin's new pamphlet, *Left-Wing Communism—An Infantile Disorder*; the English edition will be with us very soon."

Mickey scratched his head. "Well, yes, I can see that Bob may view himself as a super-revolutionary at the moment, but when has he vacillated to the other extreme?"

Theo smiled. "Comrade Lenin asked him why he had accepted nomination as a delegate to the forthcoming conference in Geneva which aims to revive the Second International. He replied that he had no intention of attending, but was unable to offer a convincing explanation of why he had agreed to attend in the first place."

"And Comrade Lenin concludes from this...?"

"That possibly Comrade Williams wishes to avoid burning all his bridges. He also seems to be rather concerned about his employment prospects once Bevin forms his new union, which to a large extent will supplant the Transport Workers' Federation." He brought his fingers down onto the table. "Hah! And you know his prediction that the new party could have as many members as the Russian within a year? Do you know where that came from? Lenin suggested that he could become a professional revolutionary *if the British party grew at the same rate as the Russian!*" He frowned at Mickey. "Why do you look so glum, Comrade?"

"Because I'm disappointed in Bob Williams, I suppose."

Theo grinned compassionately. "Ah, Mickey, you will find that such disappointments are occupational hazards for us revolutionaries."

*

The special TUC Congress at the Central Hall, Westminster on 13 July agreed to call for all British troops to be withdrawn from Ireland and for the cessation of the provision of munitions for use against Ireland and Russia, failing which strike action would be recommended, with constituent unions balloting their members.

"A step in the right direction, Theo?" asked George Sanders as they sat in the Lyons on the corner of Rupert Street.

Theo Rothstein's nod was far from demonstrative. "A step, George, yes. But one must bear in mind the wording—action will be *recommended*—and the vote—2.76 million against 1.636 million which, while giving a substantial majority, leaves a considerable minority opposed to such action. And, of course, the resolution was mainly concerned with Ireland, which is entirely understandable."

Sanders struggled to conceal his exasperation; Theo Rothstein certainly knew how to put the dampener on what was, after all, a political victory.

Perhaps sensing Sanders' disappointment, Rothstein now attempted to lighten his mood. "The second resolution was, though, short and to the point: the British government should stick to the terms already agreed by the Soviet government; any attempt by the Allies to provide military assistance to Poland was *foredoomed to failure.*" He grinned. "I like those words. The proof of the pudding, however..."

"Yes, yes..."

21

On the weekend of 31 July-1 August, at a conference in London, the project upon which Theo Rothstein had laboured behind the scenes bore fruit with the foundation of the Communist Party of Great Britain.

The only delegate whom Mickey Rice knew at all well was Bob Williams, and on the following Tuesday he was prevailed upon to address an informal meeting in the room above the Crown and Anchor.

"Think we'll get much of a turnout?" asked Mickey as he and Dick Mortlake walked to the Green from where the number 54 bus had dropped them on Clerkenwell Road. The torrential rain of Monday had given way to dry but cool weather, and a wind from the northeast, caused them to duck their heads between their shoulders.

"As long as they don't mind this bloody weather," replied Dick, "there should be a decent enough number."

"You weren't too keen on coming yourself at first, Dick."

"I fancied a night in, Mickey," he replied, hinting that the weather had had nothing to do with his reluctance.

Mickey sensed that something was amiss. There had been little conversation during their journey from Bayswater, Dick having maintained a thoughtful silence except when addressed directly. Mickey turned to him now. "Are you okay, Dick?"

Dick nodded, his eyes on the pavement ahead of him. "Yes, I'm alright. Mickey."

But he obviously was not. Mickey wondered whether there were problems between him and Gladys, but he did not know how to ask about this.

"Well, here we are." Mickey pointed to a Triumph Trusty motorcycle parked at the kerb. "George has beaten us to it."

As Mickey pushed the door of the pub and walked in, he felt the warmth envelope him. The air in the bar was hazy with tobacco smoke and laden with the smell of hops and malt and it sounded as if the fifteen or twenty men in the bar were all talking at once: George Sanders, Barney Macauley, Eric Rice, Malcolm Lewis and a couple of other committee members from Middle Row, their speaker Bob Williams, Reuben Topping from Willesden, the lay tramworkers' leader Ernie Sharp, and others to whom Mickey could not immediately put a name.

Mickey turned to Dick. "You fancy a pint before we go upstairs, mate?"

Dick, unsmiling, shook his head. "I don't think I will, if that's all the same to you, Mickey."

Mickey now began to wonder whether his friend and comrade was ill. He turned to Bob Williams. "Hey, Bob, the last time we were in this boozer you predicted that Jimmy Thomas would persuade his conference to accept the government's offer. How did it go?"

Williams looked surprised. "That was almost a month ago, Mickey. You losing track?"

"Oh, you know, married life and all."

"Ah, so it's not all bad." Bob grinned and nudged Mickey in the ribs. "You may not remember, but I was the first person you told you were engaged to that little girl."

"In fact, Bob, I have a very fond recollection of that event: it was in Hyde Park, on the day of the coppers' rally, about an hour after I'd popped the question."

"That's right: I asked you how long you'd been engaged and you said 'Oh, about an hour or so.' Anyway, Thomas." He grimaced. "Yes, he persuaded them: they voted 42 to 18 to accept."

"Jesus."

"That surely doesn't surprise you, Mickey."

"No, what surprises me is that the NUR lets just 60 delegates make the decisions for a million members. What kind of democracy is that?"

"Hardly any, comrade. If almost a third of the delegates were opposed to the offer, you can imagine what would have happened with a ballot of the membership: that minority—and I reckon we can assume that they were more active than the majority—would have been working and mobilising and the result would probably have been very different."

Upstairs, the proceedings to begin with were not so much informal as confused. In the days of the red-button Vigilance Committee, Dick would have sat on the top table to take the minutes and the cabdriver Dennis Davies would have chaired the meetings, but since the launch of the United Vehicle Workers there had been no permanent unofficial organisation of this type. As the Hirst leadership was frequently taking unpopular decisions, there was now talk of forming a rank and file body, but this step had yet to be taken. Thus, the meeting this evening lacked organisation and after a few minutes during which everyone stood around shaking their heads and shrugging their shoulders, George Sanders took it upon himself to seat himself at the top table and, having ensured that he had access to an ashtray, lit a Gold Flake and assumed the duties of chairmanship. After the briefest of introductions, he handed over the meeting to the speaker.

"There were 152 delegates," said Bob Williams at one stage during his comprehensive account of the weekend conference, "and much of the discussion was quite detailed, but at the end of the day I think everyone in the hall felt that we had achieved what many had considered impossible, and that we were now..."—a pause while he sought the words—"in the *flow* of history." Finding these words inadequate, he shook his head. "We had succeeded in bringing together the most important socialist parties and societies in our own country and would now affiliate to the Communist International, so we felt that we were now part of a powerful historical *wave* that was going to sweep our class to power in country after country!"

"What was the highlight of the conference as far as you were concerned, Bob?" asked Mickey Rice.

The dark-haired Welshman thought for a moment. "I'd have to say," he said at length. "that it was when the message from Lenin was read out. It was fairly short and pithy, but this was *Lenin* speaking directly to *us*!"

"So what did he say, Comrade?" This from Dick Mortlake who sat, arms folded, seemingly unimpressed by anything that he had heard so far. Mickey turned and regarded him with a frown, but Dick avoided his gaze.

"Well, needless to say he welcomed the plans for the formation of a communist party—his letter was dated 8 July—and said he thought the position of Sylvia Pankhurst and her party—which, interestingly, he called by its old name of the Workers' Socialist Federation—in refusing to participate in the unity convention was wrong. His own view, he said, was that the CP should participate in Parliament and affiliate to the Labour Party—as long as it receives the assurance that it will be free to conduct its own activity."

"And did the conference follow his advice?" This was Mickey's brother Eric, upon whom in the past Archie Henderson had pressed his syndicalist views.

"It did," replied Bob Williams. "The majority for involvement in parliamentary activity was overwhelming, but the debate on affiliation to the Labour Party was closely fought—some thirty speakers, and at the end of the day a narrow majority for affiliation."

"Then I regret to say," announced Dick Mortlake, "that I will not be joining."

Ah, thought Mickey, so this is what's been bothering him. He turned now to look at his friend, seeing him in a new light. No, actually it was an old light: when he had first known Dick seven years ago, he had secretly wondered how long this petty-bourgeois type would continue to play at being a worker. He had stuck with it, but now this latest development revealed, he thought, a petty-bourgeois way of looking at the world.

"Well, that's unfortunate," Bob Williams responded, taking it in his stride, "but there were a whole number of delegates who shared what is presumably your position, and they have all accepted the decision of the majority."

"I happen to believe that Sylvia is right," said Dick. "I fail to see why the new party, which will now be applying for affiliation to the Third International, should seek affiliation to the Labour Party, which has been rejected by that same International. And if anyone thinks that the Labour Party is serious about working to bring about a socialist Britain, I'm afraid they will be disappointed."

Yes, a petty-bourgeois view: better to remain pure and powerless than to risk contamination from reformists and careerists.

"The BSP was affiliated to the Labour Party," reasoned Bob Williams, "but that didn't mean that we unquestioningly accepted their policies. And, as I've said, the CP will apply for affiliation on the grounds that we will be free to conduct our own activity—which will entail struggling against the leadership when it's necessary."

"And more to the point, Dick," Mickey came in now, "Britain is almost unique in that its social-democratic party is where the organised working class is to be found. I've always argued that there's little point in us being theoretically correct unless we seize every opportunity to ensure that our theory is married up with the broader labour movement."

"My advice," chuckled George Sanders from the chair, "would be to avoid making any hasty decisions, Dick, because it's one thing for the party to *apply* for affiliation and quite another to see that application accepted."

22

For a while, it looked as if the British government and the Allies were unimpressed by the labour movement's opposition to its Russia policy. After the Soviet government stated that, if Poland applied directly to Moscow, it would be willing to discuss an armistice, the Allies at first accepted this but then issued an ultimatum, threatening to assist Poland if Soviet troops crossed the border. Krassin and his colleagues in the Soviet trade delegation received cables from the Allies, telling them not to proceed to London until a Soviet-Polish armistice had been negotiated. Although angered by this turn of events, People's Commissar for Foreign Affairs Georgi Chicherin advised London that he was prepared to meet the Allied governments there to discuss peace, but while Britain would have been willing to accept this, France objected.

Nevertheless, Krassin returned to London on 2 August. Meanwhile, however, Churchill published a virulently anti-Soviet diatribe in the *Evening News.* On 5 August, the Red Army was reported to be within 50 miles of Warsaw. Poland had sabotaged the peace negotiations in the hope that the Allies would spring to its defence. On 7 August, the *Daily Chronicle,* close to Lloyd George, ran the headline "BLOCKADE OF RUSSIA ORDERED." The same day, as the danger of a new war appeared imminent, Labour Party secretary Arthur Henderson sent telegrams to every local party secretary, calling for local peace demonstrations and resolutions to Lloyd George.

"And that's not all he's done," enthused Dennis Davies, the cabdriver who had chaired the executive council of the red-button union. Dennis, having dropped off a fare in Earl's Court at 5.30 on the afternoon of 9 August, had driven to the Earl's Court Tavern on the off-chance that he would find some comrades there. Spotting George Sanders, Eric Rice and Barney Macauley as he entered the bar, he had waved his evening newspaper enthusiastically as he approached them.

Sanders feigned surprise, eyebrows raised. "Dear God, Dennis, this must be serious! Imagine, a cab-driver coming off the road during the rush hour!"

"Of course it's bloody serious, George. Haven't you heard the news?"

Macauley nodded at Dennis's newspaper. "Let's have it, Den!"

"The emergency meeting of the TUC Parliamentary Committee,

the Parliamentary Labour Party and the Labour Party EC! You haven't heard the result?" These three bodies had met at the House of Commons in order to discuss the threat of war. Dennis opened his copy of the *Globe*. "Listen to this: the conference 'expressed its belief that war is being engineered between the Allied Powers and Soviet Russia on the issue of Poland and declares that such a war would be an intolerable crime against humanity. It therefore warns the government that the whole industrial power of the organized workers will be used to defeat this war.'"

"Bloody 'ell, that's strong stuff!" commented Eric Rice.

"There's more!" Dennis responded. "They've decided to call a conference of all the affiliated organisations throughout the country, recommending they instruct their members to down tools. They've appointed a Council of Action, which will meet Lloyd George in a couple of days' time."

Sanders allowed a long breath to escape his lips. "This is a bit of a turn-up." He frowned. "But are they serious this time?"

"I think they are. George, and there's a good reason for that: public opinion." Dennis Davies passed his newspaper to Sanders. "I probably meet more of a cross-section of people than most, and from what I can see it's only the die-hard Tories who want this war."

"And you can imagine what the men in the garages are saying," said Macauley. "Many of them were conscripted or were misguided enough to volunteer for the last lot, and I've yet to meet one who fancies doing it all over again."

"So when's this big conference, Dennis?" asked Eric Rice.

"Next Friday, mate, at Central Hall."

"Bloody 'ell, Friday the thirteenth!" chuckled Sanders. "I wonder who that's gonna be unlucky for."

*

Not being remotely superstitious, and because he wanted to see Ernie Bevin in action, Mickey Rice made sure he was available, by means of an RDX, or rest-day exchange, for the Friday 13th event. Dick Mortlake, who was rostered to rest on that day anyway, consented, after considerable persuasion—he had after all demonstrated his contempt for the Labour Party and its works just days earlier—to accompany him.

"Apart from anything else," Mickey had told him, "you've got the opportunity to witness history being made." He gave Dick a mischievous grin. "It'll be the second time for me, so you've got some catching up to do."

"Oh, you mean the police strike of 1918; well, I saw that too, so it'll be the second time for me as well."

"I wasn't counting that one, so it'll be my third time, and your second."

Dick narrowed his eyes. "When was the other time, then?"

"January 1918, when I saw Litvinov write his letter to Trotsky, introducing Bruce Lockhart."

"And where, pray, was this?"

"In the Lyons Corner House on the Strand."

"Oh, this is what Theo talked about at our wedding reception. But you never told me that you were there!"

Mickey had shrugged. "You can ask Theo if you like; I was there at his invitation—not at the same table, of course, but not more than a stone's throw away."

After a moment, it sank in: Mickey wasn't joking. "You never told me this before."

Mickey looked just a little sheepish. "No, because it was connected to some other stuff that was pretty confidential."

"I'm impressed, Comrade." Dick sighed. "Well, in the light of the decisions taken by the conference at the Commons earlier in the week, I suppose there must be a *chance* that history will be made on Friday."

"That's the spirit. And who knows? If it *is* made, you might think twice about your decision not to join the CP."

Dick, had in fact, followed George Sanders' advice and had not, as yet, made a firm decision about membership of the new party. "Well, we'll see."

Now they were at Central Hall, trying to work out how, as they were not delegates, to gain access.

"Mickey Rice!"

Mickey turned and saw, standing still as delegates swarmed past him, the bearded figure of Alfred "Tich" Smith, formerly general secretary of the red-button union and now parliamentary secretary of the UVW.

"Brother Smith!"

Smith extended his hand. "Good to see you again, Mickey and..." He turned to Dick.

"Dick Mortlake."

Smith grinned and snapped his fingers. "Middle Row branch secretary, if I recall. Anything I can do for you lads?"

"Well," said Mickey, "we were wondering how we get in without delegates' credentials. I've persuaded Dick that history will be made here today."

Tich Smith laughed. "You're not far wrong there, son!' He touched his chin with a finger. "Now, to get you in...Ernie!"

Ernie Bevin, who earlier in the year had earned the nickname of "the dockers' KC" when he had put the case for more humane employment conditions in the docks before the inquiry chaired by Lord Shaw, had the kind of figure which meant that he would never look really smart in his three-piece suit, the appearance of which was little improved by the row of pens in its top pocket.. "Morning, Tich; morning, brothers."

Mickey offered his hand. "Mickey Rice, Brother Bevin; we've met before."

Bevin frowned at him and then, as the recollection came to him, gave him a broad smile. "Leeds, 1917; the Peace Convention."

"I'm surprised you remember, Brother Bevin," said Mickey. "We were only together for about a minute."

Bevin lifted a finger and tapped Mickey lightly on the chest. "To be perfectly honest, I probably wouldn't have remembered us meeting had it not been for a little story Bob Williams told me later. Apparently, I said I hoped to be seeing more of you, and Bob told me that on the train on the way back to London you said that you probably wouldn't have any choice in the matter." He laughed heartily.

Mickey, determined not to be embarrassed, threw open his arms. "And look what has happened in the past three years: I was right, wasn't I?"

"Yes and no, Mickey, yes and no. It all depends whether you and your comrades are going to vote for or against the new amalgamation when the time comes."

"Brother Bevin, I shall be voting for the amalgamation, and I will be working hard to see that my comrades do the same."

Bevin winked. "Bob said you were a bright lad."

Well, thought Mickey, there's no time like the present. "But we want our own committee for the London Bus Section."

A smiling Bevin looked around at Tich Smith. "Bugger me, I'm being lobbied, Tich."

"You should expect a great deal more of that, if I know the London bus members. But these two lads have a bit of a problem, Ernie." It was noticeable that Tich, although Bevin's senior by twenty years, appeared to be deferring to him. "They want to know how to get into the conference without credentials. Mickey says they've come to see history made."

"Well, surely we've made provision for observers! The press has access, so why shouldn't our own members?" Bevin lifted his head and scanned the entrances. "Come with me, lads."

With Tich Smith in tow, Bevin led Mickey and Dick to an entrance at the side of the main hall. When the man on the door stepped forward to demand credentials, Bevin raised his right hand while with his left he ushered Mickey and Dick through the door.

"These two men are our guests," explained Bevin as the doorman watched them pass him.

Once in the hall, Mickey looked back to the door, intending to give Bevin a thumbs-up by way of thanks, but he had gone.

They were now confronted with a number of tables at which sat men with open notebooks before them, and Mickey realised that Bevin had led them to the corner of the hall reserved for the press. As they occupied two vacant chairs at the table nearest the door, several of the journalists turned to observe them, some with questioning frowns. One particular man—not much more than twenty years old, bespectacled and with a small moustache—almost smiled as he caught sight of Mickey but then, as if realising that he had not been recognised, returned his attention to the platform, upon which signs of activity indicated that the conference was about to begin. On several occasions during the conference, Mickey would scrutinise this individual, but although he looked vaguely familiar he was unable to put a name to him.

*

The conference was chaired by William Adamson, chairman of the Parliamentary Labour Party, a clean-shaven 57-year-old Scot who had lost a son in the war. He told the conference that they were concerned with neither the merits nor demerits of Russia's rivals nor the virtues or vices of Bolshevik forms of government. The issue was much greater. What did concern them was "the possibility of our people being committed to a policy of unwarranted interference with other people. Labour believes that it is the inalienable right of every nation to choose its own form of government." Adamson made much of the hypocrisy of the British government and its leader.

"Does the Prime Minister deny all knowledge of the Russian declaration of 28 January, vowing to recognise the independence of Poland?" He looked around the hall, as if in the hope that a reply might be forthcoming.

He threw out an arm. "Does he deny knowledge of the statement of 2 February, which repeated this vow and denied that there was any intention to force communism on Poland, as communism is only possible in countries where the vast majority of the working people have the will to secure it by their own initiative?" Once more he scanned the hall. Still no reply.

"Will the Prime Minister deny knowledge of the declaration of 7 May, which repeated this latter pledge?"

Once satisfied that no one in the hall thought Lloyd George capable of such dishonesty, Adamson thumped the table before him and declared: "The Prime Minister should understand that the British people are unalterably—*unalterably!*—opposed to war with Russia!" This earned him a rousing ovation in which Mickey Rice and Dick Mortlake participated.

Ernie Bevin presented the reports from the Council of Action.

"After the conference at the House of Commons on Monday, our first job was to tell the world what we'd done, and so we telegrammed the resolutions to France and Italy, and I can tell you that Councils of Action have now been formed in those countries—nationally, like this one, and they'll also be forming local councils as we have in Britain."

It had been surprisingly easy to form the local councils in Britain, as they were based on the Trades Councils that already existed in most towns and cities.

"When we met the Prime Minister, we told him that we were opposed to war, direct or indirect, against Russia. Moreover, we told him that the treatment of Russia since 1917 was unparalleled in human history and did not represent the will of the British people." Here was plain speaking, and it was applauded. "When Mr Lloyd George began to speak of Polish independence, we told him that we based our belief in that independence on the declarations of the Soviet government, and that we refused to build a policy on false hypotheses."

Bevin had lost most of his West Country accent, although it was still detectable to the attentive ear, and Mickey noticed a tendency to bring his teeth into contact with his lower lip, making a subtle whistling sound, when he pronounced an ess; barely noticeable for much of the time, it was plainly evident on *hypotheses*; and while Mickey had often noted this habit in men from working-class backgrounds who now wished to distance themselves from their class, with Bevin it appeared to be a natural impediment that he was doing his best to minimise.

"We then got in touch with the Russian and Polish representatives, inviting them to state their views, as a result of which Russia issued its peace terms—which were not only fair, brothers and sisters, but generous. We then saw the Prime Minister a second time, saying: 'Now you have the independence of Poland safe, and Soviet Russia with a guaranteed peace, will you please state, in equally frank, clear, and unambiguous terms, the British terms for peace with Soviet Russia?'" Bevin's gaze wandered over the conference, allowing tension to build. "And do you think that Mr Lloyd George complied with this request?" He brought his fist down onto the table. "No! Instead, he claimed to fear there was some trickery afoot!" This provoked a chorus of moans from the delegates.

Bevin sighed, indicating that the Council of Action had been somewhat exasperated in dealing not with a leading statesman but with an uncooperative child. "So back we went to the Russian representatives, who handed us a telegram dated 11 August in which Georgi Chicherin, their foreign minister, announced a peace signed with Latvia and a preliminary peace with Armenia. Mr Chicherin said that the Russian delegation had waited for the Polish peace delegation on 9 August, but it had not arrived. Instead, it was found in Siedlce when that city was taken by the Red Army." Another sigh from Bevin. "So we saw the Prime Minister for a *third* time, and asked him where the trickery was—Moscow or Warsaw!"

This brought a wave of appreciative laughter. It was, thought Mickey, almost as if Bevin were reporting back to a mass meeting of his members following hard-fought negotiations with a recalcitrant employer, explaining how he had stood up to the man on the other side of the table not as a means of singing his own praises but in order to inject some of that fighting spirit into his audience.

"And so now," he said, winding up, "this Council of Action of yours must consider what the labour movement will do if Poland refuses to accept the Russian peace terms—especially now that France has declared its support for Poland." He leaned forward, as if to share a revelation with the delegates. "And we don't need to be geniuses to work out why France has done this, do we? It has declared its support for Poland in the hope that this will force Russia to make changes to its peace offer. Our hope, on the other hand"—his voice began to rise—"is that this conference will send such a message to the Russian Soviet as will strengthen her position—that it will send out a clarion call to all the peoples of the world!"

As the applause began to die, Mickey turned to Dick. "So what do you think of your next general secretary?"

Dick nodded. "He'll do," he acknowledged, although hastening to add: "But he won't always be this progressive, Mickey."

"How can you know that?"

"Because they never are, mate."

Next up was J.R. Clynes, another self-educated man who had left school to work in a cotton mill at the age of ten and was now a Manchester MP, to make a telling point not mentioned by Bevin: the British government, which had not even made a diplomatic protest when Poland was doing well in its war on Russia, now threatened to intervene militarily when the tables were turned.

When Adamson announced that the motion approving the formation of the Council of Action would be moved by J.H. Thomas, Mickey groaned.

"Should be fun," said Dick with a grin.

"Oh, it will be."

And so, after a fashion, it was. There were, said the nattily-dressed Thomas, two principles involved. First, the executive committees represented at this conference must realise that if the motion was passed their executive responsibility would be transferred to the Council.

"In other words," murmured Mickey, "it would be the Council and not the executives of the individual unions that would call strike action."

""Is he trying to frighten them into voting against the motion, then?"

"Makes you wonder, doesn't it?"

Secondly, said the railwaymen's leader, direct action would, if necessary, be taken. He had always opposed this, but one needed to ask whether the desired outcome could be achieved by parliamentary means. "In my view," he said, "the disease is so dangerous, the situation so desperate, that only desperate and dangerous methods could provide a remedy."

Despite Thomas's best efforts, the motion was carried unanimously.

"Now it's the big one," said Mickey.

It was moved by W.H. Hutchinson of the engineering union. The motion pledged resistance to every form of military action against the Soviet government and instructed the Council of Action to remain in existence until an absolute guarantee that such action would not be used was received, all British naval forces involved in blockading activity had been withdrawn, and the Soviet government had been recognised and unrestricted trading relationships established. The motion authorised the Council to call "any and every form of withdrawal of labour" to give effect to this policy. After speeches by, among others, Bob Williams and the miners' president Bob Smillie, this was passed unanimously.

As a final item of business, the conference agreed—again

unanimously—a levy of a halfpenny per member in order to finance the Council of Action.

And then, in a surprise that capped them all, the delegates closed the conference by standing and singing the "Internationale." Mickey felt a flutter of panic because although he was very familiar with the melody and even more with the spirit which motivated the anthem, he had committed no more than a few lines of the lyrics to memory.

Arise ye starvelings from your slumbers
Arise ye prisoners of want…

For the rest of the verse, Mickey faked it, moving his lips soundlessly until he recalled a line or two. *Now away with all your superstitions…We'll change forthwith the old conditions…* He felt relief as they approached the rousing chorus, for this was impossible to forget; and he was not alone in this because, such was the increase in volume, that it was obvious that these lines were being sung by some voices which hitherto had been silent or hesitant.

Then comrades come rally!
And the last fight let us face.
The Internationale
Unites the human race.

The only journalists who stood and sang were the *Daily Herald* correspondent and the young man who had appeared to recognise Mickey.

Dick, of course, was word-perfect, standing next to Mickey with head erect, his deep voice booming with such effect that heads were turned in his direction. Looking out over the conference, hearing the delegates urge *servile masses arise* with one voice, Mickey was as moved as he had been years earlier when he, along with Dick and Dorothy, had attended a performance of Saint-Saëns' *Organ Symphony*—and for much the same reason, for although it had obviously not been the intention of the composer the soaring climax had suggested to him the moment when his class would finally take power, ushering in a future of freedom and happiness.

"You're emotional, Comrade," commented Dick as, when the last note had died, he turned to Mickey.

Mickey brushed a tear from his cheek. "Of course I'm bloody emotional! Why aren't you?"

Dick grinned. "Because I was trained not to be, Comrade. Any flautist who finds himself sobbing over a beautiful passage of music will soon find himself out of a job."

Mickey laughed. "Good point, Dick. Now answer the important question: was history made here today?"

"I think it may have been, Mickey," he nodded with a grin, "but let's see if the words are followed by action."

*

"Comrade Rice!"

Exiting Central Hall with Dick Mortlake, Mickey turned to see the vaguely familiar young journalist raising a hand to attract his attention. Having achieved this, he advanced and extended his right hand.

"Andrew Rothstein, Comrade."

"Ah, of course!" It had been several years since he had seen Theo's son. Andrew, he noted, was taller than Theo, but with a tendency to plumpness. "I didn't realise that you were a journalist now."

"I'm the London correspondent for ROSTA, the Soviet news agency," he replied with a smile tinged with pride.

"Your father will be very happy with today's result."

Andrew nodded, but there was little pleasure in the gesture. "Yes, he will be very happy—when he hears of it."

Mickey frowned. "Has he been arrested?"

Andrew cast a somewhat doubtful glance in Dick's direction.

"It's alright; Dick is a comrade."

"And a wonderful singer." Andrew sighed. "No, he has not been arrested." He paused. "Three days ago, my father left the country on a British destroyer."

"*Deported?*"

"No, he left as a member of the official trade delegation, with Comrade Miliutin—hence his mode of transport."

"Ah, he said he thought he needed to discuss a certain matter with Lenin."

Andrew nodded. "Yes, although ostensibly the reason for his voyage is to report on the progress of the negotiations with Lloyd George, he will also discuss the matter to which you refer with Comrade Lenin." His shrug was almost an indication of helplessness. "Furthermore, he has been away for almost thirty years and so he is keen to see the new Russia."

Mickey was finding it difficult to understand why Andrew looked so worried. "Then why the look of concern, Comrade."

Andrew's first sigh had been uttered as a sign of exasperation regarding his father's rash decision; the one which escaped him now might have been due to Mickey's apparent slowness in comprehending the consequences of that decision.

"Because he will not be allowed to return, Comrade. According to my sources, the British government has already declared him *persona non grata*."

There followed a silence in which a stunned Mickey digested this information. And not just the information, for it was now clear what game the Special Branch men had been playing: their purpose in providing the false allegation to Sylvia Pankhurst had been intended not so much as a means of tarnishing Theo's reputation in the movement as a device to get him to Moscow to clear himself with Lenin and, once he was out of the country, to slam the door behind him.

"Did Lenin instruct him to go to Moscow?"

"Far from it," Andrew replied, shaking his head. "In fact, after his departure, a message arrived from Lenin advising him against leaving the country, as he felt he was of great value here."

Mickey pondered that for a moment. "Should I ask my contact to bring this to the attention of Lloyd George?"

Andrew almost laughed. "There would be no point, Comrade. Lloyd George had no personal attachment to my father; he felt he needed him in this country as a channel to Lenin." He almost smiled. "Since the arrival of the trade delegation, there hasn't exactly been a shortage of Soviet officials in London, has there? To put it bluntly, as far as the Prime Minister is concerned my father's presence is no longer required, and I daresay the action of the Home Office is already known to him and was taken with his approval."

23

As it turned out, the Councils of Action were called upon to take little action. On 15 August, the Soviets were defeated in a battle outside Warsaw and commenced a general retreat. Ironically, however, a defeat on the military front led to a political victory, as the Allied united front now fell apart for, having been preparing to intervene militarily on Poland's behalf, that pretext had now disappeared. On 17 August, the Council of Action met and later issued a manifesto calling for the conclusion an immediate peace with Russia.

"But did you see the advice it gave to the local Councils of Action?" asked Dick Mortlake. They were in Dick's flat, sharing a pot of tea with Gladys and Annette.

Mickey groaned, remembering Dick's advice that they should wait to see if the words of 13 August were followed by action. "I did."

Dick insisted on spelling it out. "The local councils should act chiefly as information centres, and should certainly not usurp the power of the local union executives, especially when it came to the withdrawal of labour." He brought a finger to his chin and cast a glance at the ceiling, as if trying to recall some event. "Did I just imagine or dream that Jimmy Thomas at that conference said that acceptance of the Council would mean that the executive responsibility of each union would be transferred to the Council?"

"No, that's what he said, but what he and others like him are now afraid of is not that the Council will declare a general strike—in the same manifesto it said that this would be unlikely, as its aims could be achieved by a refusal to carry troops and munitions and the like— but that local shop stewards will jump the gun."

"Fair point," Dick conceded.

"Have you given any more thought to membership of the party?"

"I need to have a word with Sylvia."

This was the first indication Dick had given that he may have been involved in the formation of the "Communist Party, British Section of the Third International." Mickey was tempted to ask if he had been one of the people who had attended this momentous event in a small East End flat back in June, but thought better of it.

"Well, you'll have to wait a while before you do that, Dick, because she's not returned from Russia yet."

Dick's eyebrows shot up. "No? How do you know that?"

"A couple of comrades who attended the Congress gave a report-back the other evening. According to them, she arrived so late that she missed most of the actual Congress. Like several others, she had no passport and so had to take her chances as a stowaway."

"Do you know if she had the opportunity to put forward her view on parliamentary activity and affiliation to the Labour Party?"

"Apparently, she had a meeting with Lenin."

"And?"

Mickey shrugged. "I don't know, but it's said that she has mellowed somewhat."

*

It was September before Dick had his discussion with Sylvia Pankhurst.

"Well?" Mickey enquired when he saw Dick the following morning in Middle Row garage.

"You'd better give me a membership application, Comrade."

Mickey, exultant, laughed. "Really?"

Dick had raised his right foot, preparatory to climbing into his vehicle. "Really. Later this month, when her party's first congress meets in Manchester, she'll be recommending that it cooperates with the CPGB in holding another unity conference."

"So the first congress of her party will also be its last?"

Dick shrugged. "That's what it sounds like to me."

"So what brought this about?"

"The discussions at the Comintern—and her own discussions with Lenin. She's come around to the view that it boils down to a choice between unity and isolation. She's not the only one: Willie Gallacher has been converted as well, and he'll be working to involve the remaining members of his shop stewards' committee and the Socialist Labour Party up there in Scotland in the new unity conference."

Dick, seeing his conductor emerge from the output office, pulled himself into the cab and started the ignition.

*

In due course, Lloyd George advised the Polish government to accept the Russian peace terms, as these did "no violence to the ethnographical frontiers of Poland as an independent State," warning that if these were rejected, Britain would be unable to assist. The Tory press, while no longer calling for war, continued its anti-Soviet propaganda. And the Civil War, still aided, although now mainly clandestinely, by the Allies, continued.

24

"So it's looking like the miners will be out on the stones before long," Mickey remarked to Barney Macauley as they shared a drink with a few of the other lads, EC members and officers, in the Earl's Court Tavern.

They mostly stood at the bar, an indication that this would not be an all-nighter. Never much of a drinker before he came to London—or, for that matter, for a few years after that event—Mickey had grown to like the smell of hops and the feeling of fellowship to be found on occasions like this. The taste of the beer and the effect a modest ingestion of it had on his consciousness was also acceptable; but he knew he would never become a drunkard like Eric's father, the man who, three years earlier, had hurled the fact of his bastardy into his face when, knocked sideways by the death of Dorothy, Mickey had paid an ill-judged visit to Reading.

Barney nodded. "It's looking that way. Mind you, it was only early this year when they got that extra two bob a shift."

"Ah, but that was a close one," said George Sanders, joining the conversation. "The votes for acceptance only came to around 54 percent, if my memory doesn't deceive me."

"That was only in April," said Barney, "and at their conference in July they decided they were due another two bob a shift."

"That's understandable," said Sanders. "They were after three bob a shift that time around and they got two, and now, having taken a look at the industry's figures, they reckon there's more to be had."

"And it appears that we might be involved in their scrap," said Mickey.

"That's possible. Mickey. The Board of Trade dismissed their claim, and their ballot for industrial action in late August resulted in a 74-percent 'Yes' vote. The Triple Alliance"—the miners, the railway workers and the Transport Workers' Federation—"pronounced the miners' claim 'reasonable and just,' and the TUC Congress in Portsmouth went along with that view. The government wouldn't move, though, and so the miners suggested, in the interests of avoiding a strike, that the two bob per shift be granted immediately and that an examination be conducted into the industry's finances, the reasons for declining output, and the industry's wage systems—time- and piece-rates. But the Board of Trade tells them that output and wage systems can be discussed across the table with the owners, and that the finances of the industry have already been examined by the government.

"Sounds to me as if the government *wants* a strike," said Barney Macauley.

"It does sound a *bit* like that, Barney," conceded Sanders. "Anyway, Sir Robert Horne at the Board of Trade tells the miners that he won't concede the wage demand, so Bob Smillie tells *him* he can forget the union's other suggestions. Nevertheless, they meet again on 20 September, but the only progress is that Horne says the wage demand should go to an impartial tribunal which would meet immediately and conclude its business lickety-split. The following day, the miners hold a delegate meeting and agree to strike." He spread his hands. "And that's where we are today, comrades."

"So," asked Macauley, echoing Mickey's earlier comment, "do you think we'll be involved?"

Sanders took a cigarette from his Gold Flake packet and struck a match. "Too early to say," he said. He applied match to cigarette. "I had a quiet word with Bob Williams the other day. He reckons there's still a way to go and that some form of progress is possible. He also reckons that the members of the miners' executive are not all keen on striking if a way can be found to avoid it. Anyway, the Triple Alliance is meeting Lloyd George tomorrow, and so we'll have to see if the Welsh Wizard can pull something out of the hat. If it comes to a question of solidarity action, of course, a lot will depend on how Jimmy Thomas behaves himself."

Barney Macauley shook his head in an indication of disapproval. "That bugger is bound to come a cropper one of these days."

"Yeah," said Mickey. "But when?"

"Sorry, madam, no unaccompanied ladies!" This was the barman.

Mickey leaned back, peering around those standing at the bar to give him an unobstructed view of the door, through which had just walked another reason why he would not become a drunkard: Annette.

"Oh, she's accompanied alright," Mickey called to the barman.

For the staff at Transport House, the working day had extended beyond the duration of today's EC meeting, and Annette had agreed to walk down to the Earl's Court Tavern so that she and Mickey could travel home together on a number 31 bus. Her blond head approached but, after a day labouring over the ledgers, there was no twinkle in her eye.

"Can we go now, Mickey?" she asked.

He nodded to his glass, still half full, on the bar. "Just a few minutes, sweetheart. Can I get you something?"

She shook her head, pouting. "I am hungry, Mickey." A sigh. "And I have to prepare our dinner when we get home." He could sense that she felt like saying that he could have prepared it if he had gone straight home after finishing work instead of coming here.

"We could get some fish and chips," he suggested.

An unenthusiastic nod. "If you wish."

"Don't worry, I just have one more question for George, and then we'll leave."

She looked at George, who gave her a polite nod. *"Bonsoir, Madame Rice."*

At last a smile. Almost. *"Bonsoir, Monsieur Sanders.*

"What's the question, Mickey?"

"Was the amalgamation discussed today, George?"

Ernest Bevin had commenced negotiations for the formation of his super-union as early as March, meeting the leaders of several unions involved in docks and waterways

"There was a report of the Anderton's Hotel conference in August, mate. Thirteen unions in attendance."

"But not including ours."

"Not at that stage, no. Bevin put forward a draft structure for the new union, which was agreed."

"Devilish clever," commented Barney Macauley. "The country is divided into eleven areas, each of which will have its committee. But as well as those, there will be trade groups, with their own committees at area and national level—they'll have the power to deal with terms and conditions within their industries. The areas and the trade groups will have delegates on the general executive council."

Sanders shook his head. "Clever it may be," he sighed, "but to me it sounds like a recipe for divide and rule."

Macauley drew his lips together and narrowed his eyes in a thoughtful pose. "I can see how it might work like that in certain circumstances," he said. "You mean with the area delegates on the executive council outnumbering the trade groups?"

"That's what I mean," said Sanders.

"Hard to see how it would work like that," Mickey intervened. "The area reps will also be members of trade groups, and *vice versa*. It's not as if their interests will be any different."

"Bevin was quite convincing the way he explained it," said Barney, who had heard several accounts from comrades in the docks. "He said that if we didn't have the areas and their committees, the new union would be no different from the Transport Workers' Federation, and we all know how difficult it sometimes is to get the affiliates of the Fed to adopt a common position." He looked at Sanders and pulled down the corners of his mouth. "Sorry, George, but I'm convinced that it will be the areas which will get members from different industries working together, making it one union."

"Well, we'll see."

"Anyway, a few weeks after that, our own union and the National Union of Vehicle Workers joined the discussions," said Barney.

"So," asked Mickey, "which trade group will we be in?"

For once, Barney looked a little sheepish. He drew a hand over his head, as if smoothing hair that was no longer there. "At the moment, Mickey, the trade groups are what you might call a work in progress. There are only five so far, and so if that didn't change us busmen would end up in the road transport group..."

"Along with the commercial drivers, the carters and so on..."

"That's right, and that was only added after we and the NUVW joined the talks. But don't worry: we're sure to get a passenger transport group as well."

"That would be us, the tramways and the cabs?"

"Exactly. In fact, it would be like being back in the old re-button union."

"That would be good, Barney, but it still wouldn't be good *enough*. What we need..."

"Is a committee for London busworkers alone," Barney finished the sentence for him. Laughing, he clapped Mickey on the shoulder. "If you've told us once you've told us a thousand times, Mickey, and I agree that it would be a fine thing. In the meantime, there'll be a Bus Wages Board in time for next year's wages negotiations—I've told you that already, and there's no reason why that shouldn't be continued once we're in the new union." His expression turned serious. "But let me tell you, comrade, if we want any more than that we'll have to fight hard to get it, and while Ernie Bevin is all sweetness and light at the moment in order to keep everyone on board, he won't look kindly on any movement that threatens the amalgamation."

Mickey reached for his glass and drained the remains of his pint. "Then we'll fight hard for it, Barney," he said. "Won't we?"

Barney held his gaze for a while, perhaps realising that, had Mickey not agreed to withdraw his nomination for the executive seat that Barney now occupied, he might not be standing here. "We will, Mickey, we will," he said at length.

"So what's the next step?"

"Another conference at the beginning of December to smooth the rough edges, followed by a ballot of the members early in the New Year."

"And do you think you might get agreement for a passenger transport trade group at that conference, Barney?"

Barney grinned and gave him a wink. "I think we might, Mickey."

Annette was tugging at his sleeve.

"Then I'll bid you goodnight, comrades."

25

On Sunday 7 November, to mark the third anniversary of the Russian Revolution, Mickey, Annette, Dick and Gladys attended a rally at the Albert Hall organised by the Hands Off Russia movement and the new Communist Party. Apart from the resolution sending congratulations to the Soviet government on its achievements, there were a couple of other noteworthy incidents.

Bob Williams moved a resolution calling upon the Council of Action to deliver an ultimatum to the British government stating that unless all remnants of the blockade were lifted, interference in Russian affairs ended, and the Soviet government accorded recognition with full trading relations, a general strike would be called. During the course of his speech, Bob asserted that the masses had been chloroformed by the press, even though this was operated by trade union labour, and that Minister of War Churchill could have as many munitions factories as he liked but, given control of Fleet Street for a month, the movement would prove a match for him. The British revolution, he predicted, would arise not in London but in the great industrial centres of the provinces.

But it was Col. Cecil John L'Estrange Malone, MP, who provided Fleet Street with its headlines for the following day.

Before the proceedings had opened, Annette had been curious about this man with the military title, French middle name, and parliamentary designation.

"I do not understand, Mickey. Is this man a comrade?"

"Yeah," said Gladys, "I was wonderin' that meself."

It was Dick who replied. "I don't know about the French name, but he is indeed a colonel. During the war, he commanded a seaplane squadron and was a bit of a hero, by all accounts. In 1918, he was elected as MP for East Leyton..."

"But not as a communist, surely?" asked Annette.

"No, far from it. Not only was he elected as a Coalition Liberal, but he was at the time very *anti*-communist."

"So what changed his mind?" asked Gladys.

"In 1919, despite the blockade, he went to Russia, where he met Litvinov, Chicherin, Trotsky, and a number of other leaders. Civil war or no civil war, they gave him the grand tour and he was able to see for himself what conditions were like and what the people were thinking." Dick shrugged. "By the time he arrived back in Britain, he considered himself a communist."

"Not only that," added Mickey, "but he joined the BSP. Theo was a supporter of his. He attended the unity conference three months ago and was elected to the central committee."

"My goodness," Annette sighed. "So we already have a communist MP!"

"We do," said Mickey with a grin, "although whether he gets returned next time might be a bit doubtful."

Malone's speech on this occasion could only be described as incendiary. Despite pledges in Parliament and the activities of what he described as the "Council of Inaction," war was still being waged against Soviet Russia, with British officers and men donning Russian uniforms. This brought a frown to Mickey's brow, and turning to Dick he saw the same doubt expressed on his face. Malone looked forward to the day when they returned to the Albert Hall to celebrate the success of the British Revolution. People needed to decide whether they would continue to support the capitalist class, with its "scurvy agents" Churchill and Lord Curzon and their "sturdy henchmen" Arthur Henderson and J.H. Thomas. What would be a few Churchills hanging from lampposts or put against the wall compared to the thousands of Indians slaughtered at Amritsar or the hordes of patriots killed in Ireland?

"Jesus," said Mickey, "that should get him a few months behind bars." As, indeed, after Malone faced a charge of sedition, it would.

Dick nodded. "The man's a loose cannon."

*

"So the miners' strike is over, Bob?" Mickey asked the Transport Workers' Federation leader as they caught him leaving the Albert Hall. The strike had been called off a few days earlier.

"Ah, hello Mickey, Dick, ladies! Yes, it's over—for now at least."

"Listen, you lot," Gladys interjected, "if you're are gonna stand around talkin' shop, Annette and me are gonna get out of the cold."

"Okay, Glad, we'll catch up with you," said Dick, "We won't be more than a couple of minutes."

"Yes, I've heard that before."

Mickey gave Annette a grin as, perhaps against her will, she fell in with Gladys's intentions.

"Was it hard going to get a settlement?" Mickey asked.

Bob Williams laughed. "Well, I would hardly call it easy. Lloyd George got involved, and first of all he hammered away at putting the claim for the two-bob increase before a tribunal and opening talks with the owners regarding output." He pulled his overcoat about him. "A bit chilly now, don't you find? Anyway, he got the bit between his teeth on the question of output and he just wouldn't let it go: he suggested a sliding scale, a bit like what the railwaymen accepted, but this time based on output instead of the cost-of-living index. At first, the closest Bob Smillie would come to accepting that was to say that it could be considered once the two bob had been conceded. By this stage—and we're talking about late September here—the miners' leadership wasn't exactly united. Smillie recommended a second ballot, but the majority at a delegate conference wouldn't have it, although there was a sizeable minority in favour. To be honest, there were quite a number in the Triple Alliance who were keen on a settlement. But when Smillie tells Lloyd George that the strike is on, the Wizard goes berserk, refusing to believe that his proposals had been discussed in detail. The upshot of this was that the strike notices were suspended for a week while the EC and the owners discussed output.

"Long story short, the talks with the owners broke down over just where the sliding scale should start. Despite Lloyd George's urging, the boys refused to resume negotiations. The owners then came out with a better offer: an extra shilling a shift for 240 million tons, 1/6d for 244 million tons, two bob for 248 million tons, and so on. So the EC decided on a second ballot."

"What brought about the change of heart?" asked Dick.

Bob exhaled noisily, a great cloud of breath on the chill air. "The EC could see that things are changing: the boom has reached its peak, Dick; prices are beginning to fall; other economies are beginning to pick up, and so our exports are slowing; the period of high-wage work that we saw during the war and the last couple of years is coming to an end."

"But the members didn't see it like that," said Mickey.

Bob Williams chuckled. "No, they didn't, and by more than three to one they rejected the owners' offer, and so the strike started on 17 October."

"And a few days later the NUR decided on a sympathy strike," said Mickey with a grin.

"They did," said Williams, "although their general secretary told the world he didn't agree with it."

"Jimmy Thomas said that to please his parliamentary colleagues," said Mickey. "But, anyway, they called it off."

"They did," Williams acknowledged, "although to be fair that was at the request of the miners, because negotiations were about to begin again, and the EC thought it could get a settlement this time—

which, after four days, they did: the extra two bob per shift will be paid immediately, sort of on account, and wages will then be adjusted every four weeks. The EC went to ballot with a recommendation to accept..."

"But the members voted to reject..."

"By a very slim majority, they did, but the strike, which had lasted seventeen days, was called off, because according to the union's rule-book a two-thirds majority is needed to continue a strike."

"Now the important question, Bob: what will happen now?"

"My own prediction, Mickey, is that production will increase hand over fist, so the miners will probably find that their pay per shift is increased by more than the two bob they were after."

"But in the longer term..."

Bob Williams nodded. "You're right, Mickey, you're right. In the longer term, once this recession really gets underway there'll be less demand for industrial coal and so that sliding scale will start to move in the other direction."

"So we've not heard the last of it yet."

"I fear not." He shrugged himself further into his overcoat. "Damn, it's cold."

*

A few days later, in the output at Middle Row garage, discussion of the Albert Hall rally was renewed. "Did you see that the Cabinet has agreed to send a draft trade agreement to Moscow?" asked Mickey.

Dick whistled. "I didn't think the resolution passed at Sunday's rally would be quite so effective," he drawled. "Or at least so soon."

Mickey laughed. "It probably had more to do with the fact that on 4 November the Red Army took Sebastopol in the Crimea, Dick. The White armies are finished, mate. The Civil War is over."

"In which case, Malone's speech on Sunday was somewhat behind the times."

"That's true. And a further item of good news—for you, anyway: the Labour Party has denied the CP's application for affiliation."

"In which case I'd better complete that membership application, hadn't I?"

"Careful now," Mickey joked, "because we'll almost certainly try again."

Dick gave him a wink. "I'll take my chances, Comrade."

PART THREE

1921

26

The amalgamation conference on 2 December gave the thumbs-up to the proposed new union, which would be called the Transport and General Workers' Union, opening the way for the individual unions involved in the process to ballot their members. There was still no provision for a passenger transport trade group, but Barney Macauley reported back that this would certainly be agreed if the membership of the United Vehicle Workers voted in favour of the amalgamation.

"That's not what you promised," Mickey challenged Barney Macauley when they met in the Earl's Court Tavern.

"That's right, Mickey, because I didn't promise anything. I said we'd fight for it and that we might get agreement on the passenger trade group at the conference. I did fight for it and was told we'd have to wait until our union's votes had been counted in the New Year."

Early in January, the unofficial Rank and File Committee which, once the autocratic tendencies of Stanley Hirst and the majority of the Executive Council had become apparent, had been formed to replace the old red-button Vigilance Committee, invited certain full-time officers to state their views of the pending amalgamation at a meeting at the Crown and Anchor pub on Clerkenwell Green. The officers were selected on the basis of their reputations as straight-talkers, and it went without saying that they were considered to be on the left; indeed, only such officers would have had the courage to risk the ire of Stanley Hirst by attending such a meeting.

To the surprise of many, the view put forward by George Sanders was in the minority, and while many of the assembled members were sympathetic to his concerns, few were willing to agree with his apparent conclusion. Dennis Davies had an easy time as chairman, for no matter how democratically-minded the members present, many behaved themselves out of respect for the fact that the speakers were now national officials of the UVW.

Charley Carter, financial secretary, took the view that amalgamation "not only of like unions, but of all unions, national and then international, is the only method of keeping a check upon the inquisition of capitalism and to bring about its demise." That got a few cheers, but Mickey Rice and Dick Mortlake were unmoved.

"Any idea what that means, Mickey?" Dick asked, keeping his voice down.

"Your guess is as good as mine," Mickey replied, "But it sounds that Charley is a bit of a Wobbly: One Big Union."

Ben Smith, still with his bushy sideboards, stressed capital's high degree of organisation. "We must, therefore," he concluded, "create such a machine that will effectively resist any encroachment of our position, such a machine that will give us the power of attack."

"Okay," murmured Dick Mortlake, "but it's just generalities."

Mickey nodded.

Archie Henderson, brushing back his bush of red hair, took an historical view. "Chairman, whenever and wherever the workers fail it is because they lack the power and strength. These are the keys that open the door to the promised land. The land More dreamt of, Owen slaved for, Morris pictured, Hardie died for, Smillie works for, and all good, thoughtful men hope for. Our first step to power and strength is amalgamation."

"Yes, Archie, but what about *this* amalgamation?" an irritated Mickey muttered.

George Sanders, rising to his feet through a cloud of cigarette smoke, addressed that question. "Chairman and comrades, I will state at the outset that I am in favour of the principle of amalgamation—as long as it is not approached from any ulterior or underhand motive, or to foster the ambition of individuals who wish to loom large on the horizon."

There were sharp intakes of breath by several members of his audience at this, because to whom could he be referring but Ernest Bevin? Well, maybe Hirst, but certainly Bevin.

"I want to state quite frankly that I should have been more enamoured of the scheme that is now in front of the members had the National Union of Railwaymen and the Associated Society of Locomotive Engineers and Firemen been included in the list of unions for the proposed amalgamation. Whether they have been approached or not I am unable to state, but at any rate if it is at all possible to get them in it ought to be done without delay. It appears to me that an amalgamation of transport unions is not complete without these two bodies, and instead of rushing the present scheme every effort should be made to persuade them to come into the scheme, or if they have refused, it ought to be made quite clear to the members of the constituent unions who are asked to support the new scheme."

George paused and looked around the room, checking that his audience was attentive and thoughtful; it was.

"One more point needs to have the careful consideration of our members before voting, and that is that the officials of some of the unions that we are asked to amalgamate with went over to the side of the capitalist class while the late war was in progress. Seeing the terrible state this country is reduced to, they may be sorry for what they have done, but there is no guarantee that in the face of a crisis they would not do exactly the same again, and as the majority of the members of these unions probably acquiesced in their attitude, it is a point that must be looked at. It does not follow that because you ask a man 'Are you in favour of amalgamation?' if he answers 'Yes' it does not mean that he is in favour of amalgamating with everything and everybody. On the same principle that oil does not amalgamate with water, we ought to be assured that whatever fighting powers we have will not be deadened by close alliance with bodies which would stultify our efforts towards emancipation."

Another pause, this time, seemingly, to gather breath. "If the members on looking into these questions will feel confident that our interests are guaranteed, then, of course, they will vote for this amalgamation scheme." A warning finger came up, the brows lowered. "If, on the other hand, they consider that more time should have elapsed before the vote is taken then, of course, they will refuse to vote until such time as a proper comprehensive scheme is put in front of them, embracing the whole of the passenger and goods system."

"Well, let's see what they make of that little lot," said Mickey as the applause died.

But members of the audience were reticent, and when they did speak they sounded confused. Yes, they agreed that there was strength in numbers, and that greater unity was to be welcomed, but...It was as if they wanted someone to stand up and clarify the matter for them, and soon heads were turning towards Mickey in expectation. But he let them dangle, sitting with folded arms while they made their often halting contributions, hoping that someone would make a point that he could latch onto, expanding it and laying the basis for a broad consensus. He had a long wait, but finally Willesden's Reuben Topping raised his hand.

"Chairman and brothers," he began in a grave tone, "I hope you'll forgive me for speaking plainly." He shrugged. "But that's what I do—you should all know that by now." That got a laugh, and created a sense of anticipation. "We're sitting here, talking as if we don't know what the experience of amalgamation is like. Some"—he waved a hand in the direction of the officers on the platform—"seem to think that it will lead us to the gates of the New Jerusalem. Others believe that the new union will create such a bulwark that any attack by the employers is bound to dash itself to pieces against its walls." He shrugged. "Both of those outcomes would, I suppose, be possible—but only if the leadership of the new union was deeply committed to those objects and the general membership was politically educated to a sufficient level." He turned and looked around the room. "Neither of those conditions are met in our current situation, comrades.

"So let's come back down to earth. This new union, the Transport and General Workers' Union, will not be a revolutionary political party but a trade union, an organisation primarily concerned with the terms and conditions of its members. Anyone who thinks that socialism can be brought about by trade union struggle should look at what's happened to the Industrial Workers of the World—the Wobblies—in the USA, where government repression and factionalism in the labour movement is reducing its numbers. If it's socialism you want, look at how it's being achieved in Russia—not by trade union activity but by *political* struggle."

He ran his tongue over his lips to moisten them. "So we are—and will be—a trade union." He threw out his arms. "But why are we acting as if we have no experience of amalgamation? What have we been going through this last year if it's not the effects of amalgamation, of the red button coming together with the blue? And has it been a positive experience?"

"Noooo," came the moans as heads were shaken.

"Do we have as much democracy in the United Vehicle Workers as we had in the old red-button union?"

"Noooo."

"Is Stanley Hirst the kind of leader who will stand by us through thick and thin?"

"Noooo."

"And *that*, brothers, is why we can't remain with what we have now!" He nodded as this was greeted with a stunned silence. "That's right, I'm saying that we need to agree to the new amalgamation— *but on terms that will ensure that our London bus section has returned to it the democracy it lost when we became the United Vehicle Workers, and that means, among other things, ensuring that we have the final say over our terms and conditions.*"

That received the largest round of applause so far, and Dennis Davies began to pick up his pen and notebook, appearing to think that this might be an appropriate point to bring proceedings to a close. But then he looked up and saw that Mickey Rice had his hand in the air. He grinned. "Brother Rice!"

Mickey got to his feet and, seeing a number of expectant faces turned in his direction, hoped that he would not disappoint them.

"Comrades," he said, "on the ballot paper, there will be two boxes, one for a positive vote and one for a negative. But it seems that there are a number of alternatives.

"First, a straightforward negative vote will leave us with the status quo, and as Reuben has so forcefully argued, that would not be acceptable to most of us. It's not just a question of getting rid of Stanley Hirst, a general secretary who calls the police when lay members attempt to observe a meeting of the Executive Council, something which was accepted as normal in the old red-button union."

This provoked laughter from some and scorn from others as they fondly remembered those so-recently departed days.

"No, it's more than that, but I'll come back to that in a while. Then there's the formula put forward by Brother Sanders." He paused, looking directly at Sanders. "Now let me say at the outset, brothers, that I have the greatest respect for George Sanders. Nobody can question his record and the depth of his commitment—or his courage, because tonight he has come here, a national officer, and basically argued against the proposal put forward by his general secretary and the executive council of our union. Furthermore, he was of great assistance to me when I first came on the job and became active in the union, and I will be forever grateful to him for that. But the arguments he has put forward this evening, brothers, are wrong."

Mickey let that sink in as a few gasped in shock. On the platform, Ben Smith was not very successfully trying to stifle a grin.

"On the one hand, George says that when casting their votes, our members should bear in mind that some leaders of the unions involved in the amalgamation went over to the side of the capitalist class during the recent war, by which, I take it, he means that they supported that war. And that is quite true: they did. On the other hand, however, he says that the amalgamation should be placed on hold until we can secure the participation of the NUR and ASLEF."

Many in the audience now knew what was coming. "Ooooohh..." went up the cry.

"Now, correct me if I'm wrong, brothers, but wasn't Jimmy Thomas, leader of the NUR, as staunch a supporter of the bosses' war as you could wish to find?"

The room erupted in laughter, but George was taking it well, nodding with a wry grin on his face.

"But even leaving that to one side, we've just seen what happens when you amalgamate with a larger union: that larger union, by virtue of its greater number of votes, dictates who will be general secretary of the amalgamated union. The NUR has almost a million members, brothers. If it was part of the current amalgamation scheme, who do you think would be our next general secretary? Brothers, George himself said it: just because you're in favour of amalgamation doesn't mean that you're prepared to amalgamate with everything and everybody.

"However, George doesn't ask anyone to vote against the current scheme. No, he predicts that members who are not happy with it will refuse to vote until a more comprehensive one is placed before them. Now to me that sounds like a call for abstention. And what would be the result of that? There are two possibilities, brothers: either the yes vote sails home or, if there are a sufficient number of abstentions, the legal requirements for amalgamations—at least fifty percent of the total membership voting, with a twenty-percent margin of victory—are not met and the union is out of the amalgamation. If that's the case, we would be stuck with a status quo which nobody wants in the hope that the NUR would have second thoughts and, taking us by the hand, lead us into a later amalgamation—and that's something I certainly would not want! And, come to think of it, neither would Jimmy Thomas because by that time Ernie Bevin would already be general secretary of the new union!"

He paused for a breather. He seemed to be doing well. Although George was trying not to scowl, the other officers seemed to be hanging on his every word; and he certainly had the attention of the audience.

"Now, let's say a few words about Ernie Bevin. George mentions 'the ambitions of individuals who wish to loom large on the horizon.' Well, no one would dispute that Ernie Bevin is an ambitious man, but is it *personal* ambition? Bob Williams, a man who, as secretary of the Transport Workers' Federation has worked alongside Bevin for several years, and knows him as well as anyone, told me some time ago that Bevin is not personally ambitious, and I tend to go along with that. What ambition he *has* got—and there seems to be plenty of it—concerns this organisation he's building. Now, being realistic, there will probably come a time, and possibly fairly soon, when his idea of what the union should be or the direction it should be taking on one question or another, will clash with some of our views, and we'll have to have a scrap. But can you name any man who might be able to lead this amalgamation of transport workers of whom that would not be true?"

He looked around the room, nodding at the silence that greeted this question. "No," he breathed, "of course you can't." And then, raising his voice: "But I'll bet you *can* name plenty who *would* be driven by personal ambition!"

Christ, he was beginning to sound like Bevin's election agent. But never mind: press on. "And then there's the question of ability. A year ago, there was the Shaw inquiry into wages and conditions in the docks. Bevin took *eleven hours, spread over two and a half days,* to present his closing argument. *Everyone*—including Lord Shaw, who congratulated him—was impressed. They called him the dockers' KC. This man who left school when he was still a boy. But let's not dwell on this one particular performance, because it's just an example, an illustration, of the careful preparation he brings to every important issue affecting the members. Oh, you might say, he comes from the docks, so why wouldn't he make that effort! A good point—maybe. Will he take the same care and effort when the issue concerns some other section—the trams, for example?"

Mickey hesitated to allow this to sink in, for some would know where this was leading.

"Well, we'll all have the opportunity to learn the answer to *that* question, because later this month the inquiry into the tramway men's wages opens, and I for one intend to be there to see how Brother Bevin performs!

"And how would we judge Bevin's performance on the political front? He's not a socialist in the same sense as some of us are, but hasn't he done rather well politically? Last year, faced with the possibility of war against Russia, Arthur Henderson called together the Parliamentary Labour Party, the TUC Parliamentary Committee and the Labour Party Executive Committee for a meeting at the Commons. Out of that meeting came the proposal for a Council of Action. As a result of the pressure it—and the three hundred and fifty local councils of action formed around the country—brought to bear, Lloyd George told Poland they should agree to the Russian peace terms, and that it they didn't they could expect no help from Britain! Now, brothers, who was it who urged Henderson to call that meeting in the Commons? Bevin! Who suggested the formation of the Council of Action? Bevin! Who led the Council of Action in its meetings with Lloyd George? Bevin! It would probably be too much to expect him to maintain that progressive outlook as his career progresses, but can you name one man able to lead this new transport amalgamation who would have been able to achieve as much? So I don't honestly think that the personality of Bevin—no matter how large he looms—can be given as a reason to vote against this amalgamation."

The officers on the top table were nodding, and the way the applause swelled suggested that many in the audience thought that Mickey was finished, but of course he wasn't.

"There is another alternative to this amalgamation, brothers. I've heard it suggested that we should form a TOT union—Tubes, Omnibuses and Trams." He shrugged. "I would ask the people behind this suggestion a number of questions. Who would recruit and train the administrative staff for this union? Who would arrange for the lease or purchase of premises, and how would this be financed? Who has sufficient influence with the Underground staff in ASLEF and the NUR to persuade them to move across to this new, untried and untested, union? Are those members who favour such a breakaway prepared for what could be year upon year of battle with those two unions as they fought to win their members back?" Another shrug. "Well, I suppose a union *could* be formed out of the buses and the trams alone, in which case we'd be back to the old red-button union—minus the cabs. But you'd still be faced with the problems involved with establishing the new organisation. *And* you'd have a fight to get recognition. *And* there would be constant scraps with those who declined to join the breakaway. So at the end of the day, brothers, this would simply be a recipe for division—which, of course, the employers would welcome."

There were a number of relieved smiles on the top table.

"And that leaves us with the only realistic option, brothers, which is to agree to the new amalgamation—but, as Reuben has said, subject to certain conditions."

"It's too late!" called a south London man down the front. "The ballot papers are out! The branches are organising the voting!"

"So we vote in favour, brother," replied Mickey, "and once the result is known, we put our demands to the leadership."

"What leadership?" demanded the same man, whom Mickey recognized now as one of those favouring the formation of a breakaway union.

Dennis Davies now came in. "Through the chair, lads, through the chair. But I think I can resolve this little discussion: As I understand it, once the result of the ballot has been announced, there'll be a further conference of the unions that have voted in favour; at that conference, a provisional leadership will be elected."

"There you go, then," Mickey resumed. "But it's important, brothers, that we all unite behind the same demands, rather than every branch going its own way. I therefore suggest that after the ballot result is announced we have a special meeting to discuss that very point, and to agree how we put those demands to the leadership."

"Sounds as if that will be a strictly bus meeting, Mickey," said Dennis Davies, "so I'll not ask for agreement on the proposal."

As the meeting broke up, Mickey waited while the officers made their way from the top table to the door.

"Watch your step, Mickey," murmured Ben Smith as he passed. "News of this is bound to get back to Hirst."

Mickey winked. "Thanks, Ben."

As George Sanders approached, Mickey held out this hand. "No hard feelings, George."

George took his hand. "Of course not, Comrade. Congratulations on your speech."

Once the officers had departed, some of the men began to gather around Mickey, patting his back, shaking his hand, letting him know they were willing to be part of the project: Lloyd of Palmers Green, Adams of Battersea, Cassomini of Forest Gate, Lancaster of Holloway, Topping of Willesden of course, Warne of Croydon, Vernon of Morden—the one known secessionist—and a tall, thin man, all knees and elbows, who was a stranger to him.

"Glad to make your acquaintance, Brother," said this latter. "I'm Bernard Sharkey. I was a copper, sacked after the 1919 strike; George may have mentioned my name."

"Yes, he certainly has, Brother Sharkey. Pleased to meet you at last. Where are you now?"

"I'm at Willesden with Reuben."

"You're in good company there, mate."

"Why don't we form ourselves into an organising committee?" suggested Morden's Vernon. He was above medium height, well-built, and in need of a shave—which was surprising, as his head was more closely shaved than his chin.

"That's fine with me," said Mickey, "as long as it's clear what we're organising *for*: a democratic London bus section, not a breakaway."

Vernon shrugged. "That makes sense. If that fails, *then* we can talk about a breakaway."

"Mmm, maybe," mused a sceptical Mickey. "Okay, let's make a note of each other's details."

Notebooks out, they gathered around the top table and jotted down names of men and their garages.

"If we're an organising committee, our first job will be to hold a meeting after the provisional leadership has been elected," suggested Mickey.

"That's right," said Vernon. "You want me to send out the notices convening it?"

"I think Mickey should do that," said Dick Mortlake, to which there were murmurs of assent from most of the others.

Vernon affected indifference. "I was just thinking of the cost of the postage and so on."

"We have a healthy branch fund," Dick came back.

"So do we," said Vernon, "although the branch committee keeps a tight rein on it."

"Actually, that raises an important point," said Mickey. "We have to make sure that we don't end up as a bunch of individuals representing no one. If our aim is to restore our section to what it was before the last amalgamation, we need to practice what we preach, and that means fully involving our members in the decisions and carrying our branches with us all the way."

"But most of the members won't understand," objected Vernon.

"Then it's our job to make sure they *do* understand," Mickey countered.

"That's what I call hard work," said Vernon.

Mickey sighed. "Well," he said, "it's what the rest of us call democracy."

27

In December, the workers' side of the National Joint Industrial Council for tramways had submitted a claim for an extra twelve shillings a week. The municipalities rejected not only the claim itself but also the suggestion that it go to arbitration. On behalf of the Transport Workers' Federation, Bob Williams urged tram workers to "consider their position, make their protests, and send in their resolutions." A similar claim had been put in for provincial busworkers, but while George Sanders was quoted as saying that talks were proceeding "in quite a conciliatory manner," Mickey Rice interpreted this to mean that, knowing the cause to be lost, George was not pushing very hard. The Minister of Labour then intervened on the tram issue, setting up a Court of Inquiry. The Executive Council of the United Vehicle Workers agreed to attend, deciding that the tramworkers' case would be put by Ernest Bevin of the Transport Workers' Federation and John Cliff. The employers would be represented by the Municipal Tramways Association for the municipal undertakings and the Tramways and Light Railways Association for the private concerns.

As he had announced at the rank and file meeting earlier in the month, on 26 January Mickey made his way to the St. Ermin's Hotel, very close to Electric Railway House, and sat among the observers as the inquiry opened. He was not the only one, of course: Cassomini, Topping, Lloyd, and others were there from the buses, along with Ernie Sharp and a crowd from the trams. There was also a small group of provincial tramworkers which Mickey assumed were either executive council members and/or leading lights from the large undertakings like Manchester, but they were strangers to him. He spent the first few minutes nodding to familiar faces—one of which belonged to Ernie Bevin who, having ensured that his papers were in order, cast his eye about the large room and, spotting Mickey, grinned and pointed a finger at him.

Bevin sat opposite the board of inquiry: Sir David Harrel in the chair, flanked by president of the National Transport Workers' Federation Harry Gosling, chairman of the London County Council's Highways Committee George Hume, former Labour Party chairman Frank Purdy, and vice-president of the Federation of British Industry Sir Hubert Rowell. Little John Cliff sat alongside Bevin, but he would have little to do. Harrel called the meeting to order, gave a brief introduction—questions of procedure had been hammered out when the board had met in private at the Ministry of Labour earlier in the month—and let Ernie Bevin off the leash.

Bevin was thorough, detailed, and his presentation would, with a break halfway through, consume all of the first day.

Early in the proceedings, Bevin let it be known that the trade union side of the National Joint Industrial Council had proposed that the tramway undertakings be grouped into three classes, according to size—and, it was inferred, ability to pay. This appeared to be news to the members of the inquiry, and by making this announcement Bevin was on the one hand demonstrating that the trade union side was reasonable, realistic and creative, and on the other hinting that, although the claim was for twelve shillings across the board, a graduated award might be acceptable. He compared this approach with that of the employers, some of whom had failed to implement previous awards, even when, in some cases, those awards had come via binding arbitration.

There could, said Bevin, be no doubt that the earnings of tramway workers had fallen behind the cost of living. The average wage for workers on the municipal systems was £3 15s 3d per week, and for those employed by private companies £3 11s 6d. But the companies cried that they were suffering losses, and were of the view that fare increases would result in a decline in ridership and, thus, in profitability. But the tramways provided a public service, as did roads. Did the public expect the roads to return a profit? No! Then why should this be expected of the tramways?

But, on the question of profitability, the municipal systems were not performing as poorly as their balance sheets would have us believe. "Because it is only fair, gentlemen," Bevin told the Board of Inquiry, "that we take into account the use to which their revenue is put. If, as they claim, revenue is insufficient to meet all their outgoings, let us take a look at some of those outgoings! In 1918-19, the municipal undertakings paid interest amounting to £2 million." He paused to allow the figure to sink in. "Two. Million. Pounds. And please note that I did not say that they *owed* that amount, but that they *paid* it." He threw out an arm. "So the capitalists were fully compensated!

"In the same period, £1 million was set aside in reserve and renewal funds. *Half* a million pounds was charged for the rental of roads." A hand went to his forehead. "Oh, wait! It seems, after all, that I may have been mistaken when I somewhat hastily said that the public would not expect roads to return a profit! A further £553,000, gentlemen, was taken for the relief of rates—although I acknowledge that £72,000 went in the opposite direction, as aid *from* the rates. A further quarter of a million pounds, gentlemen-- £266,000 to be precise—went in income tax." He turned to the employers' representatives, who were seated at a separate table, according them a withering glance before returning his attention to the members of the board. "Gentlemen, I must congratulate the employers! They have assiduously met every charge levied upon them: the charges of the capitalists, the local authorities, and the government. The only charge they have *not* met is that of their workmen, and this cannot be permitted to continue!"

After the chairman had called it a day, Mickey joined the other UVW observers as they made their way to the exit doors.

"Well," Ernie Sharp was passing judgment, "I have to say that that wasn't bad at all."

"Yes," said Reuben Topping, "I found myself thinking of what Mickey said at a meeting we had a few weeks ago. Who else could have made a presentation like that?"

"Brother Rice!"

Mickey turned and saw Ernie Bevin walking somewhat awkwardly towards him, a bulging briefcase clasped under his right arm. "Do you have time for a brief chat?" He looked at the others in the group. "Sorry, lads, I need to borrow Brother Rice for a while."

Ernie Sharp stuck out his right hand. "Bloody well done today,

Brother Bevin."

"Thank you, Brother." Bevin nodded at his briefcase. "Will my left hand do? The right's a bit busy at the moment."

"Give it here, for Christ's sake," said Mickey.

Bevin dropped the briefcase at his feet. "You're welcome to it, Brother." He shook Ernie's Sharp's hand and then did the round of his companions.

As the others departed, Mickey tried lifting the briefcase by its handle. "Bloody hell."

"Precisely. Cup of tea okay with you?"

"A cup of tea is fine. Where's the nearest Lyons?"

"Let's ask a taxi driver."

*

"You don't strike me as the typical Lyons' customer," Bevin observed as they were seated on the second floor of the Victoria branch.

"I'm not, and in a sense that's the idea." He smiled at Bevin. "George Sanders says that whenever he wants to meet someone for a private chat he goes to a Lyons Corner House because he's unlikely to come across anyone who knows him."

Bevin laughed. "I'll have to remember that." He waved at a waitress and placed their order. "So," he said, turning back to Mickey, "what did you think of today? Do you think we stand a chance?"

"Why would you ask me a question like that, Brother Bevin? You would know far better than me."

Bevin shrugged. "Maybe, maybe not." He gave Mickey a straight look. "But I'm interested in your view."

Mickey held his gaze and nodded. "Okay. Well, you impressed us, and I daresay you impressed the board. But it will be decided by other factors, won't it?"

"Oh?"

"First of all, the composition of the board. Anyone who doesn't know the score would think that with Gosling and Purdy on the board we must be in with a fair chance."

"But..."

"But I remember the role Gosling played during the 1915 London County Council tram strike, and he was no help to us then. He sits on the LCC with George Hume, you know, the bloke who's on the Board of Inquiry with him. But you must know him far better than I do."

Bevin nodded, sighing, "Yes, I probably do," giving no indication that he disagreed with Mickey's assessment of Gosling.

"I suppose some people might think it a bit strange, even improper, that the president of the Transport Workers' Federation is sitting in judgment of a case presented by a leading member of the Fed. But there are two ways of looking at this. If we win the case, yes, the press and the right wing *will* cry that it was improper. But what if we lose? Can the tramworkers and our union leadership expect support from the TWF when its own president was party to the decision?

"And then there's Frank Purdy." Mickey shrugged. "Well, he's Labour Party, so that could mean anything."

"So you think the composition of the board means that we're more likely to lose?"

A nod. "I do. But then there are the other factors: the cost of living is beginning to fall; the steam is running out of the economy; the employing class wants to put the brakes on the growth of wages."

Bevin pulled down the corners of his mouth. "By god, we don't stand a chance, do we?"

"I honestly don't think so, Brother Bevin. I'm sorry, but you asked for my view, and that's it."

"And do you know what, Brother Rice? I agree with you!"

Mickey was nonplussed; he frowned. "Then why...?"

"Why did I throw my heart and soul into my presentation today?"

"Yes—not to mention the hours you must have spent in preparation."

"I didn't do it for the Board of Inquiry, Mickey—can I call you Mickey? No, I did it for our members..."

"Slip of the tongue there, Brother Bevin."

Bevin thought for a second. "Oh, sorry! *Your* members." He smiled. "If you're representing the interests of the members, putting forward a case on their behalf, you always have to let them see that you're doing the best you possibly can. And if possible you should also give 'em something to think about, as I hope I did today. The arguments I put forward may not win this case, but I'm sure they'll come in useful in the future."

Their order arrived: a pot of tea, two cups, a sugar bowl and small milk jug and a plate of Swiss Roll for Mickey, Bevin having patted his stomach with a grimace when Mickey had suggested it.

"But I'm guessing that you didn't bring me here to talk about the Board of Inquiry," said Mickey.

Having poured his tea and added milk and sugar, Bevin lifted his cup. When Mickey first came to London, George Sanders had told him that all great men had their flaws, and he now witnessed one of Bevin's: he slurped his tea.

"You guess right. Do you remember that little chat we had in Westminster Central Hall just before the Council of Action reported back?"

"Of course."

"Well, that's what I want to discuss with you."

"I thought it might be."

Bevin watched as Mickey used his fork to convey a portion of Swiss Roll to his mouth. "Well, I understand that..."

"You sure you won't have some of this?" Mickey nodded at the plate of Swiss Roll.

"Ohhh, go on then," Bevin growled irritably after a moment of indecision. "Just the one slice."

"I'll ask them to bring another plate."

"No, don't bother with that; me fingers will do." He reached across and took a slice. After one bite he rolled his eyes. "Mmm, I love chocolate Swiss Roll. Maybe because it was one of the things we couldn't afford when I was a boy."

"Tell me about it," said Mickey.

"You too, eh?"

"And a few million others."

Bevin chuckled, wiping his fingers on his serviette. "You know, Mickey, I feel I can get along with you." He placed the serviette beside his teacup. "That's why I don't want a falling-out between us."

That got Mickey's attention. "Oh?"

"As I was saying, I understand that you're taking the matter we discussed at Central Hall a little further." Bevin looked up from his teacup. "You've got together a little pressure group. Is that right?"

Mickey was now on his guard. Obviously one of the national officers who had spoken at the Crown and Anchor had reported back. "Ye-e-e-s. Is that what we're going to fall out about?"

Bevin lifted his right hand, waving it from side to side in a rapid movement. "No, no, no, not necessarily, although as a rule I'm not in favour of rank-and-file movements." He raised a finger, having just remembered an important point. "Oh, and let me say before we go any further that I'm grateful for the kind words you said in my support at your meeting, Mickey."

Mickey noticed that he had not been invited to call Bevin by his first name, although he doubted that this had been a conscious decision. "You're very well informed, Brother Bevin."

Bevin nodded and drained his cup. "I am, and you're probably able to work out who this information comes from."

"My money would be on Ben Smith."

Bevin winked. "No flies on you, Mickey." He moved his cup aside and placed his hands on the table. "Have you worked out *exactly* what you want from the new union? If so, I'd be grateful if you'd tell me."

"Well, *I* have, but this hasn't been discussed with the boys yet, so it's subject to change."

"I'll bear that in mind, Mickey. Fire away."

Mickey took a deep breath. Well, we'll need our own committee for London busmen, directly elected from the divisions and meeting regularly. This committee—call it what you like—would negotiate wages and conditions with the employers."

"Alone?"

"How do you mean?"

"Do you see this committee of lay members meeting the employers on their own, or with an officer?"

"Oh, I imagine the major negotiations would be led by the appropriate national secretary." He grinned mischievously. "Trouble is, we don't yet have a separate trade group for passenger transport."

Bevin brought his right hand down firmly onto the table. "At least that, I can promise you, will come. Anything else?"

"Yes, we would need our own conference, with a delegate from each garage—again, meeting regularly."

"And the purpose of this conference would be...what?"

"Obviously to receive reports from the committee on major negotiations, but also to discuss matters of common concern." Mickey, having had a sudden thought, smiled. "And if you want to discourage the formation of rank-and-file movements, this would be the way to do it, I would have thought. As I say, though, these are just my ideas; others may have a different view."

"I doubt it, Mickey, I doubt it. Is that it?"

"One more thing: full-time officers to be elected by the members."

For the first time, Bevin groaned, "That's a recipe for officers courting popularity rather than doing what's right. I have to say, Brother Rice, that I *am* opposed to elected officers."

"Then with the greatest respect, Brother Bevin, I believe you will have a problem. And I *can* say that on this matter I represent the views of the majority of active members, because this has been a principle since the foundation of the red-button union in 1913. Every attempt to move to appointments has been challenged and defeated."

Another groan. "Noted." For a moment, Bevin looked down at the table, apparently absorbing what he had just heard. He sighed and looked across at Mickey. "Now, Mickey, can we agree that this part of our conversation will be strictly confidential, at least for the time being?"

Mickey nodded. "Yes, okay."

Bevin licked his lips. "There are a couple of problems with what you're asking, Mickey. First of all, if we give it to the London busmen, other sections will want similar arrangements."

"I may be wrong, but I don't think you'll find another section with the same circumstances."

Bevin held up his palms. "Maybe, maybe. But a far more serious problem is the cost." He placed his forearms on the table and leaned forward. "Once the new union kicks off, we'll be faced with enormous costs. For example, we've said that every full-time officer in the amalgamating unions will be guaranteed his job and at least his current salary. Then there's the question of premises. It's highly likely that we'll be running at a loss for the first few years."

"So you'll be telling us the same thing as the tram operators will be telling the Board of Inquiry tomorrow: Sorry, but we can't afford it."

Bevin grinned, impressed as much by this young man's audacity as by the power of his arguments. "Oh, you're a sharp one, Mickey Rice. But the two things are not the same: here, we're talking about the workers' money, the members' money. We'll have no other source of income, and costly improvements for one section could mean *no* improvements—or worse—for others."

"Unless we did it on the cheap."

Bevin was interested. "How would that work?"

"Evening meetings with just expenses reimbursed—and as we all have free travel that wouldn't amount to much. That kind of thing." He shrugged. "Please bear in mind that I'm not speaking on behalf of anyone here."

"That's understood."

"So are you saying that you don't object in principle to the scheme I've suggested?"

"I'm not saying that at all, Mickey. In fact, I *can't* say that, can I? Quite apart from the fact that we don't know who will be general secretary of the new union..."

"Oh, come on."

Bevin ploughed on. "Quite apart from that little detail, all such decisions will be the province of the executive council—lay members elected by their comrades."

"But the general secretary—whoever he is—will be very influential."

Bevin chuckled. "So do you think you can convince Stan Hirst to back your plan?"

"If you've had a full report of our recent rank-and-file meeting you know the answer to that."

"I do, yes." Bevin drew his palm across the tablecloth before looking Mickey in the eye. "Now to the important question: What will you and those who think like you do if you don't get the structure you've just outlined? And this, Mickey, is where we could have a falling-out."

Mickey was not entirely unprepared for the question, but took a moment before replying. "In that situation, Brother Bevin, it's likely that we would not all be of one mind. Already, there are some voices calling for a breakaway union. If Ben has reported our meeting accurately, you will know that I oppose that proposal."

Bevin sighed with, it seemed, satisfaction. "That's what I wanted to hear, Mickey."

"But it would be a mistake to underestimate the strength of feeling. Many of the old red-button men are *very* unhappy with the way things are done in the UVW. If they come to the conclusion that the situation in the Transport and General Workers' Union will be in any way similar to what they have now, some of them will be gone. There's no doubt about that, and I don't think that I or anyone else would be able to stop them."

"But, if it comes to it, will you try?"

"Of course."

Bevin nodded. "Good. I can't ask for more than that." He sniffed. "Now let me tell you something about this organising committee you've formed."

Mickey was intrigued. "Go on."

"You've got a joker in the pack."

"Vernon?"

Bevin spread his hands. "Seems I'm wasting my breath. Yes, Vernon: I have it on very good authority that he is not to be trusted. Don't ask me how I know."

28

The second half of January was quite mild, but Mickey Rice took little joy in this almost spring-like weather as, after his discussion with Bevin, he travelled home by bus in the rush-hour traffic. He was dead: he had promised Annette that he would visit the butcher's on his way home and, if he arrived before her, start to cook their evening meal, but neither of these things were now possible. She would be furious and he had no idea how he would deal with the situation, apart from arriving in Alexander Street with fish and chips for two leaking oil and vinegar through the newspaper wrapping.

"So." She was standing there as he came through the door of the flat, arms folded and head tilted back, as if she were looking down her nose at him.

He had seen this stance before: she had learned it from Gladys.

He lifted the hand holding the fish and chips in case she had failed to spot them. "I've got dinner, sweetheart. We should get these on the plates before they get cold."

"You said you would bring beef."

He hurried past her, heading for the kitchen. "I was too late for the butcher's. Got delayed in town, I'm afraid."

She pursued him. "Delayed? By your friends, I suppose."

He drew two plates from the cupboard where they kept their crockery. "By Ernie Bevin, as a matter of fact."

"Oh, and that was more important than buying our dinner." He arms were still crossed.

He stopped what he was doing and slowly turned to look at her. "Yes, Annette, it was."

She bowed her head, letting her arms fall to her sides. "Oh. I am sorry, Mickey."

He began shaking the fish and chips onto the plates. "What are you sorry for, sweetheart—that you've got fish and chips again?"

Wonder of wonders: she smiled. "Yes, that also."

"Come here, Annette."

She took the one step separating them and, hands still busy, he stretched to kiss her on the mouth. "*Bonsoir, ma femme.*"

"*Bonsoir mon mari.*" She leaned closer and returned his kiss. "I will get the knives and forks."

Mickey was, as they sat down to eat, surprisingly happy. He told her of the Inquiry and his discussion with Bevin.

"So it is certain that the new union will be formed, Mickey?"

He nodded. "Certain."

She frowned. "Then why was our own union formed just one year ago? They could have waited until this new...amalgamation."

Mickey grinned. "Because Stanley Hirst wanted to be general secretary of the United Vehicle Workers."

She tilted her head. "Is that what you think, Mickey?"

"That's what I think, sweetheart."

"But it will be for such a short time."

"Unless he then becomes general secretary of the new union."

"But is that possible?"

His grin became a smile. "No."

"They tell me that I will still have a job in the new union."

"Of course: they'll need more ledger clerks than ever for such a large membership."

"But I do not think I wish to remain a ledger clerk for much longer, Mickey."

He look up sharply. "Oh? What do you fancy—secretarial work?"

"Perhaps, but I do not know shorthand. I can type a little."

"You could take a course, sweetheart."

"But I would have to leave work to do that, Mickey."

"Not necessarily: you could attend evening classes."

A frown. "But that would mean..." She bit off the remainder of the sentence and shook her head. "Oh, never mind. I will consider it."

Annette was making slow progress with her meal.

"You don't really like fish and chips, do you, sweetheart?" he said with a nod to her plate.

"I do, my love, but I am afraid that if I eat it too often you will have a wife who is *trop gros*."

He sighed and placed his knife and fork on his empty plate. "And the same might be said of me, sweetheart."

"It would be nice," she suggested brightly, "if we exercised together. We could run in Kensington Gardens, and I could come with you when you go for your swim. When is your rest-day this week, my love?"

He cleared his throat and averted his eyes. "It was today, sweetheart; I did a rest-day exchange so that I could attend the Inquiry."

The brightness vanished from her expression, and she lowered her gaze. "Ah. I see."

29

"It seems that George's popularity is not exactly on the wane," said Dick Mortlake as he sat with Mickey Rice in the Middle Row catering vehicle. He waved the latest issue of *The Record*.

Mickey looked at Dick over the rim of his teacup. "Come on, then, don't keep it to yourself."

Dick folded the newspaper. "This is a piece by the Dalston branch chairman about a visit George made to the branch on 21 January. The visit, he says, was

> the signal for an outburst of enthusiasm by the members who had packed the room to hear this stalwart on the most important questions of the day...It was a great night in the annals of Dalston, and all those who were present left the meeting feeling that the time had not been spent in vain, that there was still something to hope for, work for and live for."

"Fuckinell, Dick, that sounds more like the Second Coming than a branch meeting."

"Does, doesn't it? And I suppose one of the 'most important questions of the day' was the forthcoming amalgamation."

A nod from Mickey. "Must've been. Mind you, I doubt whether he would have come out in total opposition to it."

"No, even for George that would have been a step too far."

"Mind you, it points us in the direction of what we need to do: when we mobilise the membership in favour of an autonomous London Bus Section, we need to make them believe that there is still—what were the words?—something to hope, work and live for."

Dick chuckled. "That might be asking a bit too much, but I know what you mean. How's the organizing committee coming along?"

Mickey sighed. "To be honest, I think we're going to have a bit more on our plate before too long; I think we should delay firming up the organizing committee until we get the result of the ballot."

A frown from the branch secretary. "What are we going to have on our plate, Mickey? The wages negotiations?"

"In due course, yes, but before then I think the movement will be called upon to give some support to the miners." He held up his left hand and proceeded to count off recent development. "In January, the miners received an extra three and six per shift due to increased production. At the same time, though, fifteen collieries in South Wales were closed due to the trade recession. Under last year's agreement, the owners and the miners have until 31 March to present the government with a scheme for the regulation of wages. In the meantime, the government will continue to have financial control of the industry—which includes pumping in subsidy—until August. Just recently, the miners have refused to continue discussions on decontrol of the industry at the Board of Trade until the owners come to agreement on a permanent scheme for the regulation of wages. The main problem is that the owners want district wage-rates in the future, while the miners insist on one national rate. Their delegate conference has decided to seek the views of the districts."

"So it's heading for a fight," Dick commented. "And now they're going to have a pay-cut anyway."

Mickey nodded grimly. "That's right. Because production has fallen due to the recession, this month—February—their extra three and six a shift will be reduced to *one* and six."

"So Bob Williams was right."

"Yeah, but it was inevitable."

"I suppose so, yes." Dick folded *The Record* and placed it in his pocket. "Listen, if you've got time, I'll get myself a tea; there's something else I'd like to discuss with you."

Mickey took out his watch. "Ten minutes, Dick."

*

When, tea in hand, Dick resumed his seat, he wore a worried expression.

"If the look on your face is anything to go by, Comrade, this is going to be bad news," commented Mickey.

Dick sighed. "It's not exactly news, Mickey." He peered over at the counter to make sure that Tommy Hoskins, who provided the catering service, was not paying attention; apart from Tommy, they were alone in the vehicle. Dick looked across at Mickey from beneath a furrowed brow. "How are you finding married life, mate?"

Mickey stifled a laugh. "Christ, I thought this was going to be something serious!"

Dick looked offended. "It *is* serious, Mickey."

Mickey regarded his friend in silence for a moment before nodding. "Sorry. Okay, yes: it *is* serious. I agree."

"Well?"

"Seven minutes won't be enough for this discussion, Dick. Seeing as we finish within ten minutes of each other, why don't we go for a drink in the Eagle after work?"

Dick shook his head. "No, that would just make it worse."

"Ah, I see. Yeah, come to think of it, it probably would for me as well."

This made Dick smile. "Okay, so let's discuss it on the way home tonight; if I hang on for you, we can walk home together."

*

It was a chilly evening, with spots of rain, as they walked beside the railway line up to Great Western Road.

"I've come to realise," said Mickey, electing to go first, "that Annette is not as progressive as I thought. Her main concern arising from my brush with Special Branch was that I'd risked getting her deported."

"But," said Dick, playing devil's advocate, "isn't that reasonable, given her situation?"

"I don't think so, Dick, because the alternative would have been for me to have played the game they wanted me to play and got Theo deported."

"Which, given the fact that he's now barred from re-entry, wouldn't in fact have made a lot of difference."

"Come on, Dick, nobody knew that Theo was going to put his own head in the noose at that stage."

"Fair point."

"And do you remember a year ago, when some of us barged into the EC meeting to claim our right to be observers? Annette complained that she was embarrassed by it, because everyone in the building knew we were married. She even tried to get me to promise that I wouldn't try anything similar in the future."

"Mm, well, that *is* a bit much, admittedly."

"I suppose I was fooled by the fact that her parents are so progressive. Not that it's her fault, of course."

"No, of course not."

"I get the impression that she thinks we don't spend enough time together. She seems to resent the time I spend on the union and other movement activity."

"Well, look at it from her point of view, Mickey: she's here in a foreign country, all alone apart from you."

"But she's been here for six years, for Christ's sake!"

"Even so...Does she have any friends of her own?"

Mickey gave that some thought. In truth, he was somewhat annoyed with Dick who, having initiated this discussion, now seemed to be arguing that his marital problems might be partly of his own making; it was particularly annoying to know that he was correct. "No, I don't suppose she does—nobody really close, at least. Yes, you have a point. Anyway, I've already decided that I need to do what I can to strengthen her politically."

"Oh, that's good. And what do you think you *can* do?"

Mickey looked at Dick and shrugged. "Buggered if I know, mate."

This was said partly in jest, and if Dick had any thought of encouraging Mickey to adopt a more serious attitude he was disappointed because, as they turned into Great Western Road, a 31 came over the canal bridge and Mickey threw up his arm, running across the road as the vehicle slowed to pick them up.

Mickey gave the driver—Lenny Hawkins as it happened—a thumbs-up as he trotted in front of the cab, calling, "Drop us at The Artesian, Len!"

As they alighted, Mickey jabbed a thumb in the direction of the pub. "Quick one, Dick?"

A frowning Dick shook his head. "This is not like you, Mickey."

"I'm thinking of you, Dick: you're on next and I thought a pint—or even a half!—might relax you."

Dick forced a grin. "It wouldn't relax me, mate: I'd be worrying that she'd smell it on my breath when we get home."

They turned down Talbot Road; Alexander Street was now only three turnings away. "Let's take it nice and slow, Dick, or we'll be home before you've got it off your chest. Off you go, Comrade."

"Ohhh, to a certain extent, my problems are similar to yours: Gladys wants me home as much as possible, frowns at the very suggestion of a drink with the lads..."

"But politically she's okay?"

"Well, yes. Look, you probably know as well as I do that Gladys is undeveloped politically, but her instincts are always pretty good, although she can be a bit leftist. For example, she thought the Council of Action should have called the workers out. 'But Glad,' I told her, 'it doesn't need to. Lloyd George has backed down.' She wouldn't have it, of course." He groaned. "Ironically, I'm now having trouble convincing her that Sylvia Pankhurst is wrong to use her *Workers' Dreadnought* to fight factional battles within the party."

"Is that what Sylvia's doing? She'll get herself kicked out, surely."

"I sometimes wonder," Dick sighed, "if that's what she wants."

Upon her return from Moscow, impressed by her meeting with Lenin, Sylvia had indicated that she was now ready to lead her party into the CPGB; a second unity conference had therefore been held in January, although Sylvia was unable to attend in person as she was serving six months' imprisonment in Holloway for sedition, the *Dreadnought* having published an article which was held to have incited mutiny in the Royal Navy.

"But she's in the clink, surely."

"That hasn't stopped her. In January, the *Dreadnought* published one of her letters, arguing that the party should allow the formation of a left bloc with its own convenors and so on."

"Jesus Christ! How does she justify that?"

"According to her, Lenin found it acceptable."

"Bullshit."

"I fear you may be right."

Mickey uttered a long sigh and shook his head in exasperation. "Anyway, what are you going to do—about Gladys, I mean?"

"Oh, I don't think it's reached the point where I need to *do* anything. It's just that sometimes I feel so...trapped, I suppose."

"Do you regret getting married?"

Dick halted and regarded Mickey closely. "Do you know, that's a question that I've been afraid to ask myself. But you've asked it for me, and I suppose the answer is both yes and no: I'm glad I've been able to give both Glad and Jimmy a bit of security, but there are times when I feel I just want to escape."

"You *feel as if* you want to escape. It never reaches the point where you *actually* want to escape, then?"

"You make me feel as if I'm in the bloody witness box, Mickey. But maybe that's what I need, so no harm done." A pause. "No, I never *actually* want to escape, although I'm afraid that will come at some stage. The fact is, of course, that I won't be *able* to escape. The house is all I've got to my name, after all."

"But just think of all the married working-class men that you know and ask yourself how many of them are in the same situation."

"Probably quite a few, although of course most of them don't own houses."

"So what's to prevent them from escaping?"

"Their kids, maybe. No, *definitely* their kids."

"They're trapped in a bourgeois institution and don't know it. Of course, if they *were* bourgeois, it wouldn't be a problem for them. Bourgeois husbands have the resources to maintain mistresses and enjoy freedom within their marriages, and their wives—who have most to lose by a separation or divorce—don't dare to try to control them the way Gladys and Annette are doing with us."

"And when a bourgeois marriage *does* end in divorce, the man is usually sufficiently well-off to provide for his children, and so they don't act as a barrier to his escape."

"Well, except in the sense of the affection he might hold for them."

"Of course, Mickey. But when we say that he is able to provide for them after the divorce, where does that money come from? Think of that!"

Mickey laughed. "I see what you mean: whatever bank account or investment it comes from, it started out as surplus value, provided free of charge by workers."

"Whereas in a fairer society some of that surplus value, although it would no longer technically *be* surplus value, would be used for the provision of child-care facilities, the education of kids whether they had one parent or two, and community dining facilities which allowed women to live a full life outside the home."

"And so marriages, whether of working-class or bourgeois couples..."

"Oh, come on, Mickey, in the kind of society we're talking about there wouldn't *be* a bourgeoisie!"

"True enough. So marriages would be on a much more equitable basis. Women would be as financially secure as men and so wouldn't feel this need to control their husbands. The only reason one or the other might feel the need to escape would be if the original bonds of attraction and affection which had first brought them together faded or disappeared. And in that case the door would be always open."

Their discussion unfinished, they stood on the corner of Alexander Street, oblivious to the light rain.

"Well, Dick, we seem to have resolved conjugal problems under socialism, but that still leaves us with a problem or two in the here and now."

Dick chuckled. "It does, doesn't it? And I still have to put to you the question you asked me."

Mickey gave him a frown.

"Do you regret getting married?"

"Ah. Well, I suppose my answer is much the same as yours. No, in that the reason I married Annette—at least at the time I did—was to smooth the way for her application for citizenship. Apart from that, of course, I love her. But yes, like you I sometimes feel a bit trapped—or, rather, that Annette's attempts to keep me on a leash are a little suffocating. In my own mind, I've been hoping that she'll never force me to choose between her and the movement, but maybe that's the wrong way of looking at it. As I said earlier, I've pretty much decided that I must bring her closer to the movement, turn the sentiments she absorbed with her mother's milk into real understanding."

Dick nodded. "Yes, maybe I should work on Glad in a similar way." He brightened. "Come to think of it, we could mount a joint effort..."

"As long as it doesn't appear that way to them," Mickey intervened.

"What are you thinking of, then?"

"Well, the discussion we've just had has set the old thought process in motion. Maybe we could all attend a series of education classes—as long as one of them is on Engels' *The Origin of the*

Family, Private Property and the State. That might do for starters."

"That's a cracking idea, Comrade."

"And, bearing in mind what you were saying about the possibility of women living a full life under socialism, maybe we should do what we can to ensure that Gladys and Annette live a fuller life under *present* circumstances. Annette, for example, has her eye on a secretarial job, but she has no shorthand and not much in the way of typing skills. I've suggested that she could attend evening classes, but I get the impression she thinks that would cut down our time together even further."

"Correspondence classes, Mickey, correspondence classes."

Mickey snapped his fingers. "That's it! You, Comrade Mortlake, are a genius."

"Yes, I know, but unfortunately only some of the time."

The discussion having concluded on a positive note, they resumed their stroll towards home.

"You know, Dick," mused Mickey, "when Dorothy was working with Sylvia Pankhurst in the East End, she became very irritated with the relief work that Sylvia was undertaking—the children's nursery, the restaurant with cheap meals for working-class families, and so on. Dorothy saw it as a diversion from anti-war activity and the class struggle in general, and as something that should be provided by the government or the local authorities. Well, maybe, I said one evening, but there's surely another way of looking at this: these activities are being undertaken by hundreds of working-class women and their male supporters, and they're succeeding. Surely it's the job of Sylvia and the other leaders, I suggested, to bring these activists to understand that if they can manage tasks like these without the help of a single capitalist, they and people like them can run the whole of society."

Dick brought his palms together. "Wonderful! And how did Dorothy take this?"

"She not only saw my point but agreed with it." He shrugged. "But, of course, she and Sylvia had a falling-out and so she didn't really have an opportunity to bring Sylvia around to our point of view. And now, of course, Sylvia has abandoned that kind of work in order to become a full-time communist, as she sees it. She obviously doesn't see that the two could go together."

They were home. Dick took the front-door key from his pocket, nodding grimly. "Yes, she's in danger of becoming a very *sectarian* full-time communist, Mickey."

They stepped into the hall.

"Are you still in touch with her, Dick?"

"Yes, but not since she's been in prison, of course. When she gets out, I suppose I should really go and see her and try to get her to see sense, although goodness knows how she would greet advice from me." Raising a hand to open the door of his ground-floor flat, he paused, looking over his shoulder at Mickey. "But you know her as well, don't you Mickey?"

At that moment, the door opened and Gladys was there.

"Thought I heard you at the front door. Who's this you're talking about, Dickie?" Of late, she had taken to calling him Dickie.

"Sylvia Pankhurst, Glad." And to Mickey: "Then why don't we both go and see her when she gets out in May?"

"Or we could all go," suggested Gladys with a smile.

30

It was 7 March when the government issued the report of the tramways inquiry as a White Paper. A messenger arrived at Transport House that morning with advance copies for Stanley Hirst and John Cliff. Hirst skimmed through the document before throwing it onto his desk. What to do? He would call Cliff to his office, but first he would make a telephone call.

"I see from the look on your face, Johnny," he said as Cliff entered fifteen minutes later, "that you've had a chance to get the gist of it."

Cliff nodded grimly. "I have, Stan. Jesus, when I think of the hours Bevin and I spent on preparing for that Inquiry! A complete waste of time!" He slumped into a chair opposite Hirst. "Ernie must be spitting blood."

"Funnily enough, Johnny, he's not. I've just spoken to him on the telephone and he says this is just about what might have been expected. He says we'll have to wait until the economy improves and then pull out the stops for the tramway lads."

Cliff grunted. "All very well for him to say that: he's not the one who'll have to face the members." He sighed. "But what else can we do?"

"Why don't I call together the officers who are in the building? You can summarise the report, then we'll kick it around for a while and see if anyone has any bright ideas."

"You don't want the EC here?"

Hirst shrugged. "What would be the point? It's not as if we'll be bringing the tramworkers out on strike. No, this report tells us which way the wind is blowing—not just for the trams but for the other sections of the union as well. In that sense it will be of interest to the other officers. Let's see what they think." He cast Cliff a conspiratorial look and tapped the surface of his desk with a forefinger. "Bad news though this is, Johnny, it's not without its silver lining. If you get my drift."

A grin from Cliff. "I think I do, Stan: the dockers' KC has come a cropper."

"And in a month or two's time, once all the ballot results are in, the ECs of the amalgamating unions will be meeting to elect a provisional leadership..."

*

There were just seven of them: Hirst, Cliff, Ben Smith, George Sanders, Archie Henderson, Eric Rice and, during one of his rare absences from the Commons, Alfred "Tich" Smith, the union's parliamentary secretary. They occupied one end of the executive chamber, Sanders smoking his Gold Flake and "Tich" Smith chewing on one of his small cigars.

"There is," Cliff began, "nothing for us in this document—nothing at all! According to the report, the NJIC should examine the position of undertakings which have not observed previous agreements and arbitration awards, advising them to pay the advances in full—'if possible.' The present wages in both the municipals and the company operations, says the report, should be continued to be paid until 31 December this year. So not only do our members not get the increase they were hoping for, but they're threatened with a possible cut at the end of the year! The NJIC, it goes on to say, should consider standardisation in the near future—'having regard to the earning capacity of the undertakings, and to the interests of the travelling public.' And, finally, the NJIC should examine the circumstances of the lower-paid grades with a view to adjusting their conditions on a more satisfactory basis.

"And that, colleagues, is just about it. No decision in our favour, apart from a handful of pious suggestions and hopes, and even those are usually made worthless by the use of such phrases as 'if possible' and 'having regard to earning capacity.'"

"I thought you should hear this as soon as possible, brothers," said Hirst, "because I know a number of you have wage talks coming up and this result is likely to have a bearing on the outcome."

"Or some employers would *like* it to have a bearing on the outcome," said Ben Smith. Scratching his right sideboard. "It's becoming something of a trend, isn't it? Employers all over the shop are using the downturn in trade and the falling cost of living to try to take back what we've recently won from them. For example, Archie and I met the commercial transport employers a few days ago. And what do they want? They're arguing that the four bob advance we won last year for London drivers should be taken back in stages—two bob a time—because of the fall in the cost of living, when the fact of the matter is that the past wage-increases were insufficient to compensate for the rising prices. Anyway, we had a mass meeting at The Ring last night, and the lads agreed to take any steps necessary to resist the proposal."

"In fact," chipped in Archie Henderson, "we've already tabled a demand for a national increase, but the way things are going we'll probably have to have a scrap or go to arbitration."

George Sanders raised a hand, using the other to stub out his cigarette in an already half-full ashtray.

"Ben's right: wage-cutting is the trend. Last month, some 70,000 workers received wage-increases. Sounds good, doesn't it? Until you learn that one-and-a-half million suffered *cuts* in their wages, and half of them were miners—and I want to come back to the miners in a few minutes. But we can't escape the fact that prices *are* falling. From January last year to this, across the country as a whole, wholesale prices fell by 17 percent, and there was a further fall of six percent in the first six weeks of this year."

"Still taking notes from *The Times*, then George," observed Ben Smith with a smile, perhaps recalling the wage negotiations at Electric Railway House in 1919.

"Of course, Ben," replied Sanders, adding, as he directed his gaze in the direction of Hirst and Cliff, "After all, somebody has to do it, don't they?" He sniffed. "Anyway, this report will be warmly welcomed by all of the employers in the passenger transport sector, and we'll be meeting the largest of 'em in a month or two: the London General Omnibus Company. Funnily enough, though, I don't think we'll do too badly when it comes to cash, as long as we make them know we're not going to lay down and let 'em have their way with us. No, it's the conditions we'll have to safeguard, the ten-hour maximum spreadover in particular.

"But listen, colleagues, today's report is bad news for the tram lads, and it's another indication of the way the wind is blowing. But winds have been known to change direction, and this particular wind is not a force of nature but a product of the system under which we live. If the employers are on the offensive, it's because they feel confident; but our movement has the power to shake their confidence. I'm thinking, colleagues, of the forthcoming battle that the miners will have to fight. They're already suffering wage-cuts, and this month falling production has meant that the extra payment per shift won in last year's strike has been completely eliminated. And the government has announced that financial control of the industry will end not on 31 August as originally agreed, but at the end of *this* month."

"How does this have a bearing on our situation?" interjected John Cliff. Stanley Hirst, seated at his side, nodded.

"If the miners—over a million of 'em, don't forget—go down to defeat, it will affect not just us but the whole movement, but if you hang on just a moment, Brother Cliff, I'll tell you what it means in a more practical sense," replied Sanders. "There's not a snowball's chance in hell that the miners and the owners will come up with a new wages scheme by 31 March, as the owners are saying that they'll have to go to a district system, and that the 1914 wage-rates would form the base line below which no one would be allowed to fall."

"And yet there's no talk of a strike ballot," commented Eric Rice.

"They won't need one," explained Sanders, "because if the current wage system is going to end on 31 March and they don't agree a replacement, the owners will be legally bound to give the miners notice of termination. On 1 April, in effect, they'll be locked out. And when that happens, you can be sure that they'll call on the Triple Alliance for support." He looked around at his six colleagues. "Let's be honest about this: on their own, the miners will be defeated. With the members of the Triple Alliance out in support, however..."

"The miners, the railways and the Transport Workers' Federation," Hirst counted off the members of the Triple Alliance on the fingers of his left hand. "If they were to come out together it would, given the other industries that would be affected, amount to a general strike."

"That's true," said Sanders, "and it would surely stand a great chance of success. It's why the Alliance was formed in the first place. The important result for us, however, would be that the confidence that the employer class is currently feeling would evaporate overnight and our own battles would become that much easier to win."

"And are we sure that Jimmy Thomas and the NUR will play ball?" asked Ben Smith.

"The wages of the membership of the NUR are also on a sliding scale, Ben, and as it's linked to the cost of living they can expect a reduction in the near future."

John Cliff was frowning. "I'm not at all sure, George, what you're suggesting."

"What I'm saying, colleagues, is that we should start mobilising our members for the inevitable."

"Ah, now, that would be a decision for the EC," said Hirst.

"Of course," said Sanders, "and that's really what I'm suggesting."

Hirst chewed his bottom lip. "I'll give that some thought, George, but I really don't think we should be jumping the gun before the miners have called for our support."

Sanders made a mental note to contact Mickey Rice; perhaps he would talk to Eric after the meeting and ask him to pass a message to his brother.

31

The message from George Sanders was quite simple: the official leadership of the United Vehicle Workers was obviously going to drag its heels over mobilising support for the miners, and so the task would need to be undertaken by rank-and-file activists.

In theory, this looked easy enough. Dick Mortlake, who had acted as secretary to the former Vigilance Committee of the red-button union, still had the address-list of contacts and activists, but of course this covered only the membership in buses, cabs and trams; a shorter list of activists from the commercial transport sector who had attended unofficial meetings since the amalgamation existed, but this would need to be expanded if the campaign was to be effective; a further shortcoming lay in the fact that, wide as this net might eventually become, it would cover only the greater London area. Then there was the question of finance. Mickey and Dick got together with Malcolm Lewis, their branch chairman, and agreed a possible way forward: the next meeting of the Middle Row branch would be asked to endorse a plan in which, subject to initial funding by the branch, Mickey and Dick would call a meeting of the contacts which were already in the bag, and that meeting would plan an expansion of the campaign, agree funding, and provide volunteers for addressing envelopes and other minor administrative tasks.

It was, therefore, Wednesday, 30 March before the inaugural conference took place. At 7.30 on the evening of that day, the meeting room of the Crown and Anchor was packed, with every seat taken and activists standing shoulder to shoulder at the back of the room. Most of the London General and Tillings branches were represented, as were all the tramway branches and cabs, and there was a fair representation from commercial transport firms. The movement was, however, technically leaderless, although Mickey Rice and Dick Mortlake, having convened the meeting, sat at the top table. It was Dick who stood and asked for nominations for a chairman, whereupon several voices shouted Mickey's name.

"Any other nominations?" asked Dick.

"Brian Vernon!" called one brave busman.

There being no further nominations, Dick suggested that as many would be unfamiliar with Vernon he should stand and make himself known, which, to the accompaniment of several remarks about his closely-cropped head, he did. When Dick called for votes for Mickey, a forest of hands went up; Vernon attracted three votes.

"Brothers," said Mickey as he stood to address the meeting, "we're here because I think we all realise that the membership must be fully mobilised in readiness for the moment when the miners— unless there's a miracle—call upon the support of the Triple Alliance in defence of their livelihoods. Time has almost run out for a settlement to be reached, tomorrow being the last day on which that will be possible. If there's no settlement tomorrow, the notices which the mine-owners have issued the miners will take effect, and they'll be on the stones. Oh, yes, the owners have said that these notices were issued simply to fulfill a legal requirement, and that they have no intention of terminating anyone's employment. But the fact of the matter is that if there's no agreement tomorrow, on Friday—1 April— the employment of every miner in this country *will* be terminated.

"And why should this concern us, brothers?" He looked around the room. "Obviously, it should concern us because we're trade unionists, and solidarity is one of the first principles of trade unionism! But there's another reason, much closer to home: if the owners and the government get away with this, the wages and conditions of every worker in this country will be under threat— make no mistake about it!"

The low growl which arose from the crowded room told Mickey that these activists agreed with his analysis.

"It's probably worth pointing out, though, that throughout the period, news from elsewhere has done nothing to cheer up the miners. Earlier this month, a joint meeting of the manufacturers' associations stated its opposition to the miners' plan for the unification of wages and argued that there could be no revival of trade unless the price of coal was drastically reduced. I think there's only one way to read that, brothers: the ruling class is closing ranks against the miners.

"Then the cost of living figures for last month were announced: the index had dropped by a further ten points.

"Finally, a week ago it was announced that the wages of the railwaymen, which as you know are on a sliding scale, will be reduced by four bob a week." He shrugged. "I suppose there are two ways of looking at that: on the one hand, it's another indication of the way things are going; on the other, it just might put some backbone into the rail lads when the miners call for strike action from the Triple Alliance."

Mickey sighed and picked up a newspaper clipping from the table. "Just to wind up this introduction, brothers, Frank Hodges, secretary of the Miners' Federation, had an article in *The Times* today." He looked up and grinned. "If you've all seen it, just say so and we'll save a bit of time."

He waited for the laughter to die.

"According to Brother Hodges, the pay-cuts proposed by the mine-owners will vary enormously: ten percent in some areas, fifty percent in others. The industry as a whole, he says, is insolvent, but it could be restored to health by a lesser reduction spread evenly throughout the country. In normal times, such a scheme could be negotiated, but these are not normal times, and what is needed is government subsidy for a period.

"Now listen to what he says about wages, because this is important. Hodges says that miners would not object if, after a fall in the cost of living and a lowering of the price of coal, their wages were reduced by the same rate, but that they *do* object to a reduction *before* a fall in inflation. He says, though, that the owners aren't listening, and that only the government can prevent a stoppage on 1 April."

He replaced the cutting on the table and looked around at his audience. "So, brothers, we have to conclude from this that there *will* be a stoppage on Friday. As I see it, our job tonight is to launch a movement that will ensure that *our* union, at least, will respond positively when the call from the Triple Alliance comes. Our comrade Dick Mortlake has a few suggestions to put to you." He turned to his branch secretary. "All yours, Dick."

"Our job, then," began Dick, "is to mobilise our members behind the demand to support the miners. How do we do that? We make sure they're fully informed about the issues. Are we able to do that?" Between thumb and forefinger, he took a sheet of paper, printed on both sides, from the table and held it up. "We have a leaflet. Brothers, we have *thousands* of leaflets, and we want you to carry them away with you when you leave and make sure every single member of your branches gets to read one. However, these leaflets are professionally printed, and the cost so far has been met by the Middle Row branch fund. So we're asking you to get your own branches to contribute a few quid—to reimburse us for the cost of the leaflets and pay for the printing of more when we need them; to pay for the hire of this meeting room and any other venue we need during the course of the campaign."

"How about posters?" came a voice. "A few posters would be useful, with a simple slogan, like 'ALL OUT FOR THE MINERS.' That sort of thing."

"Even better," called a tramway worker, "would be 'THE MINERS' FIGHT IS OUR FIGHT.'"

Dick, exulted by the enthusiasm of the meeting, laughed. "You want posters? Okay, you'll have posters, but don't forget that the branches will have to pay for them.

"And there's something else, even more important, that you'll have to get your branches to do, brothers! The reason we're here, after all, is because when it comes to support for the miners the leadership of our union is dragging its heels." Usually undemonstrative, Dick banged the table with his fist. "Every branch represented here should—without delay—send a resolution to the EC, demanding that it works within the Transport Workers' Federation to ensure that the whole Triple Alliance is out when the time comes!"

After the cheers this received had died away, the meeting turned its attention to more mundane business: the need to reach out to those branches which were not represented here, persuading them to join the campaign; how, in particular, to make contact with the commercial transport branches in the London area and, at the very least, to provide them with leaflets; and how to break out of the London area and ensure that UVW branches elsewhere were urged to put pressure on the EC. With regard to this latter matter, there was some discussion, it being decided that it would be far too ambitious to think of a national vigilance committee at this stage and that, instead, letters should be sent to all those provincial branches whose addresses were known, encouraging them to form their own local vigilance committees.

"And while we're about it," suggested Rueben Topping from Willesden bus garage, "why don't we make contact with branches of other unions—particularly the rail unions and dockers?"

"And let's give ourselves a name," called Dave Marston of Lewisham. "I suggest the Southeast District Vigilance Committee!"

Agreed.

*

Afterwards, Mickey Rice was inclined to blame himself for calling for any other business rather than just thanking everybody for attending and closing the meeting; but, he consoled himself, Vernon would still have found a way to make his point.

"Thank you, Chairman," said Vernon, "there is a matter which I feel I have to raise here, and which should be of interest to all present." He sniffed. "As I recall it, Chairman, the last time you and me was in this room you were saying how wonderful Ernest Bevin was, and how he was the only one fit to lead the new union. Well,"— he took a folded newspaper from his jacket pocket and shook it open—"while you was reading *The Times* today, I was reading *The Record*, the *union* newspaper. Now, as this is hot off the press, you may not have had a chance to see it yet, but there's a very interesting article in it by George Sanders."

Mickey turned and raised his eyebrows at Dick, who shrugged: he had not seen it, either.

"It also reprints something from the *Weekly Dispatch*, which talks of a secret dinner held by something called the National Alliance of Employers and Employed, which seems to be a group of capitalists and union leaders. Now, if you're scratching your heads, wondering what these people can have in common, I'll tell you: they want industrial peace! This is what the *Dispatch* says:

> 'The moderate men in the labour movement appreciate the difficulties of the industrial position, and are anxious to meet the employers in a mutual endeavour to remove them, but the wild men prefer the coercion of the strike threat to the round table method of conciliation.'

"What kind of capitalists were at this dinner? Big ones: Sir George Murray of Armstrong, Whitworth; Sir Vincent Callard of Vickers, Ltd.; Sir Robert Hadfield of Hadfields. There was even a director of the Bank of England!"

Vernon took a breather at this point and then, frowning and lowering his voice to give it an air of confidentiality: "But more to the point, Chairman, who were the trade union leaders who attended this dinner? Charles Duncan, MP, of the Workers' Union."

This was greeted by laughter and moans, as some in the audience remembered that during the war Duncan had been known as the

Angel of Death, due to his practice of touring the country to persuade workers to volunteer for the Army.

"W.A. Appleton, of the General Federation of Trade unions."

Silence.

"Arthur Pugh, of the Iron and Steel Trades' Confederation."

Another silence.

"J. O'Grady, MP, of the Furnishing Trades' Association."

A few groans this time, probably provoked by the man's parliamentary status.

"Coming a bit closer to home now, Ben Tillett, of the Dock, Wharf and General Labourers' Union."

This time the laughter and groans, occasioned by Tillett's former pro-war stance, were joined by gasps of amazement because this was, after all, one of the unions—Bevin's union!—leading the push for amalgamation.

"And this is what George Sanders says of this secret dinner:

'The name that interested me most was E. Bevin...'"

Uproar.

Mickey turned to Dick, muttering, "I fucking knew it!"

Vernon stood calmly, in silence, until the rage and disappointment of the activists was spent. "'The name that interested me most,'" he then repeated,

> 'was E. Bevin, who on several occasions has come into close contact with vehicle workers...If it was true that Mr Bevin accepted the invitation to dinner with the idea, as it states, of using his influence to curb rash confreres, it does not appear to fall in line with the views expressed by E. Bevin on the Council of Action...I do think that Ernie Bevin ought to let us know whether the account as written in the *Dispatch* is a true one from his point of view.'

"This is the man, Chairman, who will in all likelihood lead the new amalgamated union, and anyone who thinks that London busworkers will be able to achieve autonomy from such a man must be living in cloud cuckoo land. That being the case, we have to rethink the outcome of our last meeting and start preparing for a breakaway!"

Mickey was on his feet. "That's quite enough, Brother Vernon. This is not a meeting of London busworkers, and so your last comment is out of order. You can put forward your point of view at the next meeting..."

"And when will that be?" demanded Vernon.

"It will be when we've concluded the business which brought us here tonight and not before! And in that regard, Brother Vernon, I do have to say that your contribution has been extremely unhelpful. You will have noticed that before you got to your feet this meeting was full of enthusiasm and commitment, and you seem to have deliberately done what you could to sabotage that positive mood. Frankly, I'm beginning to ask myself what side you're really on."

Vernon began to get to his feet. "If you think I'm going to sit here..."

"Yes, I *do*"—Mickey struck the table with his fist—"think that you're going to sit there and take it, because if you don't you'll be thrown out!" Encouraged by the wave of laughter and cheers that greeted this, Mickey ploughed on. "This movement we're launching is the result of several weeks of hard work, and if anybody thinks they can come along and attempt, by trying to sound more left than the rest of us, throw a spanner in the works, they can expect a few nasty shocks." He struck the table again and raised his voice a notch or two. "Why are we doing this? For ourselves? For our own self-interest? No, we're doing it for the miners and for the whole movement!"

The reception this received was so positive that Mickey was almost grateful that Vernon had made his intervention. Well, he thought, as they're in the mood, let's hammer home another point.

"And Ernie Bevin? At the meeting to which Brother Vernon refers—for the benefit of other sections, it was an unofficial busworkers' meeting in this very room—I don't recall anyone claiming that Bevin was the reincarnation of Jesus Christ or Karl Marx. What I do recall being said—because I was the one who said it!—was that it would be a mistake to believe that he would maintain a progressive outlook throughout his career." He threw open his arms. "Brother Bevin has attended a dinner with capitalists who see him as a potential moderate. So what! Does that mean that the rest of us will suddenly be transformed into right-wingers when the new union sees the light of day? Of course it doesn't! Brother Bevin may have a great many strengths, but when all is said and done he's just a man, like the rest of us.

"But what is the response of those who consider themselves lefter than left? Defeatism! Oh, we can't survive in the same organisation as Ernie Bevin! We must form a breakaway! Defeatism, brothers— before a single shot has been fired!" He looked around the room and, his voice dripping with contempt, concluded: "Yes, form a breakaway and do the employers a favour by dividing the movement!" He chuckled. "I don't think so. No, brothers, I think you will agree with me when I say that this movement we've launched tonight will carry out the tasks before it, and come the new amalgamation people like you will work to ensure that our union is progressive and that the lay members will decide policy—no matter where Ernie Bevin has his dinner!"

32

Bob Williams witnessed some of the events of the next two weeks.

He was at Unity House, the NUR headquarters on the Euston Road, when the EC of the Miners' Federation, having held its own meeting at its Russell Square offices on that first Friday, arrived to meet the leaders of the Triple Alliance, urging them to come to their aid. This appeal met with a positive response, although the leaders of the NUR and the Transport Workers' Federation were in no position to take a decision without consulting their members and affiliates.

"I hate to say this, Bob," Bevin muttered at an early stage, "but I think we'll see some games being played during the next week or two."

Williams was silent for a few moments, somewhat irritated by Bevin's scepticism. Eventually he sighed and whispered in reply, "I hope you're wrong, Ernie."

"So do I, Bob, so do I."

As Jimmy Thomas, the railworkers' leader, was at a meeting in Amsterdam, the NUR's position was put by the union's industrial general secretary, Charlie Cramp. His executive council, he announced, was impressed by the gravity of the situation, seeing the attack on the wages of the miners as the forerunner of a general campaign by the employers to abandon national negotiations and push down wages, and the NUR would be calling a delegate conference for the following Wednesday, 6 April. For the National Transport Workers' Federation, Harry Gosling echoed this: "We regard this as an attempt to get back to the old days of district negotiations rather then national negotiations, which would affect us in the same way as the miners." The executive members of the TWF affiliates, he announced, would be meeting on 5 April.

Bob Williams spent the weekend alone, brooding about the state of the movement, the country, and his own prospects. The country was sliding towards crisis. A million men were locked out of work and yet the rest of the movement had yet to spring into action. Rumour had it that Lloyd George would soon invoke last year's Emergency Powers Act. The press, meanwhile, was busily wooing minds away from any idea of supporting the miners, those men who were callously forbidding the maintenance men to set the pumps working and maintain the safety of the mines that had given them their livelihoods. They're even prepared to let the poor pit ponies die! Yes, they're faced with heavy reductions in their living standards, but with the steep recession in trade we're all making sacrifices, aren't we? Williams wondered whether the movement would be able to withstand this propaganda. Would the Triple Alliance have sufficient belief in its own strength and values to hold together? More to the point, would it have the strength to exert some measure of control over the leadership of the Miners' Federation, which throughout the negotiations had kept the Alliance at arm's length— something which Williams and Bevin had warned about earlier in the year? There were rumours that Bob Smillie had resigned the presidency not due to ill-health but because of the uncompromising stance of the majority of his EC.

His visit, as a member of the Labour Party and TUC delegation, to Soviet Russia the previous year had made a powerful impact on him. Socialism was no longer an idle dream. It *could* be built and it *was* being built! And oh, what a hard time of it the Soviet comrades had! But despite the problems, despite the hardships, they stuck to the task, organised and committed. Those men and women were heroes; the word was entirely appropriate. And, of course, he had had a two-hour meeting with the man who led and inspired them: Vladimir Ilyich Lenin.

Williams had been asked—contracted, in fact—to write a series of four articles about his Soviet visit by, of all things, the *Daily Mail*. He had left that paper's foreign editor, G. Valentine Williams—no relation—in no doubt that the articles would be pro-Soviet, but he had been told to go ahead. And so he had, as a result of which the *Mail*, having received the first two articles, returned them unpublished. Bob had then stitched them together into a sixpenny pamphlet called *The Soviet System at Work*, published by the newly-formed Communist Party.

He had returned to Britain full of enthusiasm, keen to impart that same zeal to British workers, convincing them that they too could do what their Russian brothers and sisters were doing. But what had happened? He had met with that quality which, often concealed beneath militant slogans and high-minded phrases, seemed to characterise the British labour movement: inertia. What had happened since his return? There had been the formation of the Council of Action which, of course, had been called upon to take no action; there had been last year's miner's strike which, although seemingly successful, had merely paved the way for this current crisis; and there there was the calamitous inquiry into the tramways. He cringed now to recall the prediction he had made upon his return—and repeated in his pamphlet—that the membership of the new CP could reach 650,000 after a year of correct, dedicated and sustained work. But, after nine months of existence, what was the membership? In truth, nobody knew, as accurate records had not been kept, but it was doubtful that it came to more than 3,000. This meant, of course, that there could be no question of him becoming a "professional revolutionary" as Lenin had half-jokingly suggested. And with the slow but steady progress being made by Bevin's Transport & General Workers' Union project, the chances of him continuing to be a professional trade unionist were not much brighter.

If the Triple Alliance came to the aid of the miners, what would be the possible consequences for the movement—and for himself? It was being said that, given the number of workers directly and indirectly involved, such a struggle would take on the aspects of a general strike, and would directly challenge the state. What would success look like? With so few serious-minded socialists in the leadership of the trade unions, and with a communist party that was still in its infancy, success would certainly not look like socialism. No, success would surely take the form of further government subsidy. This would be a sound defeat for Lloyd George, but Williams could imagine him chuckling as he watched the miners return to work, gratified that he had demonstrated that the British working class, even after mounting a successful challenge to the state, had no thought of taking the whole cake, being quite satisfied with maintaining the size of its own slice.

Defeat, now: that was another thing entirely. With the Triple Alliance out, Lloyd George would certainly invoke the Emergency Powers Act, and that could mean real bloodshed. Just two years earlier, in Amritsar, India, a peaceful demonstration had been fired upon, killing almost 400 people and wounding countless others. Could such an atrocity occur here? Why not? The same Prime Minister was in office, and he had offered no apology for the massacre. Defeat would come about by either the retreat of our leaders or the crushing of our movement.

*

On the Monday, Williams learned that various branches and sections of the National Union of Railwaymen had met over the weekend, calling for support of the miners. Charlie Cramp was quoted as saying he didn't think the miners and the railwaymen could win on their own, but if all transport workers joined in there would be a chance of success. "If they can be successful," he was quoted as having said, "they ought to have a shot at being successful." He made it sound like a game of chance, thought Williams.

And, sure enough, it was on Monday that Lloyd George did indeed invoke the Emergency Powers Act, so that the following week's issue of *The Record*, the UVW journal, would write: "The London parks are armed camps, and three times three round the streets dash stage batteries of artillery, while lumbering up and down Oxford Street, twice daily and one performance in the evening, are the various breeds of tanks." The Act also provided for the banning of public meetings considered to be sufficiently subversive.

Tuesday's meeting of the Transport Workers' Federation was found to be inconclusive—as it was bound to be, thought Williams, as the NUR's delegate conference had not yet been held. Havelock Wilson, the seamen's leader, argued that the miners were not the only workers suffering wage-cuts, hardly an augury
of forthcoming solidarity action.

*

"You seen what the Army is draggin' 'round London, Mick?" asked Lenny Hawkins. He was finishing an early turn; Mickey had just signed on for a late one.

"Caught sight of some of it last night," said Mickey, "down Oxford Street."

"Who they thinkin' of using that against, then?"

"Us, if the strike turns into a revolution," Mickey replied. Seeing that this seemed to have caused some concern among the other men in the output office, he smiled. "But it won't come to that. No, those guns and tanks are just to scare us. But I'll tell you this: not one of those weapons can drive a bus."

The door opened and Dick Mortlake entered the output.

"Ah, just the man!" cried Mickey. He picked up a rolled document he had left on the counter while signing on and handed it to Dick.

"For the union notice-case, Branch Secretary!"

Dick took the document and unrolled it, revealing a poster with the message THE MINERS' FIGHT IS OUR FIGHT! He turned it around and showed it to the seven or eight men in the output. They cheered, bringing a smile to the faces of Dick and Mickey.

"How's the campaign goin'?" asked Lenny Hawkins.

"Well," said Mickey, "the posters and leaflets have mostly disappeared, so you'd have to say it's doing well."

"And we've had financial contributions from loads of branches—bus and tram branches, mostly," said Dick.

"And according to my spies," added Mickey, "the branch resolutions have begun to arrive at Transport House."

"So when will we be out?" asked Lenny.

"Just as soon as the Triple Alliance issues the call," said Mickey.

*

Negotiations with the government resumed and so the miners' EC asked its fellow Triple Alliance members to allow them to attend a meeting with Lloyd George and his ministers alone. The Prime Minister asked that, now they were around the table again, the pumpmen be allowed to work and the pit ponies rescued. Herbert Smith, acting president in the absence of Bob Smillie, who had resigned the presidency earlier in the month, told him that if he wanted a truce it would have to be on the basis of the wage-rates of 31 March and on condition that the government and owners accept the principle of a national wages board and a national pooling of profits. Deadlock.

*

"Has word come? Are we out?" Throughout their working day, these words were thrown at Mickey and Dick by other crews on the road and in the canteen at Liverpool Street—and not just by Middle Row men but also by men from other garages who recognised them.

Their replies were always the same: "Not yet, Brother. Hold tight; won't be long now."

*

On 8 April, the second Friday since the lockout began, Lloyd George told the Commons that volunteers would be sought to pump out the mines; they would need protection, so he was also seeking volunteers for an emergency defence force, and would be calling out the reserves. In a further indication that the state was standing firm, the Industrial Court denied an appeal against the refusal to pay miners unemployment benefit, even though they had had their contracts terminated as opposed to being on strike.

The Triple Alliance agreed to strike from midnight the following Tuesday, 12 April, unless negotiations were resumed in the meantime. The Transport Workers' Federation conference gave the ECs full power and then dispersed to await the strike call. The miners, meanwhile, turned down the offer of a conference made by Lloyd George as he was insisting that the safety of the mines should be the first topic of discussion. Although, therefore, a settlement looked unlikely, that same evening Jimmy Thomas told the Paddington branch of the NUR that he would do whatever he could to secure peace, even if some considered this a "betrayal of trust."

*

"We're out!"

"When?"

"From next Tuesday at midnight!"

"About bloody time!"

These exchanges, shouted from bus to bus, tram to tram, were repeated across London, to the consternation of some passengers and the delight of others. When the crews began to arrive at their garages the following morning, they were greeted by posters in their union notice-cases making it official:

ALL OUT IN SUPPORT OF THE MINERS

FROM MIDNIGHT, TUESDAY 12 APRIL

THEIR FIGHT IS OUR FIGHT!

*

On the Monday, the mine-owners and the miners met. Lloyd George's previous insistence on discussing safety questions first had been withdrawn and it was now announced that the conference would discuss "all questions in dispute." The transport and railworkers' leaders had argued that it was important that the miners should not lose public support, and so the miners had indicated that they would instruct their members not to interfere with safety work; and the government was willing to offer some financial assistance in areas where the proposed wage-reductions were steepest. Given these signs of movement, however slight, by all parties to the dispute, hopes arose in some quarters that a settlement could still be reached. Both sides put their cases and then adjourned until the next day, giving Lloyd George the opportunity to study and digest them. leading the Triple Alliance to postpone its strike.

The Triple Alliance issued a manifesto in which it argued that the principles at stake were vital to the whole trade union movement; the document accused the government, which claimed impartiality, of secretly siding with the employers, of talking peace while encouraging war.

*

"It's off—postponed!"

"Don't gimme that, Mickey! What's their excuse?"

"Negotiations ongoing, mate."

"Do the miners honestly think they'll get an agreement from the owners—or Lloyd George, come to that?"

"Well if they don't the strike will be back on, won't it?

The first poster was taken down and replaced with a new one:

STRIKE POSTPONED

Due to extended negotiations between the Miners' Federation, the mine-owners and the Government, solidarity strike action by the Triple Alliance has been postponed until further notice.

*

On the afternoon of 12 April, the allegation levelled by the Triple

Alliance in its recent manifesto was echoed by Herbert Smith, acting president of the Miners' Federation. This was after Lloyd George had said that a national pool for the equalisation of wages would be impossible without renewed state control of the industry—something to which the government would not agree—and so there was no alternative to district wages. "This scheme," thundered Smith at 10 Downing Street, "is absolutely the owners' scheme. If you had copied the words from their scheme, it could not be put in more explicit language." If the owners were determined to return to their pre-war ways of behaviour, "we will be starved into submission before we accept it."

The following day, the Triple Alliance met and decided that the strike of railwaymen and transport workers should go ahead. Making this announcement, Jimmy Thomas added that several other unions had offered to join the action; what he did not say was that Bob Williams had been forced to argue at length with him before he had agreed that ASLEF, the other rail union, should be allowed to join the Alliance.

*

"It's back on! The strike's back on!"

"When?"

"This Friday at 2200 hours. And the union has called midnight mass meetings all over London for the day before, Make sure you're there, brothers!"

The third notice went up in the union notice-case at Middle Row garage:

ALL OUT IN SUPPORT OF THE MINERS!

STRIKE FROM 2200 HOURS, FRIDAY 15 APRIL.

MIDNIGHT MASS MEETING, THURSDAY 14 APRIL,

KILBURN PICTURE PALACE

*

On the afternoon of 14 April, the TUC General Council and the executives of the Parliamentary Labour Party and the Labour Party assembled in the Grand Committee Room of the House of Commons and questioned representatives of the Triple Alliance, Bob Williams among them. Williams watched the to and fro of the interrogation, conscious that at this stage of the proceedings it was still possible for the strike to be thrown off-course by a negative or even lukewarm resolution by the National Council of Labour, as constituted by the three bodies here. But the National Council ended by pledging support to the miners and the Triple Alliance.

That same afternoon, Harry Gosling and Jimmy Thomas, for the transport workers and railwaymen respectively, went to see Lloyd George at No 10, specifically to answer the question the Prime Minister had, via the press, posed to them: "For what reason are you imposing this blow on your fellow countrymen?"

Given the records of both men, this meeting too was not without its risks. But Gosling and Thomas stood firm, Gosling turning the tables on Lloyd George by asking him why *he* was imposing this blow on his fellow countrymen and insisting that in order to help themselves they had no choice but to help the miners. Thomas spoke in a similar fashion.

It was close to midnight when it became apparent that something was amiss.

*

At 2345 hours the crowd outside the Kilburn Picture Palace on Belsize Road, just off Kilburn High Road, had grown to unmanageable proportions. Mickey Rice recognised men from a number of bus garages—Willesden, Cricklewood, Dollis Hill, the Bush and, of course, Middle Row—as well as tram men from Holloway, identifiable by their uniforms, a sprinkling of cabdrivers and a contingent of commercial drivers. And men were still arriving. The crowd would have been perfectly manageable—in fact, there would not have been a crowd at all—if the theatre doors had been open. But they were not. The police had been given adequate notice of the mass meeting but, anticipating no complications, had sent only a token force, and so they had now closed Belsize Road to what little traffic there was at that time of night. The bus branches had dipped into their branch funds and had travelled to Kilburn on buses obtained from their own garages on a private-hire basis, and at first these had parked in Belsize Road outside the picture palace, but the police were now directing the later arrivals to park up on the High Road, forcing the men to walk to the theatre. And then it began to rain.

"Fuck this for a game of soldiers, Dick!" Mickey oathed as he attempted to shoulder his way to the front of the crowd.

"What do you intend to do, Mick?"

"I'll see if I can wake someone up inside the theatre."

"There's still five minutes to go; someone from Emperor's Gate is sure to turn up soon."

"But they won't have bloody keys, will they?"

After a struggle, Mickey found himself at the doors of the theatre. He peered through the glass and, raising a fist, pounded on the wood panelling.

"Oi! Steady on, sir, steady on."

Mickey turned his head to the right and saw a large police sergeant scowling at him.

"You 'ave a go, then!"

"'Ave a go at what?"

"At seeing whether anyone's inside!"

"They've all gorn 'ome, mate."

"Gone 'ome? Why, for Christ's sake?"

The sergeant moved closer and lowered his head, as if about to let Mickey into a secret. "On account of the meetin' bein' cancelled, mate."

"Cancelled?"

"Keep your voice down or we'll have a riot on our 'ands!"

"Who says it's been..."—Mickey, feeling that the policeman might have a point, then lowered his voice—"cancelled?"

"I've been here since eleven-fifteen, mate. Five minutes after I arrived, the theatre staff came out and said they'd had a telephone call from your union, saying that the meeting had been cancelled."

Mickey brightened somewhat. "Ah, but that doesn't necessarily mean anything. I recall a few years back when one of our colleagues rang the Euston Palace of Varieties to say that a meeting had been cancelled, but it hadn't been: it was a ruse by someone who didn't want the meeting to go ahead."

The sergeant sighed. "That may well have been the case, but if this one was goin' ahead, shouldn't your leaders 'ave arrived by now?"

Mickey nodded grimly. "Yeah, you're right. But why didn't you tell anyone that it had been cancelled?"

"Because I don't want to be the one to create the riot. My idea was to just leave it, and sooner or later everyone would get fed up of waitin' an' bugger orf 'ome."

Mickey fell into thought. After some twenty seconds, he raised his head. "Listen, sergeant, these mass meetings are supposed to be taking place all over London. We need to know if they've *all* been cancelled." He inclined his head. "Is there any way you could find out whether they have?"

The sergeant shrugged. "Not without going to the station, no."

"You want a lift?"

"You gonna drive me?"

"No, I'll be responsible for crowd control while you're away. I'll get you a driver." Without waiting for the sergeant's reply, Mickey peered into the surging crowd in search of Malcom Lewis, who had driven one of the Middle Row private- hire buses. "Malcolm! Malcolm! Got a job for you!"

*

The sergeant stood at the front of the lower saloon, immediately behind Malcolm Lewis so that he could shout directions to him.

"We're facing the wrong way, driver, so you'll have to turn around."

"Nah, there's not room here—too many buses parked up."

"Alright, drive straight ahead down Belsize Road until you cross Abbey Road. Stop there and I'll see you back. You know Abbey Road?"

"Of course: I'm on the 31s!"

"Off you go, then."

"This is like being back at the training school."

Once the vehicle had crossed the junction, the sergeant alighted and stood in the centre of Abbey Road, holding up the light traffic while Malcolm reversed round to the left. The sergeant then boarded again and trotted to the front of the saloon. "Okay, back down Belsize Road and turn right onto Kilburn High Road!"

Reaching the picture palace, Malcolm was forced to sound his klaxon to part the crowd, which raised a cheer from the assembled multitude. As he passed, he saw that Mickey had climbed aboard one of the vehicles and was about to address the troops from the top deck.

"Driver," the sergeant directed once Malcolm had turned onto the High Road, "now you want to turn left onto Brondesbury Road; then straight ahead and you'll see the station on the corner of Salusbury Road."

*

Malcolm and the sergeant were back within twenty minutes. Malcolm joined Mickey on the top deck of what had become the speaker's platform and imparted his news.

"Comrades!" What with the numbers present and the rain, which was persistent but not particularly heavy, he doubted whether they would all hear him, but he would just have to do the best he could. "As we suspected, the mass meeting was cancelled by the powers that be at Emperor's Gate, the headquarters of our union—although maybe that address should be changed to Traitor's Gate!"

They liked that. As he looked down at them, he saw that their bodies from the shoulders down appeared to be melded into one dark mass, while the light from the gas lamps fell on hundreds of rain-washed faces as they lifted their heads and cheered the appropriateness of this new address before relapsing into expressions of anger and frustration.

"And comrades, it's worse than that! *All* of the mass meetings have been cancelled, every single one, right across London! That can only mean one thing: they've cancelled the bloody strike as well!"

Rainfall, illuminated and sparkling in pockets of gaslight, disappeared from view as it descended onto the men.

"Why would the strike have been cancelled? Two possible reasons: either the miners' case has been settled…or the miners have been betrayed. When Malcolm here"—he reached behind him, as if knowing that Malcolm would still be there, and placed a hand on his shoulder—"and the sergeant got to the police station, they were told that all the mass meetings had been cancelled. *But when Malcolm asked the officer if the miners' case had been settled he was told that there was no news of that!* SO THE MINERS HAVE BEEN BETRAYED, COMRADES!"

As hundreds of fists and voices were now raised, the police sergeant, who had followed Malcolm onto the top deck of the bus, leaned forward and shouted in Mickey's ear: "Is this what you call crowd control?"

Mickey turned to him, issuing a curt "Wait!" Then, mellowing, he turned back to him and raised a finger. "Watch me, Sergeant."

He turned back to the crowd, gripping the rail with both hands. "Comrades! There may be no mass meeting tonight, but there *will be a* mass meeting very soon! If our leaders have no satisfactory explanation for what they've done, they will be made to pay the price! And to discuss what that price should be, the Southeast District Vigilance Committee will call a mass protest meeting of its own!"

"When?" came a voice from down below.

"Within a week!" Mickey shouted back.

"Where?"

"Keep an eye on your union notice-cases! You'll have posters giving the date, time and place."

"You don't seem to realise," shouted a Shepherd's Bush man, "how bloody angry we are, Brother Rice!"

"Of course, I realise you're angry. Do you think I'm not angry? A word of advice, brothers: *stay* angry. Save up your anger and bring it to the protest meeting with you—and I hope you'll all be there. For now, there's nothing for us to do tonight but go home and get some shuteye."

Already, men were shuffling back to the buses.

"One last thing before you go, comrades!" A brief pause as they turned back to him. He raised a fist. "Victory to the miners! Victory to the miners! Let's hear you!"

"VICTORY TO THE MINERS!"

Mickey turned to leave and almost walked into the police sergeant. He looked up at his bewhiskered face and shrugged. "See? Crowd control."

The sergeant grunted his begrudging assent. "There'll be a few complaints from the neighbours, though."

33

Ernest Bevin folded his newspaper, laid it on his lap, then leaned his head back and closed his eyes, listening to the sounds of morning rush-hour traffic as the taxi entered the Euston Road. On an impulse, he retrieved the newspaper and was about to open it when he sighed. What would be the point? He had read the report twice already and a third reading was unlikely to change the news or reveal a previously overlooked insight. Another sigh. Well, if the miners were going to settle, well and good, but he felt uneasy, suspecting that this would not be straightforward.

He left the taxi outside Unity House, and as he walked to the entrance he spotted Bob Williams just in front of him.

"Bob!"

"Morning, Ernie."

Bevin held up his newspaper. "Have you seen the news?"

"Haven't had a chance yet, Ernie."

Bevin took him by the sleeve and guided him to a spot just to the left of the main entrance to the NUR headquarters. "It seems a crowd of back-benchers had a couple of meetings on the mining crisis late last night. First they heard Evan Williams for the owners. Apparently they weren't too impressed with him and so they got hold of Frank Hodges, secretary of the Federation. He went down rather better— so well, in fact that a group of MPs formed some kind of *ad hoc* committee and scuttled round to Downing Street for a midnight meeting with the Welsh Wizard."

"So what did he say to them—Hodges, I mean?"

Bevin slapped his copy of *The Times* against Williams's chest. "Here, you can read it yourself, but in brief he said his members were willing to discuss wages as long as there was no question of a *permanent* district basis. Lloyd George thought this was so significant that he told the owners they'd better meet the Fed EC this morning. He wrote to Frank Hodges, inviting the miners to meet, making it clear that they would be discussing a *temporary* wage settlement, and that the question of the national pool could be discussed when the question of a permanent settlement came back on the agenda. The owners have put out a statement saying that they're keen to meet, and that they're prepared to forego *all* profits for the next period."

"So the strike's off?"

"I don't know, Bob." He blinked and looked up at the big Welshman. "Do you remember me telling you that we'd see a few games being played before this matter was put to bed?"

"I do, yes."

"Well, I've a nasty feeling that today will be the day. Come on, let's see what's happening."

*

At first, everyone was milling around and no one knew anything. Then the executives of the three components of the Triple Alliance assembled formally, at which point the EC of the Miners' Federation indicated that it would withdraw in order to give consideration to Lloyd George's invitation. During this lengthy hiatus, there was much informal discussion, in which James Sexton, general secretary of the National Union of Dock, Riverside and General Workers, and an MP, let it be known that when Hodges had addressed the back-benchers the previous night several miners' MPs had been present and they had raised no objection.

After ninety minutes had passed, Bevin got to his feet, telling

Gosling and Williams, "I'll go and see if they've reached a decision."

He was soon back, reporting, "Dear, oh dear, what a sight! There's Hodges sitting in a room on his own and the EC members are arguing the toss in the corridor. They've rejected Hodges's scheme by a majority of one, with three executive members absent. Hodges has resigned, but they've rejected that, too." He shook his head. "They'll be up here in a few minutes."

And back they came, led by a bristling Herbert Smith, their acting president, who without further ado, made a brief statement.

"It is our intention, brothers, to reject Lloyd George's invitation to meet today. And now, if you don't mind, we'll return to our offices in Russell Square to draft our reply to his letter."

Jimmy Thomas was on his feet. "But Brother Smith, let's talk about this. I think you'll agree that the decision of your EC leaves us in a somewhat tricky position. It needs to be discussed."

But Smith was already gathering up his papers. He turned to Thomas, almost snarling, "Get on t' field. That's t' place."

"I'm not fluent in the Yorkshire tongue," murmured Bevin to Bob Williams, "but I think we've just been told that we should call out our members if we want the right to discuss the conduct of this dispute."

*

The hours ground by. At Unity House it was decided to send a message to Russell Square, seeking to delay the dispatch of the miners' reply until it had been discussed by the full Alliance. After time had passed and this had received no reply, Bevin got to his feet.

"I move," he said, "that we elect a small sub-committee to meet the miners' EC."

This was duly done and the sub-committee, led by Harry Gosling, made its way to Russell Square, where it was shown into a waiting room. When eventually admitted into the presence of the EC, Gosling urged the miners to meet with the owners and government and come to a temporary agreement on wages.

"Brother Gosling," boomed Herbert Smith, "t' letter to Lloyd George is bein' typed."

"Might we see it?"

"No, you can't. Let me meck it plain for ye: there'll be no further negotiations, either wi' Lloyd George, the owners, *or the Alliance.* Our demands are clear, an' we're standin' by 'em. An' let me say, Brother Goslin', that we expect the Alliance to stand wi' us, just as you've agreed, an' that you'll call out your members tonight."

*

"I have to say," fumed Jimmy Thomas when this was reported back, "that this is hardly the way to treat allies."

"Be that as it may, this is not the time to take personal offence," Bevin responded. "Let's not lose sight of what we've been telling our members throughout the piece: a defeat for the miners will be a defeat for the whole movement, and employers throughout the country will be lowering wages. Bearing that in mind, it's surely worth making a final attempt to bring us all together. I therefore move that we ask the miners' EC to return to Unity House on the basis that the Triple Alliance will be announcing to the press that we're finalising arrangements for the strike."

"Our union will need to consider that alone," said Thomas, who clearly did not favour the proposal.

"The game," said Bevin to Williams, "is about to be played."

*

"Our EC," announced Thomas upon his return, "has considered very carefully the motion put forward by Brother Bevin. Needless to say, we wish to see a victory for the miners—both for their own sakes and for the sake of the rest of our movement. But the motion calls for the miners' EC to return to Unity House, and we have absolutely no confidence that the miners would comply with this. That being the case, it would obviously be impossible for us—as a *Triple* Alliance—to make any plans for the strike. Our EC has therefore voted—by a substantial margin—against the proposal."

"How substantial?" came a voice from the ranks of the Transport Workers' Federation.

"Twenty-eight to twelve!" responded an NUR EC member before Thomas could forestall him.

"And furthermore," Thomas continued, "we move that the proposed strike action be cancelled."

Bob Williams got to his feet. "No one can doubt," he began in his deep baritone, "that this Triple Alliance of ours today faces its most severe crisis. Many in this room will blame the EC of the Miners' Federation for this, and in truth they must shoulder part of the blame. But in truth,"—he looked around the room—"in *truth,* brothers, are we not all to blame? Some of you may recall that in February this year I wrote a lengthy document in which I argued that unless we returned to first principles, this alliance was bound, sooner or later, to come to grief. What did I mean by that? When we first formed this alliance in 1914, it was clearly understood that we would discuss and agree our demands and plans *jointly* before any question of action; those demands would then be tabled to the employers at the same time. Has that that happened on this occasion? No, it has not—nor anything like it! The same could be said of the miners' dispute last year, which is why I put pen to paper in February.

"The Miners' Federation formulated its demands entirely without reference to the Alliance; when it met the owners or the government it insisted on doing so alone as, our members not yet being on strike, we were not qualified to join them. And that attitude has persisted until today, when they have refused to even show us the text of their reply to Lloyd George. Is this an alliance in which we are all equally involved, or are we to be dragged along, at the tail, willy-nilly, of the Miners' Federation? For this uncomradely behaviour, there is no one to blame but the miners themselves. But none of this would have occurred, brothers, if we had insisted upon returning to the principles and procedures upon which this Alliance was founded! And for that we are *all* to blame!"

"Chairman," insisted a brave voice from the ranks of the NUR, "we have defeated a motion to call the miners back to Unity House and we are now asked to consider a motion to cancel the strike. But there is surely another option: to simply continue the strike as previously agreed, without calling the miners back or issuing a statement to the press on behalf of the Alliance."

"And there's another option: simply postpone the strike until we can talk some sense into the miners!" This was Charlie Cramp!

Jimmy Thomas's face was not a pretty sight. "I would remind the members on this side of the room," he snarled, "that the organisation of which they are members have taken a decision and that they are bound by it!" He sniffed. "Anyone favouring an alternative option will obviously have to vote against the motion which is now before this meeting."

"I think it's time for some plain speaking," said Ernie Bevin once the commotion caused by the previous intervention had died. "We in the Transport Workers' Federation find ourselves in an almost intolerable position, Chairman. On the one hand, we have the miners, who while they believe in unity in action, obviously have no time for unity in counsel. But on the other hand we have the

National Union of Railwaymen, which by the decision it has just taken has virtually dictated our own position. For how can the transport workers be expected to go it alone? To do so would be to invite disaster. Part of me agrees with the NUR dissident who has just complained that other options were not explored, but let me tell you quite candidly that even if the strike were to go ahead, with all of us in it together, it would not have been without problems as far as we were concerned. This federation of ours is not like the Miners' Federation or the NUR: our organisation consists of over thirty unions, some better organised than others. While we know that many of our members have decided to strike tonight, we know of others—and I'm talking about commercial drivers here—who have offered themselves to the government's volunteer services. We were willing to take a chance on a strike if we were to be united—miners, railwaymen and transport workers. But to go ahead without the NUR would risk the destruction of our federation and even some of the unions in it. You leave us with no alternative but to vote for the motion you have placed before us.

"And Chairman"—here Bevin raised his head and looked Thomas straight in the eye—"I don't want my frankness here to be the excuse for any finger-pointing, or accusations of weakness, because that's a game that can be played by two. This past week there have been rumours that some railwaymen were reluctant to strike for the miners. And I daresay that the news of their general secretary telling one of their biggest branches that he would do whatever he could to bring peace did little to firm up their resolve!" Bevin sat down, batting away with the back of his hand the few insults which flew as a result of his closing remarks.

When the motion was put to the vote, there were only three votes against—and they came from the ranks of the NUR. At four o'clock, Thomas stepped outside the building and announced to the waiting press that the Triple Alliance strike was cancelled.

*

The following morning, Mickey Rice and Dick Mortlake went to the union notice-case in Middle Row garage and displayed a new poster.

THE MINERS BETRAYED!

YESTERDAY, ON BLACK FRIDAY, 15 APRIL, THE
MINERS WERE BETRAYED WHEN THE NATIONAL
UNION OF RAILWAYMEN AND THE TRANSPORT
WORKERS' FEDERATION CANCELLED THE STRIKE
DUE TO COMMENCE THAT EVENING.

THE TRAITORS WILL BE CALLED TO ACCOUNT!

WATCH THIS SPACE FOR DETAILS OF OUR
PROTEST MEETING!

SOLIDARITY, BROTHERS, SOLIDARITY!

Their job done, they closed the case, locked it and prepared to make
their way into the output office to sign on. As they turned, however,
they saw Victor Wiggins, the garage superintendent, standing a few
yards away with arms crossed, surveying their work.

"Good morning, Driver Rice, Driver Mortlake," he nodded. "A very
pungent message, if I may say so." He smiled. "Do you know, as a
result of yesterday's decision, I don't think it will be long before the
company starts putting up a few posters of its own."

Mickey and Dick ignored him and entered the output.

34

Six days later, Mickey Rice sat at the head of the fifty protesters
who had taken over Transport House the previous day,
confronting the national officials and executive council of the
United Vehicle Workers. The officials and the executive members sat
at the head of the room, while the protesters sat, unevenly spaced,
facing them.

"Well," sighed Stanley Hirst, "you've got us all here, so we'd better
hear what you have to say for yourselves." He held up a finger. "Only
let me make this clear: there will be no free-for-all. You've had the
run of this building for two days, striking terror into the staff and
turfing the officers onto the street, but in front of your executive

council you'll behave yourselves, and..."

The free-for-all Hirst had sought to prevent was now provoked by both his words and his attitude. Some protesters stood. Arms were waved, voices raised.

"We're the injured party here!"

"Terror, my arse!"

"Who does he think he is?"

"Are we wasting our time here, Mickey?"

*

When they had occupied the building on the Thursday morning, 21 April, they had evicted the officials but had given the staff a choice: they could either stay and continue their work, or leave. When the press arrived, Mickey told them that this occupation had been decided by a protest meeting the previous evening at which 12,000 members had been represented. This was true, although it disguised the fact that attendance had been much poorer than expected. Any journalist worth his salt would have calculated that if the branches represented had each contained an average of 200 members—and some were known to be larger than that—the attendance at the protest meeting would have been a mere 60; allowing for the probability that more than one member per branch had attended, the numbers would still only have reached hundreds, not thousands. The poor attendance, Mickey and several others agreed, was undoubtedly because spirits had been dampened by the decision by the Triple Alliance to call off the strike.

A few wild voices—Vernon was present—had, perhaps predictably, called for the formation of a breakaway, but they had been told that such a demand was not particularly logical, for the midnight mass meetings had been called off by the United Vehicle Workers, a union that would within months cease to exist. Representatives from Nunhead, Merton and the Old Kent Road appeared to settle for a compromise, vowing that their branches would withhold their contributions. Most of those present seemed to find this just as irrational as the formation of a breakaway, but there still remained the question of what action should be taken. How would the "traitors" be "called to account?" In the end, it was Harry Beard of Nunhead who came up with the proposal.

"Do you recall," said Harry, "that some of us was chucked out of Traitor's Gate last year when we told 'em we was gonna sit in at the EC meeting?" Nods and murmurs. "But do you know *why* we was kicked out?" He stood with folded arms while he awaited a reply.

"Well," said New Cross's Ernie Sharp, "they said we had no right to be there."

"Oh, yeah." Harry came back. "That's what *they* said, but what was the *real* reason? I'll tell you: they kicked us out because there wasn't enough of us to *stop* 'em kicking us out!"

This gave rise to a certain amount of laughter as the audience could see what was coming. "So you're suggesting what, Harry?" asked Mickey Rice from the chair.

"I'm suggesting, Mickey, that we get fifty or sixty big lads to turn up at Traitor's Gate tomorrow morning and completely take over the place!"

That got him a round of cheers. Mickey, although smiling, nodded slowly. "And then what?"

"And then we put the officials on the street where some of 'em belong!"

The cheers now were louder and more numerous.

"I can see that's a popular suggestion," persisted Mickey, "but what then? We surely have to have a demand or two!"

Ernie Sharp, thin and tubercular-looking, got to his feet. "Mickey," he said, his voice almost a growl, "you remember the old red-button days and how we used to deal with officials and executive members who thought they could do as they pleased, never mind what the members said. On one occasion, for those of you who don't know,"—he looked to the left and the right—"we forced the resignation of the entire EC. Of course, that was at a Special Delegate Meeting, constitutionally called, in 1916. Now, whatever we might think about Harry's proposal, we'd have to say that it's highly *un*constitutional"—a wave of laughter—"and so we can't expect to be in a position to force anybody's resignation. But as Mickey says we have to have a demand." He hunched his shoulders and lowered his voice into little more than a hoarse whisper. "Picture the scene, brothers: there we are, occupyin' Transport House; Stanley Hirst pleads with us to leave; we reply No, Stan, we're not leaving until..." He lifted his palms and resumed his normal voice. "Until what?" He turned to Mickey, addressing him directly. "I suggest, Mickey, that we refuse to leave until the whole EC has been called to listen to our complaints and the leadership gives a complete explanation as to why our mass meetings were cancelled and why the strike in support of the miners was called off."

As the members cheered and applauded, Mickey looked about the hall. "Will that fit the bill, brothers?"

Agreed.

*

"Do I recall you telling me that Annette gave you a hard time after you and the others gate-crashed the EC meeting in February last year?" asked Dick with a grin as they made their way home.

"Yes, Dick, I did tell you that," Mickey replied with a straight face.

"So how will you get away with this one?"

"For a start, mate, I'm not going to give her advance warning, so I'd be grateful if you say nothing to Gladys until it's all over."

"Won't that make it worse?"

Mickey shrugged. "We'll see."

*

And so, at ten o'clock the next morning fifty big lads—*The Times* the next day described them as being "mostly men of stalwart build and demeanour"—had turned up at 45, Emperor's Gate, Kensington and told the man on reception—still the same medically-retired tram motorman—that he could take the rest of the day off if he wished. They then went through the headquarters, floor by floor, office by office, telling the officials to vacate the building and the staff to continue with their work if that was their preference. Mickey made a point of not going near the ledger department, and Malcolm Lewis told him later that Annette had said that as she had not voted to go on strike she would remain at work; she had not asked about Mickey and her face, said Malcolm, gave nothing away.

"I see Brother Vernon is not with us this morning," Mickey remarked.

Malcolm grinned. "Probably feels it's a bit too dangerous for him."

Stanley Hirst had arrived outside the building at 10.30, initially thinking that the officials crowding the pavement must be engaged in some protest of their own. "Come on lads, this is no way to behave, break it up, break it up," he muttered, trying to work his way to the entrance.

"You'll not get in there, Stan," John Cliff advised. "We're locked out."

"Locked out?" Hirst was dumbfounded. "Locked out? How can we be locked out of our own building? Who's responsible for this?"

"It's the London lads again, Stan," said Cliff, "only this time there's a good sixty or seventy of 'em." George Sanders, Eric Rice and Ben Smith, London lads themselves, looked on in silence.

Hirst cast his eye over the building, catching sight of unfamiliar faces at some of the upper windows. "Bloody hellfire,"—*hell-fi-er*—he oathed. "Has nobody called the police?"

"For what?" asked Ben Smith.

"To get the buggers out, of course!" Enraged, the diminutive general secretary was beginning to perspire in his heavy overcoat and hat. The day, like so many others that year, was turning warm.

Ben Smith spoke calmly. "Stan, they must have known that the police would be called—some of 'em have had prior experience of this sort of thing—and so equally they must be intent on staying where they are until they get what they want. Besides, you don't want to see the building wrecked, do you?"

"Well, we'll have the police here anyway," insisted Hirst. He turned to Cliff. "Johnny, make the call."

"Where from?"

"Where *from*? Where the bloody hell do you think...? Oh, aye, I see what you mean. Well, nip down to the High Street and see if you can find a copper, will you? And tell him he'll need reinforcements."

Later in the morning, Mickey peered through a window and saw Hirst in conversation with a police sergeant on the pavement; a constable stood a few feet away, next to the railings. Hirst, still in his overcoat and hat, dwarfed by the policeman and looking more like Mr Punch than ever, was using his right hand to emphasise certain points, which the sergeant appeared to find unconvincing. The other officials seemed to have drifted off, probably to the nearest café.

"Were the men who took over your building armed, sir?"

"Armed? Of course they weren't armed, Sergeant!"

"Do you consider them to be dangerous, sir?"

"Not in the way that a policeman would understand the word, no."

"Do you believe them to be intent on robbery?"

"Not at all, Sergeant."

"Are the staff in any danger, sir?"

"I very much doubt it."

The sergeant, blinking thoughtfully, touched his chin with a forefinger. "Then, if you'll pardon me, sir, I'm blowed if I can see what the problem is." He cleared his throat. "In fact, wasn't there a similar incident early last year?"

Hirst wagged a finger as realisation struck. "Ahhh, yes! You were the sergeant who attended on that occasion!"

The sergeant, pouting, nodded. "I was indeed, sir." A finger went to the peak of his helmet. "And that incident, if you'll pardon me for saying so, turned out to be a storm in a teacup. Which is why there is only two of us on this occasion. So I ask again: what is the problem?"

"The problem, Sergeant, is that these men—seventy or eighty of them—have illegally occupied the building and are preventing me and my officials from doing a day's work!"

"Seventy or eighty, you say?"

"I do say. Huge brutes according to my colleagues."

"In which case, sir, I think we'll wait until they begin to tire before we storm the building."

Hirst took a step backwards and looked up at the policeman, eyes narrowed. "Do you think this is some sort of joke, man?"

"Well, to be honest, sir, I'm not at all sure what it is. What do you think it is?"

"How do you mean?"

"Well, last time, if I recall, a few men were insisting on witnessing one of your meetings. What is this lot after?"

"I'm damned if I know, Sergeant." Hirst shook his head. "I'm *damned* if I know!"

"Do you not think it would be wise to ask, Mr Hirst?"

"Ask?"

"Yes, ask." He sighed and folded his arms across his substantial chest. "You know, most of the problems a policeman is called upon to deal with are pretty humdrum. When you've been on the job as long as I have, however, you've probably come across a few of the more major items: murder, armed robbery and—yes!—occupations of this nature. Now in my experience, when a building is forcibly occupied, the occupiers always have a set of demands. Why else would they be doing it? Now, once we've ruled out retaking the building by force...Have we ruled that out, by the way, Mr Hirst?"

Hirst grimaced. "My colleagues are of the view that it would be inadvisable."

"Mm. Yes." The sergeant regarded Hirst in silence for a moment. "Well, once that is ruled out, the next step is to ascertain the demands of the occupiers."

"So when will you do that, Sergeant?"

The policeman frowned. "As far as I am aware, Mr Hirst, the occupiers have no demands on the Metropolitan Police. I suggest you contact their leader without delay and ask him what they want."

"I don't know who their leader is."

"Not even the slightest suspicion?" The policeman winked at Hirst and nodded encouragingly. "Go on, have a guess."

"Alright, here we go." Hirst backed into the middle of the road and looked up at the building. "BROTHER RICE! BROTHER RICE!" For such a small man, Stanley Hirst, a veteran outdoor speaker, had a loud voice.

"Coming, Stan, coming," came a faint voice.

"That Rice bloke must be a bloody ventriloquist," commented the sergeant. "I would've sworn that voice came from behind us."

Hirst turned and saw Eric Rice trotting up the street, and behind him the other officials, hands in pockets, sauntering in leisurely fashion after their second breakfasts.

"Not you, you pillock! It's your brother I want!" He threw an arm in the direction of the upper stories of the building. "See if you can attract his attention."

"MICKEY! MICKEY! IT'S ERIC HERE! STAN WANTS A WORD! OPEN THE WINDER SO HE CAN TALK TO YOU!"

From above, there drifted down the distant slap of shoe leather hastening from one part of the building to another and muted cries of "Mickey! Mickey!"

Eric turned to his general secretary. "That should do it, Stan. I think he'll be with you in a tick."

In due course there came the sound of a sash window being hauled up and Mickey Rice leaned out.

"How can I help you, Brother Hirst?" he called down.

"Well, you could meck a start by vacating my bloody building!"

"*Your* building?" The window came down.

"No, no, no, Mr Hirst," counselled the sergeant, "you'll need to be a bit more diplomatic than that. And when it comes to language you might consider the fact that this is a respectable neighbourhood."

Eric Rice tried again. "MICKEY! MICKEY! GIVE STAN ANOTHER CHANCE! HE SAYS HE'S SORRY!"

"No I don't!" seethed Stanley Hirst.

"Yes you do!" hissed the sergeant.

The sash was drawn up once more. "Yes, Brother Hirst?"

"Look, could you tell me...Just give us some idea..."

He was silenced by a raised palm from the sergeant, who then took over as lead negotiator. "Good morning, Mr Rice. I believe we met here last year."

"So we did, so we did. Nice to see you again, Sergeant."

"Look, lad, Mr Hirst would like to know what your demands are. Tell him that and he'll know how to respond. Are you with me?"

"Of course, Sergeant. Our demand, Brother Hirst, is that you, the other leading officers and the executive council give us a full explanation of why our mass meetings were cancelled last week and the solidarity strike was called off."

Another window went up. "And," called a commercial driver, "we want to know if there's any truth in the rumour that you lot have agreed a wage-cut with the London haulage employers."

"Yes," said Mickey, to whom this additional demand was something of a surprise, "that too."

"We-e-e-ll..." Stanley Hirst suddenly became avuncular, arms outstretched, palms upturned, a smile on his face. "If that's all it is, there's no problem. I'll *personally* meck sure it's in the next issue of *The Record*."

"No, no, no, we want to hear it from you and the EC *directly*—before we leave this building."

"Oh, come on now, Brother Rice. This is not how we do business in our union—you should know that."

"And *you* should know it *is* how we red-button men do business!"

There came the sound of cheers from the building—most obviously from the men standing behind Mickey Rice, but also from those on other floors.

"Mmm, sounds to me as if you were right, Mr Hirst," murmured the sergeant. "Sounds like a good sixty or seventy of 'em." He sniffed, "Well, sir, what do you intend to do?"

Hirst held up a hand. "Give me a moment, Sergeant." He turned to address the still-open window. "Just a minute, Brother Rice!"

The other officials had by now gathered on the pavement. Hirst gestured to Ben Smith, who stepped forward.

"Ben, did you hear what he's asking for?"

"I did, Stan."

Hirst paused for a moment, as if in the hope that Ben would follow up his brief reply with a denunciation of the proposal. Disappointed, he leaned forward and spoke confidentially. "But it would take me at least 24 hours to get the whole EC here."

Ben scratched his right sideboard. "Well, there's your opportunity, then: tell him that and say that you'll call a meeting for tomorrow if he and his lads vacate the building now."

Hirst pointed a finger at Ben Smith's chest. "Good thinking, Ben." He stepped back a few paces and looked up at the window. "Brother Rice, if you vacate the building now, I'll call the EC together for tomorrow. How does that suit you?"

"Not a chance. We'll leave when we've had the discussion with you and the EC."

"What's the matter? Don't you trust me?"

"No."

The other officials, with the exception of John Cliff, were hiding their faces. Fuming, Hirst turned and walked fifty or sixty paces down the street and back again, then repeated the manoeuvre.

"If you look closely," whispered Archie Henderson, "you can see the steam rising from him."

"That's probably why they call it letting off steam," said Eric Rice.

When Hirst returned to the fold, he was relatively calm. He looked around the group. "It seems to me," he said levelly, "that he has us by the knackers. If anybody has any bright ideas, now's the time to speak up." Silence. "Just as I thought. Right!" He stepped into the road and looked up at the open window.

"Brother Rice!"

"Brother Hirst?"

"Is my secretary still in the building?

"As far as I know, yes."

"Then have her come to the window, if you please, and tell her to bring her dictation pad."

Moments later, a middle-aged woman appeared at the window.

"Doris, you need to send a telegram to all members of the executive council: 'Emergency EC meeting Transport House tomorrow Friday 22 April. Crucial you attend. Stanley Hirst.'"

"Will that be all, Mr Hirst?"

"Just one more thing: tell the staff that they should leave for home at the usual time this afternoon and report for work at the normal time tomorrow morning, as if nothing untoward was occurring. I will see you tomorrow, Doris, so good day to you. And good day to you, Brother Rice."

And with that Stanley Hirst walked in the direction of Kensington High Street, followed by the other officers.

*

What were they to do for food? Transport House had a canteen, but the solution this provided was not totally satisfactory, because priority had to be given to the staff—readily agreed by Mickey in discussion with the canteen supervisor—and then the estimated surplus proved insufficient.

"The problem is," said Enzo, the Italian supervisor, "the only meal we serve is lunch, and then a snack—biscuits, pastries—mid-morning and mid-afternoon. Every morning we buy supplies, just enough so it's fresh." He shrugged. "Maybe we got enough for some extra lunches today, but not for all of you."

"The problem is bigger than you think, mate: we'll be here until tomorrow."

Enzo slapped his forehead. "Oh, bloody hell!" He spent a few moments in deep thought. "No, no, no, I don't see no way to feed you."

"Look, how would it be if we made do with a snack for lunch, and then you get in supplies to serve us a proper meal just before you leave this afternoon? That should see us through until tomorrow morning."

Enzo fixed him with a suspicious look. "You gonna pay for this the same as the staff?"

"Of course we are! And listen: we'll pay you in advance, so you can use that to buy the stuff."

Enzo shook his head. "No need for that. We got accounts with the local butcher and grocer. Pork chop and two veg suit you?"

"Fine. And make sure there's plenty of tea and milk."

"Of course. And you want breakfast tomorrow morning, I suppose."

"If it's available."

"It will be, if you pay."

"We'll pay."

"Okay, now I got to phone for those deliveries. But first I got to clear all this with the finance office."

"Why's that?"

"You want us to cook you a meal for late afternoon, then you want breakfast tomorrow: that means overtime for my girls."

*

As he left the canteen, Annette, accompanied by two of her colleagues, was about to enter it for lunch. He had known that it was inevitable that they meet, and so he was prepared. He assumed that she had made her own preparations, for when their eyes met there was no indication of surprise or disquiet; there was, possibly, little warmth in her smile but it was at least a smile. He touched her forearm to detain her as her colleagues entered the canteen and the strangest thing happened: there came that jolt of electricity that he had often, in the early days of their relationship, felt when touching her. Stranger still, it was obvious that she felt it also, for her lips parted and her eyes misted over. He took her hand in his and smiled, gratified that something precious had been confirmed, or, he thought, regained, even. Regained? Had this intimacy been lost, then?

"Sweetheart, I hope you understand..." he began, drawing her into a deserted corridor.

Flushed with both pleasure and embarrassment, she waved a hand dismissively. "Oh, don't worry about that, my love."

He was in earnest, though. "But I *want* you to understand, Annette. It's…"

She placed a small, soft hand on his mouth. "I *do* understand, Mickey. At least I understand why you are doing this." She gave her blond head a subtle shake, a small amused grin on her lips. "But I do not understand what you hope to gain from it." She shook her head, more emphatically this time. "But it does not matter. Because I love you, Mickey."

He touched her cheek, gently. "Oh, Annette, do you know what I would like to do now?"

She laughed and placed a palm on his chest. "Yes, of course, Mickey, but you would be expelled and I would be dismissed." She sighed. "So you will not be coming home tonight?"

"No. I'm so sorry, sweetheart."

"It is alright, Mickey. I will see you tomorrow."

"Yes, tomorrow we may be able to travel home together, if our business here is finished."

"I hope so, Mickey, I hope so." She leaned up and kissed him on the lips. "Now I must go."

When Mickey re-joined his comrades, he was whistling gaily.

*

And now, on Friday afternoon, a week—almost to the very hour—after Jimmy Thomas's announcement from the steps of Unity House, the protestors were in confrontation with Stanley Hirst, his colleagues, and the executive council.

Mickey Rice stood. "Brother Hirst," he said, after the latter's outburst had provoked outrage from the floor, "with all due respect, your attitude is not helping matters. The staff were not terrorised, and we've taken very great care to ensure that no damage was done to the building or anything in it. We're here because a very great injustice has been done to one million miners, who are locked into a dispute which we could have helped resolve—that we *wanted* to help resolve and we *would* have helped resolve. But the Transport Workers' Federation, to which our union is affiliated, and the National Union of Railwaymen decided to cancel their solidarity strike at almost the last minute, with not a word of explanation. As our mass meetings were called off, we are sure that our own union must have been a party to the decision of the Triple Alliance to call off the strike itself." He heaved a sigh. "And *that*, Brother Hirst, is what brings us here. We want an explanation, and we're not leaving this building until we get it.

"In addition to this, there's the issue of the proposed wage-cut for commercial drivers. Some of our members suspect that the cut has already been agreed by the leadership of our union, and they wish to be assured that this is not the case."

"Is that it?" asked Hirst, as if he were expecting more.

"It's enough," replied Mickey.

"Well, let's take your last point first. You say the commercial drivers want an assurance that the wage-cut proposed by the London employers has not been agreed by the leadership of this union. I hereby give that assurance!"

Mickey groaned and climbed to his feet once more. "Brother Hirst, I suspect that our commercial members are expecting a little more than that. Anyway, if I'm not mistaken, you have a national organiser and national organising secretary for the commercial sector on the platform with you. Isn't this a question for one of them?"

Hirst called over his shoulder. "Brother Smith!"

Ben Smith walked to the front of the platform. "Brothers," he began, "as most of you know, I'm an old red-button man—as, for that matter, is our national organiser Archie Henderson."

"After he was a blue-button man," an irritable Hirst muttered audibly. Archie had defected from the blue-button union during the London tram strike of 1915.

"Does anyone honestly think that two former red-button men would agree a wage-cut behind the backs of the members?"

Maybe not, Ben, thought Mickey, but I recall the time you endorsed a set of minutes in which you agreed that the union would not support members who went outside the agreement.

"That," Ben continued, "would be against everything we believe in and have practiced for years." He smiled. "Now, I know you lads haven't had the chance to see a newspaper today, but if you had, you would have seen a little story to the effect that the joint committee of our own union and the National Union of Vehicle Workers met on Wednesday and decided to place the matter before the members in order to get a decision. In the newspaper I saw, Will Godfrey of the NUVW has announced that there will be a delegate conference of both unions *next* Wednesday at Friars Hall, Blackfriars."

"Okay?" asked Hirst.

Mickey looked over his shoulder at Neville Bramley, the commercial driver who had, so to speak, placed the matter on the agenda, receiving his nod.

"Okay."

"Now to the far more complex—and probably contentious—matter of the decision taken by the Triple Alliance a week ago today." Hirst sighed heavily and drew a hand over his face. "Believe me when I say, brothers, that we all wanted to help the miners over the enormous difficulties they face. To be honest, however, the miners themselves—or the EC of their union—didn't make it easy for us. And I have to warn you, brothers, that I'm constrained in what I can say in this regard, because even after the decision to call off the strike was taken we agreed that publicly we—our union and the NUR—should say nothing that might
reflect badly on the miners."

Hirst had calmed down considerably and was now addressing his audience as if this were a perfectly normal, legitimate conference. This could only be, thought Mickey, because he wanted desperately to be believed and for this unexpected problem to go away.

"You will have read in the press that on the evening of 14 April Frank Hodges, secretary of the Miners Federation, addressed a meeting of back-benchers in the House of Commons. At that meeting, in reply to a question, he said that his EC was willing to discuss wages—wage-*cuts*, in plain language—as long as it was understood that the district system of determining wages would not be permanent. Now, it is a fact that he said it, and Hodges himself doesn't dispute that he said it. In fact, our parliamentary secretary Tich Smith was *there* when he said it, as were several of the miners' MPs, none of whom said a dickey-bird."

He sighed. "That's the first thing. The second point that has to be made is that the next morning, after the miners' EC received the letter from Lloyd George suggesting a further meeting with the owners, they left the meeting-room and went downstairs to decide on a reply. At that point—or any other point, come to that—the miners wanted no input from their partners in the Triple Alliance. After they had been gone for two hours, Brother Bevin went to look for them. He discovered, brothers, that they had debated the proposal suggested by Hodges at his meeting with the back-benchers and had rejected it"—he paused for dramatic effect—"by a single vote." He extended a finger. "One vote! And at the same time, there were three EC members not in attendance, so it's anyone's guess as to how the vote would have gone if they'd been present.

"They came back into the meeting and announced that they had decided to reject Lloyd George's offer and were going to their offices in Russell Square to compose a reply to him. Suggestions were made that they stay and discuss the situation that had now arisen, but they declined.

"Later, a deputation, led by Harry Gosling, was sent to Russell Square, but they were told in no uncertain terms by Herbert Smith, the miners' acting president, that there would be no further negotiations and that their partners in the Triple Alliance were expected to honour their commitment to strike.

"Later still, Brother Bevin moved that they send a message to Russell Square, asking the miners to return on the basis that the Triple Alliance would announce to the press that it was meeting to finalise preparations for the strike. That message was never sent, brothers, because the NUR insisted on debating that motion on their own, with the result that they rejected it and moved instead that the strike be cancelled permanently."

Moans of dismay now arose from the floor, and Mickey saw Hirst's lips tighten in what would have been a grin, had he not swiftly composed his features.

Hirst thumped the table in front of him. "If there are to be allegations of *betrayal*, brothers, you now know where they should be levelled!"

Dick Mortlake was on his feet. "But, Brother Hirst, is it not true that the whole of the Transport Workers' Federation delegation then voted in favour of that motion?"

Hirst was not fazed by the question. He raised his upturned palms. "Without the railwaymen, what were we to do? Quite apart from anything else, if we had gone ahead on our own the government would have been free to switch its full attention onto us, sending in its soldiers and volunteers to drive buses, trams and commercial vehicles. And make no mistake, brothers, that would have weakened us. And nobody should doubt that with unemployment as it is there would have been thousands of volunteers. We were left with no choice, brothers."

Some of the protesters were by now turning to each other with frowns and shrugs, wondering whether Stanley Hirst and the rest of the leadership might after all be in the clear. Surely even Mickey would have difficulty in attempting to turn the situation around.

He did try, however.

"Brother Hirst, can you tell us what time the decision was taken to call off the strike?"

"It was some time before four o'clock, because that was when Brother Thomas made the public announcement."

"And that was on Friday, 15 April." Even to himself, Mickey sounded like a barrister addressing his remarks to the occupant of a witness box.

"It was, Brother Rice."

"And that was the decision by the Triple Alliance, or two components of it."

"Correct again, Brother Rice." Hirst was almost amused, failing to see how this line of questioning could lead him into trouble.

"Tell me, Brother Hirst, did the United Vehicle Workers' Union, as opposed to the Transport Workers' Federation of which it is an affiliate, take any previous decision in opposition to the strike going ahead?"

Hirst now became wary. "I'm not sure I get your drift, Brother Rice."

Michael Rice, K.C. long-suffering interrogator of the powerful and not particularly bright, paused to look Stanley Hirst in the eye, letting him know that he had him in a corner. "It's a perfectly simple question, Brother Hirst. The joint decision of the NUR and the Transport Workers' Federation was taken at some time before 4 p.m. on 15 April—for the sake of argument, let's say 3.40 p.m. Would that be about right?"

"Yes, it would have been around that time."

"The question, then, is whether the leadership of our own union, the UVW, adopted a position in opposition to the proposed strike prior to that—let's say in the previous 24 hours?"

"Oh, no, we made no such decision."

Mickey Rice narrowed his eyes. "Are you sure that is correct, Brother Hirst?"

Hirst now lost his temper, feeling that this bus driver had accused him of lying. "If I say a thing, then I am sure it is correct, Brother Rice!"

Mickey sprang at him immediately, leaning forward and pointing, his voice loud and authoritative. "Then how could it be, Brother Hirst, that some sixteen hours earlier, when our leadership was still in favour of the strike, and when nothing was known of the speech by Brother Hodges to parliamentary back-benchers, the midnight mass meetings which were to have been held throughout London were cancelled by this same leadership, leaving us standing in the rain? Doesn't this mean that a decision *had* been made to oppose the strike?"

Tumult. Thunderous applause. Oaths thrown at the platform. The debate no longer concerns the miners but is about the red versus the blue, and Mickey has done it! The red-button days have been recaptured! And look at those faces on the platform: Hirst blinking with his mouth half open, unable to come up with a reply; George Sanders and Archie Henderson standing at the back, grinning broadly; the EC members, with the exception of Barney Macauley and one or two others, frowning as they contemplate the possibility that their leaders have been guilty of betrayal.

And yet it is a former red-button man who punctures this balloon.

The bearded Albert "Tich" Smith, parliamentary secretary, comes forward and stands at the edge of the platform, hands gripping his lapels, perfectly calm as he surveys the pandemonium before him, possibly finding this reminiscent of occasions in previous years at the Club and Institute Hall, Clerkenwell Road, when red-button conferences had got the better of a wayward executive council. As no one behind him seems prepared to do it for him, he raises a palm to quieten the discordant voices and gradually the tumult subsides.

"Brothers, I think it would be prudent if I began by congratulating Brother Rice on his bravura performance; on several occasions when he was on the executive of the old red-button union, by the sharpness of his mind he managed to bring clarity where there had been confusion."

The applause which this brought was, of course, for Mickey rather than for Tich.

"On this occasion, however, he is incorrect in the conclusion he draws."

This was greeted by a wave of disbelieving groans.

Tich took this in his stride, smiling indulgently where Stanley Hirst would have scowled. "Mickey has made a mistake—an understandable mistake, maybe, but a mistake nevertheless—and so I would ask, brothers, that you listen carefully to what I have to say."

He raised his right hand to smooth his moustache and beard, both streaked with grey. "First of all, you need to understand that cancelling the mass meetings is not the same as cancelling the strike. True, there *might* have been a connection, but on this occasion there was not. I know, because as far as the cancellation of the mass meetings go, I was as responsible as anyone." A pause to allow the murmurings to die. "As Brother Hirst told you, I was present when Frank Hodges addressed that meeting of back-benchers on the evening of 14 April. 'Yes,' he said, 'we are prepared to discuss wage-reductions—as long as the system of district wage-negotiation is not permanent.' Everyone supposed that the miners' EC had authorised Brother Hodges to make this statement, and so the prospect of a settlement immediately appeared before us. It was on this basis that a group of the MPs hurried down to Downing Street to get Lloyd George out of bed.

"It was my view, brothers, that this placed our own union in a bit of a spot. All over London, mass meetings would be taking place at midnight. Being an old red-button man myself, I knew what midnight mass meetings could do. Usually, they do exactly what we want 'em to do, winding the members up to fever pitch so that the action we're preparing will go off with a bang!" He turned down his mouth at the corners and regarded his audience dolefully. "But how would the members feel if, having been brought to the boil at the mass meetings, it turned out that the strike was off because negotiations were underway again? I daresay they wouldn't be too happy. That being the case, I telephoned Brother Hirst and we agreed that the mass meetings should be cancelled. At that stage, as far as we were concerned the strike would still go ahead if negotiations failed to be resumed, or if they ended up in deadlock again. Before the afternoon of 15 April, there was no suggestion that the strike be cancelled." He held his arms wide at his sides, palms exposed. "That, brothers, is the long and the short of it."

The mood in the room had changed dramatically: the anger had subsided; the sense of triumph of just minutes ago dissipated. For some moments, the only sound was, for those with a liking for metaphors, that of the air escaping from the balloon.

Mickey stood and, looking around the room, located Harry Beard, who had made the suggestion that they occupy the building. Mickey raised his eyebrows; Harry shrugged. Mickey then turned back to face the platform.

"What Brother Smith has just told us makes sense," he acknowledged, "but it comes a week late. Why were we left waiting in the rain when a brief explanation would have sent us back home?"

"The only people we could contact," explained Tich Smith, "were employees of the picture palaces and theatres where the meetings were due to take place. It seemed somewhat risky to me to leave a message with someone who might get it all wrong in transmitting it to our members."

"And the week since then?" Mickey persisted. "Do you think we would be here is we had received your explanation earlier in the week? Would branches—three to my knowledge—have taken the decision to withhold their contributions if they'd been given an explanation?"

"They've *what*?" Stanley Hirst, reddening, was out of his seat.

"Decided to withhold their contributions. I thought that might get your attention, Brother Hirst. But the question is: why no explanation until now?"

"Here," said Tich Smith in a rare show of disloyalty to his general secretary, "you may be on firmer ground, Brother Rice. I'll hand you over to Brother Hirst."

Stanley Hirst followed Tich Smith with smouldering eyes while he resumed his seat and then turned back to the audience. "I didn't send out an explanation because I hardly thought it necessary!" he snapped. "We notified the branches—at considerable expense, I might add—that the strike was off, and anyone who read a newspaper knew what was happening." He shrugged. "What else could be required?"

"An expla*nation*!" shouted tramworker Ernie Sharp. "An account of what our union did and what it didn't do, and why! Jesus *Christ*!"

"Alright, it'll be in the next issue of *The Record*."

"You need to put out a branch circular," said Malcolm Lewis, "something that everyone can read in the union notice-case."

Hirst began to shake his head, saying, "Do you know how…" but by this time several EC members were standing behind his chair, bending their heads to his.

"Alright! A branch circular will go out on Monday."

Mickey sighed. The occupation had not, then, been a complete waste of time. He stood and looked around at his followers, nodding. Time to go home, lads.

*

As previously planned, Mickey and Annette walked the short distance along Kensington High Street and caught a 31 bus as it exited from Earl's Court Road. They were at ease with each other and they both knew that when they arrived home they would make love. First walking together and then sitting together, that electricity they had felt on Thursday was still there, still exciting them. Something had changed for the better, and he did not know what it was. He wondered how she would have reacted if he had suggested a drink in the Earl's Court Tavern before catching the bus, but in his present mood there was no possibility that the suggestion would be voiced.

"Did you get what you wanted, Mickey?" Annette asked as, sitting on the top deck, they were jostled together towards Church Street.

"Yes, I think so, sweetheart." He turned to look at her. "When we met yesterday, why did you say that you didn't know what we hoped to gain?"

She shrugged. "Because I truly did not know, my love. What was it that you wanted?"

"An explanation of why our mass meetings were cancelled."

"And did you get an explanation?"

"Yes, sweetheart, although not the one we were expecting. We suspected that our union had already decided to pull out of the strike, but that was not the case. The mistake they made was not explaining their actions. Now they *have* explained and that explanation will be sent to the members."

"It seems a little result for such a struggle, my Mickey."

"Well, we also wanted to teach them that if they ignore the members, they must expect trouble. I think we achieved that."

She snuggled closer to his arm. "Oh yes."

*

As soon as the door of the flat closed behind them, Annette threw her arms around Mickey's neck and brought her mouth to his. He fumbled at the buttons of her coat, but then placed his hands on her shoulders, restraining her. Seeing her questioning expression as she looked up at him, he smiled. "I have to wash, my love. I've been sleeping on the floor of Transport House and haven't washed properly in two days."

"Be quick, my sweet, be quick."

When he came from the bathroom wrapped in a towel, Annette was waiting for him on the living-room sofa, wearing a lightweight dressing gown, her legs tucked beneath her. At the sight of him, she sprang to her feet and fell against him, pressing her body to his and with one hand loosening the towel about his waist.

"What is this, my love?" he chuckled. "Where did this tigress come from?"

"She has been here all the time," she replied. The towel having fallen away, she gripped his penis. "And she wants this inside her."

*

Later, as they lay in each other's arms, he stroked her head and asked, "Sweetheart, when we invaded the executive chamber last year, you were angry and embarrassed, but when we took over the whole building these last two days you seemed to support us."

"Yes, that is true, my Mickey."

"So what changed your mind?"

"You do not know, my love?" She tugged gently at his testicles with her right hand, as if to see whether this might call his soldier to attention once more.

"If I knew, I would not ask, sweetheart."

"Because of the staff, *mon chérie*."

"The *staff?*"

"The staff do not like Brother Hirst very much, Mickey, and so they thought you were a hero. Oh, I was so proud!"

Mickey's groan of disappointment was interpreted by Annette as one of pleasure as she played with his genitals, and taking this as encouragement she dropped to her knees and took his aroused soldier in her mouth.

*

Later that evening, there was a knock on the door.

"Who is it?"

"Who do think it is, for Christ's sake? It's me, Dick."

"Okay, give me a sec. Is it urgent?"

"You could say that."

Following their lovemaking, Mickey and Annette had, after the necessary ablutions, eaten a sparse meal and gone to bed, falling asleep immediately. Bleary-eyed and disoriented, Mickey now pulled on the nearest pair of trousers and stumbled to the door of the flat.

"Sorry if I woke you, Mickey."

"Nnnggh. I must look a sight."

Ignoring both this comment and Mickey's appearance, Dick strode into the flat, spun around and delivered his news: "The party has expelled Bob Williams."

"They've *what?*"

"The executive must have taken the decision sometime in the last few days. His expulsion was approved today at the party congress in Manchester. There are some snidey references to it in the evening press."

Mickey fell onto the sofa, waving Dick into the armchair. "But *why*, Dick?"

"For his role in Black Friday, of course." It was difficult to tell from Dick's tone whether he considered this a reasonable sanction; maybe he was simply awaiting Mickey's reaction.

"His role?" Mickey threw open his arms. "*His* fucking role? What else could he have done? Jimmy Thomas had already persuaded the NUR to sabotage the strike!"

"Why are you swearing, Mickey?" Annette, rubbing her eyes, had come to the bedroom door in her dressing gown.

"The party has expelled Bob Williams because of Black Friday."

"Oh my goodness!" She came to sit next to Mickey on the sofa, elbows resting on her knees, a palm to each side of her face. "But that cannot be right. Does the party think that he should have isolated himself even within the Transport Workers' Federation? From what you have told me, Mickey, the strike was already abandoned by the time the Federation voted."

Despite his exhaustion, Mickey smiled at his wife and threw an arm about her shoulders, kissing her on the forehead. Annette had just demonstrated that she was, after all, rather more than a hero-worshipper.

35

It was around this time that the first of the new K-type buses put in an appearance at Middle Row garage. There was just one of them, as this would be used for training purposes, a driving instructor taking out four drivers at a time and giving them each thirty minutes at the wheel, for which a three-hour overtime payment had been negotiated.

Mickey arrived in the garage at 0945, fifteen minutes early, to find Lenny Hawkins already there.

"Morning, Lenny. What you on today?"

"Type training first, then a middle turn."

"Oh, me too."

"I wonder how they came up with the name: type training."

"Yeah, I was thinking about that too. There hasn't been a new type since before the war, so I suppose they didn't need to call it anything until now."

"Well, there was the B-type as well as the X-type."

"True enough, but they would've called that B-type training or X-type training wouldn't they?"

"I dunno. Can't remember."

"But now there's gonna be a few new types, they must have felt the need for a term that was more...What's the word I'm looking for, Dick?" Dick Mortlake had just come into the output, having finished his first half.

"Generic," said Dick.

"Yeah, a more generic term."

"If you say so, Mickey."

Soon Mickey and Lenny were joined by Malcolm Lewis and Johnny Sutcliffe, a fairly new driver. At two minutes to ten, they heard the vehicle enter the garage and went out to meet the instructor, a gaunt middle-aged Scot called Mr MacPherson.

"Alright, gather 'round lads while I tell you about your new bus," said Mr MacPherson, a tall man who stood with arms folded. "Say hello to the K-type. Believe it or not, she was first designed ten years ago, but then along came the war. She has a four-cylinder, 30-horsepower engine, and three-speed crash gearbox, and you'll find to your great delight that the clutch is a lot smoother   than you're used to."

While Mr MacPherson droned on about the technical specifications, Mickey drifted off. This stuff might be of interest to an engineer, but to a driver? Not really.

"You'll note that the driver is now situated next to the engine, and that has allowed more room in the saloon, so the passengers can now sit facing the front. And the seating capacity is 46, as opposed to the previous 34."

"Alright, lads, any questions before I put one of you in the cab?"

"Just a couple, Mr MacPherson," said Mickey.

The instructor seemed surprised that there should be a question at such an early stage, but he nodded. "Very well, go ahead, Driver."

"When will the company design a bus with a closed-in cab? We're sick and tired of being exposed to rain and snow and everything in between. You have no idea what it's like!"

Mr MacPherson threw back his head and laughed. "Oh, I have a *very* good idea what it's like, Driver. D'ye think us driving instructors come fully formed? But it's a good question. The problem is that if the cab was enclosed with glass, you wouldn't be able to clear the screen of rain and snow..."

"Wipers, Mr MacPherson. Cars are now being fitted with windscreen wipers."

"Aye, cars maybe, but the technology is still new. If ye have a problem with the wipers of a car, all ye have to do is pull over. But with a bus? Besides which, you've got maybe thirty passengers sitting behind you and if there's a safety problem...Then again, glass shatters easily, and that would be another safety issue."

"Laminated glass is your solution there, Mr MacPherson; Henry Ford started using it two years ago."

The instructor tilted back his head as if to get a better view of Mickey Rice. "Have you made a study of this subject by any chance, Driver?"

"Yes and no, Mr MacPherson, yes and no. I'm union rep here, and so I listen to the complaints, and then I look for solutions."

Mr MacPherson wagged a finger at Mickey. "Ah, of course, you're Mickey Rice, are ye not?"

"I am. Now, Mr MacPherson, you say this bus was designed ten years ago. The war may well have delayed its production, but couldn't that time have been spent in looking for ways to *improve* that design?"

Mr MacPherson sighed. "You may well be right, son, but I'm a mere driving instructor and have no authority over such things. This, I think, might be a question that the union leaders might wish to take up with the company."

"And it's another open-top bus, so the poor bloody conductor is even more exposed to the elements than the driver."

"Ah, but you know that's the fault of the Metropolitan Police rather than the company. They reckon that if you put a roof on a double-decker it would be in danger of toppling over."

"I know that, but why doesn't the company do something about it—design a prototype to prove to the police that they don't know what they're talking about?"

"Another excellent point, Driver Rice, and one which the union leadership might well want to take up." He pulled out his pocket watch and gave it a glance. "Now, if I'm going to get you lads trained and have time for a cup of tea before my next batch..."

*

Mickey went first, followed by Lenny and Johnny Sutcliffe. Malcolm was last, and as he drove back from Marble Arch along the Bayswater Road, he engaged Mr MacPherson in conversation not directly related to the task in hand.

"You say this bus will take 46 passengers, Mr MacPherson, compared to the old 34?"

The instructor stood at the front of the saloon, directly behind the driver, and thus was able to issue instructions and advice. "That's right, Driver. Keep your eyes on the road, now. Check your mirror if you're pulling out."

"So that's an increase of almost a third."

"That's correct, Driver. Ignore that pedestrian." A man stood on the pavement, hand extended as the bus approached. "Some of 'em will stick out their hand for anything as long as it's red. Can't he see there's no destination-board or route-number?"

"So revenue per bus will increase by that same amount."

"Well, roughly, I suppose. It will all depend on the loadings, surely. Now, Driver, we'll be turning into Ladbroke Grove, and you've got traffic turning right here at Notting Hill Gate, so get onto the left until you're past them and then back onto the right."

"In fairness, then, we should be up for a thirty-percent wage increase."

"In fairness, maybe, but my advice, Driver, would be not to pin your hopes on it."

Ten minutes later, as Malcolm drove into garage, he noted something of a crowd around the union notice-case. "Something's going on here, Mickey," he called over his shoulder. "You might want to take a look at it."

Mickey hopped from the bus and eased his way to the front of the crowd around the notice-case. Someone, not having a key to the union notice-case—obviously Victor Wiggins—had covered it with a company notice announcing a wage reduction of three shillings a week starting in October.

Having parked the training bus, Malcolm walked towards the crowd with the instructor. "I thought you wanted a cup of tea, Mr MacPherson," said Malcolm.

At this moment, Victor Wiggins emerged from his office.

Mr MacPherson lifted his chin, peering over the heads of the crowd. "Oh," he crooned, "I wouldnae miss this for the world, never mind a dish of tae."

"What's the meaning of this?" Mickey demanded, whirling to face Wiggins.

"Do you not recall, Mr Rice," said the garage superintendent, a faint smile on his face, "that when you posted your notice concerning what you called Black Friday, I predicted that it would not be long before the company began posting a few notices of its own? Well, this is the first of them."

"But this is our union notice-case!"

Wiggins shrugged. "We may have granted you the use of it, but it's still company property, surely."

"Oh really?" Mickey reached for the notice and ripped it from the front of the case before tearing it into four and hurling it at Wiggins's feet. "That's what I think of your poster—and the company's proposal! You can tell your superiors that there's a procedure for proposals regarding wages and conditions, and this is not it!" Up came his forefinger as he was struck by an afterthought. "And I speak as a member of our union's Bus Wages Board!" This was true enough: the proposal for the new negotiating panel had been agreed by the EC and in the elections held earlier in the year Mickey had gained a seat.

Victor Wiggins feigned dismay, adopting an expression meant to convey a sense of horror. "Oh, Mr Rice, I regret to say that you have just earned yourself a divisional office disciplinary hearing. If this is not gross misconduct, I don't know what is." He turned to the driving instructor. "Ah, Mr MacPherson! I'm sure you would appear as a witness, would you not?"

"Be glad to, Mr Wiggins, glad to." Feeling Malcolm Lewis's attention on him, Mr MacPherson turned and gave him a subtle wink.

"Mr Rice, you are suspended from duty pending a disciplinary hearing."

Malcolm Lewis walked towards the garage superintendent. "I'd like to thank you, Mr Wiggins."

Wiggins frowned in disbelief. "Thank me? What for, Mr Lewis?"

"Many of the lads in this garage had prepared themselves for a strike on 15 April and were bitterly disappointed when it was called off." He shook his head. "God only knows what that can do to a man's nervous system: one minute you're up, raring to go, and the next minute you're down; you've been told you have to stay still, but your pulse is still racing because you're that keen on joining the scrap. The pressure that's built up in you has to be released if you're not to explode or suffer a heart attack, and you, Mr Wiggins, have just opened the valve that will let that pressure out. If Mickey Rice is suspended, then so are all bus services from this garage!" He turned to the men gathered around the notice-case. "Lads, get yourselves to the changeover points and tell 'em to run their buses in. We're on strike!"

Wiggins's hands went to his head, clutching the carefully assembled forest which grew on top of it. "Wait! Wait! Wait!"

The men who had been making for the garage door now halted and turned.

"Second thoughts, Mr Wiggins?" asked Malcolm, eyebrows raised.

"You're not the rep, Mr Lewis! Driver Rice is the rep! You have no authority…"

"You, Mr Lewis, have for no good reason just *suspended* our rep.

In the absence of the rep, the branch chairman acts on his behalf—and that's me!" He turned to the men. "Okay, lads, off you go."

"No!"

Once more, the men hesitated.

"No good reason? What do you mean, no good reason? You all saw him destroy the company notice!" It seemed to occur to Mr Wiggins that it might be a mistake to rely on the evidence of men who appeared keen to get the strike underway, and so he turned in the direction of the driving instructor. "And Mr MacPherson has said that he will be my witness!"

"Oh, now just hang on, Mr Wiggins," counselled the driving instructor, who had been following events with arms folded. "I agreed to be *a* witness at a disciplinary hearing. I didnae say I'd be *your* witness. It seems to me that provocation was involved here."

A red-faced Wiggins, teeth clenched and eyes protuberant, began to emit a high whining sound, although this, being drowned by the cheers of the men, was audible only to those closest to him. "Alright!" he said eventually. *"Alright!"*

Mickey cocked his head to one side. "Alright what, Mr Wiggins?"

"The suspension is lifted and you are reinstated, Mr Rice, but I insist that in future you show more respect for company property." He turned and walked swiftly to his office.

"And you show more respect for our notice-case!" Malcolm called after him.

Mr Wiggins hesitated at the door of his office but, obviously dismissing any thought of turning back, entered the office, slamming the door behind him.

Amid the renewed cheers of the men, Malcolm turned to the driving instructor. "Well, Mr MacPherson, you were proved right."

"About what, son?"

"I shouldn't be pinning my hopes on any big pay-rise!"

36

Shortly after this incident, the two panels sat opposite each other in Electric Railway House. On the employers' side, Messrs Shave, Lansdown and Mackinnon for the London General, Mr Wolsey for Tillings, and Mr Kipping for British Automobile Traction, a company in which Tillings was a major shareholder. On the union side, Robert Williams for the National Transport Workers' Federation and the members of the UVW's Bus

Wages Board: George Sanders, Willy Hammond, Chris Platten, Walter Worsley, Johnny Mills, Barney Macauley, Bill Brosman, Tom Warne, Bill Modley and Mickey Rice.

"I very much hope, Mr Shave," said George Sanders at the outset, "that you will agree that the posting of such notices as this"—he lifted a copy of the wage-cut poster and let it fall from his fingers in apparent distaste—"is not the proper way to conduct industrial relations."

Since the promotion of H.E. Blain to the position of assistant managing director in January, George Shave had been appointed as operating manager, and as such was leading for the employers' team at today's meeting. Sanders felt more comfortable with Shave, a man with experience of actually making things—he came from the engineering works in Walthamstow—although he had no illusions concerning the road which lay ahead.

"As you know, Mr Sanders," replied Shave, "the notices were removed after we received a very sharply-worded complaint from Mr Williams on your behalf. As for the original posting of the notices, I concede that the action was ill-judged, and I trust we may leave the matter there."

"There was almost a strike at one garage, you know."

"Yes, I am aware of that, Mr Sanders," said Shave, the beginnings of a grin on his face as he directed a glance down the table at Mickey Rice, "and were you to offer the opinion that the actions of the local official in that case were even more ill-judged, I think I would have to agree with you."

Sanders laughed. You couldn't help liking the bloke. "Alright, let's leave it at that."

George Shave patted the document which lay before him and then looked across to Sanders. "Needless to say, Mr Sanders, we have given your submission the most careful consideration." His eyes closed for a moment. "But with the best will in the world, I have to say that, given the state of the economy and the situation in which the company finds itself, your aspirations are far too ambitious."

"Well, it's true enough, Mr Shave, that our members are ambitious, but I'm afraid you'll have to be rather more specific if I am to understand you."

"In past negotiations, Mr Sanders, you and Mr Williams"—a nod to Bob, seated beside Sanders—"have given numerous examples of other industries where wages have been raised and the hours of work reduced. Now, I don't mean to throw this at you..."

"But you'll do it anyway."

"I don't mean to throw this at you as a cheap shot, but it *is* the case that the reverse has been true for many months now..."

"You certainly cannot point to an industry where basic hours have been extended," said Bob Williams. "The forty-eight-hour week is protected by legislation."

"That is quite true, Mr Williams, and we have no intention of proposing an extension of working hours, although we *would* like to explore the *arrangement* of those hours."

"As you and Mr Blain have been telling us ever since you agreed the ten-hour maximum spreadover two years ago."

"Well, you are correct in that we wish to discuss maximum spreadover time, and our chief schedules officer, Mr Mackinnon, will explain our position in due course."

Sanders grinned across at Mackinnon, a technician rather than a manager. "Yes, I didn't think that you'd brought Mr Mackinnon along just to make up the number."

"Haha. Very amusing, Mr Sanders. On the question of wages, however, we are seeking a modest reduction. As the cost of living has reduced, wages have been lowered in industry after industry. Indeed, one must assume that the decision by your Triple Alliance to call off its solidarity strike was conditioned by a realisation that a reduction in the miners' wages was inevitable."

If Bob Williams had been a bull, this would have been the red rag waved before him. "I can assure you, Mr Shave," he said, his cheeks filled with colour, "that our decision was made on quite other grounds. We considered—and *still* consider—the mine-owners' proposals to be callous and ill-founded!"

Shave raised his palms. "I'm sorry if I have misunderstood the situation, Mr Williams. Perhaps I should confine myself to matters of which I have a greater knowledge: the wages of our operating staff, for example. Now, it is a fact that the operating staff of the companies represented here are the *only* group of workers in the country who continue to receive the *full* war-wage. The war bonuses were awarded in order to compensate for the rising cost of living in war conditions, and these conditions continued to exist for some time *after* the war. Now, however, the cost of living is falling, and in industries like the railways, it has been agreed that the war wage should be reduced on a sliding scale—so much for every five-point reduction in the cost-of-living index. It seems to us that such a reduction would be just and equitable, and would entail no reduction in the living standards of the staff."

"That might be so if the official figures could be considered trustworthy," said Bob Williams, "but you are probably aware that in most negotiations of this nature they have been questioned by the trade-union side."

"If, however, the company finds itself embarrassed by the fact that London busworkers still receive the full war-wage," George Sanders came in, "our members would have no objection to its reduction, as long as the same amount was transferred to the basic wage."

"And that would be acceptable as an annual increase?" George Shave seemed interested.

"Oh, no, Mr Shave, I merely suggest that as a means of reducing the war-wage. Quite apart from that, our members expect to be compensated for the additional wealth they've created for the company."

"Additional wealth? How have they achieved that, Mr Sanders?"

"By carrying—and collecting the fares from—a maximum of 46 passengers as compared to the previous 34, Mr Shave."

"Ah, I see. But you can't have your cake and eat it, Mr Sanders."

Frowning, Sanders looked to the other members of his team to ascertain whether they might be able to interpret this comment and, receiving no enlightenment, gave an exaggerated shrug. "You've lost me—us—there, Mr Shave."

"Well, earlier this morning I was glancing over the minutes of our wage negotiations for the past two years—as one does in preparation for the next battle, so to speak—and I noted that you had used the argument of the improved seating capacity of the new vehicles in 1919. Can't have two bites of the same cherry, can you, Mr Sanders?" Shave regarded his adversary with a faint smile, confident that he had got the better of him.

Sanders laughed. "Leaving aside the question of whether we're talking about a cake or a cherry"—laughter from the trade union side, averted looks by those seated about George Shave—"I can acknowledge that you're right, Mr Shave."

The thunder that had descended on Shave's brow at the allusion to his mixing of metaphors now lifted, replaced by a satisfied smile.

"But only partly. Yes, in the course of the 1919 negotiations I *did* mention the larger vehicles, but a more careful reading of those minutes will reveal that I did so in order to demonstrate that the additional revenue generated by those vehicles would assist the company in meeting the financial calls upon its resources, which Mr Blain was attempting to convince us were so onerous as to rule out major improvements in the terms and conditions of our members. I quite deliberately made no mention of the share of that additional revenue which should go to our members. How could I? The additional revenue did not then exist. Now it *does* exist, and therefore this is the time to talk about it."

A junior member of the management team, not long out of his teens by the look of him, was furiously turning the pages of a document—obviously the minutes of the 1919 negotiations. Knowing precisely what he was doing, the members of both teams fell silent while he did it. Silent, that is, in that nothing was spoken across the table; demonstrating his confidence to the other side, Sanders turned to Bob Williams and murmured, "I'm fair dying for a fag, Bob, so we'll have to see if we can create the conditions for an adjournment in a minute or two."

"I think you may already have done that, George," Williams whispered in reply.

The junior management man left his seat and walked to Shave's side, bending to whisper in his right ear, where his lips could not be read by the trade union side.

A subdued George Shave nodded silently, spent a moment gazing at the table before him and then, making no mention of the reverse he had just suffered, smiled across the table at Sanders. "Apologies for that brief interruption, gentlemen. Now, where were we? Ah yes, the new vehicles! A few minutes ago, you referred to the extra revenue *generated* by the K-type. I believe that term to be entirely appropriate. The extra revenue *is* generated by the *vehicles*, not by their crews, and so why should they be compensated for something they have not done?"

It was Sanders' turn to nod. Grinning lightly, he cast his mind back to a meeting held at the headquarters of the old red-button union in Gerrard Street in...oohhh, it must have been as long ago as 1914. He had invited Theo Rothstein to address a meeting of members on the causes of the war which had just begun, and Theo had, in simple language easily understood by busworkers, explained the role of surplus value. Surplus value: the new value created by the worker, on top of that needed for his own wages, during the course of his working day.

"Well, Mr Sanders?" George Shave thought that Sanders was stumped for an answer.

"Sorry, Mr Shave, I was taking a little trip down memory lane, recalling something I once heard a very clever man say." He gathered himself, placed his elbows on the table and pointed a nicotine-stained finger at Shave. "I challenge you, Mr Shave."

"To what, Mr Sanders?" Shave was bemused, one part of his mind thinking that Sanders had lost the thread of the argument, another part warning him that it was usually a mistake to underestimate this man.

"I challenge you to accompany me to the nearest bus garage. We'll find a K-type that's parked up, and then I'll ask you to instruct it to start generating revenue. Talk to it the way you would talk to a horse: 'Giddyap! Come on, let's see you generate some revenue! Giddyap!'"

There was laughter of both sides of the table in which even George Shave joined. Some of the laughter on the trade union side, however, was more knowing, because men like Barney Macauley and Mickey Rice had been present at that 1914 meeting and so knew what was coming.

"But that's ridiculous, Mr Sanders!"

"Of course it is, Mr Shave, but it's really your suggestion, not mine. While I might agree that these new vehicles might *make possible*, rather than generate, extra revenue, that revenue, *all* revenue, is *realised* by the operating staff. It's not until the driver climbs behind the wheel and starts the engine, and the conductor stands on the platform and starts welcoming passengers aboard, that revenue is realised. If that is *not* the case, why pay drivers and conductors *anything*? And if they realise *more* revenue—the conductor by collecting more fares, the driver by expending more of his energy and exercising more of his skill by driving a larger, heavier vehicle with a greater number of passengers around the streets of London—then surely it is only just and logical that they should receive higher *wages*!"

This went down very well on the trade union side, the busmen in particular smiling and nodding in appreciation, while those on the management side of the table were clearly concerned that their aim of cutting wages was being diverted into its opposite.

George Shave now launched an attempt to reduce the damage.

"You are aware, of course, that we have not yet replaced the whole fleet. The new K-type is being used on the busier central London routes, while the old B-type is assigned to the smaller routes on the periphery. This being the case, if—and this is an *enormous* if—we were to accept your suggestion that the men be rewarded for the greater capacity of the K-type, it would logically lead to the creation of a two-tier wage structure. Would you be comfortable with that?"

"No, Mr Shave, we would not be comfortable with that. It is obviously your intention to *eventually* replace the entire fleet with the larger-capacity vehicles. Indeed, in view of the argument put forward by Mr Blain in 1919, we're surprised that that hasn't been achieved already. Rather than a two-tier wage structure, we would propose that we first agree on a sum—per driver and per conductor; *every* driver and conductor—which would be appropriate compensation for manning the larger vehicles, and then we reduce that by the proportion of the fleet that still has the B-type; when the whole fleet is converted, that reduction would then be restored."

Shave, eyes narrowed, regarded Sanders carefully. "Are you sure, Mr Sanders, that you have the authority of your committee to negotiate along these lines?"

"Mr Shave, when one is about to enter into what you have termed a new battle, one—as one does—attempts to anticipate each turn that the battle may take and to formulate appropriate responses."

George Shave, who had obviously neglected to anticipate much of Sanders' argument, looked grim. "I think we'll take an adjournment at this stage, Mr Sanders."

*

"Well, George," said Barney Macauley once the employers' team had left the room, "I would say that we're doing surprisingly well."

"We're not doing bad, Barney, but let's not fool ourselves: George Shave has been given a job to do, and he's called this adjournment because he knows he's not doing it very well."

"A word of advice, George," counselled Bob Williams. "Try not to take the piss out of him quite so much. I think he's always struck both of us as a man who can see sense. If we make any progress, it'll be down to him to convince Blain, and maybe even Ashfield, that they should give a little. He's already an adversary, but you don't want to turn him into an outright enemy."

Sanders expelled a lungful of smoke. "Yes, good point, Bob." He grinned. "Trouble is, sometimes I can't help meself."

"So what do you think he'll do now?"

"I think, Bob, that he'll drop all mention of wages and get Mackinnon to tell us why they need twelve-hour spreadovers."

Bob Williams, who looked somewhat pale and drawn, nodded. "You're probably right. Listen, George, I'm going to stretch my legs for a bit if that's alright with you."

*

During the adjournment, Bob Williams took a walk through the corridors of the upper floors of Electric Railway House until he found a window with an unobstructed view.

There he stood, looking out over the roofs of Victoria and Pimlico and once again pondered the excruciating situation in which he found himself. Black Friday had been a devastating setback for the labour movement, but he had never in his worst nightmares thought that he would be singled out for special punishment. Just last year he had sat with Lenin in the Kremlin, and yet here he was, expelled from the party. Expelled! And for what? For not breaking ranks with the rest of the Transport Workers' Federation representatives who voted against a strike that had already been torpedoed by that fop Jimmy Thomas! Had his been the lone NTWF hand raised against the NUR motion when the vote was taken in Unity House he would, presumably, still be a member of the Communist Party of Great Britain. And yet what would his position have been in the Federation? Such an act would have given the right wingers such as Havelock Wilson, the seamen's leader, the excuse to attack him and attempt to unseat him as secretary. He had endured several of their attacks in the past, as in 1917 when at the Fed's national conference he was taken to task for not only speaking at the Leeds Convention but for adopting a position—the creation of soviets throughout Britain—which had certainly not been decided by the Fed. Not for the first time, he had been defended on that occasion by Bevin, who told the delegates that he was sick and tired of these attacks on the secretary, despite the fact that Bevin himself had virtually poked fun at the programme agreed at Leeds.

And what about all of those plans and visions of his? His prediction of a mighty communist party after just the first year of its existence had already fallen foul of the more modest reality, but now he was not even in a position to influence its development. He recalled Vikha telling him that, as his job was to wage revolution in Britain, they would probably never meet again. And now? Now she would presumably consider him a pariah. He had little doubt that, through the Comintern press, she would know of his expulsion. And so too, of course, would Lenin, although presumably he would learn of it by more direct means. Oh Jesus bloody Christ! He felt his mind being enveloped by a dark cloud which squeezed and squeezed and squeezed until he thought that he must lose consciousness.

He shook his head to clear it and concentrated for a moment not on the roofs basking in the early May sunlight, but of the hard, shadowed pavement immediately below.

"Don't do it, Bob!"

Williams started at the sound of Sanders' voice. "Don't do what, George?"

"Jump, of course!"

"Haha. Things may be bad, George, but they're not that bad."

Sanders stood before him, studying him coolly. "Well, I certainly hope not, Bob. Listen, I told the lads that you'd probably got lost so I'd better come and find you, but I really wanted a quiet word with you. We haven't had a chance to talk since the congress took that bloody awful decision, but I just want you to know that I and most of the people I know in the movement don't think for one minute that you betrayed the miners. I certainly understand the position you were in and I can't imagine me doing any differently." He placed a hand on Williams's shoulder. "You're still a comrade as far as I'm concerned, Bob, and we'll continue to value your input into these negotiations. Talking of which…"

As Sanders turned to lead the way back to the meeting room, Williams touched his arm. "Wait, George."

Sanders turned.

Williams offered his hand, which Sanders took. "Thank you, George. Thank you."

*

"I think it best, gentlemen," said George Shave when the meeting resumed, "if we leave aside the question of remuneration for a subsequent meeting and turn to the matter which has been bedevilling us like no other: the maximum length of the spreadover." He raised his palms as if to quell an expected outburst of indignation. "Now, I realise that you are quite right when you say that it is only two years since we agreed upon a maximum of ten hours from sign-on to sign-off, but it cannot come as a surprise to you that we seek to reopen the matter now: we after, after all, raised it twice during those two years."

This was true, and on the last occasion, during the 1920 wage negotiations, Sanders had refused to discuss it, walking out of the meeting and taking his team with him. He hoped that the fact that he showed no sign of walking out today would not be taken by George Shave as a sign that his aim could be accomplished with ease.

"And it will not come as a surprise to you, Mr Shave, when I tell you that the men are as opposed to a longer spreadover as they ever were."

Shave nodded. "I realise, of course, that the proposal will not be popular, but quite frankly we have no alternative." He turned to his chief schedules officer. "But let me ask Mr Mackinnon to explain our position."

Mackinnon, looking studious, sat with his fingers laced before him—a man in complete mastery of his subject had no need for notes—and smiled across at George Sanders and Bob Williams. "Good morning, gentlemen. I trust that the fact that I am only asked to attend these meetings in order to deliver bad news will not affect our cordial relationship."

Sanders returned his smile. "No, Mr Mackinnon. I realise that you are the man who cuts the schedules according to management's specifications, not the one who draws up those specifications." His smile broadened. "So no need to worry: you have nothing to fear from us."

"Thank you, Mr Sanders." A clearing of the throat. "As you know, the major aim of the long spreadover is to ensure that both morning and afternoon peaks—the so-called rush-hours—are adequately covered. Quite simply, the ten-hour spreadover doesn't do it, I know you're familiar with the argument, as I've put it to you before: a crew starting at 0700 will cover the morning peak but will sign off just as the afternoon peak is underway; conversely, a crew covering the afternoon peak signing off at 1930 will be unable to contribute to the morning peak as 0930 is the earliest it can sign on. Both of those duties, however, are at work in the late morning and early afternoon, times when at least one of them is not required, due to the lower level of demand."

"But as I recall, Mr Mackinnon," Bob Williams came in, "in 1919 several flexibility measures were agreed which would take some crews off the road during those periods of low demand."

"This one is for Mr Shave, I think," said Mackinnon.

"You are correct, Mr Williams," said Shave. "But there are only so many trips to the bank during the day, only so many trees that require lopping, and only so many bus movements that require to be undertaken." He shrugged. "The flexibility measures did not make the impact we thought they might."

"And so those measures will be discontinued in the event of a more satisfactory solution?" Williams again.

Sanders, gladdened that Bob appeared to be climbing out of the despondency in which he had been enveloped, was content to let him lead. This was the thing about negotiations: once you saw the possibility of making an advance, no matter how modest, your spirits lifted as you became fully engaged, and very often other problems which might have been troubling you tended to fall away, at least for the time being.

Shave stroked his moustache. Williams seemed willing to concede the principle in return for movement elsewhere, and that must be viewed as a positive sign, although he knew that Sanders would need to be won to this view if real progress was to be made. "It would very much depend on the nature of that solution, Mr Williams, but yes, it's possible."

"I think you should put your cards on the table, Mr Shave. Last year, you asked us to agree that 25 percent of all duties should have a maximum spreadover of twelve hours. Is that still your intention?"

"Not quite, no." Shave, looking almost embarrassed, spent a moment regarding his hands, which lay before him on the table. "Look, Mr Sanders, already I sense that we are separated by a very wide divide. For example, would you believe me when I say that the submission you have put forward would, if granted in its entirety, add a million pounds to our costs? A million pounds, Mr Sanders!"

"Well, I did say that our members are ambitious, Mr Shave." If Shave had expected Sanders's mouth to fall open, he was disappointed.

Shave cleared his throat. Look, I wonder—*we* wonder, as we discussed this possibility during our adjournment—if it might be better if we adjourned now until another day. During the adjournment, we will draw up a set of counter-proposals for your consideration. Would that be acceptable to you?"

"And you would send us these proposals several days before the next meeting, so that we will have time to consider them in depth?"

"Oh yes, have no fear of that. Far better that you come to the meeting fully prepared."

Sanders looked to his left and right to get an indication from his team; most shrugged. "Well, Mr Shave, it seems as if the idea of the adjournment is acceptable; it remains to be seen whether that can be said of your counter-proposals."

*

"Well, lads," said Sanders as, the employers having withdrawn, he lighted a cigarette, "I think we can assume that something's afoot."

"It's interesting, George," said Tom Warne, "that when you asked him whether they still wanted twelve-hour spreads, instead of answering yes or no he said *not quite*. So what are they after—eleven hours?"

Mickey Rice laughed. "Given the circumstances in which these negotiations are taking place, I very much doubt that the employers will be asking for less than they've asked for before. No, brothers, they'll be coming for more, not less."

37

"How do you understand Lenin's New Economic Policy, Mickey?" asked Dick Mortlake, waving a sheet of paper before him.

Gladys was down the road visiting her mother, and so Dick had taken the opportunity to come upstairs for a chat. They were both on late turn, and Annette was at work.

"No chance of a bit of foreplay before launching into the main course, then?" As was often the case, when Dick had something on his mind he dispensed with small-talk.

Dick grinned. "Not on this occasion, Comrade: life's too short."

Mickey had just finished washing up after lunch. He dried his hands on a tea-towel as he sank onto the sofa, waving Dick into what used to be Dorothy's armchair. "Well, as I understand it, it's Lenin's view that Russia needs to ensure that it has a firm material base on which to build socialism. That being the case, swift economic growth is required, and so peasants are now allowed to sell their produce on the open market, small industrial and retail enterprises can be privately owned and even publicly-owned factories are expected to make a profit; foreign capital is allowed in, subject to strict control." He shrugged. "That's about it."

"And does this mean that Russia is returning to capitalism?"

"Of course not. What it does mean is that Russia is going to *use* capitalism to rebuild the economy, but a capitalism always controlled and directed by the state and for a limited period only." He looked across at Dick and raised his eyebrows. "Have I passed the exam?"

A nod from Dick. "Just about, which is more than I can say for the author of this little gem." He passed the sheet of paper he had been holding to Mickey.

"Lenin: We address you as representative of the Russian Soviet Government and the Russian Communist Party. With deep regret we have observed you hauling down the flag of Communism and abandoning the cause of the emancipation of the workers. With profound sorrow we have watched the development of your policy of making peace with Capitalism and reaction. Why have you done this?"

Having read the single paragraph Mickey, holding the paper in his left hand, pointed at it with his right and raised his eyebrows at Dick. "Who?"

"Any guesses?"

Mickey sighed. "Sylvia?"

"Bull's-eye!"

"And this is the woman you say we should visit and try to talk sense to."

"I didn't say it would be easy."

"When does she get out?"

"Next Tuesday, 10 May."

"Around about the time of our next amalgamation conference. So when should we visit her?"

"The following Saturday?"

"Maybe we should give it two or three weeks—give her a chance to get her feet back on the ground."

"So to speak," Dick laughed. "It'll have to be a weekend, by the way. Or an evening."

"Why?"

"Didn't she tell you?" Dick waited a couple of seconds and then, receiving no response, continued, "You'll recall that Gladys invited herself. Well, she and Annette have obviously been comparing notes, because it seems Annette has also been recruited."

The expression on Mickey's face could almost be described as one of disbelief. "I'm not sure how I feel about this," he murmured.

"Me neither."

38

The next amalgamation conference took place on Wednesday, 11 May in the Venetian Room of the St. Pancras Hotel. That evening, Barney Macauley gave an informal report-back in the Crown and Anchor, Clerkenwell Green.

"The Transport and General Workers' Union," he announced to what was less a full rank-and-file meeting than a left-wing get-together in the bar, "will commence life on New Year's Day."

"So Barney," asked Mickey Rice, "the fact that our union was a part of today's conference obviously means that we voted in favour of the amalgamation, so why haven't they made the result public?"

"It'll be officially announced at our Annual Delegate meeting in Sheffield later this month," replied Barney, "but I can tell you that the vote was 65,407 in favour and 5,455 against."

Eric Rice whistled through his teeth. "Blimey, a landslide!"

Mickey looked at George Sanders, who nodded soberly, accepting that his advice had largely been ignored.

"So who is to lead us?" asked Dick Mortlake.

"Well, bear in mind that the elections today were for officials in a *provisional* capacity. Proper elections will be held later. Anyway, Harry Gosling was nominated for president, with no opposition."

"And general secretary?" This came from several of those present; they couldn't wait.

With a mischievous grin, Barney Macauley decided to string it out. "Next came the vote for treasurer. There were four nominations, and Brother Kay, who holds that post in the Dockers' Union, was elected."

The urgent cry was repeated: "And general secretary?"

"Well, there were three nominations: Bob Williams, but he withdrew..."

Bob Williams was actually present, and all eyes turned to him. "Why did you do that, Bob?" asked Reuben Topping.

Williams shrugged. "Because I could see that I had no chance of being elected."

"The other two nominees," Barney continued, "were Stanley Hirst and Ernie Bevin. Now, I should explain that it was a card vote..."

"And?"

"Hirst received our own union's 130,000 votes, and Bevin received the support of the other nine unions, with 225,000 votes. I think that Hirst was under the illusion that as the tramway inquiry went against Bevin, he would lose support, but those who were there all agree that he was brilliant. Besides, as it was a card vote it didn't really make any difference one way or the other."

Presumably pleased that their own general secretary had been unsuccessful, most of those present uttered sighs of relief.

"Well, that's that, then," said George Sanders. "But there are one or two things here that strike me. First of all, a vote like that brings home the relative size of our own union in this amalgamation. Imagine: the UVW with 130,000 members and the other *nine* with less than double that. Now, bearing that in mind, it surely can't be right that all three of the top positions have gone to men from docks and waterways."

Macauley nodded. "You have a point, George, and it's something that will have to be put right in the New Year. I think Bevin realises it's a bit lopsided, and if we keep at him over the next few months I'm sure he'll do something about it. You have to realise, though, that the upshot of this will probably be that Hirst will get a position."

"Do you recall, Barney," asked Mickey Rice, "that EC meeting when we were trying to get Hirst to pledge the blue-button's support for the strike for the women's war bonus?"

"I do, Mickey; remember it well. As I recall, Tich was on the blower to him and Hirst was complaining about the possible financial consequences."

"And Frank Mead said..."

Barney snapped his fingers. "That Hirst should be a financial secretary rather than a general secretary." He laughed, joined by the others. "Yes, that would be a possibility. He couldn't do us much harm as financial secretary, could he?"

"And what about your own position, Barney?" asked George Sanders.

"Ah! Thought you'd never ask! Yes, I'm a member of the provisional executive council, brothers."

"Well," sighed Reuben Topping, "I suppose now is the time to get our campaign for a democratic London bus section up and running."

Mickey nodded. "Yeah, I'll start making the arrangements for a meeting, Reuben."

"You know there's another way of doing it, Mickey?"

"All ears, Barney."

"In the next few months Bevin will be circulating all branches with the draft rules; the branches will then be able to submit proposed amendments to a rules conference later in the year." He shrugged. "Isn't that the best way of achieving what we want?"

Mickey gave this a moment's thought. "Wouldn't we be taking a bit of a chance doing it that way, Barney?"

"In what way, mate?"

"The rules conference will be made up of delegates of all ten unions involved in the amalgamation—and possibly more will have joined by then. How many of them will understand and support what we're asking for? And don't forget, Barney, that what we're asking for is something that none of the other sections will have."

"And what would be the upshot if the rules conference rejected the proposals?" asked George Sanders. "There'd surely be no coming back from that, would there?"

"No," Barney was forced to agree, "that would be an end to the matter."

"In which case," said Mickey, "I think we'll stick with our campaign, Barney."

"Fair enough, Mick, but you'd be advised to hang on until after the rules conference."

George Sanders wagged a finger. "Barney has a point, Mickey: if the branches start sending in resolutions now, Bevin will simply tell them to submit amendments to the rules conference, and you could end up with the very thing you've just decided to avoid."

Mickey Rice and Dick Mortlake exchanged glances. "That means," said Mickey, "that we'll need to rein in Vernon and the breakaway crowd."

39

They entered the premises of the *Workers' Dreadnought* at seven o'clock on a Tuesday evening, setting the bell a-jangle and thus drawing their arrival to the attention of Sylvia Pankhurst, although she was nowhere in sight. While most people, knowing that a newspaper had a Fleet Street address, would have expected premises of more generous proportions, the two bus drivers had been prepared for the more modest reality, having made a point of looking out for the dingy office while working rest days on route 15. The front office was poorly-lit and dusty; small piles of back numbers—probably returns—sat on the counter and about the floor. But no Sylvia.

Mickey was not really looking forward to this meeting, as he expected it to end in discord. Dorothy had told him enough about Sylvia to give rise to this expectation. So why had he come? At first, because he had had the feeling that Dick wanted his support, but then because Annette had been added to the party, after which there could be no backing out. He had his eye on Annette now, wondering how she would react to these surroundings. But of course her father Emile was a printer and possibly she had visited premises as shoddy as these in Liege; while she looked around, it was out of mere curiosity, with no trace of distaste on her lovely pale face. Gladys, on the other hand, was casting a frown over the four walls as if wondering why, if this enterprise was dedicated to the cause of the working class, it was not more spick and span. Dick, who in past years had ample experience of Sylvia's East End premises, was completely indifferent.

"Maybe she forgot we was comin'," suggested Gladys in a whisper.

"No, she wouldn't have left the front door unlocked," said Dick. He cleared his throat and raised his chin. "Sylvia!"

"Coming, coming, coming," came the muted reply from somewhere on the other side of the counter.

A door opened and there she was, hair awry and eyes bearing signs of exhaustion. "Ah, Richard! How nice to see you again. And Comrade Rice, if I'm not mistaken! And—oh, you seem to have made a family outing of the occasion!"

"I did say, Sylvia, that we would be accompanied by our wives, both of whom were keen to meet you," said Dick.

"Yes, yes, of course you did," Sylvia said after a fleeting moment of reflection, moving from behind the counter. "Now you must introduce us."

Dick did as he was bidden, and Mickey found himself wondering, as Sylvia cast an eye over the substantial figure of Gladys, whether Dick had acquired his taste for large working-class women during the time he had worked with Sylvia in the East End.

"I am so glad to meet you, Comrade Pankhurst," said Annette as her fingers, still somewhat stained from her pen extended to those of Sylvia, which were also stained, presumably from her typewriter ribbon.

"Oh, you are French?" exclaimed Sylvia as she heard the accent.

"Belgian, Comrade."

"Well!" Sylvia sighed, looking around at the four of them. "Let's go to where it's a little more comfortable—not a much, but a little," she laughed.

She led the way to an office towards the rear of the building which had at least the advantage of a sufficient number of chairs. Seated on one of these, behind an oak desk upon which he worked, apparently proofreading articles for the next issue of the *Dreadnought*, was an almost bald, chunky man of Latin appearance in his early forties. Sylvia took the seat next to him, directing the two couples to desks facing her.

"This, comrades," she said by way of introduction, "is Mr Silvio Corio, our printer. You can speak freely in front of Silvio, as he is a comrade."

Given the kittenish smile which accompanied this introduction, Mickey suspected that Silvio Corio was rather more than a printer and a comrade. Signor Corio now inserted two fingers into the pocket of his waistcoat and pulled out a business card, which he flicked in the direction of the guests. Mickey caught it and saw that Silvio Corio ran a local business called The Agenda Press at 19, Wine Court.

Dick placed his elbows on his desk, clasped his hands before him and regarded Sylvia sympathetically. "How was it this time, Sylvia? Holloway, I mean. Are you recovered?"

Sylvia shrugged. "Oh, you know..."

"You surely weren't on hunger strike this time?"

"No, no," she said wearily, as if that kind of thing were behind her, "but I *was* ill towards the end of my sentence. I was struck down with colitis, of all things."

Dick frowned. "Colitis?"

"If you don't know already, Richard, I have no intention of telling you what it is."

Dick, suspecting a female ailment, blushed.

"But I'm sure you didn't come here to enquire about my health." She raised her eyebrows as a thought struck her. "By the way, do you still both work on the buses?"

"We do, Sylvia."

"Of course, my own view is that industrial struggle has had its day," she somewhat loftily declared. "I have been re-evaluating my experience in the East End and I'm tending to the view that the projects we undertook could form the basis for soviets."

"It's funny you should say that," said Mickey, "because I once suggested to Dorothy that the kind of activities in which you were involved—the workers' restaurant, the crèche, the babies' feeding centre, the toy factory and so on—could be used to show the men and women involved that if they could achieve these results without the involvement of a single capitalist they should perhaps aim a little higher and think of running the whole country."

"How interesting. But Dorothy never mentioned this to me, Comrade Rice." Her laugh was not quite as relaxed as, perhaps, she intended it to be. "I can assure you that I have not stolen your idea."

"I wasn't suggesting that you had, Comrade. I think the disagreement you had with Dorothy probably came before she had the chance to discuss it with you. At the time, I would have been quite happy for you to adopt the idea." Irritated by her defensive stance, he decided that this required qualification. "Of course, I wasn't thinking of soviets, as the word was unknown to us then. And with the greatest respect, while your activity in the East End might have provided a sound basis for the formation of a soviet, that basis didn't exist in most other areas, and still doesn't."

"Well, we'll see about that," she replied. "But tell me: if you weren't thinking of soviets, what *were* you thinking of?"

"Raising the consciousness of the people involved," Mickey replied without hesitation.

"With a view to what—recruiting them into your party?"

"I probably hadn't thought that far ahead, but that wouldn't have been a bad thing, would it? The British Socialist Party had made a clean break with Hyndman and was the only revolutionary party with a national membership."

"And that is where you are *wrong*, Comrade Rice. The BSP may have broken with Hyndman the man, but it was still wedded to his ideas—involvement in the bourgeois parliament, for example. And this Hyndmanism is now in the Communist Party, just as it was in my own little party."

"So you consider Lenin to be a Hyndmanist?"

The question was not intended seriously, merely a means of pointing out where Sylvia's broad characterisation might lead, but there was now little chance of stopping her.

"Yes!" Sylvia slapped the desk before her, causing Silvio to jump. "He proposes Hyndmanism for Britain—parliamentary activity and affiliation to the Labour Party—and who is to say, once the capitalist forces regain strength under his New Economic Policy, that he will not concede bourgeois political forms in Russia!"

The four visitors, shocked by this outburst, sat in silence for some moments. Then Annette began to raise her hand, but Dick got in before her.

"Sylvia," he said softly, "we did not come here to have a row with you. We were concerned—*I* was concerned—about some of the material that has been appearing in the *Dreadnought* and so I hoped to discuss the matter calmly with you. I can see there's a possibility that you will find yourself isolated, and I think that would be a great shame. Having previously worked with you—several years ago now, it's true—I have a great regard for your abilities and your sincerity, and I've come here to offer the hand of comradeship. Let's not fall out, Sylvia."

There was a silence during which Sylvia considered this plea, which Mickey thought far more polished and diplomatic than anything he would have been able to deliver. He wondered which of its three strands—the implied criticism of the *Dreadnought*'s content, the danger of her isolation, and the offer of comradeship—Sylvia would focus upon; but he already knew, he really knew.

Finally, having maintained a calm exterior for several seconds, she stiffened; Silvio gave her a sidelong glance, one eyebrow raised; she lifted the fingers of one hand, presumably to assure him that she was not in need of assistance, following which he returned to his proofreading.

"And what material did you have in mind, Comrade?"

"Well, for example the matter you've just touched upon—the NEP—and the fact that the *Dreadnought* provides space for Russia's so-called Workers' Opposition; the fact that you continue to fight against Labour Party affiliation and parliamentary activity." Realising that he was reciting a litany of sins which would only serve to provoke Sylvia further, he changed tack. "But more generally what is the party's attitude to all of this? It surely can't be very happy about it."

She scrutinised Dick through narrowed eyes. "Have they sent you? Is that why you're here? Did the party central committee send you?"

"No, Sylvia, of course not. I asked you what the party's attitude is because I genuinely do not know. Presumably there'll be something in the next issue of *The Communist*."

She fell silent for a moment, regarding her hands, which were drawn into fists, on top of the desk. "Yes, presumably there will be." For the time being, the hands relaxed. "I was called before a sub-committee—*summoned*, just the way my sister Christabel summoned me to Paris in order to dismiss me from the suffragette movement which she and my mother ran like a military organisation—and told that I must do one of two things: either I must hand over the *Workers' Dreadnought* to the party, which would then appoint an editor, or I must fold it up completely. I refused to do either. Why? Because the *Dreadnought* had never been a party newspaper." Her voice rising, she now stood. Silvio had by now put aside the sheets upon which he had been working and was giving the discussion his full attention. "It had always been *my*"—striking her chest with the flat of her hand—"newspaper. *I* was the one who launched it, *I* was the one who nursed it for eight years, *I* was the one they prosecuted for it!"

"Forgive me, Sylvia" said Mickey, using her forename rather than *Comrade* lest he sound like a member of the committee which had interviewed her, "but wasn't the *Dreadnought* the organ of the CP (BSTI), which has now joined the CPGB?"

Silvio was looking at him the way a barman might regard a potential troublemaker.

"I *loaned* the paper to the party; it was never the *property* of the party!" She was still standing, haranguing the four comrades as she had over the years harangued prosecutors and judges. After a deep breath, she fluttered her fingers in the direction of Annette. "But why are you men monopolising the discussion? The wife of Comrade Rice indicated several minutes ago that she wished to speak."

"Thank you, Comrade," said Annette softly, inclining her head. She sniffed. "Comrade Sylvia, you must forgive me but I am confused, although I cannot believe that these things are managed so differently in the British communist movement."

Sylvia smiled indulgently. "What exactly do you mean, dear?" she enquired, demoting Annette by this form of address to the status of one of her non-political helpers in the East End.

"You are, Comrade, now a member of the Communist Party of Great Britain, yes?"

Sylvia's smile faded as she became wary. "Ye-e-e-s."

"And is not the principle of democratic centralism followed in this party?"

Sylvia sighed. "Yes it is, but my position is that open discussion on the left is vital for the health of the party. Certainly, right-wing deviations should be suppressed, but on the left..."

"My understanding, Comrade Sylvia," Annette persisted, "is that with democratic centralism, there is open discussion *before* a decision is made, but *once* it is made all party members should close ranks. Now, it is true that I have not read many issues of your newspaper—only what my friend and comrade Gladys has shown me—but from what I have heard this evening it would seem that you are using this newspaper to argue against some very basic policies of the party which were decided at its congress. Not only that, but that you oppose the economic policy of the Russian comrades and allow its *Russian* opponents to have a voice in your pages. Oh, Comrade Sylvia, do you not understand that our Russian comrades are implementing a *revolution,* and that your arguments assist those who would *destroy* that revolution? This is not left-wing, Comrade Sylvia—or, rather, it is so far to the left that it is objectively on the right! This is wrong, Comrade, and you must stop it. I implore you to stop it!"

From the way in which Silvio glared with open hostility at Annette, it was clear that he shared Sylvia's view of the world and, thought Mickey, he may have played a part in fashioning it. Both hands were on the desk, elbows akimbo as if he were about to rise, as he growled, "I think it is time for your friends to leave, Sylvia."

Sylvia calmed him with a pat on his forearm, although she was herself anything but calm, for she appeared to view this intervention from the distaff side as little short of betrayal. "Don't you *dare* tell me to stop what I am doing! Do you know the sacrifices I have made for this movement of ours? *Do* you?" She threw out an arm. "*You,* who can know little of conditions in this country!"

"Oh, and I suppose Rudolph Valentino here knows *all* about conditions in this country!" At last, Gladys had found her voice. She jerked a thumb at Silvio, her upper lip curled in a sneer.

Silvio, pushing himself to his feet, seemed intent on advancing on Gladys.

Mickey pointed a finger at Silvio. "Careful, pal. Sit down before..."

Silvio laughed. "Before what? Before you knock me down?"

"No," said Mickey, tilting his head in Gladys's direction, "before *she* does."

Gladys was on her feet. "Don't worry, Mickey, I can handle this one."

Three voices, two male and one female, were raised in alarm: "GLADYS! NO!"

*

"Well, that went rather well, didn't it?" said Mickey as they waited for a number 15 bus.

"Very droll, Mickey, very droll," Dick responded. He sighed. "I accept the blame, though. It was really my fault for suggesting the visit in the first place."

"It's certainly cured me of Sylvia Pankhurst, anyway," declared Gladys.

"Ah, you see, so it was not time wasted at all," said Annette.

"So what is colitis?" asked Dick. "Anybody know?"

"Sylvia," chuckled Gladys, "had the shits."

"And so did Silvio when he saw you coming at him, Glad," said Mickey. He threw his arm around Annette's shoulders and squeezed, letting her know that he was proud of her.

40

"Yesterday," said Mickey Rice, "Johnny Gill was called to a meeting of all the journal editors involved in the amalgamation..."

"And sacked?" guessed Malcolm Lewis.

The two friends were walking home after their early turns, the fierce sunshine of late June slowing their pace in this year of drought.

"Not really, Malc. They were told that all the journals should wrap up their operations. The last issue of our *Record* will appear on 6 July and a new TGWU journal will come out on 1 August."

"How do you know this, Mickey?"

"Eric called last night."

"Ah. So is Bevin doing this to shut us up for the rest of the year while the amalgamation goes through? What does Johnny Gill think about it all?"

"According to Eric, Johnny thinks it's a sensible move. But the effect, of course, will be just as you say: we're hardly likely to get our arguments for a democratic bus section published in a TGWU paper, are we?"

"That's true. What's the new paper gonna be called?"

"Guess."

"Oh, I dunno. Probably something like *Transport Times*."

Mickey grinned. "*The Record.*"

"Geddaway! So they're keeping our title!"

"Yes and no, Malc: the journal of Bevin's union is called the *Dockers' Record*."

"Ah, now it makes sense."

They had reached Great Western Road and here they paused before Mickey turned right and Malcolm swung left, headed for home across the Harrow Road.

"Still nothing on the wages front, then Mick?"

"Not a dickey-bird, although George thinks we might be back at Electric Railway House next week."

"So what's takin' 'em so long?"

Mickey sighed. "They're probably arguing between themselves about how much they think they can get away with. They'll be looking to strike a balance: an attack on our wages and conditions that will takes us down a peg or two but which, after a few amendments, we'll be persuaded to accept."

"I'm sorry I asked now, Mick."

41

It was Friday 8 July before the two sides met again at Electric Railway House, the employers having forwarded copies of their counter-proposals to the union earlier in the week. The teams were unchanged, with the exception of Bob Williams, who was absent on this occasion, it being thought that the TWF's presence was only required at the opening of negotiations, for the signing-off of an accepted package, or when there was a crisis.

"Well, Mr Sanders," George Shave began, "you have had an adequate opportunity to study our proposals. May we assume that you're prepared to accept the document on general principles?"

Mickey Rice had to struggle to prevent himself bursting out in laughter. What a nerve the man had! Not only were they proposing that ten percent of duties be scheduled to a maximum thirteen-hour spreadover, but that the wages be subject to a sliding scale. True, they had thrown in a couple of sweeteners—an increase in annual leave entitlement to eight days from the current six, and time-and-a-quarter for Sunday duties—but the long spreadovers and the wage-reduction proposals were an outrage! Mickey watched carefully as George Sanders replied. A moistening of the lips, the eyes drilling the document before him before lifting to meet those of George Shave. But the expected explosion did not come.

"No, sir," came the mild reply, "it is far too early to make that assumption. We have spent three to four days studying this document; it is quite possible that we could submit it to our members, if amended."

Sanders, Mickey noted, gave not the merest hint of the document's original reception by the Wages Board: the fury, the raised voices, the oaths hurled at the absent London General Omnibus Company and its junior allies. And was that *sir* entirely necessary? Sanders was giving the impression of a man who knows he will be defeated. Indeed, during those days spent studying the document, Sanders had persuaded his team that they would have to give way on the twelve-hour spreadover, as he was convinced that it was necessary for the companies, and that the important thing now was to ensure that it was adequately compensated. Mickey too understood why, for reasons of adequate coverage of the peaks, the companies considered it necessary, but here they were, taking the piss by demanding ten percent at thirteen hours *in addition to* twenty percent at twelve hours. George really should have given them both barrels.

"As we pointed out at the previous meeting, Mr Sanders," said Shave, "your own proposals would have added a million pounds to our costs and are, therefore, quite out of the question."

"Taking the question of spreadover length," said Sanders, "we now propose that 75 percent of duties be worked within a maximum spreadover of eight hours, thirty minutes, inclusive of a thirty-minute meal relief; twenty percent within a spreadover of eleven hours; five percent within a spreadover of twelve hours. You see, we have conceded the principle of the long spreadover." A brief pause. "But it would be sheer madness to suggest a thirteen-hour spreadover to our members."

"But ten percent is such a small proportion," murmured Shave. "At most, a man would work a thirteen-hour spreadover once in ten weeks."

"The men have a dread, Mr Shave—a *dread*—of going back to the old conditions. On wages, if I may continue, we suggest two shillings and one penny an hour for drivers and one and elevenpence for conductors. With no sliding scale."

Shave came right back, feeling himself to be on firm ground. "I am afraid, Mr Sanders, I have no alternative but to say that we must insist on a sliding scale. You are the only concern with whom the sliding scale has not operated, and we are prepared, if you agree to these proposals in principle, not to touch your wages until the end of the year, You are receiving a higher rate than any other undertaking in England."

"There has been talk, I believe, of a fare-increase."

Shave was quite happy with this area of discussion; Mickey suspected that he had rehearsed. "There is a limit to what people will pay in fares," he declared. "You get to a certain point beyond which if our fares are raised another halfpenny you lose those travellers who make the difference between profit and loss—that is, those who ride in the slack hours of the day; not the workers, those who are using the two peak loads—the difference between profit and loss with this undertaking is made up of those who do not actually have to ride but who ride purely as a convenience; and if you raise fares beyond a certain limit those travellers will not ride, but walk."

Mickey conceded that Shave had got the better of this exchange, although it was quite possible that the employers were asking for more than they needed in terms of a reduction; we can surely whittle the figure down.

Sanders decided to change the subject. "Let's return to the question of spreadover, Mr Shave. How would you compensate the men for the extra hours?"

"Oh, I think you misunderstand, Mr Sanders: the men would not be *working* extra hours. No, no, it is *non*-working time that would increase by two or three hours—but only in a minority of cases."

George Sanders almost groaned. "I understand perfectly well, Mr Shave. What I am asking is how you propose to compensate the men for those two extra hours of non-working time. I say *two* hours because, as I have indicated, it would be quite impossible to get the men to accept a thirteen-hour spreadover."

"Then perhaps it is I who do not understand. What possible reason would we have for compensating a man for *not* working for an extra two hours?"

"Because you're keeping him hanging about for those two hours!" Mickey came in, angry that the man affected not to understand the case. He took a deep breath, calming himself. "Let's suppose a man signs on at seven in the morning and finishes his first half at eleven-thirty and is not required to start his second spell until three-thirty. He has four hours at his disposal. Four hours! At the moment, the longest spell of non-working time is two hours, and the man might well look upon this as an extended meal relief—time to have a meal and read his newspaper from cover to cover. But *four* hours!"

"He could invest in a more substantial newspaper," Shave suggested and, although it drew a chuckle or two from his side of the table, he immediately regretted it.

Mickey treated this with the contempt it deserved. "You think that you're purchasing a man's labour. In fact, however, you're purchasing his labour *power*. The fact that you're unable to use that labour power for four hours is due to the way you've chosen to organise his working day. Does he suffer as a result of this? Of course he does, and in two ways: first, at the end of his shift he is considerably more exhausted than if he had worked a normal duty with a ten-hour maximum spreadover; secondly, whereas in the latter case on his second spell of duty he would have experienced a lower level of passenger traffic, now he is in the thick of it once more—to use Mr Sanders' term, realising far more revenue than would otherwise have been the case. He deserves to be compensated for that."

"But we've never paid our staff for non-working time," Shave persisted.

"Oh yes, you have," said Sanders.

Up went Shave's eyebrows. "I beg your pardon, Mr Sanders?"

"In the 1914 agreement, the companies agreed to pay a shilling per duty to compensate for spreadovers in excess of twelve hours. This was before you moved over to the operating side, I believe, Mr Shave. In addition, because payment for an eight-hour is currently guaranteed and—despite the undoubted skill of Mr Mackinnon and those who work with him—it is not always possible to schedule all duties up to that eight-hour maximum, you are required to pay for the non-working time this entails."

Shave looked taken aback, and he seemed to be unfamiliar with this aspect of the agreement.

"And we note," added Sanders, "that you now propose to reduce that guarantee from eight hours to seven! This will entail a considerable loss of earnings and is certain to be rejected by the men. We won the eight-hour guaranteed day in 1919 and now you propose to take it away."

Rather than attempt to resolve each issue as they came to it, Sanders and Shave were, Mickey noticed, simply setting out their positions on an issue and then moving on. The hard bargaining would come later. On some issues, there was an opportunity for humour, as when they discussed the flexibility clause, which the employers intended to retain, even though Shave had acknowledged that its usefulness was limited. Here, Sanders suggests the addition of "which does not interfere with the regular work of any other employee."

"There are certain men," said Johnny Mills, "who are set to clean out the lavatories."

"That is true socialism," joked Shave.

"No," said Sanders, "filling them is socialism."

"No," insisted Shave, "true socialism is where we all have to take a turn."

"But I know some," said Mills, looking straight at Shave, "who will not take their turn."

Before the meeting, the Wages Board had agreed that they should attempt to limit rest-day working, as men earning a seventh day's wage were less likely to press for an improvement in basic earnings. Sanders now surprised the employers by suggesting that the clause outlawing compulsory rest-day working be expanded to rule out penalty payments for those who volunteered.

"Now, declared Sanders now, "there's a concession for you!"

"But who will work on their rest-days?" asked Shave.

"Oh," said Walter Worsley, "you'll get more than you need."

"Yes," said Mackinnon, revealing a less appealing side of his character, "Jews and Scotsmen."

"Yes, that's right," replied Worsley.

An appalled Mickey Rice leaned forward and frowned down the table at George Sanders in the expectation that he would protest against this slide in standards, but George was pretending not to have noticed.

Once the whistle-stop tour of the document had been completed, Sanders threw up his hands. "Let me be straight with you, Mr Shave: the agreement as put forward by the companies stands no chance of acceptance. If our amendments are accepted by you it would stand a much greater chance, but even then there could be no guarantee. But we want to get the completed document in front of the members as soon as possible. Can you meet us at 4 p.m. this afternoon?"

"When the proposals are put in a form that you find acceptable, Mr Sanders," replied Shave, "will you be recommending acceptance?"

"Until we see what you have to say, Mr Shave, you can hardly expect me to answer that."

*

"I'm having second thoughts about this Shave character," said Mickey Rice as they enjoyed a late lunch in the Adam & Eve pub.

"How do you mean, Mickey?" asked Sanders.

"There are so many things he has no understanding of; you'd think he'd never read the agreement. There's the shilling spreadover allowance we got in 1914, the guarantee of payment for eight hours a day..."

Sanders nodded soberly. "I know, I know." A sigh. "I tend to agree with you, Mickey. You know, it's sometimes a damn sight more difficult negotiating with a half-decent man who has no real grasp of the issues than with a hard man who at least understands what he's talking about."

*

When they reassembled, Shave made the first real movement. On maximum spreadover length, 70 percent of duties would be within 10 hours, with a nine-hour average, 20 percent would be within 12 hours, and 10 percent within 13 hours. But there would be penalty payments: a shilling for every duty between ten and twelve hours, and one shilling and sixpence for duties over twelve hours.

"It's useless," said Walter Worsley, "to go to the men with 13-hour spreadovers."

"But we're hoping to keep them down to five percent," said Shave hopefully, "even though the agreement will specify ten percent."

"This morning," said Chris Platten, "Mr Sanders suggested that 70 percent of duties should have a maximum spreadover of eight-and-a-half hours, inclusive of a 30-minute meal relief. We haven't had a reply to that."

Of course we haven't, thought Mickey Rice, because it was put forward in the knowledge that we wouldn't get it; it was to show the members how high we had aimed on their behalf. Fool.

Mackinnon was in like a shot. "It is quite impossible."

"Couldn't be done," agreed Shave.

And that was that.

When the discussion turned to wages, Sanders put his cards on the table. "I think the time has now arrived when I ought to state that our feeling on this side is this: I do not think it is any good disguising the fact any longer that we think it is very inadvisable— at any rate you will stand a very poor chance of getting the agreement through—if you demand *both* the spreadover *and* the sliding scale."

There followed a lengthy discussion on the sliding scale, with Shave pledging that, with the safeguard that the companies were prepared to give, even if wages hit the limit below which there would be no further reduction, wages would still be 52 percent above the 1914 level.

"But it's not just on the hourly rate that you're attempting to claw back our wages," said Mickey Rice. "You also propose that if the fortnightly hours exceed 96, rather than the current weekly hours exceeding 48, overtime rates will be paid for any excess. That's a further loss of earnings for us."

"We're prepared to delete that," said Shave, "at the cost of £25,000."

"Which is what it would have cost us if you'd left it in," said Mickey.

That was a relatively minor point, as was the next one: Shave agreed with Sanders' suggestion that 25 percent of annual leave, as opposed to the current 20 percent, could be taken in the summer months.

But then they returned to the question of guaranteed payment for a daily duty: would it be eight hours or seven? If the latter, it was pointed out, it would mean that seven hours could be worked one day and nine hours the next, with no overtime payment for the latter. "This," said Chris Platten, "shatters any hope of getting the agreement accepted."

Shave adjourned for fifteen minutes and upon his return suggested they call it a day until Monday.

*

At 3 p.m. on Monday, 11 June, they opened on the vexed question of the guaranteed payment for the day.

"Understand our position," said Johnny Mills. "If your proposal was implemented, a man working three days at seven hours and three days at nine hours would lose eight shillings in overtime payments. This is what you pay at the moment. This is what you agreed in 1919."

My god, thought Mickey Rice, just look at Shave now, reddening, blinking like mad. Totally at sea. Lost.

"I simply cannot understand," blustered the operating manager, "how this was ceded in the first place."

Well, you were there, thought Mickey; you may not have been operating manager, but you were there with Blain.

"To my mind it seems immoral that there should be an understanding at all to pay for hours not worked!"

Immoral, for Christ's sake! But it's perfectly moral for the companies to pocket the surplus value we've created for them! Mickey thought of wading into the discussion, but George had it.

"You have the right," said Sanders, "to use the men's services for eight hours; it's not our fault if you choose not to."

After a long discussion, Shave appeared ready to bow to immorality. "Look," he said, "if we concede this we cannot give you what we've promised on the other clauses. It's for you to say which we should take off."

Oh, yeah, thought Mickey. Fat chance!

When they returned to the sliding scale, George suggested a slight increase in the lower limit to one and ninepence an hour for drivers and one and sevenpence for conductors which Shave, presumably relieved at having won acceptance of the principle, agreed.

There was then a further example of Shave's inability to understand the business.

"You propose in Clause 9," said Sanders, "that this agreement 'shall not apply to employees of the companies engaged in connection with any services outside the Metropolitan Police Area.' We ask that the word 'entirely' be inserted here."

"It's in the present agreement," said Worsley.

"I cannot see the point," said Shave.

Is the man thick, Mickey asked himself, or is this an attempt to pull the wool over our eyes? Tell him, Worsley!

"What we do not want," said Walter Worsley, "is on the 10B route, let's say, where at Epping Town you go a good distance outside of the Metropolitan Police Area. And if we do not have that word put in, immediately we pass the Bell on Epping Common we're on a lower rate of pay although we've done the best part of our journey from the Elephant inside the area."

"Is that what you really fear?" asked Shave.

Isn't it bloody obvious, thought Mickey?

"Yes," said Worsley, "that's what we fear."

After a short adjournment, Shave agreed that the first reductions, if any, would take place in the first payroll week of April 1922.

"But if we leave the eight-hour guaranteed day as it is, we will have to remove the time-and-a-quarter for Sundays."

It's bluff, George! We can have both if we give him something for the Sunday payment. What? Don't worry, he'll tell you soon enough.

"Although you give may us concessions on what you originally wanted us to accept," said Sanders, looking thoroughly fed up at the games being played, "at the same time we are losing something all the way through the piece."

Chris Platten came in: "Withdraw the thirteen-hour spreadover, leave in the time-and-a-quarter for Sundays and you are almost home."

Shave folded his hands on the table and looked directly at Sanders. "If we concede the time-and-a-quarter for Sundays, will you recommend acceptance?"

There it is, George: that's the deal, thought Mickey. Watch your step now, George.

Sanders almost smiled. "Let's wait until we have the redrafted agreement."

"Alright," Shave sighed, "let's have one more meeting to go through the agreement. We'll send you copies beforehand and we'll meet on Thursday afternoon."

Agreed.

*

The meeting on Thursday 14 July was fairly short and was used to ensure that both sides had the same understanding of what now appeared in the redrafted document. George Shave began by expressing the hope—forlorn as it would turn out to be—that this would be the last meeting of the 1921 cycle, and concluded by congratulating Sanders on his conduct of the negotiations. "I hope, Mr Sanders," he said, "that your committee will give the document its blessing, if not a recommendation."

I'm not at all sure, thought Mickey Rice, that it's a good sign when the employer congratulates you on your conduct of the negotiations. Doesn't that mean that he's heaving a sigh of relief that you've stopped well short of wringing him dry? And he still wants us to give the document a nod of approval when we put it before the lads. Let's see how George responds to this.

"After the way you have met us this afternoon," said Sanders, "no word will go out from us, at any rate, towards accentuating the difficulties of getting it through."

This is not the George Sanders I used to think I knew, mused Mickey. So where have we ended up on the major items? On maximum spreadover, 75 percent of duties will be within 10 hours, the average not exceeding nine hours; 20 percent will be within twelve hours, carrying a penalty payment of a shilling per duty; and the remaining five percent will be within 13 hours, with a penalty payment of one shilling and sixpence.

On pay, the hourly rate for a driver will from January 3 1922 be two shillings, and for a conductor one shilling and ninepence, thus eliminating the awkward five-eighths of a penny both grades currently earn on top of that by levelling up the conductors' rate and levelling down the drivers'; these rates will then be reduced or increased, on a quarterly basis, by a farthing for every five points the cost of living index varies from 140, with a minimum guarantee of one shilling and ninepence for drivers and one shilling and sevenpence for conductors. If the cost of living ever falls that low, then, a driver will lose 12 shillings a week.

Guaranteed payment for a scheduled duty will remain at eight hours, and Sunday working will be paid at time-and-a-quarter.

Once the agreement is signed, all members will be given a clean record.

But will it be signed? We'll have to see what George means when he promises to avoid "accentuating the difficulties of getting it through."

This became clear the following day, when George Sanders met the rest of the Wages Board at Transport House to decide the form in which the proposals would be presented to the members.

"We need a pamphlet," said Sanders, "containing the proposals, the verbatim notes of the meetings, and a foreword in which we give our thoughts on the matter."

"Jesus wept," said Barney Macauley, "you're talking about a hundred pages or so, George! Do you think Stan Hirst will agree the funding for that?"

"He won't have to, Barney. I reckon that the whole thing will come out at just over seventy pages. I've had a word with Caledonian Press in Swinton Street and I reckon we'd break even if we sold it at threepence a time."

"So we'll be asking the members to pay for the rope that hangs them!" said Mickey Rice.

This got a few chuckles, but there was also unease; eyes were averted.

Sanders took a deep draw on his cigarette before stubbing it out in the ashtray at his side before replying, in a cloud of blue smoke, "We can do without talk of that sort, Mickey. You were there the whole time, you know we tried our damnedest and I hope you'll agree that the members should also know that."

"How many members do you think are going to wade through seventy pages?"

"Probably not all of them," Sanders acknowledged, "but hopefully enough of them to make an impact." He raised his eyebrows at Mickey. "Besides, what harm can it do?"

"I can't see the verbatim notes doing any harm, George, but the foreword needs to be given careful thought."

"Agreed," said Sanders. "So are we all agreed on the *principle* of the pamphlet?"

As Mickey looked around the table, he felt he could read their thoughts as they cast their minds back over the July days of negotiations, assessing their performances and if, like Johnny Mills and Walter Worsley, they felt they had done well, nodding in assent. Mickey laughed good-naturedly and joined the majority.

"Alright," said Sanders, "so to the foreword. I've written a draft. Here, see what you think." He passed copies around the table.

Mickey began to read, and the more he read, the more his heart sank. There were just six paragraphs, but five of those six contained a broad hint that the draft agreement should be accepted.

In the opening paragraph, we hope that "every consideration will be given to the economic conditions prevailing in the industrial world at the present moment."

"We think," said the second paragraph, "it quite safe to say that trade unionism at the present moment is at the lowest ebb it has ever been in our lifetime...On every hand, we find that the workers are being beaten on the industrial field...Most of the large unions have agreed or are negotiating big decreases in wages without effective protest..."

Paragraph three: "Having full knowledge of the facts, and knowing that it would be useless to expect help from other sections of the workers..."

The fourth paragraph advised the members to disregard the pessimism of the weaklings and the enthusiasm of the strong and come to their own conclusions.

"It may be humiliating to the majority of the class-conscious bus workers," said paragraph five, "to have to yield something already won, but right through the ages one has to realise that the strong majority have had to suffer on account of the apathy, the indifference, and the ignorance of the huge majority."

Closing his eyes, Mickey let the single sheet fall from his fingers onto the table. Looking around at his colleagues, he could see no enthusiasm for the document but feared that most would go along with it.

"Well?" Sanders snapped once they had all finished reading.

"It's as weak as piss," hissed Mickey Rice, "and it's certainly not what I would call leadership. You might just as well have come out and recommended acceptance instead of expecting the members to swallow this."

It was immediately apparent that Mickey was in the minority. Most members of the Wages Board shrank back at his words, as if he had doused them with boiling water. "Oh, there's no need for that!" cried Platten. Even Macauley sat there shaking his head, murmuring, "Mickey, Mickey..."

"Are you moving that we recommend acceptance, then?" asked Sanders.

"You may fancy moving acceptance of long spreadovers and a pay-cut," said Bill Modley, "but I sure as hell don't!"

"And that's the problem, isn't it?" said Johnny Mills, surprising everyone by seeming to join Mickey. "We're so worried about getting elected to positions in the new union that we think it would be suicidal to recommend acceptance. But this form of words..." He gestured at the sheet before him. "Mickey's right: it just makes us look weak." He shrugged. "Mind you, I can't see the way out of it. Can you, Mickey?"

"I'm not in favour of recommending acceptance at all, brothers," Mickey responded. "It's all very well to point to the defeat of miners, and to the fact that the railwaymen have accepted cuts, and to mention the weak state of the whole movement. All of that is true! But we need to focus our minds on *these* employers and *their* circumstances. I'm in favour of moving rejection, brothers! And why? Because I suspect that they *have* got more to give, that we haven't pushed them quite hard enough. During the negotiations, George, you reminded them that last year Blain said they wanted no more than the twelve-hour spread. Give us that and we'll ask for no more. Did you see their faces when you put that to 'em? And the best they could come up with was 'Oh, Mr Blain must have been ill-advised.' No, they had some in reserve, George. Now, I'm not saying that this occurred to me at the time, because if it had done I would have said something. No, what convinced me that they'd been bluffing was when, right at the end, Shave congratulated you on your conduct of the negotiations, George. I don't think he would have done that if we'd had him against the ropes. So I move, brothers, that we recommend rejection."

George Sanders had paled. "And what do I say to Shave, after I've told him we won't say anything to make difficulties for getting the agreement accepted?"

"Do you recall, George, the arguments we had with Harry Bywater over the 1914 negotiations?" This was Barney Macauley making a diplomatic intervention. No one else on the Wages Board had been present at those negotiations, and so they were in no position to know that Barney's question was not exactly flattering to Sanders.

Sanders cast his mind back. In 1914 the membership had rejected the company's proposals on two occasions, and Bywater, then the general secretary, had told the committee that he felt like Oliver Twist, going back to ask for more. One particular officer had thumped the table and suggested that the managing director, then plain Albert Stanley, be told that the red-button union, unlike the London General Omnibus Company, was a democracy, and that its officers took their orders from the members. The officer who thumped the table had been George Sanders. Had he, over the past seven years, evolved into a version of Harry Bywater? He hoped desperately that this was not the case. Besides, the lay leadership had been with him yesterday when he had made that promise to George Shave. Bywater, on the other hand, had on two occasions met Stanley privately, telling no one. So no, he was not another Bywater.

"The conditions in 1914 were somewhat different, Barney," he replied eventually, regaining his poise. "The trade union movement was very much on the offensive, and had been since 1910, whereas today we are, like it or not, on the retreat. In today's circumstances, it would be a grievous mistake to recommend rejection and then find that we're unable to make further headway."

"But whether we recommend it or not," said Mickey, "the members will reject these proposals. Didn't you yourself, George, tell the company that it would be madness to put a thirteen-hour spread before them? Didn't other members here make the same point? Were we the ones who were bluffing?"

Sanders sighed and dug into his Gold Flake packet for another cigarette. "Well," he said, "if these proposals are rejected, someone else will have to take the lead when we go back to the company."

At the end of the discussion, the foreword suggested by Sanders was accepted.

42

It took a few days for the pamphlet to be printed, and after that a fortnight was allowed before the ballot, enabling the members to read the thing and absorb the not very subtle message in its foreword. During that period, the branch resolutions began to arrive at Transport House.

"It seems the branches want the Wages Board—including George Sanders—to resign," said Malcolm Lewis when the Middle Row branch committee met to discuss the matter.

"Well," said Mickey, "I can't say I predicted this, but I'm not surprised."

"Are you sayin' that you were against the document?" asked Lenny Hawkins, lean–faced and serious.

"Yeah, at the last knockings I argued against that bloody foreword and even moved that we recommend rejection."

"On what basis, Mickey?" asked Dick Mortlake. Sharing the same roof as Mickey, he already knew Mickey's position but was keen to ensure that the committee also heard it.

"On the basis that I think there's more to be had," said Mickey.

"But you put your name to that document," said Charley Adams.

"Of course I did, because I lost the vote. It's called collective responsibility, brothers."

"So you reckon that the branch should recommend rejection to the members?" asked Malcolm.

"I can't say that, can I? Collective responsibility again. I'm bound by the decision of the Wages Board: each member should make his own decision."

"What's the point of electing leaders who won't lead?" sighed Dick.

"That's pretty much what I told 'em."

"Well, fuck that," said Lenny. "I'm all for recommending rejection."

"On a personal level, that's fine with me, but you realise I can't be a party to it."

"So," said Dick, scribbling in his minute book, "one abstention."

*

In early August it was announced that some eighty percent of the London bus membership had voted to reject the companies' proposals.

"So what are your feelings on the matter, George?" asked Stanley Hirst. It wasn't hard to see that Hirst was not particularly upset that the bus membership had given Sanders a black eye.

"I'm wondering whether I should give those branches which have sent in resolutions what they want," said Sanders.

"What do you mean? Resign?"

"Of course."

"Don't be so daft, George. Do you think I haven't been in the same position? Think back to the tramway negotiations last year." It seemed that Hirst, while happy enough that Sanders had been taken down a peg or two, did not wish to get rid of him completely.

"Well, if negotiations are resumed there's no way that I can take the lead. In fact, I told the Wages Board after the last negotiations that if the proposals were rejected someone else would have to take the lead."

Hirst shrugged. "No problem, George; we'll call in Bob Williams."

Everyone expected the two teams to reassemble at Electric Railway House in the near future, but that did not happen. It turned out that Lord Ashfield, even if he did not attend the negotiations, wanted to be available, and he was about to go on holiday. A further complication lay in the fact that Stanley Hirst took the view that if there was a chance that Ashfield would attend, he should be there also, and in September his hands would be full preparing for the new union's rules conference. It would, therefore, be over two months after the ballot before battle was resumed.

43

"So did you have a chance to take the waters, Barney?" asked Mickey.

They were in the Crown and Anchor and Barney Macauley had just returned from the three-day rules conference in Leamington Spa.

"You're joking! Almost two thousand amendments to wade through!" A sniff. "Had a chance to saunter through the town, though. Some lovely Regency architecture up there."

"So how did we do?" asked Reuben Topping.

Mickey had called just eight of the provisional organising

committee together on a very informal basis; if Brian Vernon later asked why he wasn't invited he would be told that it was not a meeting of the committee as such, just an informal chat with Barney and the most local lads.

"We did alright, Reuben. We've got the Passenger Group for buses, trams and cabs, so you can go ahead with the campaign for a sub-section for London buses. In fact Harry Gosling, the provisional president who opened the conference, said that no one should think that they would be leaving the conference with a perfect set of rules, so the way is open for improvements."

"How did Bevin perform?" asked Dick Mortlake.

"I have to say that he was excellent. Mind you, he was on his best behaviour because he knew he couldn't afford to upset any section at this stage of the game." Barney chuckled.

"Okay," said Lloyd from Palmers Green, "so do we call a meeting of our organising committee and get our campaign for the London Bus Section on the road?"

"The problem there," said Mickey, "is that we're probably going to be tied up with the wages question in the next week or two, aren't we? That could end up in a strike ballot, of course."

"Surely we can take on both questions at once," Dick protested. "In fact, it could work to our advantage: if the members are mobilised and ready for a scrap on the wages front, they'll surely be in the mood to make demands on Ernie Bevin at the same time."

Mickey nodded. "That's a fair point. Okay, but how about if we give it to the end of October before we make a move?"

Reuben Topping took a whistling intake of breath. "That's cutting it a bit fine, Mickey. By that time we'll have just two months before the Transport and General is up and running."

"I honestly think that'll be time enough. The handful of branches that are withholding their contributions will presumably still be doing that, and those few who are agitating for a breakaway will most likely still be on the go. With regard to the breakaways, by the way, and *strictly* between us few, I think it would be an idea if we gave them their head for a while before cracking down on them."

Lloyd frowned. "Why would we do that, Mickey?"

"It'll add a bit more pressure on Ernie and the provisional executive. If it looks like getting out of hand we'll have to step in sooner, but I think it'll be quite manageable."

Lloyd nodded. "As long as you're sure, Mickey."

"So I'll call a meeting for the end of October. That should give us plenty of time. What do we have to do, after all? Mobilise the branches to send in resolutions to Bevin, and generally make a lot of noise. We'll have bags of time. Meanwhile, if any of the others start getting impatient, tell 'em to sit tight for just a few weeks."

"And in the immediate future," said Barney Macauley, "Mickey and I will have to be prepared for another trip to Electric Railway House."

"When do think that will be?" asked Reuben Topping.

"Week after next, I should think. God knows why they're taking so long."

"We all know there's been talk of holidays and other commitments," said Mickey, "but I suspect that the companies have been wondering if they could get away with imposing the agreement we rejected. At the end of the day, the size of the majority against the proposals have probably convinced them that would be a mistake."

*

In the second week of October, they were back at Electric Railway House before George Shave. The union side was led by Bob Williams and Ben Smith, the latter in the capacity of not a UVW senior officer but an executive member of the Transport Workers' Federation. There was movement, but not much: whereas previously the companies had said that the sliding scale would commence whenever the cost of living index fell below 140, but Shave now agreed to amend that to 135; Ben Smith tried to get him to agree to 120, but to no avail. In addition to this, Shave proposed that the maximum length of spreadover would be 12 hours, 30 minutes rather than the previous 13 hours; the union side, emboldened by the previous ballot result, rejected this.

It was therefore agreed that the two sides would meet again—for the eleventh time this year—on 14 October and that the employers would be led by Lord Ashfield.

44

The UVW team was now joined by Stanley Hirst who would contribute nothing to the negotiations, speaking only when the employers posed a question to him, and the UVW president, Ernie Plinstson. Bob Williams and Ben Smith led for the union side, while George Sanders' only real contribution came when he defended the foreword he had written. The lay members would also be silent for most of the time, Hirst having pointed out before the meeting that the frequent lay interventions he had seen in the verbatim notes would have no place in any negotiations in which he played a leading role. Only one person would break ranks on this: Mickey Rice.

As they arrived, Bob Williams gave Mickey a nudge, saying quietly, "Did you see the party's made another expulsion, Mickey?"

"Yeah, Sylvia, about a month ago."

"If they go on like this, we'll soon have enough to form our own party," Williams joked.

"But Sylvia would probably get herself expelled from that one, too."

Bob grinned. "Maybe, Mickey, maybe."

Mickey sat next to Barney Macauley at the outer extremity of the union line, as far away from Hirst as possible.

Last to enter was Lord Ashfield, tall and dignified. Before taking his seat next to Mr H.E. Blain—another addition to the employers' team—, he placed his papers on the table before him and nodded to the other side. "Good afternoon, gentlemen." Running his eye down the union line, he suddenly started and, shading his narrowed eyes as if regarding Mickey from a great distance, enquired, "My goodness, is this Mr Rice I see before me?"

"Well, it's certainly not Macbeth, Chairman," replied Mickey. "Good afternoon."

Ashfield laughed. "Forgive us, gentlemen," he said to Bob Williams and Ben Smith, "but Mr Rice and I are old sparring partners. We usually spar with quotations from Shakespeare. Do you have anything appropriate for this afternoon, Mr Rice?"

"Yes, Chairman, I believe I do: 'Heat not a furnace for your foe so hot that it do singe yourself.'"

More laughter from Ashfield. "*Henry VIII*, I believe. Yes?"

"Correct!"

Of those present, only two men did not join in the laughter: Stanley Hirst because the vow of silence he had sought to impose on the lay members had already been broken, and H.E. Blain, who thought Mickey guilty of discourtesy.

"Mr Rice," said Blain, "I think it quite improper that you should address our chairman in such a manner. He is Lord Ashfield and should be addressed as such."

Ashfield seemed to find this even more amusing. "Now, now, Mr Blain," he said, placing a restraining hand on Blain's forearm, "it is quite in order for Mr Rice—or anyone else—to address the company chairman as Chairman. In fact, as I am confident that Mr Rice heartily disapproves of titles such as Lord and Lady, it seems to me that he has hit upon a quite ingenious compromise." He turned in Mickey's direction. "But the quotation you have chosen, Mr Rice...Ohhh, *very* biting. Tell me now, did that line just occur to you, or had you pocketed it for future use some time ago?"

Mickey laughed. "Chairman, I spent two hours combing through Shakespeare last night until I stumbled upon it."

"Aha! Splendid, Mr Rice, splendid. 'No legacy is so rich as honesty.'"

"All's well that Ends Well?"

"Oh, very good, Mr Rice!" He cleared his throat. "Well, if this meeting is going to end well, I suppose we had better get on with it."

Mickey knew that Ashfield's geniality was quite genuine, but he also knew that he was employing it to win the union side to the view that he was a warm, friendly bloke who wished to do them no harm. Well, he thought, we'll see.

*

"I have," Ashfield began, "read the notes of the proceedings you have had with Mr Shave, who has been dealing with this matter for Mr Blain and myself. From these, and from what Mr Blain and Mr Shave have told me, I believe that you have not succeeded in coming to an understanding."

"That is so," said Williams."

"Well, it is a great pity."

"I told Mr Shave that."

"It is a great pity for two reasons. First, I was congratulating myself that here was a matter with which I did not need to burden myself." A glance at Mickey. "Yes, yes, Mr Rice: Uneasy lies the head, etc. Secondly, I was congratulating both sides on the amicable and friendly way the negotiations had been carried on—until the last meeting. At that point—and it is not disclosed in the notes—a very great change took place. While the negotiations were conducted amicably, there was running through the proceedings that same spirit of suspicion and distrust which has almost always prevailed when we have been discussing matters affecting the interests of the busmen. I do not know how new you are to this, Mr Williams."

Bob shrugged. "I come in and out, just as you do, Lord Ashfield."

"I would give a great deal," Ashfield continued, "if that distrust could disappear. I have no objection whatever to a difference of opinion between us, but I cannot understand why there should be distrust between us."

Barney Macauley leaned towards Mickey, whispering, "Get your handkerchief ready, mate, because this bloke will have us in tears before long. I've seen it before."

Ashfield then advanced an argument which was wholly unexpected. "I can see no hope whatever of any better situation developing as long as the kind of report upon the proceedings which was sent to our men continues to exist. It was thoroughly bad; if I may say so, it was unfair."

"You mean the verbatim report?" asked Bob Williams.

"No, I mean the foreword, which must have been looked upon by the men as a précis of all these negotiations, but more than that as an indication of what they ought to do."

Mickey began to shake his head in disbelief. How was it that all members of the Wages Board had recognised that foreword as a veiled urging to accept the agreement while the company chairman, reputed to be possessed of a towering intellect, interpreted it as a recommendation to reject? Can't he see that the members voted to reject not because of the foreword but because of the four pages which followed it, containing the proposals?

"If one can read English plainly, it was an indication that you repudiated the offer which had been put to the men. It carried with it this—which is the sting of it—that those who represented the men had done all in their power to secure as favourable terms for the men as possible—which they rightly always do—but that in this case they were confronted with task masters who were so impracticable, so determined to squeeze the last penny they could out of these negotiations, that all they could do was simply go to the men and say, 'We are sorry; we have met a hopeless position; we can do nothing whatever with them; they put to you an absolutely hopeless proposition, and we really recommend that you have nothing to do with it.' "

Mickey watched as George Sanders scribbled a note and passed it to Bob Williams.

This would have been an appropriate point for Ashfield to pause and allow Sanders—as he obviously wished—to respond to his comments about the foreword, but on he went, first asserting that surely no one, given the current circumstances, would argue that there should be *no* changes to wages and conditions, while claiming that it was not the companies but the travelling public who, by its resistance to higher fares, dictated these changes. He went on to state that the omnibus was at last capable of providing the kind of service which the public desired and deserved, referring to the admiration expressed by the people for the way in which the busmen performed their duties—the skill with which passengers were conveyed through the streets of London and the work performed by the conductors.

"But if the men fail to recognise the situation in dealing with the current problem, if they fail to cooperate with us, it will simply be impossible. And I find room for disappointment in the thought that as far as I can judge, there has not been on the part of those who were speaking for the men a real attempt to aid us in finding a solution to this problem.

"We will always take the view that the first charge on our undertakings is a fair and reasonable wage for our men. But there is a limit to it. I hope, therefore, that you will come to an agreement with us and then say to the men: 'Whether you like it or not, we, with our knowledge of the facts, have no hesitation in recommending it.'"

"Want to borrow mine, Mickey?" murmured Barney Macauley.

"Your what, Barney?"

"Handkerchief."

A dry-eyed Bob Williams indicated that George Sanders had something to say about that foreword. Hirst looked uncomfortable at this. He had made it clear that if Sanders had not withdrawn from the lead role in these negotiations, he would have insisted on it. It was he who, realising that there needed to be a UVW officer sitting alongside Bob Williams, and presumably lacking the confidence to do the job himself, had instructed Ben Smith to step in, albeit wearing a Transport Workers' Federation hat.

Sanders, clearly irritated, waved a copy of the pamphlet before him. "Perhaps more than any other," he said, "the English language lends itself to a host of interpretations. I have read this document again and I fail to see how anyone"—looking straight at Ashfield now and repeating the word to dispel any doubt about whom he was talking—"how *anyone* can say that it shows bias." He quoted a passage from the foreword. "I want to say on behalf of the Wages Board that we find ourselves between two stools. We come here today and are lectured because we did not take up our position as leaders in a certain respect." He threw out a hand. "On the other hand, our Board has received resolutions asking the executive council for our immediate resignation—of myself and the whole Wages Board—for seeming to recommend here the men's acceptance of the agreement. That is a very peculiar position to be in.

"That is the position. We tried to make it so this foreword could not be construed either too much one way or the other. It makes me wish that we *had* shown bias and indicated that the men ought to vote for the agreement."

Jesus, George, what are you saying? Perhaps feeling that it would be too demonstrative to place his hands over his ears, Mickey Rice closed his eyes and sighed.

"Sitting around this table are working busmen. Since they became organised in 1913 you have paid decent wages in the London General, but you know the conditions before that were very bad; and the men are very much afraid that they may have to go back to the conditions against which they put up a spirited fight. *That* is the idea running through the minds of the busmen, and I think the men here intelligently echo their concerns." He paused, then lowered his voice. "I felt that I should say those few words on behalf of the board because I don't think they will be saying much today."

Ashfield let it pass; if he realised that his interpretation of the foreword had been erroneous, he wasn't admitting it.

Bob Williams squared his shoulders and proceeded to paint a picture of the terrain as he saw it.

"I have come in for the same reason as you appear to have been brought in, Lord Ashfield. There appeared to be a hitch, and my colleagues thought I might pull an ounce more strength or exert an ounce more force, and so I came in. If I have a little more influence, though, I feel that that influence will carry with it a little more responsibility, and so I have told my colleagues again and again that if we arrive at an agreement they will have to share the general measure of responsibility with me.

"It seems to us that we are faced with one of two alternatives: either extended spreadover or a cut in wages. I have told my friends frankly that in view of all the national and international circumstances they will have to face up to one of these two alternatives."

Clever stuff, Bob, thought Mickey, because we all know that the companies want both of those alternatives, and you're obviously trying to put Ashfield in the frame of mind where he'll consider, given *our* circumstances, that just one would be acceptable. I'm not sure that you'll succeed, but I wish you—us!—luck.

"Now," said Williams, "I understand that the overwhelming majority of the men are unalterably opposed to any extension of the spreadover system, and so they are forced to consider a wage-cut."

There now took place a long discussion regarding comparisons between conditions on the buses, trams, railways and mines, but this hardly moved the business forward. Ben Smith had pointed to the appalling level of unemployment, arguing that longer spreadovers would exacerbate this situation in that less men would be required; in response, Ashfield pledged that longer spreadovers would not result in the unemployment of any London General men, but this had not really been Ben's point.

Bob shifted the discussion to wages, suggest the cost-of-living index figure of 100 as the starting point for reductions of a shilling a week for every point below that. A bob a week per point seemed bloody steep, thought Mickey, but how likely was it that the cost of living would fall to the 1914 level? The chances were that with this formula there would be no wage-reductions at all; and for that reason Ashfield would certainly not accept it. At the previous meeting, when Shave had suggested the index figure of 135 as the starting point, Bob had been forward the compromise of 117.5, but Shave had then said that he had no power to make such a recommendation.

"Wages and the spreadover hang together," Ashfield now said.

Bob effected a shocked expression. "Are you saying the men have to face the longer spreadover *and* the wage-cut?"

Ashfield, as practiced an actor as Bob Williams, hesitated, looking regretful. "Yes," he breathed finally, "I am afraid so."

"In that case, I think we need a few minutes on our own, Lord Ashfield."

*

"It seems to us," said Bob Williams after the employers had returned at 4.25, "as if we are starting all over again—*de novo*, as it were."

"Is that Welsh?" Barney Macauley muttered to Mickey.

"If this is the case, just tell us what you have in mind for working conditions."

"Are you prepared to make a recommendation?" asked Ashfield.

Mickey jotted down a note—"New offer on the way"—and passed it to Macauley.

"First of all, we want to hear your suggestions."

Ashfield lowered his brow, lips pursed. "We want to be as decent about this thing as you are."

"You can try," said Bob, causing laughter on both sides of the table.

"Yes, as near as we can get." With a fleeting glance at Sanders, Ashfield decided to risk a little sarcasm. "There may be some bias attached to it, but we try not to have it." A smile. "I would like to know, once this thing is threshed out, if you think it acceptable will you make a recommendation to the men?"

Ashfield must have been on the same negotiating course as Shave, thought Mickey. Will you recommend, will you recommend?—and always before he's put anything before us *to* recommend.

"Yes," sighed Bob, "I have already said that."

"And which in the circumstances is one in regard to which we could not ask the company to do more..."

Now he's writing the recommendation for us, for Christ's sake!

"If we think it is the best, we will obviously do that."

Ashfield got to his feet. "Alright, we'll send you a note with our proposals and you can discuss them."

That did not take long, and after just twelve minutes the employers were called back.

"These proposals," protested Bob Williams, gesturing at the single sheet before him, are little different from those put at the last meeting with Mr Shave." He shook his head. "We could not recommend these, Lord Ashfield."

Ben Smith came in. "If the spreadover system is so indispensable to you, I assume you are prepared to pay a penalty."

"Yes, we have suggested that," Ashfield replied.

"But we object to that form of penalty. This began with the shilling in 1914, but the men said that as soon as the schedules went up they saw that the company was cutting into it by a minute."

"Really, Mr Smith, is this what you're afraid of?" enquired Ashfield. "Come now, this smacks of distrust."

Ashfield made the mistake of glancing in Mickey's direction, giving him the opportunity to quote from *Troilus and Cressida*: "Modest doubt is called the beacon of the wise." Having no time for this game now, Ashfield waved a dismissive hand.

"Would you suggest another form of penalty?" asked H.E. Blain.

"On the railways, only five percent work it, and if any others work it they get paid as if time worked. I suggest that the spreadover should be paid on the basis as if time worked."

"I cannot see how it could be worked. I cannot see your point," said George Shave.

"He never bloody can," whispered Mickey to Barney Macauley.

"Earlier," said Ben, "Lord Ashfield said that the omnibuses had never been able to meet the public's requirement. If you have never done it on the basis of a maximum spreadover of 15 hours, 10 minutes a weekday and a maximum spreadover of 14 hours, 20 minutes on Sunday, you could *never* meet it unless you had the whole 24 hours!"

Broad smiles on the union side. Bulls-eye, Ben!

But no, Ashfield is also grinning. "It was not a question of spreadover but of vehicle type."

"I want to put this to you, Lord Ashfield," said Ben. "Are you prepared, first of all, to increase the proportion of 10-hour spreadovers from 75 percent to 85 percent, with an average over the route of nine hours?"

Ashfield's reply was so swift in coming that it was obvious that this had been tucked up his sleeve for some time. "I will agree that the ten-hour spreadovers will remain at 75 percent and that the twelve-hour spreadovers be increased from 20 percent to 25 percent over the route."

There it was: the 12-hour-thirty-minutes spreadover was gone. A certain amount of hubbub now arose on the union side, during which Mickey murmured, "Told you there was a new offer on the way, didn't I?"

"Took longer than expected, though," said Barney Macauley. "And bloody George Shave, who told us that the 13-hour spread was a necessity, ain't even blushing."

"He was probably trying to make a bit of a name for himself," suggested Mickey. "Came unstuck, though."

Following that achievement, and an undertaking from the employers that they would do their utmost to ensure that each twelve-hour spreadover had only one lengthy period of relief, Ben Smith turned the discussion back to wages.

"Assuming we can get agreement on the spreadover, I take it you would accept our figure with regard to the cost of living index figure of 120 before any reductions occur. That is a very fair offer, Lord Ashfield."

"What I will do," replied Ashfield, is consider the date when it is to come into operation."

"But assuming a steep redduction in prices, it means a very big drop in wages when it comes. I would rather a figure of 120. Assuming the figure of 135 and the implementation of the sliding scale in April, if the index reaches 100 it will mean a drop of seven shillings a week. Wallop! With rents as they are and so on, it is a horrible drop."

"It is regrettable, but we can do nothing, I will help if I possibly can."

Leaving the sliding scale for the moment, Ben Smith suggested that the penalty payment for all spreadovers in excess of ten hours should be one shilling and sixpence; the employers said that they would look at it.

This was eventually conceded, as was an amendment to the proposed wage-reduction for conductors, who would now lose only one-eighth of a penny per hour for every five-point reduction in the cost-of-living index.

*

"So what do you think, Mickey?" asked Barney as they gathered their papers together."

Mickey grinned. "Could have been a lot worse, couldn't it? The sliding scale will mean that if the cost of living index hits 100, drivers will, as Ben says, lose seven bob a week and conductors three and six. But in real terms we'll still be better off because of the lower cost of living. Yes, we've conceded the 12-hour spread, but in return for one and six per duty—that's nine bob a week if you work six spreads. Like I say: could have been a lot worse. You fancy a drink, Barney?"

"I would," said Barney, "if I wasn't meeting Sandy."

"Sandy?"

"Alessandra—the tall waitress who served at your wedding at Guido"s."

"But that was almost two years ago."

Barney winked. "That's how long we've been going out, mate."

45

"There was a letter from Papa today," Annette announced as they sat at dinner.

"Oh?"

Annette nodded emphatically. "Yes. We now have a communist party in Belgium."

"Well, that's good news. Isn't it? You don't seem very happy, sweetheart."

She shrugged. "It is very small. Perhaps five hundred members."

"But what is the population of Belgium?

"Approximately seven-and-a-half million."

Mickey closed his eyes and did a rapid mental calculation. "So your five hundred in Belgium would be the equivalent of something under three thousand in Britain." He smiled. "Your party is probably bigger than ours, sweetheart."

She brightened. "True. I had not looked at it in that way."

After dinner, the washing-up done, Mickey sat on the sofa reading *The Times* while Annette sat at the table studying the latest lesson in her correspondence course.

"I think I need cheering up, sweetheart."

"Oh? Well I think I might be able to do that, my love." She looked up from the exercise upon which she was working and gave him a twinkle.

"I'm sure you could, love, and maybe a little later we might put it to the test, but I was really thinking of something that would cheer both of us up."

"Yes, what I have in mind would make me happy also."

"Alright, you've convinced me, but what I have in mind would involve us leaving the house."

"This evening?"

He glanced down at his newspaper, which was open at the entertainment page. "No, Saturday evening, sweetheart."

"Are you going to tell me, my Mickey?"

"Saturday evening, the Albert Hall, Saint-Saëns' *Organ Symphony*."

"Oh yes! Yes please, my love! This is the symphony we have on the records."

"That's right, but to hear it played at the Albert Hall is another thing entirely. I went with Dick and Dorothy...six years ago. My goodness, six years! You will love it, sweetheart."

"And shall we ask Dick and Gladys to accompany us?"

He gave that a moment's thought. In truth, he did not want the occasion to resemble too much the 1915 visit with Dorothy. "No, just the two of us, sweetheart."

"Ohhh...Have you finished with the newspaper, my Mickey?"

"Why, do you want it?"

She pushed aside her books and stood. "No, my love, I want to come over there and cheer you up."

*

As in 1915, they sat in the western circle, although not this time in the front row. Six years ago, Mickey and Dick had looked across the theatre at the boxes opposite and spied Albert Stanley, as he was then, with his wife and party. Now, Mickey cast a wary glance at the boxes and received a jolt when he saw, in a box to the right of the one he had occupied in 1915, Lord Ashfield, his wife and two teenaged girls who he assumed were his daughters. As he and Annette were seated in the third row from the front it was unlikely that Ashfield would be able to identify him at this distance, but he took the precaution of concealing his face behind his programme before whispering to Annette, "You see the man in evening dress in the box almost opposite us? Yes, with the woman and two young girls. That's my employer, Lord Ashfield."

"Oh, he is *tres distingué*. Mickey."

"Well, yes, I suppose he is."

"You told me that you saw him here in 1915, Mickey. Why do you think he has come again?"

"Because he obviously likes it. Same as me. But we're here to cheer us up and he's here to celebrate."

"What has he to celebrate, Mickey?"

"A twelve-hour spreadover and a wage-cut, sweetheart."

The *Organ Symphony* was, when it came, wonderful. In the fourth movement that mighty C major chord hit Mickey in the chest, making him gasp at the wonder of it and he could sense that, sitting close to him and gripping his arm in excitement, Annette's whole body was alive. Then that rippling piano. And the sheer majesty of the final passages, led by the largest pipe organ in the world!

It suddenly came to him that his dissatisfaction with the piano recital he and Annette had attended just after their wedding had arisen from the fact that it would make little difference whether one listened to that music alone or at a concert, as it was aimed at the intellect rather than the emotions. Music such as the *Organ Symphony* or Tchaikovsky's *Violin Concerto*, on the other hand, although they could be heard from a gramophone, *demanded* to be appreciated in the company of a large audience so that one's spirits rose along with those of the multitude, combining with them until one felt that one's heart would burst with the cry: *we are humanity!*

He realised, of course, and had always realised, that this was illusory, for he was sure that this music meant different things to different people. To Mickey, the triumphant finale had always been the anthem to be played at the moment his class came to power, whereas that would not be true of tonight's audience, any more than it had been of those who had sat in this hall in 1915; then, for most it would have conjured visions of military victory over the Central Powers and tonight...what? A continuation of imperial greatness, or merely a return to better times? Both of these were, he considered, unlikely. And what was in Ashfield's mind as he rose for the almost obligatory standing ovation? The triumph of the mighty Traffic Combine? Possibly.

When they stood, Annette fell against him, throwing her arms about him. "Oh, Mickey, I have *never* heard anything like that before!"

As they made their way to the exit, Mickey walked slowly, almost dawdled.

"Mickey, why are you so slow? Are you alright?"

"I'm fine, sweetheart. I just want to avoid you-know-who."

Annette's mouth fell open. "But why, Mickey? Didn't you meet him here in 1915?"

"That was then, sweetheart. It would not be proper now."

46

"I see you've sent out the notices for the meeting of the organising committee," said Dick.

"Yep," replied Mickey. "Friday 28 October at the Crown and Anchor."

"Do you know that Brian Vernon has stolen a march on us?"

"In what way, mate?"

"He's arranged a breakaway meeting for the Wednesday and claims that he'll have tube men there to prove that a Tubes, Omnibuses and Trams union is a real possibility. His group is also campaigning against the wage proposals."

"Ah, that's just opportunism!" declared Mickey.

"I know, but he'll get a following. You realise there's a real possibility that the 14 October agreement will be rejected?"

"Of course."

"And then Vernon will claim that the result was due his group, and that in turn will build the breakaway movement."

Mickey was silent for some moments, brow furrowed. "Fuck it!" he oathed finally. "Okay, how are they mobilising for this meeting on the 26th?"

"They seem to be inviting anyone who's not connected with us," replied Dick. "They've got all sorts: some are genuinely convinced that a breakaway is the best option, some have never been to a meeting in their lives, others are disaffected for personal reasons—they didn't get elected to the position they thought they deserved, or they blame the union for the fact that they received a disciplinary award from the company or lost an appeal. Like I say, all sorts."

"Well, we need to get some people to that meeting—men who have perhaps attended one or two of our own but who are not firmly identified with us. Any ideas?"

"Well, there's the ex-copper who came to one of our meetings with Reuben."

"Sharkey. Yeah, he'd fit the bill. Let's see if the lads can rustle up a few more to go with him."

"And what do we want them to do once they're there?"

"Good question." Mickey gave it some thought. "Well, it depends on the size of the meeting, I suppose. If it's small, I would say they should get on their hind legs and argue against the breakaway scheme. Otherwise, just watch and listen, make a few notes and ask one or two awkward questions if the opportunity arises. But they'll really have to play it by ear." A pause. "Now what about these tube workers? Do we know who they are?"

Dick shook his head. "Not a clue, Mickey."

"Alright, I'll see if George can do some digging for us."

*

By arrangement with Bernard Sharkey, Mickey arrived at the Crown and Anchor thirty minutes early on the 28th.

Sharkey arrived a minute later, all knees and elbows, and made his way to the table where Mickey sat.

"Good evening, Brother Sharkey," Mickey greeted him, handing him a pint. "How did the so-called TOT meeting go?"

Sharkey scowled. "Only twenty in attendance, Mickey. It's Bernie, by the way."

Mickey smiled. "Okay, Bernie; and where was this?"

"A pub in Clapham. I suppose they decided to meet south of the river because that's where most of their support is. And, of course, it would be less likely that any of us would be there. From what I could make out, there were men from Plumstead, Old Kent Road, Merton, Morden and a couple of other south London sheds. Vernon blamed the poor attendance on the short notice."

"You think he was bullshitting?"

Sharkey took a sip of bitter. "Difficult to say, Mickey. Vernon claimed that the union hierarchy is more worried than they make out, says they know damn well that the TOT movement is strong and growing."

"But there were no tram men there?"

"A couple, I think."

"Was one of them Ernie Sharp from New Cross. You know him?"

Sharkey nodded. "Yeah, I know Ernie, and he wasn't there."

"In which case, their movement ain't growing on the trams. How about tube men?"

A shake of the head. "No, Vernon said he thought it would be a mistake to have 'em along at this first meeting, as he suspected the turnout wouldn't be up to much. He says he'll make sure they're at the next meeting."

"The other day, I asked George Sanders to have a word with his contacts in the NUR and ASLEF. George says they don't know of anybody who's interested in a breakaway." Mickey let his pensive gaze rest on the table between them for a moment before raising it to meet Sharkey's. "Do you think we've got anything to worry about, Bernie?"

"I think," said Sharkey slowly, frowning thoughtfully, "that we should be cautious."

"Sound advice, Bernie," Mickey nodded. "So tell me, how did Vernon back up his claim that the union hierarchy is worried about the breakaway movement?"

Sharkey dipped into the bag he carried on his shoulder and drew out the pamphlet concerning the July negotiations and opened it at the relevant page. "He used this, Mickey—the verbatim notes, where George suggested the insertion of a line agreeing that all platform staff should become and remain members of the union. Let me read it for you.

"'Mr Sanders: You tell them now that they have to be members of the union.

'Mr Shave: Yes, but we cannot put it in the agreement. We have done that,
and Lord Ashfield has told you that it is being carried out; but I do not want to put it in the agreement. There is no need to emphasise it.

'Mr Sanders: "The reason we put it in is, bluntly, because this committee thought it would have a great bearing on the members in getting this agreement through.

'Mr Shave: "It might do that; but we cannot agree to it.'

"So Vernon was claiming that George was so worried about the breakaway movement that he was asking the employers to put the closed shop arrangement in black and white, so that it would be clear to everyone that anyone who wasn't in the UVW would be out of a job." Sharkey shrugged. "You have to admit it's clever stuff."

"Were it not for the fact that Vernon missed out the bit where George explained that it was about silencing the handful of non-members who were always causing trouble."

"Yeah, but he was on safe ground there, because how many members have read the whole pamphlet?"

Mickey laughed. "Good point. So do they intend showing up here tonight, Bernie?"

"Oh yes! Vernon urged them all to attend and try to win the meeting over to the breakaway idea."

"And when is their own next meeting?"

"They're looking at a month's time, when they've had a chance to win over a few more. They're convinced the wage package will be rejected and they'll be using that to strengthen their case."

Mickey looked across the bar at the street door, through which men in London General uniforms were now beginning to enter. "Okay, Bernie, our audience is arriving, so we'll leave it there for now. But listen: no matter what nonsense the secessionists come out with tonight, keep your head down because we may need you to keep in with them—if that's alright with you."

Sharkey gave him a wink. "No problem."

*

Once they were assembled in the upstairs meeting room, Mickey saw that there were around thirty-five or forty of them, with no sign of the secessionists as yet.

Not wanting to be both chairman and main speaker, he nominated Ron Vickers of Shepherd's Bush to take the chair, and this met with the meeting's approval.

"Some of you must be wondering," Mickey began, "why we've left it so late to call this meeting. There were a couple of good reasons, brothers. First of all, if the branches had started to send in resolutions in September, the EC would simply have told them to submit amendments to the rules conference. Any amendment that was rejected by that conference, however, would be stone dead, and we couldn't afford to take that risk. Secondly, we've still got the wages question before us; many of us thought that would have been settled one way or the other by now, but the EC has taken its time in arranging the ballot.

"Any questions so far?"

At this moment, the door to the meeting room burst open and the secessionists—all seven of them—swept in and immediately demonstrated that they were intent on disruption.

"Any questions!" roared Brian Vernon. "Any bloody *questions*! Bloody loads of 'em, mate! How come you're only holding this meeting now? Why are you all listening to a man who negotiated the wage-cut?"

Ron Vickers, a big man in his early fifties, rose to his feet and thumped the table. "Enough!" He threw out his right arm, the forefinger aimed at Vernon. "You find a seat, and tell your gang to do the same."

"Or what?"

"Or you'll be thrown out!"

"Who by?"

For answer, Ron Vickers stepped from behind the table and began to stride towards the rear of the hall.

"Alright, alright, we haven't come here to fight," protested Brian Vernon, his hand raised, palms outward.

The chairman walked back to the table, winking at Mickey, and resumed his seat. "Continue, Brother Rice!"

Mickey put forward the package of measures which, he suggested, they should be demanding from the Transport and General Workers' Union: their own bus committee, a quarterly conference, the election of full-time officers...The meeting discussed these item by item, agreeing each; during this, the secessionists bided their time, saying nothing.

"And now comes the question," said Mickey, "of what we do to achieve this package."

Brian Vernon now sprang back to life. "Easy! When we form our own union, this is the structure we'll adopt! Many thanks for working it out for us, Brother Rice."

Mickey laughed at him. "You think it's as easy as that, Brother Vernon? Have you any idea how much this structure will cost? No, of course you don't, because you haven't given it a single thought! In all probability, this bus sub-section will *only* be possible within the TGWU, because the rest of the union will be subsidising us. Oh, I suppose if you went on your own you *could* do it by increasing the dues. Today, a driver pays sixpence a week. Are you going to tell them that it'll cost them double that if they join your breakaway, Brother Vernon?"

"Nonsense!" Vernon came back, demonstrating that he might have given the matter *some* thought. "Once we reduce the salaries and expenses of the full-timers there'll be no problem."

More laughter from Mickey. "So you think men will want to be full-timers at reduced wages in a union with no members?"

Grinning, Vernon stood and drew a copy of the pamphlet on the July negotiations from his pocket. "I think it's time we put this one to bed, Chairman. The UVW hierarchy, lay and full-time, are putting it about that we don't have a following. If that is the case, why did George Sanders ask the employers for a formal closed shop agreement in July?"

"Alright, Brother Vernon," replied a seemingly unperturbed Mickey, "tell us what Brother Sanders said. Read it!"

Vernon then repeated the few lines he had read to his own meeting two nights earlier, at the conclusion of which he held out the pamphlet in his left hand while pointing to the relevant passage with his right forefinger. "There it is, in black and white! Now why would he have made that request if he wasn't worried about our group?"

"And some of us, Brother Vernon," said Mickey Rice with narrowed eyes, "are asking ourselves why, if this was the case, George Shave turned him down flat!"

Most of the audience greeted this with a prolonged "Ooooo..." as they realised the implication of Mickey's riposte.

"But that to one side, Brother Vernon, why have you not quoted the entire exchange? Why have you left out the sentence where Brother Sanders *explains* his reason for making the request?" He picked up his own copy of the pamphlet from the table and turned to the relevant page. "This is what he said: 'There are one or two hardly worth talking about who cause trouble, who persistently refuse for reasons best known to themselves; they like to take the benefits from the organisation, but they do not want to pay their quota; those people cause a lot of trouble in the garages...' It is clear, Brother Vernon, that you have been misleading your few followers, because Brother Sanders was not talking about you at all!"

Surprisingly, Vernon was not at all knocked off his stride. "No, I agree he wasn't talking about us *openly*, but it was us he was worried about; it was because of us that he made the request." He chuckled and looked around the audience. "How much trouble is caused by the handful of non-members—if there are any—in your garages, brothers?" When this was greeted by almost total silence, he nodded. "That's right: none at all. But there have been other occasions, Chairman, when Brother Sanders has *explicitly* warned of the danger of a breakaway. Not a nuisance! Not a small problem! The *danger* of a breakaway, brothers. Now, if we're so small, how can we be a *danger*?"

Got you now, thought Mickey. How are you possibly going to justify this claim? "So tell us, Brother Vernon," he said, brimming with confidence, "where Brother Sanders is supposed to have said this!"

"At the Annual Delegate Meeting in Sheffield. Bear in mind, now, that the ADM was held in May. If we were a danger in May, what must we be now, when it's almost November!"

Mickey turned to frown at Ron Vickers, who had been a delegate to the ADM. "Did George say that, Ron?" he murmured.

A grimace from Ron. "He did, Mickey."

Mickey turned back to Vernon. "Then he was obviously ill-advised!"

Vernon seemed to find this hilarious. "Ill-advised? Ill-bloody-ad*vised*? I'll tell you when he *was* ill-advised!" he shouted, shifting the focus of his attack. "He was ill-advised when he placed that damned agreement before us with a foreword that even a blind man could see was a recommendation to accept! He was even *more* ill-advised when he *actually* recommended that we accept the latest offer! And you're a party to that, Brother Rice, as a member of the Wages Board."

"Then you know what to do about it, don't you?"

"Oh, we'll vote to reject alright—thousands of us!—but we'll do more than that."

"Brother Vernon," warned Ron Vickers, "there will be mass meetings on the wages question in a week or so where you'll have the opportunity to make your points. *This* meeting was called for one specific reason, and that is not it, so let's get back to the subject under discussion."

"Ah, but it's all connected," persisted Vernon. "Even if you get the structure you're looking for, you'll be no better off in the Transport and General Workers' Union, because the chances are the same people will be pulling the strings. We want the resignation of the Wages Board, including George Sanders—a clean sweep. And if that's not possible we'll have a completely new union—one which will refuse to negotiate with the companies on the questions of longer spreadovers and lower wages!"

"So you'll just strike until they drop the demands?"

"Of course."

"How's your strike fund? Pretty flush, is it?" Mickey was grateful that Vernon had switched the focus, as he now had the opportunity to regain some ground. He turned to Ron Vickers. "Chairman, it's fairly obvious that Brother Vernon is out of his depth here, so I agree with you that we should return to the matter in hand. How do we impress our ideas for a London bus sub-section on the leadership? What we must do, surely, is to..."

Vernon was on his feet. "You're all wasting your time here!" he declared, addressing the audience directly. "The only way forward is to get together with the tubes and the trams and form a union that will have the strength to stand up to the Traffic Combine! Follow me if you agree!" With that, he walked to the door followed by the six companions who had arrived with him and, after a nod from Mickey, Bernard Sharkey. But Mickey was watching the audience carefully and he could see that a few of the less regular attendees of these unofficial meetings were tempted.

47

"I need to ask you something, George."

George Sanders looked up from his desk and saw Mickey Rice standing at the door. He gestured in the direction of the chair on the other side of the desk. "Then you'd better come in, Mickey."

"I'd be interested in your assessment of the breakaway movement, George," Mickey asked once he was seated.

"Do you want my assessment of its size, its quality, or its chances of success?" Sanders was bent over a pad, swiftly covering its surface with a scrawl; he didn't look up.

"Its chances of success," Mickey replied, "although I don't suppose you can really discuss that without consideration of the other two."

"No, probably not." Sanders pushed the pad away from him. "Still write my correspondence in longhand," he explained. "I just can't get comfortable with shorthand."

"Do you think they're dangerous, George? Are they in with a chance?"

"I think they're in with a chance of causing a lot of disruption that will play into the hands of the companies, Mickey, so in that sense they're dangerous. But of forming a TOT union?" He shook his head. "Nah."

"So back in July, when you put forward the suggestion of writing the closed-shop arrangement into the agreement, did you have them in mind?"

"Of course I did."

"But you said nothing to us."

"At that stage, I saw no point in causing alarm unnecessarily, but I could see that, a bit further down the line, the secessionists might become a problem."

"Vernon has latched onto that, you know."

"Onto what?"

"Your request to have the closed shop spelled out in the agreement. He's picked it up in the verbatim notes we included in the pamphlet and is claiming that it's clear evidence that he had us worried. He's also using what you said at the ADM as further evidence."

Sanders shrugged. "Well he's right in a sense. I'm worried that he and his followers will cause disruption—and at a critical point, what with the wages problem."

"I've been wondering why Shave was so firm in his rejection of your suggestion, George." Mickey studied Sanders closely, wondering whether the same suspicion had appeared in his mind.

"Well, very often closed-shop agreements are verbal; you won't find too many in the written agreements." But then Sanders caught Mickey's look. "Ohhh, you think the companies turned down my suggestion in order to *help* the secessionists?"

"The possibility has crossed my mind, George."

Sanders chuckled. "Anything's possible, I suppose, but I would be surprised if Shave would involve himself in that sort of thing. And Ashfield certainly wouldn't."

"Shave commanded the London General's special constabulary during the war, so he must have plenty of contacts in the security forces."

"True enough, but...No, I can't see Shave playing dirty like that. *Some*body in the company maybe..."

Seeing that Sanders was not convinced, Mickey shifted the focus. "So what's your estimation of the *quality* of the secessionists?"

"From what I understand, they're mostly malcontents led by an opportunist."

"You've been speaking to Bernie."

Sanders smiled. "I have, Mickey. I see you've put him into the secessionist camp as your spy—smart move, that."

"Thanks. But to be honest, George, Bernie's assessment is on the basis of his attendance of *one* secessionist meeting. I think there are a few honest and sincere men who have become involved with Vernon and quite a few more who are thinking about it; and that's what worries me."

"If they're really honest and sincere, Mickey, the sooner we can expose Vernon for the chancer he is, the better."

Mickey chuckled. "I think of almost nothing else, George. I've asked around, and he seems to be a bit of a mystery man: came on the job less than two years ago, completed his first year's membership and then stood for rep and started putting himself about. On the wages question, of course, he's campaigning for rejection."

"Of course. But will he succeed?"

"I think the package will be rejected, but not that his group will necessarily be responsible for it."

Suddenly, Sanders looked grim. "Is there that much opposition to it in the garages, Mickey?"

Mickey nodded. "Of course, George. Twelve-hour spreads and a wage-cut: just a year ago you were as opposed to that sort of thing as anyone."

"And I still am, for Christ's sake! But it's one thing being opposed to something and another to find a way to defeat it." He sighed. "So you're convinced that the package will be rejected. Then tell me this: once it's rejected, will the members vote for a strike?"

"To be honest, George, I wouldn't put money on it."

Sanders sat up straight. "Oh? What makes you say that, Mickey?"

Mickey thought carefully for a moment. "The old fighting spirit is no longer as widespread as it used to be, George." He grinned. "Funnily enough, our successes are partly responsible for that—the 1919 agreement in particular." For some time now, Mickey had thought that the unity of the men had been diluted by the improved conditions. No longer bound together by common misery and the need to struggle against it, some had drifted into a new conformity.

Sanders reached for his pad and pulled it to him. "Okay, Mickey, thanks for coming in to cheer me up. Next step, the mass meetings."

Mickey nodded at him. "Good luck, George."

"Yeah, I'll need a bit of that by the sound of it."

*

A few days later, Mickey came across Ron Vickers in the canteen at Liverpool Street station; Ron, like Mickey a rep who did not avoid driving a bus whenever possible, was working on route 11. As they left the counter, Ron pointed to a table in an almost deserted corner of the large canteen—an indication that he wanted a quiet word.

Through a sea of blue uniforms and tobacco smoke, the big man led the way with what could only be described as a lumbering gait, nodding now and then to acquaintances; he was widely liked and respected and had a presence that was authoritative, such that Mickey was usually surprised when Ron deferred to him.

Ron placed his tea on the table and, taking out his tobacco tin, began to roll a cigarette. He raised his eyes to Mickey. "This Vernon cunt," his deep voice rumbled, "is turning out to be more of a problem than we thought." He licked the edge of the paper and gave the cigarette a final roll. He struck a match and brought it to the cigarette and, narrowing his eyes against the smoke, took a drag. "He's got a few in my garage taking up his cause. One of 'em tells me that he's arranging a number of local meetings in various parts of London, building up a network."

Mickey's tea sat before him, untouched. "So how many has he got at the Bush?"

"Five or six."

"And what's their story, Ron?"

Ron sighed. "That's what makes me so bloody mad: they're good men, loyal as the day is long."

"So how has he hooked 'em?"

"It's this damned package we'll be voting on next week!"

"So it's not that they particularly want a different union?"

"Nah, not at all." He checked himself. "Well, *hardly* at all: they want a union that will save 'em from long spreadovers and lower wages, and if the one they've got can't—or, as they see it, won't—do it, they'll be interested in an alternative."

"So do they think that we can force the company to withdraw this package?" Mickey raised his eyebrows. "Do *you* think we can, Ron?"

Tapping the ash from his roll-up, Ron flashed his eyes at Mickey. "Listen, Mickey, I'm not completely fuckin' daft. The company is always shouting the odds about us being the only group of workers who still receive the full war wage. If they thought that we were gonna fight like hell to make sure we *continue* to get it, the company—and the government—would pull out the stops to make sure that didn't happen. Come that day, this canteen would be full of squaddies having their meal reliefs off of route 7 and route 11. They would starve us back to work like they did the miners back in June." Ron shrugged. "And who would come to our support? Jimmy Thomas? Don't make me laugh!"

"Have you told 'em this?"

Ron grinned. "Not yet. After the ballot will be the time for that."

"Surely you mean *before* the ballot, Ron."

"No, I think the package should be rejected, and that's how I'll vote." He tapped the table-top with a fingernail. "Look,'—first listen, now look: perceive—"I know what the company is going to do to me but I'm damned if I'll give 'em my permission to do it!"

Mickey nodded. Yes, he perceived. He glanced around the room and saw several heads turned in their direction: if two reps, one of them a member of the Wages Board, were engaged in a private discussion, there must be something afoot.

"So you think the Wages Board is wrong to recommend acceptance?"

"I do, because you've ended up turning a good part of the members against you." He leaned forward. "I *know* that you've got from the company all that it's prepared to give. But that's not a reason to recommend acceptance."

"Then the company would accuse us of not having the courage to tell the facts of life to the membership."

"Who *cares* what the company says! Besides, if you tell 'em *why* you're recommending rejection—the way I just explained it to you—they're bound to respect that. Then comes the ballot for strike action: *that's* when the members will have to be told the facts of life."

"But if the members don't vote for a strike the company will just impose the package."

"That's right, but they'll be under no illusion that they have our permission to do it. *And*, more important, the members will know that and respect you for it. At the moment, it seems to them as if George Sanders and the Wages Board have agreed to help the company out in difficult times, and that's a major reason why Brian Vernon is picking up support, Mickey."

"Ah well."

"What?"

"It's too late to change the recommendation now."

"That's right, Mickey. But it's as well you know why you're in the pickle you're in."

No deference today, then. Mickey smiled. "And I thank you for that, Ron."

48

On Wednesday, 9 November, the Middle Row members attended the mass meetings at Cricklewood Labour Club at 10.30 in the morning and at Cricklewood Council School at 7.30 in the evening; both were in Cricklewood Lane. There was, Mickey knew, a reason for this arrangement, and for similar ones across London: to hire theatres and picture palaces would have meant midnight meetings, but these were held when the union was on the offensive, whereas today it was on the back foot; the usual purpose of a midnight meeting was to wind the members up to fever pitch, whereas the aim today was to keep them calm.

The upshot was that the venue was barely able to contain the members from Middle Row, Cricklewood, Willesden, Shepherd's Bush and Dollis Hill, and when Mickey arrived at 10.25 he had to shoulder his way in. He looked around and saw many people he knew, and not just from Middle Row. But it was the figure of George Sanders who sat at the table at the head of the room that got his attention.

Sanders looked as tired and worn as Mickey had ever seen him, much older than his 50 years. George was like the midnight mass meeting: you used him when you needed to get the members in a mood to fight; but he had little experience of advising the members to retreat, and he was clearly uncomfortable with the prospect. Furthermore, George was a man wedded to the principle of the election of full-time officers, and because he *was* elected he had in the past taken chances in defying the authority of those above him, and so the recent resignation calls had placed an additional strain on him, shaking his self-confidence. The ashtray at his side already contained several stubs and he was surrounded by a blue haze.

Eventually, Sanders uttered a long sigh, pushed himself to his feet—he seemed, in fact, to have to *force* himself to stand—and began to take them through it, emphasising that the company had first proposed to make a cut of three shillings a week in October— *last* month—whereas now their earnings were safe until next April. And if reductions were made, it would be in the war wage, not in the basic wage of a shilling and twopence an hour, or 56 bob a week, established in the 1919 negotiations. For every five points that the cost of living index fell below 135 points, the war wage, currently 10 and five-eighths pence per hour, would be reduced by a farthing for drivers and an eighth of a penny for conductors: a shilling a week and sixpence a week, respectively, the adjustments to be made quarterly.

The purpose of these meetings was to explain the proposals, and so Sanders was not so much making a speech as delivering a tutorial, and after each major point he would pause for questions.

"I thought," said one conductor, "that it was the job of the trade union to negotiate improvements in our wages and conditions, so why have you come to us with a *worsening*?" This cheap shot—or maybe, thought Mickey, the conductor genuinely did not understand the situation—received a predictable ripple of applause.

"I'll make two points," said Sanders, his tone more spirited now as he rose to the challenge. "First of all, it is not the trade union that is making these proposals, but the company! What we're placing before you is what's left of the *company's* proposals after we've argued the toss with them for six months. Secondly, the brother says that it's our job to get improvements in your wages and conditions. And that is what we did throughout the war years when prices were going through the roof, and sometimes we had to have a scrap about it. That was how we got the war wage. Now, though, the boot's on the other foot and prices are falling. Should we be surprised that the company now wants some of its money back? Of course not! We may not like it, but we shouldn't be surprised. It becomes a question of *how much* they take back. If we end up persuading them to take back less than they advanced in the war wage, you're better off, aren't you? Not in cash, but in real terms.

"Let me explain what I mean. According to the company's proposals, if the index goes as low as 85, the reductions will be a farthing an hour, or a bob a week, for everyone. So, with prices at 85—a sixth less than in 1914—your hourly war wage—let's take the driver for the sake of this example—would be reduced by...how much? Is there a mathematician in the house?"

He actually had them laughing.

"Well," said Willesden's Reuben Topping, "85 is 50 points lower than the 135 starting point, so that's ten reductions at a farthing a time: tuppence-ha'penny."

"Exactly!" said Sanders. "Thank you, Reuben. So that would mean that while prices were almost a sixth less than they were in 1914, you'd *still* be getting just over eightpence an hour in war wage. What's that if it's not the same as a wage-rise?"

Mickey found it interesting to watch the various reactions to this: some—possibly conductors, more accustomed to mathematical calculations than their drivers—were nodding to indicate that, yes, this made sense, while some others frowned or shrugged.

"Sounds alright when you say it like that, maybe," cried one dissident, "but that tuppence-ha'penny works out at ten bob a week!" This proved a rallying-point for those who were determined to resist the proposals regardless of any persuasive explanations.

Sanders shrugged. "At a time when your weekly expenses might have reduced by *fifteen* bob!" he responded.

"I seem to recall," said a Cricklewood driver, "that whenever we applied for a war bonus, we ended up at the Committee on Production. So why don't we take this little lot to arbitration?"

"Because," Sanders replied in a flash, "the arbitrator would do the same calculation we've just done and send us away with a flea in our ear."

This got him some laughter and all of a sudden he seemed to be almost enjoying himself, as he seemed to have convinced a large part of the meeting that they would, in fact, be better off in real terms under the proposed sliding scale. But Mickey knew that it couldn't last.

And it didn't, of course, because he next dealt with the twelve-hour maximum spreadover. Surprisingly enough, he started off by repeating much of the company's argument as to why the long spread was necessary—the need to provide an adequate service in both the morning and afternoon peaks, the impossibility of doing this with a spread of ten or eleven hours, and so on. "In all of this," he said, "we have to remember that the travelling public pays our wages, and so their interest has to be considered." He was, Mickey considered, making a mistake by pursuing this line, as he was sounding more like a company spokesman—even if what he said was correct.

"Now just remember," Sanders advised, 'that they started out by demanding thirteen hours, then they came down to twelve-and-a-half and eventually settled at twelve. Now I know how you all feel about this..." The clamour coming up from the meeting demonstrated that he had that right. "...But we've made sure that this won't be anything like a return to the old conditions. Gone are the days when you would be expected to work on three or even four buses during a long spread. Gone are the days when the non-working time would be split into two or three useless breaks. You will work on two buses and have one long break—with the exception of five percent of duties, which will give the schedulers a bit of flexibility if they need it. Furthermore, the company will ensure that you'll not be booked to work a long spread in consecutive weeks; on average, it'll come around once in every four weeks. And you'll be compensated: one and sixpence for every duty with a spreadover in excess of ten hours. So if you do six long spreads in your working week, you'll be nine bob better off."

Opinion was divided on this, with the more recent recruits savouring the thought of an extra nine shillings every four weeks and the older hands recoiling from memories of the utter exhaustion to which long spreads had reduced them during the war.

First on his feet was a bearded driver from Willesden. "Brother Sanders, I joined the red-button union as soon as it was formed in 1913. And I know that the one demand which that union consistently put forward was to reduce spreadover length. Year after year the demand was made, and year after year the company knocked it back, until in 1919 we finally achieved the ten-hour maximum spread—even though we wanted nine hours. And here we are, just two years later, and the United Vehicle Workers is prepared to throw it away!" He looked about the room, palms outstretched. "For some time, Brother Sanders, there has been talk of forming a TOT union—getting together with the trams and the tubes—but I paid no attention to it." A pause while his glare swept the room. "But now—NOW, Brother Sanders—I'm beginning to think that this might be the way forward for us. And, let me tell you, I'm not the only one who's thinking along these lines!"

This evoked a murmur of assent from a disturbingly numerous section of the meeting.

"You're missing a number of points, brother," Sanders replied. "First, the twelve-hour spread will be limited to 25 percent of duties. Secondly, the whole of the life of the red-button union was spent in a period when the labour movement was on the offensive, and that's certainly not the case at the moment! Then again..."

The Willesden man would not let him finish. "Do you think the company's finished with us? They tried to get you to agree to twelve-hour spreads for the past two years, and this year they came back and got it. And how did they start off this year? By demanding thirteen hours! Don't you see that they'll be back next year to make sure they get it?"

"Then they'll have a fight on their hands, won't they?"

"Will they? I don't see any signs of you blokes offering to lead a fight this year, so why would you change your spots in 1922?"

This set the tone for the remainder of the meeting, with Sanders doing his best. As much he tried to direct their attention to the lesser elements in the package, they insisted on coming back to the twelve-hour spreadover, and it was clear to Mickey that this would sink the package. It seemed to be clear to Sanders also, for he had lost whatever bounce he had gained during discussion of the sliding scale and when he closed the meeting his reminder that the Wages

Board was urging acceptance in Friday's ballot was almost perfunctory.

*

The following Monday evening, Stanley Hirst, George Sanders, Ben Smith and the Wages Board assembled at Transport House and witnessed the tally of the ballot results which had been sent through the post by each garage branch. Before the tally began, the members of the Wages Board compared notes on the twenty mass meetings which had been held at ten locations, and it seemed that most had gone the same way as the one at Cricklewood Labour Club, although breakaway sentiments had not been expressed at all of them. The tally was conducted by a couple of staff members on overtime, one calling out each result and the other chalking it up on a blackboard in the executive chamber. As the tally progressed, it was clear to all present that the package would be rejected. The final result: 3,134 for acceptance and 6,832 for rejection.

Mickey Rice kept his eye on Stanley Hirst, as his reaction was bound to be entertaining. If Hirst had been wearing a hat, thought Mickey, he would have snatched it from his head and hurled it on the floor, stamping on it in impotent rage. "Damn and buggeration! There are times when I regret this bloody amalgamation! What do the London busmen want, for God's sake?"

"It's more a case of what they don't want," said Sanders.

"Well, what do we do now? I suppose we'll have to have a strike ballot. And then, even worse, bear the expense of strike pay!"

"The next step," said Sanders, "will be a return to Electric Railway House to see what the companies intend to do."

"And what will that be, d'ye think?"

"I think they might impose the agreement. That'll be the time to talk about a strike ballot."

"Bloody hellfire!" Hirst placed a hand on his forehead then whipped it away as another thought occurred to him. "And I suppose you know they're bombarding Ernie Bevin with branch resolutions, calling for their own section in the new union!" The hand flew out in Mickey's direction, while his eyes remained on Sanders. "All encouraged by your apprentice here!"

"Hang on, Stan," intervened Johnny Mills. "There's nothing wrong in what Mickey's doing. Unless you'd prefer to have a breakaway!"

Hirst seemed to have overlooked the fact that he was surrounded by busmen, and he was now forced to retreat as others entered the discussion to support Mickey. Mickey looked across at Mills and gave him a grin and a nod. Thanks, Johnny.

"Breakaway? *Break*away?" Hirst echoed. "That's all a load of talk. I've come across plenty of that in my time, I can tell you!"

"Well, it wasn't all talk in 1915 was it?" said Mickey. "Although that wasn't strictly speaking a breakaway, of course." No, it was when a huge number of London tramworkers in Hirst's blue-button union, disgusted with that union's failure to speedily declare its support for the tram strike of that year, had come over to the red-button.

Hirst reddened, glaring at Mickey. "In my book," he seethed, "you're no better than the secessionists. You won't be satisfied until you get back to your red-button ways of doing things."

How to bring Stanley Hirst nearer to explosion? Give him a smile. "You're right enough with that last observation," Mickey conceded with a smile. "But the secessionists are a mixed bag, and although some of them might be perfectly sincere, if they want a return to the red-button days they're going the wrong way about it."

The explosion did not come. Instead, Hirst sat staring at Mickey and breathing deeply until the sparking fuse fizzled out. In those moments, Mickey saw, Hirst had been forced to come to terms with his own impotence, realising that whatever control he might have over Mickey Rice—and that was not much—would completely disappear in six weeks' time.

"However," said Mickey, offering something of an olive branch, "I think you may get away without paying a penny in strike pay."

"Why do you say that, Mickey?" asked Ben Smith, coming in when Hirst seemed averse to talking to Mickey.

Mickey shrugged. "Because I don't think we'll get a majority for a strike."

Ben looked around the table. "What do the rest of you say? Is Mickey right?"

"It'll be close," conceded Johnny Mills with a nod.

"Yeah, I agree with that," said Willy Hammond. He turned his palm from side to side. "Could go either way."

"Wouldn't like to say," said Chris Platten.

No one declared their belief that a majority could be achieved for a strike.

"Well now," said Stanley Hirst, warming to the subject, "that *is* interesting. But why? Why wouldn't the two-thirds that have voted to reject the new terms, not also vote for a strike?"

"The other day, I had a chat with one of the reps in my division," said Mickey, "and he told me that he would be voting against both the new terms *and* a strike. When I asked him why, he said that the company and the government would use all means available to crush a strike, but he was damned if he would give the company his permission to worsen his terms and conditions."

There were nods and chuckles from the other members of the Wages Board, who could see the logic of such a position.

"Now, I'm not saying that there are many members who share that view," Mickey continued, "although the rep in question said that he'd be arguing that position in the event of us holding a strike ballot. But in addition to that, as I was saying to George in a recent chat, I get the impression that the improvements we made in 1919 have softened the men; there's not that anger and bitterness they used to display during the war years when the company was working 'em half to death."

Sanders laughed. "Yes, I remember you saying that Mickey, but when I took those two mass meeting in Cricklewood last week I got the impression there was still quite enough anger and bitterness to go around!"

"Yes," Mickey agreed, "enough to reject the new terms by a two-thirds majority but not enough, I'll bet, to secure a majority in a strike ballot."

"Well listen," said Hirst, "if we're all convinced that we won't get a majority, what will be the point in holding a strike ballot anyway?"

"Oh, I haven't heard anyone say they're *convinced* there wouldn't be a majority," said Ben Smith. "And let's face it, if the companies tell us they're going to *impose* the new terms, we're duty bound to hold a strike ballot. Imagine if we didn't! Who would be the villains in the eyes of the membership? *Us!*"

That settled it, although the EC would have to take the formal decision, if that became necessary.

*

It did become necessary, of course.

The LGOC used the press to advise the public of its complete surprise at the ballot result, coming as it did after six months of negotiation and potentially thwarting company plans to provide enhanced levels of service during the peaks and introduce reduced fares during the midday slack period in an attempt to encourage greater ridership. On the Friday of that week, the company and its allies met the United Vehicle Workers and the Transport Workers' Federation at Electric Railway House.

Lord Ashfield gave this one a miss, as did Stanley Hirst, but Blain was back to lead the employers' side.

"You probably don't need me to tell you, gentlemen," said H.E. Blain, looking stern and determined, "how everyone on this side of the table—and, indeed, throughout our companies—was shocked, surprised and disappointed at this ballot result…"

"Shock and disappointment I can accept, Mr Blain," said George Sanders, "but you can only have been surprised if your local officials were completely out of touch with the feeling of the men. We"—both arms outstretched to indicate the men either side of him—"said we would recommend acceptance of your terms—not because we thought them wonderful but because we were convinced that you would make no further movement—and we did that, hard as it was. And it was clear to us that the ballot result would be rejection. So we were not surprised by that result, and I doubt very much whether you were."

Sanders was speaking out of turn, as Ben Smith and Bob Williams should have been leading for the trade union side, but neither gave any sign of objection.

"Then maybe," said Blain, "I should have said that we were surprised by the feelings of the men."

"But we made it abundantly clear," said Ben Smith, "that there was a great fear of a return to the bad old days, and that this fear was caused by your insistence on the twelve-hour spreadover."

Blain fell silent for a few moments, regarding the men on the other side of the table. Then, obviously concluding that further discussion would be fruitless, he cleared his throat and made the announcement the trade union side had expected. "Well, gentlemen, you have left us with no alternative. I have to advise you, therefore, that new schedules incorporating the changes contained in the last document we issued will come into operation at the end of this month."

"Your announcement was not unanticipated," replied Bob Williams. "You, in turn, leave *us* with no alternative, and I therefore advise that the executive council of the United Vehicle Workers will be balloting the operating staff members employed by your companies for strike action."

Blain stood. "I see. In that case, good afternoon, gentlemen."

49

The following week, Mickey was on an early turn which finished at just after two. He liked these winter afternoons when, having several hours to himself, he would return to the flat in Alexander Street, prepare and consume a light lunch and then sit before the gas fire, dozing over a book until it was time to prepare the dinner for himself and Annette. Upon arrival on the Tuesday afternoon, however, he found a note which Annette had placed on the dining table before leaving for work that morning: "Dear Mickey, in the first post this morning I received a letter from a friend in Camden Town, where I used to live. After work, I will be going to see her and so I will not be home until seven or seven-thirty. I will explain everything when I see you. Love, Annette."

Mickey stretched luxuriantly. Almost five hours to himself!

He expected Annette to look weary and a little drawn, but not a bit of it: having let herself in, she looked over her shoulder as she closed the door and he could see that while the way she was biting her lower lip indicated a degree of trepidation, there was about her eyes a twinkle which promised a pleasant surprise.

He went to her and helped her off with her coat. "What was the problem, sweetheart? Was your friend ill?"

Turning to him, she gave her head a vigorous shake. "No, no, Mickey, nothing like that." She looked up at him and placed her palms on his chest. "Please do not be angry."

He grinned. "I promise."

"I have been to see an apartment, Mickey. The letter from my friend told me that this apartment—quite close to where I used to live with my parents—was for sale, and..." She broke out in a wide smile, eager now to convey her news. "And, Mickey, it is so lovely! Two bedrooms, a very large living room, a very clean and spacious bathroom..."

"Furnished, sweetheart?"

"No, my Mickey, it is not for rent but for sale..."

"Oh, yes, so you said. So how much?"

"£300."

"Oh, I don't know, sweetheart..."

"But Mickey, you agreed that we would need a larger place if we were to start a family."

"Yes, but you're not...Are you?"

"Yes, Mickey!"

*

They left their dinner to get cold and stepped down to Westbourne Grove to take a taxi to Camden Town. Sitting in the back of the cab, Mickey could not take his eyes off her. He had never seen her look so happy. When she had confirmed her pregnancy she had been— the only word for it!—radiant. She sat now, clasping his hand in hers, now and again squeezing it, swallowing, shaking her head as if unable to believe the double good fortune that appeared to have descended on her. Ridiculously, he found himself wondering how he would explain the accident to the cabdriver if she wet herself.

And how was Mickey taking it? He was, understandably, swollen with pride. He recalled how he had once had a desire for a child— eventually—with Dorothy, a desire which had remained unvoiced because he had lacked the confidence that she would share it. And yet here he was, unplanned by either of them, or so he assumed, an expectant father. He smiled contentedly and suddenly understood the convention—so he had been led to believe—for men in his situation to indulge in a cigar.

Then there was the apartment. As they passed the zoo, practical considerations began to announce themselves. What about work? He could transfer to Chalk Farm, of course, but the Farm already had a pretty good rep. Or he could buy a bicycle and continue to work at Middle Row. How would he pay for the apartment? He still had £500 of the money left by Dorothy which had been gathering interest since her death in 1917. He could use that, but he had promised himself that this would be, as Dorothy had intended, used for the movement. He and Annette were a prudent couple and they had a healthy little savings account, and so they could put down a deposit and take out a small mortgage. But why pay interest to a bank when it was unnecessary? In addition, there would be furniture to buy. Then again, there would come a time when Annette would not be earning. While he recalled Bob Williams reporting that women in Soviet Russia were afforded generous maternity leave arrangements, he knew for a fact that few if any British employers considered this an obligation. But did this extend to trade unions? He was forced—somewhat ashamed—to admit that he simply did not know whether his wife's employer, the United Vehicle Workers, soon to be the Transport and General Workers' Union, granted paid maternity leave to its female staff. These factors persuaded him that if they were to buy this apartment he would need to dip into Dorothy's money and maybe replenish it over a period of years.

By the time they reached Camden Town, such considerations had somewhat dampened his enthusiasm for the venture.

"What are you thinking, Mickey?" asked Annette, puzzled by his pensive silence.

He smiled reassuringly, squeezed her hand and brought it to his lips. "I was thinking, sweetheart," he said, "that I might need to buy a bicycle."

*

Whatever qualms Mickey might have had were quickly dispelled when he saw the apartment—actually a maisonette with its own green street door next to a stationary shop on Greenland Street, just off the High Street. While Mickey paid off the cab, Annette used the knocker to summon the owner, a middle-aged railway official called Gower who was, he explained as he led them upstairs, being transferred to the north.

The door at the top of the stairs opened directly into a spacious living room which, apart from the small kitchen at the rear of the building, occupied the whole floor. Here they met Mrs Gower and the couple's teenaged son, both of whom stood awkwardly when the strangers entered. As he closed the door behind him, Mickey's attention was drawn to the wall between the door and the front of the house, which was completely occupied with bookshelves. Many of the volumes were, he saw, concerned with railway history and the technicalities associated with that field of endeavour; there was a set of encyclopaedias—obviously the son's—and various novels by Dickens and the Bronte sisters.

"If you're a reading man, Mr Rice," said the homeowner, "I can leave the bookshelves for you; if not, I'll just take them down and dispose of them, as they obviously won't fit in our new place in Leeds."

Mickey chuckled. "Oh, we're a reading couple, Mr Gower, and so if we end up taking the place I'm sure we'd be very grateful if you would leave them." He turned with the intention of obtaining Annette's agreement on this point, but found that she had gone with Mrs Gower to the kitchen. He stood back and regarded the room in silence, imagining the two of them here on a winter's evening like this one, reading or listening to music on the gramophone.

Upstairs, they saw that the bathroom, which sat over the kitchen, was just as Annette had described it, spacious and clean. Mickey turned on one of the faucets at the washbasin and let it run for a few seconds before testing it with his fingers. He nodded in satisfaction. "Nice and hot. What are the gas bills like, Mr Gower?"

"Oh, quite reasonable, Mr Rice, quite reasonable. I can show you the last couple if you'd like me to."

Given the space required for the landing, the two bedrooms were not quite half the dimensions of the living room; even so, they were more than adequate and Mickey thought that the modest bookcase they had purchased for the flat in Alexander Street could be installed in their bedroom.

"Have you made a decision, Mickey?" asked Annette after Mr Gower had returned to the living room in order the give them a few moments alone.

Mickey nodded. "Yes, I have, sweetheart."

"What is it, Mickey?" Her hands were on his forearm, squeezing, urging, imploring. "Please tell me, *mon chérie.*"

"Are you ready for this, my love?"

"Yes!"

"I've decided to buy a bicycle."

*

The following afternoon, Mickey visited the office of solicitor Sidney Landles in Notting Hill Gate. Sidney was a comrade and his flat in Gloucester Terrace was often used for education classes and party branch meetings.

"Mickey!" he cried as the bus driver, still in uniform, entered his private office; he was the kind of solicitor who wore his glasses on the end of his nose so that he could peer over them at you. "What brings you to this centre of bourgeois legal expertise?"

"I need a bourgeois legal favour, Sid," replied Mickey cheerfully. He sat opposite the solicitor at his desk, thinking that this was a bit like being in the garage superintendent's office.

'Well, judging from your high spirits, I doubt whether you require representation in one of His Majesty's courts, so..." Having thought for a moment, he threw up his hands. "I'm blowed if I know, Comrade. How can I help you, Mickey?"

Comrade he might be, thought Mickey, but it had obviously not occurred to Sidney Landles that a mere bus driver might be an aspiring homeowner. "I need a cheap conveyancing, Sid." He grimaced in self-deprecation. "I hope I'm not one of a long line of comrades asking you for this particular favour."

"As a matter of fact, Mickey," replied Landles, masking his surprise, "you're not: those of our members who are comfortably off don't need it, and most working-class comrades are in rented accommodation. Lowering his head, he peered over his glasses. "Got a mortgage?"

"I'll be paying cash, Sid."

This time, the solicitor's surprise could not be so easily concealed. "Ah, I keep forgetting that you busmen are now up there with the aristocracy of labour."

Mickey hoped he wouldn't now ask why, if he could afford to pay cash, he was seeking cut-rate conveyancing services.

"Haven't fallen out with Dick and Gladys, have you?"

"No, Sid, Annette's pregnant, so we'll be needing a little more room."

Landles sprang to his feet and proffered his hand across the desk. "Oh, congratulations Mickey! My heartiest congratulations!" He sank back onto his chair and, grinning, pointed a finger at his new client. "Just as well you told me that, Mickey, because I was about to turn you down, but for Annette I'll do it!"

*

That evening, Mickey and Annette broke the news to the couple downstairs.

Advised of Annette's pregnancy, Gladys embraced her, pouring out her congratulations while sober Dick, a broad smile on his face, pumped Mickey's hand.

"The bad news, however," said Mickey, "is that we'll be moving."

"Oh, bugger!" said Dick, "I hadn't thought of that. But there's no rush, surely."

Mickey outlined the events of the past twenty-four hours. "As Mr Gower already has his property in Leeds arranged and I don't have anything to sell, Sid Landles reckons contracts could be exchanged within three weeks, so we could be in Camden Town by Christmas."

50

In the days leading up to the strike ballot, the London General sought to ensure that Londoners withheld support for the busmen by pointing out in the press that they were the only section of workers in the country still receiving the full war wage, and that under the proposed sliding scale they would lose a mere shilling—an even more paltry sixpence if they were conductors—for every five-point decline in the cost-of-living index. As most of them doubted whether a strike in the current circumstances could be won, the union leaders were less than energetic in their efforts to counter this propaganda. And those opposed to a strike had a strange ally.

"Seen this, Mick?" Malcolm Lewis, having just entered the output office at Middle Row, handed Mickey a small one-sided leaflet.

Mickey ran his eye over its contents and snorted in contempt. "Where d'you get this, Malc?"

"Bloke was dishin' 'em out in the canteen at Liverpool Street."

"So now they're calling themselves the Campaign for a TOT Union," observed Mickey.

"So it seems."

Mickey read the leaflet again.

VOTE AGAINST THE STRIKE!

The Campaign for a TOT Union continues to grow!

London busmen need a union that will stand up to the Traffic Combine and say no to wage-cuts and longer hours!

The so-called United Vehicle Workers has made a mess of the negotiations and cannot be trusted to lead a strike it does not believe in!

We need a union that combines the Tubes, Omnibuses and Trams—a TOT union!

Our campaign argued strongly against acceptance of the new terms demanded by the companies, and the result showed that a large majority of you agreed with us.

We now call on all London busmen to vote NO in the forthcoming ballot for strike action and save their strength until we have a union that believes in its members and in the action that they will call for when the time is right!

Our campaign will be holding local meetings all over London in the next few weeks. We urge you to attend and join our Campaign for a TOT Union!

UNITY IS STRENGTH!

"What do you think, Mick?"

"It's a load of bollocks, Malc. You see here that they're claiming credit for the rejection of the new proposals. You and I *know* that they weren't responsible. Next, they'll be claiming responsibility for the rejection of the strike, because believe you me"—he moved away from the allocation window and lowered his voice—"that will be the result of the ballot, with these clowns or without 'em. They claim they want a TOT union. How many tram men have they got? How many Tube men?"

Malcolm looked concerned. "Everything you say is true, Mick. But they *are* growing."

Mickey sighed. "I know. We've let 'em have too much leeway and now we'll have to see if we can rein 'em in. If they're serious about these local meetings we'll have to mobilise our people to attend and make sure our arguments are put."

"Which are?"

There was in the look Mickey gave Malcolm both impatience and disappointment. Did he really have to be told? "For a start, we can use this leaflet. They're calling for rejection of a strike. Doesn't that put them in the pocket of the employers?"

"But we're not so keen on it, are we?"

"But we're not calling for bloody rejection, Malcolm, are we? Then again, where are these Tube men they say are supporting their campaign? They should be pressed to produce them! And when they can't we call them what they are: bloody fakers. But finally, our basic argument needs to be hammered home time and again: the answer to our problems is not a breakaway union but a democratic London bus section, and we can get that from the Transport and General."

"Good morning, Mr Rice!"

The greeting came from Victor Wiggins, who had appeared in the allocation office.

"Good morning, Mr Wiggins."

"A little bird tells me that you will soon be submitting a change of address form."

"Depends on the result of the searches, Mr Wiggins."

"Yes, of course." The garage supervisor seemed almost gleeful. "Well, I hope it all goes well for you. If so, I imagine that your change of address form will be followed by a transfer request."

"No such luck, Mr Wiggins! If it all goes through I'll be purchasing a bicycle."

His hopes dashed, Victor Wiggins's visage assumed its usual sour expression.

*

The ballot result was announced at the tail-end of November: for the strike, 4,095; against, 5,144.

The following morning, Dick Mortlake found Mickey in front of the notice cases in which the schedules were posted, jotting down the details of his jobs for the coming weeks.

"So you weren't all *that* confident that the lads would vote against a strike," Dicked teased.

"What makes you say that, mate?"

"If you had been, you would have taken your jobs down as soon as the schedules were posted."

A chuckle from Mickey. "Ah, I see what you mean. No, it wasn't that. I couldn't very well be seen taking down jobs before the ballot, could I? I was supposed to be calling for a Yes vote, after all."

"No, I suppose not. Anyway, what have you got?"

"Next week, a twelve-hour spread."

"Oh, I bet the bastards made sure you were one of the first to get a long spread, Mickey."

Mickey turned to his friend with a grin. "Actually, Dick, it suits me: I'll be able to use that four hours off in the middle of the day to shoot up to Camden Town and buy some furniture. Annette and I did some window-shopping at the weekend, so I've got my instructions." He turned from the notice-case and placed his notebook in his inside pocket.

"So it's all settled? The place is yours?"

"As of yesterday, mate."

"So you've got a busy week coming up. Give me a shout if you need a hand, Mickey."

"Thanks, Dick, but it's in the evenings that I'll need a hand."

"Why's that?"

"Brian Vernon and his gang are holding a local meeting next week—Kilburn on Tuesday night. Then on the Saturday night they're holding a big one—so they hope—at the Crown and Anchor. We need to make sure they get a warm welcome."

*

It was a few minutes after eight o'clock when Mickey arrived at the Kilburn meeting on Tuesday evening, and he was feeling the effects

332

of his day. After finishing his first spell of duty at 10.45 that morning, he had caught a number 31 bus to Camden Town where he visited a shop on the High Street specialising in carpet oddments. He presented an assistant with the dimensions of his living room and the two bedrooms but, finding that there was no piece large enough to fit the living room, he borrowed a tape measure from the shop and visited the flat, taking measurements for *two* carpets—one for the living area and one for the dining area.

"You want us to fit 'em, sir?" enquired the assistant once the carpets had been cut.

Mickey nodded eagerly. "Yes, please."

"That'll be extra, of course."

"Of course. Can you do it today?"

The assistant, a thin young man in a brown smock, took a blue-covered ledger from beneath the counter and flipped through the pages. He ran his finger down a column of what presumably were appointments and grimaced. "Naaah, our fitters are all booked up today, sir. Tomorrow?"

"Late morning, about 11.15?"

As the assistant turned the page and surveyed another column, the grimace was repeated, reinforced with a shake of the head. "Naaah, four in the afternoon is the earliest they could make it. Thursday at 11.15 looks alright, though."

Mickey's spirits sank as he witnessed the rapid disappearance of his week of spreadovers. "Thursday, then. How long will the fitting take? I need to know because I'll be having furniture delivered early in the afternoon."

"Are the rooms clear, sir?"

"Completely empty."

The young man pouted and narrowed his eyes. "Then I would say an hour and a half at the most, sir."

Then to Bowman Brothers in the High Street. Mickey wanted a double bed, a wardrobe, a small dining table and chairs, and a couple of armchairs. From the moment he entered, however, he noticed that the staff, male and female, were giving him questioning looks, as if implying that he really shouldn't be here. It was the uniform, of course.

"Good afternoon, sir," purred a pinstriped, moustachioed gent in his forties. "May I be of assistance to you?"

Yes, thought Mickey, you can wipe that smirk off your face before I knock it off.

"Oh, thank you, guv," said Mickey, presenting his palm. "Lend us a fiver."

"Ha ha. One assumes that sir is joking."

Mickey nodded. "As sir probably earns more than you, he must be, mustn't he?"

That straightened his face out and Mickey told him what he wanted. When he and Annette had walked around the store the other Saturday afternoon—no uniform then, of course—they had chosen the pieces they liked but had not asked the prices. Their choices had been light, modern and, Mickey now learned, expensive. He therefore resolved to visit a second-hand furniture shop further down the High Street for the living-room furniture and the wardrobe, but would buy the bed and two sets of pillows—the notion of a second-hand bed did not appeal to him—from Bowman's, arranging delivery for 1 p.m. on Thursday.

By the time he had concluded his business at the second-hand shop it was almost 2 p.m. and he had just over an hour left before starting his second spell of duty. When he had arrived in Camden Town that morning, a nip in the air despite the bright sunshine, he had been alert and looking forward to completing his tasks; now he felt that subtle prickling under the skin that told him he was beginning to flag. Ravenously hungry, he had bangers and mash and a cup of strong tea in a café before catching a 31 bus back to North Paddington, where he climbed into the cab of his number 7 and commenced four-and-a-half hours of labour between Liverpool Street station and Wormwood Scrubs. Any busman would tell you that it was never any fun having to work the longest spell on the second half of the duty, especially on a spreadover, and by the time he came off at just after 7.30—1935 hours—Mickey was hardly in the mood to attend the secessionists' meeting but he nevertheless pushed himself to walk up to Westbourne Park and catch a 31 to Kilburn High Road.

*

There were only twenty in the meeting, and at least six of those— Dick Mortlake, Malcolm Lewis and Lenny Hawkins from Middle Row, a likely lad from Cricklewood, Reuben and Bernard Sharkey from Willesden—were anti-secessionists. When Mickey arrived, Brian Vernon was under pressure from Lenny, and he made the gloomy realisation that no harm would have been done if he had skipped the meeting. But then Vernon made the mistake of provoking him.

"Ah," said Vernon, doubtless welcoming the opportunity to shift attention away from Lenny, "so good of you to join us, Brother Rice. Pity you couldn't make it on time." That was his first mistake.

"I've just finished a twelve-hour spread," Mickey replied, sinking onto a chair, "so let's have none of your sarcasm, Brother Vernon."

"Well, you've only yourself to blame for that!" declared Vernon. "Aren't you a member of the Wages Board that recommended it?" That was his second mistake.

Mickey shot up from his seat, an arm aimed like a rifle at Vernon. "Don't give me that shit, Vernon! You and your pals campaigned against the strike, so when it comes to long spreads you're as guilty as anyone!" Although quite aware that, given his own position on the strike, he could be accused of outrageous hypocrisy, Mickey's anger was both boiling and perfectly genuine, and he was grateful to Vernon for having provoked it. "Just who do you think you are? You've been on the job five minutes and yet you set yourself up as some kind of super militant, passing judgement on people who've done what they consider to be their best for the membership! What are your qualifications? What is your experience? You came on the job after we'd won the 1919 agreement, so you have no experience of fifteen-hour spreadovers. You have no real understanding of what angers our members, of what motivated them to vote against the new terms. But you have the nerve to claim responsibility for that vote!"

He paused for breath, passing a hand over his mouth. "And what have *you* done? What have you done for the members at Morden in the few months since you conned them into electing you rep? Are your schedules better than anyone else's? No, they're a damn sight worse, aren't they?" Mickey was advancing towards the top table. "*Aren't they?* Answer me, damn you! AREN'T THEY?"

Lenny Hawkins stood up. "Steady on, Mick, steady on."

"What do you know about our schedules, and what business is it of yours!" Vernon protested.

Mickey halted in his advance to the top table, suddenly calm. He leaned forward, head lowered like that of a cat about to pounce and, lowering his voice, said, "What do I know about your schedules? Much more than you think, Vernon." His voice began to rise again. "I had someone go to your garage and check 'em. Not only are they worse than most, Vernon, but some of 'em—*some* of 'em—breach the agreement that people like me negotiated, and *that* makes it my business!"

Finally, one of Vernon's acolytes, a thin man with straw-coloured hair unknown to Mickey, came to Vernon's assistance. "This meeting is not about schedules! We're here to discuss a TOT union, so let's get on with it!"

This, too, played into Mickey's hands. "Yes, let's talk about this TOT union of yours!" He looked around the sparse gathering. "Where are the tram men? Where are the Tube men?"

Now Malcolm came in. "Yeah, for weeks now you've been saying that Tube men are on board, so when are we gonna see 'em?"

Dick: "Really, Brother Vernon, you can't go on making these claims with no proof."

Lenny: "It's about time we saw 'em, Vernon!"

A Cricklewood man: "Time to put your money where your mouth is, Brother Vernon!"

Vernon, forcing a grin, stood up. "Alright! Our Tube leaders will be at the Crown and Anchor, Clerkenwell Green, on Saturday night! And the schedules? Yes, our schedules steward let me down. Needless to say, he's no longer the schedules steward! Now let's get on with this meeting."

Mickey laughed. "Let's see what you produce on Saturday night, Brother Vernon. Until then, I wish you goodnight. Anyone else coming?" He turned and walked out, followed by most of the meeting. Passing Bernard Sharkey, who remained seated, he mouthed the word "Saturday" and received a wink in return.

As they walked to the High Road, Lenny Hawkins posed the question everyone wanted answered. "So who went down to Morden to check the schedules, Mickey?"

Mickey gave him a wink. "No one, as far as I'm aware, Len."

"Then how did you know?" asked Malcolm Lewis.

A shrug from Mickey. "Shot in the dark, mate. You often find that reps like Vernon, all mouth and trousers, make a complete mess of the job back at the garage. And I doubt whether his branch has a schedules steward, or that the branch was ever given an opportunity to discuss those schedules."

A gale of laughter arose from the group and Mickey realised that he no longer felt so exhausted.

*

The following day, Dick advised him that he had received a circular from the provisional executive of the Transport and General, calling a delegate conference—three delegates from each London bus branch—for Tuesday, 13 December.

On Thursday, Mickey travelled once more to Camden Town after his first half and was pleasantly surprised when it all went like clockwork: the carpet fitters arrived on time, followed by first the men from Bowman Brothers—they had to disassemble the bed to get it upstairs—and then the pieces from the second-hand shop. After the last man had departed, Mickey sank down into one of his armchairs and uttered a satisfied sigh. This was to be home. He cast his eye around the room, imaging the bookshelves filled with his and Annette's books, the gas fire casting its glow on a gloomy winter afternoon. He was tempted to take a nap but controlled the impulse, glancing at his pocket watch and pushing himself to his feet. Before returning to work, he once again had bangers and mash in the same café he had visited on Tuesday.

That evening, at the emergency branch meeting called by Dick, the delegates to next Tuesday's conference were elected: Rice, Mortlake and Hawkins.

During his break on Friday, he walked from home to Queensway, where in Whitely's—London's first department store and the largest shop in the world, so they said—he purchased blankets, bed sheets and pillowcases. Dorothy's money was by now almost gone.

*

On Saturday evening, Mickey and George Sanders stood in a doorway across the green from the Crown and Anchor and watched as busmen arrived for the meeting.

"This is not exactly my idea of a Saturday night out, Mickey," complained Sanders as a light rain began to fall. "And now, just to top it all, I'm gonna get a wet arse when I climb astride the bike." His Triumph Trustee motorbike was parked at the kerb. "Why are we standing in bloody doorway when we could be across the road having a pint?"

"No, it's not my idea of a Saturday night either, George, but we need to get a look at these Underground men and I want to get an idea of who we'll be up against over there...Here, who's this?"

A small black car circled the green before driving into Aylesbury Street.

"I thought that might be them," said Mickey. As first one car door slammed, then another, he held up a hand and then came the sound of well-shod feet on the wet pavement. Sure enough, the two men who came into sight were wearing Underground uniforms.

"Well, well, well," said Mickey.

"Ah, the guests of honour," remarked Sanders.

They watched the two men, one tall and one short, enter the pub, and now busmen were arriving in some numbers.

"Looks as if Vernon may have a decent meeting," said Mickey, "although of course it's difficult to know how many of these blokes are our people."

"Psssssst!" This came from their left, and turning Mickey saw Bernard Sharkey, who had walked up from Clerkenwell Road. He waved him to approach.

"Well blow me down!" exclaimed Sharkey as he spotted Sanders. "What you doin' here, George?"

"As this is supposed to be the secessionists' big meeting, Mickey thought we should bring out the big guns. All I'm doing at the moment, though, is catching a cold."

"Mickey certainly gave Vernon a roastin' the other night in Kilburn!" Sharkey told Sanders. "I'm surprised he's volunteerin' for another one, to be honest."

Sanders sniffed noisily, drawing attention to his discomfort.

"Why don't you go in now, George," suggested Mickey.

As Sanders nodded and stepped out of the doorway, Mickey placed a hand on Sharkey's arm, detaining him.

"A word, Bernie. Two Tube men arrived a few minutes ago. Don't go into the pub until the meeting has started. When you get upstairs, stand at the back and try not to be seen by the men on the top table. Get a good look at the Tube men, and if they look familiar to you, shoot back over here and let me know."

"You not comin' in, then?"

"Can't risk it, mate," he replied and, seeing the confusion on Sharkey's face, added: "All will be explained, Bernie."

*

Mickey Rice stood well back in the doorway, glad that he had decided to wear his uniform greatcoat, and waited. There were a few late arrivals at the Crown and Anchor, one of whom was Steve Mason, a former rep at Dollis Hill who, having failed in his application for an inspector's job, had challenged Mickey for a seat on the EC of the red-button union. Also failing in that, he had attempted to break the strike of the women conductors in 1918, but the only thing broken was his nose, when Gladys had visited his garage and knocked him onto the seat of his pants. His next application for an inspector's job had been successful and here he was, seeking to widen the divisions in the union. If this was the kind of man the secessionists were attracting to their ranks, thought Mickey, they would not go far.

Presently, the lights in the Crown and Anchor's meeting room came on and the rumble of voices could be heard, even at this distance. Five minutes after this a man came running, all knees and elbows, across the green.

"They're not bloody Tube men!" protested Sharkey, squeezing into the doorway alongside Mickey. "They're bloody…"

"I know, I know," said Mickey. "I thought I recognised them when they went past, but I wasn't absolutely sure. Where did you come across them?"

"First time, it was on Tower Hill, during the strike in 1918. By the time of the second strike the following' year, of course, they'd switched sides, and were goin' from station to station, tryin' to put the frighteners on us and wheedle out what information they could about our union and its plans."

"Okay, but keep this under your hat, Bernie."

"*What?* But we've got Vernon by the bollocks, Mickey!"

Mickey grinned. "Yes, we have, Bernie, but we need to hang onto this information until it will do the most damage. I'm thinking of next Tuesday's delegate conference, but if it gets out before then Vernon will stay away. Besides, I want to see if Vernon leaves with 'em tonight. If he does, we'll follow 'em."

"We?"

"Me and George, on his motorbike." He nodded at the Triumph Trusty at the kerb.

*

Ninety minutes later, George Sanders and Mickey Rice watched as Vernon and the two "Tube men" left the Crown and Anchor together and began the short walk to Aylesbury Street. Sanders walked to his motorbike, swung his leg over the saddle and turned to Mickey. "Climb aboard, Mick."

They followed the small black car to its destination and then turned, heading back to Central London. Entering Parliament Square, the Triumph Trusty skidded on the wet—now becoming icy—surface and off they came. As Mickey slid towards the central reservation, thoughts passed through his mind in rapid succession: he was now doubly thankful that he had worn his greatcoat, as it had broken his fall; then fearful because he had no helmet; if both he and Sanders were badly injured, who would drop the bombshell on Tuesday?; if he was disabled or merely had to take time off work, how would Annette, three months pregnant, cope?; if he was still off work when she had to take maternity leave, would they need to sell the maisonette and fall back on Dick's generosity?

Finally, he simply closed his eyes and prepared for the impact.

51

The origins of Anderton's Hotel, standing at 162-165, Fleet Street, extended at least as far back as the early fifteenth century when the site was occupied by an inn known as the Horn in the Hoop; rebuilt in 1880, its bright front of red brick and stone had been dulled by the subsequent introduction of the internal combustion engine. Several of Ernest Bevin's amalgamation conferences had been held there and today—13 December, a dull Tuesday—it was host to the special conference of the London bus section convened by the provisional general executive council of the Transport and General Workers' Union in order to hear the grievances of the bus branches, each represented by three delegates, and hopefully arrive at a resolution which would quell the secessionist sentiment which had spread throughout the section.

Although the conference was being convened by the provisional executive of the new union, it had been demanded by the branches themselves, over twenty of which had submitted resolutions to this effect. Thus Bevin, Harry Gosling and Ben Smith, who acted on behalf of the hospitalised George Sanders, had sent a circular to all branches in which they recognised that "a good deal of the prevalent grievances are very real," and announced the holding of the conference.

By the time Harry Gosling opened the conference, there were still only two delegates from the Middle Row Branch—Dick Mortlake and Malcolm Lewis; although Mickey Rice had promised to be present, these two assumed that he was not feeling sufficiently recovered. This was of concern to several delegates, because no could put forward the needs and demands of the London bus section as powerfully and clearly as Mickey.

To begin with, Gosling and Bevin let the delegates off the leash, allowing them to state their grievances without interruption or reply.

Predictably, the recently-imposed new terms, or more especially the way they had been arrived at, came in for heavy criticism.

"What gave our leaders the impression that they had a mandate to negotiate away the gains of the 1919 agreement in the first place?" demanded Peter Cassomini of Forest Gate. "Negotiation was no use unless they had the men behind them, and if they *had* the men behind them negotiation was unnecessary. The men are dissatisfied with the incompetence of the officials!"

The company, moreover, was ignoring the positive aspects of the agreement. "What does that document say about systematic overtime?" demanded Lloyd of Palmers Green. "It says there won't *be* any! And yet what happened when route 20 was opened up? The company sent twenty-two of my members to work their rest-days at Chalk Farm. In fact, brothers, there have been no rest-days this year at Palmers Green! So much for the so-called agreement!"

"He's right, Chairman!" declared Battersea's Adams. "What happens when the company operates summer schedules? They force crews to work their rest-days! And that, brothers, allows them to operate 200 extra buses without employing a single extra man!

"But one of our main grievances concerns the officials—their high salaries, and the expenses they draw, which are sometimes higher than their salaries. We have no control over the officials, and so what is needed is rank-and-file officials with rank-and-file control."

"Brother Adams has hit the nail on the head!" said Lancaster of Holloway. "The members have lost constitutional control over our section; our position has been weakened because of the amalgamation with the old blue-button union, so what we need is a structure that will return that control to us. And if we don't get it...Well, I think you know what will happen."

Next came Warne of Croydon, one of the branches which had clearly stated its intention to secede. "The officials need to be stronger, men who will carry out the mandate of the members and not be swayed by this section or that. Now let me tell you, brothers, if Croydon fails to get satisfaction we will have to say: we're sorry but we must adopt our own methods, just as we did when our union was a red union."

One of the Plumstead delegates drew attention to the circular convening the conference. "Now, according to that, there are *one or two branches* talking about secession. One or two? *One or two?*" He looked around the hall. "We all know that the number is far in excess of that, don't we?" A growl of agreement rose from the floor. "And we also know that the secessionist movement has been going on for some time, but the executive council of the United Vehicle Workers has done nothing—nothing!'"

Brian Vernon now rose to his feet. "And I would be very surprised," he said, "if the provisional executive of the new union will do anything either! They've brought us here today to let us voice our grievances and get it all off our chests in the hope that we'll be good little boys and go back to our garages and carry on as usual. Brothers, I tell you we're wasting our time here!"

Harry Gosling now intervened. "I would advise you, brother," he said, "to await our response at the end of this discussion before you jump to conclusions like that."

Ernie Bevin stood. For a couple of seconds, his gaze rested on Vernon, before wandering over the rest of the conference. "I wonder," he began, "if any of you have had the opportunity..."

BANG!

All eyes went to the double doors which had flown open to reveal a man entering the hall backwards; as he swung around, it became apparent that he was pushing a man in a bath chair, a plastered leg extended before him. When the conference recognised the man in the chair as Mickey Rice, a cheer arose. Ernie Bevin had halted in mid-sentence and was watching Mickey's entrance with interest and amusement.

"Well," said Bevin with a laugh, "welcome to the conference which, if my information is correct, you have done so much to bring about, Brother Rice! I won't suggest you take a seat because it seems you already have one."

"Thank you, Brother Bevin. And Chairman,"—Mickey turned his attention to Harry Gosling—"I apologise for my late arrival. We had a bit of a job persuading the hospital authorities to let me out, following which my driver—allow me to introduce Morris Frankenberg, a leading member of our cab section—had difficulty in finding a parking space."

"Apology accepted," nodded Gosling good-naturedly. "I suggest that you find a parking space for your current vehicle by the front row. However, your arrival has interrupted Brother Bevin, who was about to..."

"Oh no, Chairman," Bevin said with a wave of the hand, "I feel sure that Brother Rice wishes to make a contribution..."

"I do, Chairman, but I think Brother Bevin should continue with his remarks, as long as he wasn't intending to make a full reply to this discussion at this stage."

"Thank you, Mickey," said Bevin, unconsciously falling into this more informal form of address. "I think you in particular will be interested in what I have to say." He lifted his head to take in the rest of the conference. "Now, brothers, you will recall that shortly before the arrival of Brother Rice we heard from Brother Vernon that—in his own opinion—this conference would be a waste of time because the provisional executive would give you nothing. I was then about to ask the conference if any of you have had the opportunity of reading *100%*, the recent novel by Upton Sinclair. In this novel, a young man is pressured into becoming a spy and an agent provocateur for the authorities, and eventually he finds he has a taste for it. So you often find that those who boast of being extremists are often on the side of, or inspired by, the employers. Now, I make no accusations, but I know that some of the inspiration of the secessionist movement has come from Electric Railway House."

This allegation gave rise to uproar, with one half of the delegates shouting "Prove it, prove it! Where's the evidence?" at Ernie Bevin while the other half turned on Brian Vernon, demanding to know whether he was a spy.

Mickey Rice raised his arm and was recognised by the chairman.

"Chairman," he said once the conference had settled down, "I may be able to throw some light on this. First of all, let me say that I have no knowledge of company involvement in the secessionist movement, whether by activity or inspiration."

He paused to let that sink in. Bevin looked uncomfortable; behind him, Mickey heard a buzz of speculation.

"It's even worse than that, brothers. Far worse." That put a grin on Bevin's face. Vernon, who obviously knew what was coming, got to his feet. "I'm not going to listen to..."

"Yes you are," ruled Gosling. "Sit down!"

Mickey manoeuvred the bath chair until he was facing the audience. "For some time," he resumed, "Brother Vernon had been claiming that his plan for the formation of a TOT union had the support of Underground workers. The problem was, he had never produced any evidence of this. Oh, he would say, they can't afford to reveal themselves publicly because they'll be expelled by the NUR or ASLEF." He chuckled. "This never made a lot of sense to me, because if these men were preparing to break away from those unions in any case, it surely wouldn't have made much difference if they were expelled.

"Eventually, however, the pressure on Brother Vernon was so great that he obviously realised that he would have to come up with the goods. He agreed, therefore, to bring a couple of representatives—one NUR and one ASLEF—along to a meeting. That meeting was held last Saturday evening, brothers, and I suppose a few of you might have been present. If you were, you will know that the two Underground men were introduced as Ron Albert, driver, and Kieron Duffy, guard. As they probably explained, these weren't their real names. No, they couldn't possible use their real names because word might get back to Jimmy Thomas of the NUR and Jack Bromley of ASLEF. That's what they told you, anyway. Is that right?"

There were sounds of assent—embarrassed groans, really—from six or eight men.

"Well, that was only half true. Those weren't their real names. Perhaps I should explain that I saw these two characters arrive for the meeting. I was standing across the street with George Sanders. Why? Because George had been unable to get any confirmation from the NUR or ASLEF that any of their members were seriously involved in this TOT adventure, and so when we heard that Brother Vernon was going to produce a couple out of the hat, we decided to try and get a glimpse of 'em. And so we did. They arrived in a car, which they parked away from the Crown and Anchor in Aylesbury Street, and walked to the hall. They were in uniform...Oh!" He clasped a hand to his forehead and looked at the platform. "Perhaps I was wrong, Chairman, when I said I knew of no company involvement: the uniforms must have been supplied by someone in the Traffic Combine, after all. And, believe it or not, as I watched them walk to the hall, I felt that these men were in some way familiar...but I'll come back to that.

"So, brothers, you've probably worked out by now that these fellows were not really Underground workers. So what were they? Policemen! Yes, brothers, they were policemen!"

"Oh, this is ridiculous!" cried Brian Vernon.

"How do you know, Mickey?" asked Willesden's Reuben Topping.

"Yeah, come on, Mickey, where's the evidence?" shouted someone at the back.

"A driver I know—and someone that George Sanders has known for some years, since the man concerned used to be a copper himself—was at the meeting at my request. Within five minutes of the start of the meeting, he came out and darted across the road. He told us that he had recognised both men—and for that reason he couldn't remain in the meeting in case they recognised *him*. The tall ginger fellow pretending to be a guard is Detective Constable Jack Dunleavy; the shorter, tubbyish men is Detective Sergeant William Huntley; and they are both Special Branch men! As soon as I was told this, I remembered where I had seen them before: these were the men who dragged me to Harrow Road police station last year and tried to frighten me into setting up the Soviet Ambassador."

Not surprisingly, Brian Vernon was now the centre of attention; he now changed his tune. "The bastards! If I ever see those bastards again I'll..."

"Are you saying that this is news to you, Brother Vernon?" asked Harry Gosling from the platform.

"Of *course* it's news to me! What do you take me for? I know I may have rubbed up some people in this room the wrong way, but you surely can't believe that I would..."

"Well, Brother Vernon," said Mickey, "I think we're entitled to believe that you *would* knowingly collaborate with Special Branch. As far as we know, you may be a member of that fraternity yourself."

"Now, now, Brother Rice," counselled Harry Gosling, "I'll have to ask you to justify that remark."

"Here you are, then: George Sanders attended the meeting while I waited until it ended—not a comfortable thing to do in December. Vernon left the hall with the two coppers and walked to their car with them. The three of them drove off together..."

"So what!" bleated Vernon. "They was givin' me a lift."

"George and I followed on George's motorbike. Their destination was New Scotland Yard on the Embankment; all three entered together. George turned the bike around and drove us back towards town, with the intention of dropping me in Oxford Street so that I could catch a number 7 or 15 bus. The road surface was wet and somewhat icy, and at Parliament Square George, possibly due to the excitement at our discovery, accelerated too quickly and we ended up on the deck, sliding towards the central reservation."

Vernon decided there was only one thing for it. He sprang to his feet and ran for the double doors, followed by howls of contempt, insults and two delegates intent upon assault.

On the platform, Bevin was laughing, heartily enjoying himself. "Well," he told the conference, "I suppose that's the last we'll see of him!"

"Or of the TOT union!" added Ben Smith.

"Brothers," said Bevin, rising to his feet, "I think we all owe Brother Rice a vote of thanks." He extended the flat of his palm in Mickey's direction. "To Mickey Rice, brothers!"

They stood, cheering and applauding, but Mickey didn't want it, and it crossed his mind that Bevin might be deliberately engineering this acclaim in order to reduce the impact of what he intended to be his main contribution to this conference.

"Well, brothers," Harry Gosling was saying, "it seems to me that this might be an appropriate time to call an adjournment to allow us to consider all you have told us and..."

"With due respect, Chairman," said Mickey, "there are one or two things I'd like to say before you do that."

Gosling fell silent, as if in two minds as to whether he should allow Mickey back in. This created a certain amount of tension in the hall, and Mickey now saw that Bevin had, whether intentionally or not, done him a favour, because the conference, having demonstrated its support, was now like a coiled spring ready to pounce if Gosling dared to deny him the chance to speak a second time. Bevin turned to Gosling and murmured something.

"Alright, Brother Rice," said Gosling, "please proceed."

You could feel the relief in the hall, almost sense the muscles being relaxed, hear the sighs of the delegates.

Mickey nodded. "Thank you, Chairman." He had turned his bath chair so that it faced the platform, and it was to the platform rather than to the delegates that he addressed his remarks.

"Chairman, I came to this conference today with two intentions. My first intention was to see that the secessionist movement was defeated. That would have been my intention even if Special Branch had not been involved because, even though some honest and sincere men had given their support to that movement, objectively it favoured the employers. Division always favours the employers. My second intention was—and is—to find a way, alongside my brothers here, of ensuring that such a movement never arises again in our section.

"If we are to achieve that, we have to understand why it arose in the first place. Increasingly, the men—both the men here and those they represent back at the garages—felt that they weren't being listened to, that they were being ignored. I'm talking here, Chairman, of the last two years, since the formation of the United Vehicle Workers. Now, fortunately or unfortunately, depending on your point of view, we London busworkers have a history, a culture that was developed in the seven years in which our union was the London and Provincial Union of Licensed Vehicle Workers—the red-button union!" A great cheer came up from the delegates. "At one stage, we too had leaders who ignored us, who shut their eyes to policies adopted at democratic conferences. And so we got rid of them, Chairman." Another great cheer. "For a good part of those seven years, we were fighting not just the employers but our own leaders as well. Leaders who decided that the results of wage negotiations should not be submitted to the members. Leaders who tried to do away with elected full-time officers and have them appointed. But we won each of these battles.

"Imagine how we felt, when, after our amalgamation with the old blue-button union, it felt as if we were back where we started! But did we take it lying down? We did not. Instead, we began once more to organise unofficially. Now, I know from a discussion I had with Brother Bevin back in January this year that he is opposed to unofficial movements, to rank-and-file movements. But if workers have no effective *official* machinery by means of which they can make themselves heard and get their policies adopted, they have no *choice* but to organise *un*officially!

"Let's be quite honest about it! *This conference is taking place today because we organised unofficially and exerted pressure for it!* Sometimes unofficial movements *are* necessary. They are less *likely* to be necessary, however, if official channels exist that allow the members a voice and an opportunity to fight their corner. And that's what brings us here today."

A scrutiny of the platform told him that he still had their attention and that they—particularly Bevin, who had begun to jot notes—now anticipated that he would put forward his main points.

"So what does the London bus section need? What are its demands? What might a democratic London bus section look like? Let me say here, that the demands I will outline have not been agreed by the section as a whole. No, because we had no other way of doing it these demands have been agreed only by those who chose to attend our unofficial meetings. This conference should, as it has been convened by the provisional executive of our new union, be considered official, however, and the delegates will be able to tell us whether what I have to say is acceptable to the section as a whole.

"First, the section needs to be recognised *as* a section, or perhaps a sub-section of the Passenger Group. It should have its own elected committee of lay members to negotiate with the employers on all major questions; that committee should meet regularly, perhaps monthly. There should also be a regular London bus conference, with a delegate from each garage branch, to which the bus committee would report and be accountable. You may ask if such a conference would have sufficient business to occupy it. Believe me, Chairman, that would not be a problem: major schedule changes, infringements of the agreement by the employers, to say nothing of wages and conditions demands, would give it plenty to do. Finally, full-time officers must be elected by members of the section, ensuring that they represent the interests of, and are accountable to, the members who pay their wages.

"If we want to ensure that a secessionist movement will never arise again, Chairman, surely this is the way to do it, by making sure that the London bus section is a self-governing democracy."

Harry Gosling looked up at the conference as it applauded Mickey Rice. "I think, brothers," he said, "that we'll now take that adjournment and report back to you in an hour or so."

*

During the adjournment, several delegates crowded around Mickey to enquire about his health, wish him well and pat him on the shoulder in recognition of his contribution to the conference.

"If that don't do it," rumbled Ron Vickers, "I don't know what will, Mickey."

"If we get that bus committee," enquired Reuben Topping with a grin, "will you be standing, Mick?"

"One step at a time, Reuben, one step at a time," replied a modest Mickey.

A more practical Dick Mortlake frowned down at the invalid. "Does Annette know that you're out of the hospital?"

Mickey pretended to cower. "No, but I'll be back in there this afternoon: I haven't discharged myself. Why, do you think she'll be angry?"

Dick gave that some thought before shaking his head. "No, I think she'll be proud of you, Mickey—depending on the outcome of this conference, of course."

"How is George?" asked Malcolm Lewis. "Will he be alright?"

Mickey nodded. "I wouldn't say he was okay at the moment, but he'll be alright in a week or two."

During this time, various hotel staff had been coming in and out, laying plates on the long tables which ran down the right side of the hall, next to the entrance. Now came a waitress pushing a trolley upon which sat something which could only be a tea urn. Following her came Ernie Bevin, grinning at his oversight.

"Brothers!" cried Bevin, gaining instant attention. "No, no, I don't have a reply for you yet. We won't be too long, but in the meantime, please help yourselves to the buffet."

Suddenly, Mickey was alone. He looked over his shoulder at Morris Frankenberg, who had remained seated in the front row. "Nosebag time, Morry! Go on, don't be shy. And you can bring me a plate as well, if you can manage it."

"No need, Morry," said Dick Mortlake, approaching with two plates.

"Well, this looks nice," observed Mickey as he accepted his plate. "Sandwiches *and* a chicken drumstick. I bet this was none of Stanley Hirst's doing, Dick."

"No," chuckled Dick, "probably not. I'll get our teas in a bit, Mickey."

"Do you think Ernie might be intending this as a consolation prize, Dick?"

"I suppose that's possible. It's more likely, though, that he's making a statement: Welcome to the Transport and General Workers' Union."

"I hope you're right, mate."

After the delegates had cleared the buffet tables and drunk the tea urn dry, Gosling, Bevin and Ben Smith returned to the hall and made their way to the platform. "Didn't leave much for the staff, did they?" quipped Gosling as they passed the buffet tables.

Following the trio's arrival on the platform, there was the expected shuffling of papers and murmured comments. Apart from this the silence in the hall was total, and if any of the three had lifted his gaze he would have seen the delegates erect in their seats or leaning forward in expectation, their expressions clenched and intense. The one exception to this was Mickey Rice, who leaned back in his bath chair, his eyes on the ceiling. In his mind, he was listening to the fourth movement of the *Organ Symphony* of Camille Saint-Saëns.

"Brothers," announced Harry Gosling, "thank you for your patience. I now call upon Brother Bevin to reply to this morning's discussion and advise you of our recommendations."

As Bevin stood, a four-handed piano played that exquisite rippling melody. "Conference, I have to say that the complaints you voiced this morning made a deep impression on us, and we are agreed that they must be investigated. We therefore recommend that such an investigation should be conducted by an *ad hoc* committee of twelve, elected by ballot and reporting back to a further delegate conference."

The music now began to swell.

"Brothers our provisional executive council wanted to find a way to link the busmen with the tram-men, a real coalition, so that a combined effort might be brought into being, not to drag down the busmen to the trams, but to raise the trams up to the busmen's level. Thus, we placed the busmen in the same trade group as the tram-men."

The organ now entered and picked up the theme.

"We have, however, considered the representations made this morning and we have arrived at a recommendation. In this, I should add, we are all three agreed."

A mighty clash of cymbals!

"We will recommend to the executive that especially for London a bus sub-section should be created, with its own committee and conference."

That organ! The cymbals! The brass! The music filled Mickey Rice's whole being, rendering him deaf to all else until someone in the front row leaned forward to clap him on the shoulder and he became aware that the whole conference was cheering and applauding, many of the delegates standing. He turned his bath chair and was presented with a scene of jubilation, and it was plain to him that the delegates were not celebrating a gift from Ernest Bevin or thanking him for it but, very conscious that this had been *their* achievement, were basking in their own success; some, to judge by the wide-eyed expressions on their faces, were surprised by their accomplishment. Mickey Rice had no choice but to replay that passage again: Organ! Cymbals! Brass! Since he had first heard this music he had imagined it as the backdrop to the conquest of power by his class, an anthem of triumph and celebration, and he knew that what he was feeling now was not quite the same as what he would feel when that day came.

But it was close.

AUTHOR'S NOTE

As with the previous two volumes in this trilogy, the main events are based on those documented in my *Radical Aristocrats: London Busworkers from the 1880s to the 1880s* (London: Lawrence and Wishart, 1985). *The Times* Archive has been extremely helpful throughout and, indeed, during the period in question *The Times* certainly lived up to its reputation as a "newspaper of record," often reporting speeches in Parliament and at trade union conferences verbatim, as it did with negotiations at 10 Downing Street between trade union leaders and Lloyd George.

The detail regarding Madame Ravitch in Chapter 15 is from Emma Goldman's less than friendly *My Disillusionment in Russia* (New York: Doubleday, Page & Company, 1923).

Chapters 14-16 are partly based on the accounts in "British Labour Delegation to Russia, 1920: Report" (London: TUC and Labour Party, 1920) and Robert Williams: *The Soviet System at Work* (London: CPGB, 1920). I am grateful to Kenny Coyle for confirming that the Comrade Sverdlov who accompanied the delegation to the south was, indeed, the brother of the late Yakov Sverdlov and that Williams' use of the term "Commissar of Ways and Communications" arises from the fact that in Russian "railways" is translated using these two words, "ways" and "communications." Bob William's outburst in Chapter 17 is also based on his argument in *The Soviet System at Work.*

Details of Soviet Russia's efforts to gain recognition by the British government were provided by W.F. and Zelda K. Coates, *A History of Anglo-Soviet Relations* (London: Lawrence and Wishart/The Pilot Press, 1943), which also discusses the international diplomatic activity following the unprovoked Polish attack on Russia.

Harry Pollitt's account of his involvement in the anti-interventionist activity on the London docks are based on on his *Serving my Time* (London: Lawrence and Wishart, A Worker's Library edition, 1941).

For knowledge of Sylvia Pankhurst, I turned to Mary Davis, *Sylvia*

Pankhurst: A Life in Radical Politics (London: Pluto Press, 1999), and Shirley Harrison, *Sylvia Pankhurst: Rebellious Suffragette* (London: Sapere Books, 2012).

The debate on the merits or otherwise of amalgamation in Chapter 26 did not take place, but the comments of Carter, Smith, Henderson and Sanders, here abbreviated or slightly edited, appeared in *The Record*, 5 January 1921.

In the novel, Brian Vernon, the secessionist leader, works at Morden bus garage. In reality, of course, there was neither a Brian Vernon nor a Morden garage. Was either Special Branch or the Traffic Combine involved in the secessionist movement? Evidence is lacking; however, it is a fact that, at the delegate conference for the London bus branches held at Anderton's Hotel in December 1921, Ernest Bevin did suggest that delegates read *100%*, the novel by Upton Sinclair published the previous year, in which a young man acts as a spy and provocateur on behalf of capitalist interests. Bevin also claimed that Electric Railway House provided the inspiration for the secessionist movement.

Details of Theodore Rothstein's involvement in the British socialist movement can be found in David Burke, *The Spy Who Came in from the Co-op* (Woodbridge: The Boydell Press, 2008) and *Russia and the British Left, from the 1848 Revolutions to the General Strike* (London: I.B. Taurus, 2018). Details of the formation of the Communist Party of Great Britain were provided by James Klugmann, *History of the Communist Party of Great Britain, Volume One: Formation and Early Years, 1919-1924* (London: Lawrence & Wishart, 1968).

Some of the information regarding Black Friday was provided by Alan Bullock, *The Life and Times of Ernest Bevin, Volume One: Trade Union Leader, 1881-1940* (London: Heinemann, 1960). The comments by Robert Williams to the Triple Alliance (or what was left of it after the miners had departed) in Chapter 33 are based on a memorandum he had written in February 1921 and his remarks at the annual general council meeting of the National Transport Workers' Federation, June 1921. Bevin's remarks at the meeting of the Triple Alliance on 15 April are based on his speech at the annual General Council meeting of the Transport Workers' Federation, June 1921. I have seen no evidence that he was rude to J.H. Thomas, but *The Times* edition of 16 April described the meeting as "acrimonious."

The results of all the negotiations with the London bus companies are historically accurate. However, the actual *conduct* of those negotiations before July 1921 have been wholly invented. For the negotiations in July and October 1921, some dialogue is based on the verbatim records, for access to which I am grateful to Jim Mowatt, director of education at Unite the Union, the staff of the Modern Records Centre at the University of Warwick, and Dr James Fowler of the University of Essex.

The comments of some of the delegates to the delegate conference held at Anderton's Hotel in December 1921 are based on the minutes of that conference. George Sanders was, indeed, absent on that occasion as he had been injured in a motorcycle accident, although he had not, of course, been hunting for spies at the time of that accident.

It may be of interest to some readers to be advised of the subsequent lives of some of the historical figures featured in the novel:

- Lord Ashfield remained chairman of the London General Omnibus Company and associated Traffic Combine companies until 1933 when the semi-public London Passenger Transport Board, of which he also became chairman, was formed. He resigned in 1947 and died the following year at the age of 74.
- Ernest Bevin was General Secretary of the Transport & General Workers' Union until 1940, when he became Minister of Labour and National Service in the wartime coalition government; he became a notoriously anti-communist Foreign Secretary in the post-war government until he died in 1951 at the age of 70.
- Peter Cassomini was elected as Schedules Officer of the London bus section in 1925.
- John Cliff was elected National Passenger Secretary of the TGWU and in 1924 became Assistant General Secretary. In 1933 he was appointed as a part-time member of the London Passenger Transport Board, and two years later resigned from the TGWU to take up full-time duties on that body.
- Archie Henderson became National Secretary of the TGWU's Road Transport Commercial group in 1922.
- Stanley Hirst became Finance Secretary of the Transport & General Workers' Union
- J.J. Mills was elected as the London Bus Section's London District Secretary in 1923.

- Sylvia Pankhurst withdrew from communist politics but became staunchly anti-fascist, in particular opposing the Italian invasion of Abyssinia (Ethiopia). In 1956, at the invitation of Haile Selassie, she relocated to Ethiopia where, after her death in 1960, she was given a state funeral.
- Harry Pollitt was general secretary of the Communist Party of Great Britain, 1929-39 and 1941-56. He died in 1960 at the age of 69.
- Andrew Rothstein was a lifelong communist, publishing numerous original works as well as English translations of Lenin and Plekhanov. In 1988, the re-established Communist Party of Britain presented him with its card number 1. He died in 1994 at the age of 95.
- Theodore Rothstein was appointed as Soviet ambassador to Persia (Iran) soon after his return to Russia. In 1922 he became a member of the People's Commissariat for Foreign Affairs and was appointed director of the Institute of World Economy and Politics. He died in Moscow, aged 82, in 1953.
- George Sanders was defeated by John Cliff in the election for the TGWU's National Passenger Secretary. He was later appointed National Officer in the General Workers section, a post he held until his death by cancer in 1932 at the age of 61.
- Bernard Sharkey became a member of London's Central Bus Committee and was active in the London Busman's Rank and File Movement in the 1930s.
- Albert "Tich" Smith was elected as MP for Sunderland in 1929 and died in 1931 at the age of 69.
- Ben Smith (or Sir Benjamin as he later became) was elected as MP for Rotherhithe in 1923 and in 1945 was appointed as Minister of Food in the Attlee government until he resigned in the following year upon his appointment as chairman of the West Midlands Coal Board.
- J.H. "Jimmy" Thomas became Secretary of State for the Colonies in the first Labour government in 1924 and Lord Privy Seal with responsibility for employment during the second Labour government in 1929, and the following year became Secretary of State for the Dominions. When he joined the National Government of Ramsay MacDonald, he was expelled from both the Labour Party and the National Union of Railwaymen. In 1936, he was forced to resign his position as Secretary of State for the Colonies after he was

found to have leaked details from the forthcoming Budget to stock exchange speculators.

- Robert Williams re-joined the Labour Party following his expulsion from the CPGB but, although becoming chair of the party, failed to get into Parliament. In 1936, unable to find secure employment and plagued by what Bevin's biographer Alan Bullock refers to as "personal problems," he drowned himself.

ABOUT THE AUTHOR

In the first ten years of his working life, Ken Fuller was an office boy, a baker, and a merchant seaman. He then drove a London bus for eleven years, followed by twenty years as a full-time official in the Transport & General Workers' Union. His first published book was *Radical Aristocrats: London Busworkers from the 1880s to the 1980s* (London: Lawrence and Wishart, 1985), upon which some events in *Red-Button Men* are based.

His other published work is as follows:

- *Forcing the Pace: The Partido Komunista ng Pilipinas, From Foundation to Armed Struggle* (University of the Philippines Press, 2007). This was a finalist for a National Book Award (Manila Critics Circle), 2008.
- *A Movement Divided: Philippine Communism, 1957-1986* (University of the Philippines Press, 2011).
- *The Lost Vision: The Philippine Left, 1986-2010* (University of the Philippines Press, 2015). This was a finalist for a National Book Award (Manila Critics Circle), 2016.
- *The Long Crisis: Gloria Macapagal Arroyo and Philippine Underdevelopment* (commercially published as an e-book by Flipside, Quezon City, in 2013, and in 2019 republished as a paperback via Kindle Direct Publishing).
- *Hardboiled Activist: The Work and Politics of Dashiell Hammett* (Glasgow: Praxis Press, 2017).
- *Foreigners: A Philippine Satire* (paperback and e-book via Kindle Direct Publishing, 2019).
- *Love and Labour: Red-Button Years, Volume 1* (paperback and e-book via Kindle Direct Publishing, 2019.)
- *Romance and Revolution: Red-Button Years, Volume 2* (paperback and e-book via Kindle Direct Publishing, 2020).
- *A Mad Desire to Read: Books and their Authors* (paperback and e-book via Kindle Direct Publishing, 2020).
- *Raymond Chandler: The Man behind the Mask* (paperback and e-book via Kindle Direct Publishing, 2020).

Since 2003, Ken Fuller has lived in the Philippines.

Made in the USA
Middletown, DE
19 November 2021

52901750R00203